THE FORGOTTEN DAWN

BOOK ONE, THE SHATTERED SKY SAGA

LAURA A BLAKE

Copyright © 2024 by Laura Blake. First published in 2025.

All rights reserved.

No part of this book may be reproduced in any form or by any electronic or mechanical means, including information storage and retrieval systems, without written permission from the author, except for the use of brief quotations in a book review.

Cover Design by An-Nhien Nguyen

Line Editing by Tabitha Chandler at Tabitha Does Editing

Developmental Editing by Valeria Eden

Map by Andrés Aguirre Jurado

ELDARA
POOL OF VITALITY
ETERNAL COURT
NORTHERN RIDGE
TACTRAS MOUNTAINS
COURT OF WHISPERS
WESTERN RIDGE
MAZIMA
HESUM
IESALIA
EASTERN RIDGE
SAMINA
ESCALIA
GATES OF AZMEER
RICCIA
AZMEER
THE CENTER COURT
SOUTHERN RIDGE
COURT OF SHADOWS
HYDRATAS SEA
COURT OF REFLECTION

For Esmay.

For those who have danced with darkness—
and for those who watched them shine all the brighter because of it.

PROLOGUE

Everything was still. I basked in the silence before the world was born.

I gazed upon the darkness of the void as the first whispers of creation stirred.

Chaos swirled at my fingertips, yearning for the embrace of order to define its essence and being.

Then it called to me. A beautiful song only I could hear.

I orchestrated the Celestials.

I shaped the heavens and earth as I wove strands of light and energy into existence.

I was the creation.

A canvas of life unfurled before me. A foundation upon which worlds and empires would rise and fall.

The very core of my being infused the earth with vitality. From my soul came the world.

I was the conductor of tempests, the serenity in waves, the warmth within flames, and the salt in the soils of the earth.

I illuminated the cosmos, the inception, the dawn.

A herald of days, the sunrise on the horizon.

I was the beginning.

I was the foundation upon which the world stands, yet they have forsaken my memory.

My name is a silent whisper in the wind, sounds lost to time so long ago.

I was once the Primal of days, and now I am forgotten.

A Dawn awaiting its Dusk.

CHAPTER ONE

The kettle's whistle pierced the still air, dragging me from the fog of exhaustion. There was no time for sleep. I measured the herbs, echinacea for his immune system, turmeric for inflammation, peppermint for his pain. Grinding them released their familiar, earthy scent, mixing with the quiet dread I carried. I wasn't a healer, but I had my research and wasn't ready to let go. Each dose felt like a tiny rebellion against the illness trying to steal my father.

Carrying the steaming tea, I forced a smile and entered Dad's room. He lay propped up against a stack of pillows, looking smaller than I ever remembered. Dr. Vager was there, his face drawn with fatigue and concern. He took the cup from me, his fingers warm against mine, and handed it to Dad.

"Brida, could we talk for a moment?" Vager's voice was gentle but held an edge of urgency. My heart sank, but I nodded and followed him into the hallway, the wooden floorboards creaking beneath us.

In the dim kitchen, Vager leaned against the counter, his shoulders slumped. "I've done all I can," he said quietly, his words hanging heavy in the air. “Based on what I’m seeing, I’d estimate a year.”

A year. The words echoed in my mind, an impossible sentence. My grip tightened around the edge of the counter. “No, that can’t be,” I insisted, shaking my head. “He was fine just a month ago.” My voice cracked, the frustration and fear spilling over. “There must be something we haven’t tried. Azmeer has healers with knowledge we don’t have here.”

Vager sighed, running a hand through his hair. “It’s possible, but we’re out of options locally. Without knowing exactly what’s wrong...”

“There has to be something!” I cut him off, my desperation mounting. “There are herbs, treatments, something we haven’t thought of yet. I can’t just give up.”

Vager studied me for a moment, a flicker of pity in his eyes. He reached into his bag and pulled out a list. “These are the strongest remedies we have available. They might help with the symptoms, but...”

“But they won’t cure him,” I finished, my voice hollow. I took the list, my fingers trembling. “I refuse to believe he only has a year left. He was fine—he was fine.” The tears I’d been holding back burned at the corners of my eyes, but I blinked them away, swallowing the lump in my throat. “There has to be a way.”

Vager nodded, a resigned look on his face. “Please let me know if you need me.”

I stumbled back to Dad’s room. The gentle rise and fall of his chest was a small, bittersweet comfort, a reminder that he was still here, even if only just. I left a note on his bedside table, a promise of my return, before grabbing my coat and heading into town.

The familiar trip into town took mere minutes, our home just on the fringes. Escalia wasn’t a large city by any means; it could hardly be called a city at all. We were a moderate-sized town in the Northern Ridge, largely ignored by Azmeer. Yes, they would send their tax collectors each year, and the new decrees for the year would be read, but for the most part, we were forgotten.

The sounds of horses whinnying, children playing, and the locals at the tavern already engrossed in their daily debate, despite it being barely midmorning, filled the air as I made my way along the streets. As was customary on my visits into Escalia, I drew stares from its residents as I walked by. "*Your hair makes you special, Brida. You may not see it now, but you'll appreciate it one day.*" My mother's words echoed in my mind as I moved through the crowd. Women glanced at me, their eyes lingering with a mixture of curiosity and unease. My hair—a deep shade of almost black, threaded with subtle crimson—made me stand out starkly among the locals.

Growing up, I had felt like an outsider, constantly aware of the curious stares and whispers behind my back. Children can be cruel, and I had endured more than my share of taunts and teasing. "Red-eyed witch," they called me, and "darkling," as if my unusual appearance marked me as something otherworldly. As a child, all I had wanted was to blend in, to be like everyone else. I had spent countless nights wishing my hair would lighten, that I could walk through the streets without drawing attention. I'd come to the realization now that it would never be the case, not unless I left.

At the apothecary, I reached into my pocket and pulled out Vager's list, smoothing the crumpled paper with careful fingers. The air inside was thick with the mingling scents of dried herbs and tinctures. I felt the weight of the shop assistant's gaze—a hard, assessing stare. Her eyes, cold and unforgiving, swept over me as I scanned the shelves. I spotted the milk thistle first, its vibrant purple petals dried and fragile. My hand paused over the jars of turmeric, the golden powder gleaming in the dim light. As I added each item to my basket, the assistant's lips tightened, her expression growing sharper as if my mere presence offended her. I kept my focus on the list, resisting the urge to meet her gaze, and continued gathering the ingredients, each movement deliberate and unwavering.

I thanked her, as I always did despite the treatment. With my nails digging into my palm, I made my way onto the covered porch.

"It's going to be in a couple of weeks!" The shout from a boy cut through the thick hum of market noise.

I barely registered it at first, distracted by the sight of shoppers moving from stall to stall and smells of freshly baked bread swirling around me, but there was something about his voice that made me pause.

"If I get an invitation, I'm going. I bet I'd do well in Azmeer." Another boy, older, swaggered as he spoke, his friend answering with a playful punch to the arm.

Azmeer? My ears pricked up, my attention shifting away from the dusty market stalls, and focusing instead on the scattered conversations drifting through the air. I caught snatches of excitement, the underlying thrill vibrating beneath the words. Something was stirring, something important.

A vendor arranging his wares nearby murmured to his partner, "I heard the invitations are already going out. Only a thousand or so... no one knows the exact number."

My chest tightened. *Invitations?*

I slowed my steps, glancing around, trying to catch more of what they were saying. A thousand invitations. A thousand...to what? The Courting. The word struck like a hammer, and suddenly, everything clicked into place, the scattered pieces forming a picture in my mind. The Courting, the elusive chance to prove oneself worthy of Azmeer.

My heart stuttered in my chest. *The Courting.*

The realization settled in slowly, creeping up from the edges of my mind, and with it came a rising sense of panic. The invitations were already out. They'd been sent. Each fragment of conversation confirmed it; everyone was talking about it, everyone except me.

Why hadn't I heard anything? Why hadn't...no. No. This couldn't be happening. I couldn't have missed this. This was the opportunity I'd been waiting for, the way out, the way to help my father.

My pulse quickened, a sharp urgency replacing the dull thrum of the market around me. I pushed through the noise, zeroing in on a cluster of children nearby, my voice cutting through their chatter before I even realized what I was saying. “Excuse me,” I blurted, barely able to hide the tremor in my words. “Where did you hear that the invitations had already been sent out?”

The boys turned, startled by my interruption. One of them, with an easy smirk, looked me over as though deciding if I was worth responding to. He must’ve found me harmless enough because he shrugged, his voice casual. “Some of the older kids are already talking about it. They’ve seen the invitations and can’t wait to check their mail. We don’t have any yet, though.”

I nodded, not really seeing them anymore. His words tumbled through my mind, over and over. The invitations *had* been sent. There might be one waiting for me. I could feel the weight of that possibility like a physical thing, heavy and dangerous.

There might be one. There had to be one.

Without another word, I spun on my heel and hurried back the way I came. My breath was shallow, each step faster than the last, fueled by a quiet determination that pulsed through me like a drumbeat. *Azmeer.* This was my way in. My way to help Dad.

I didn’t know how or when, but I would seize it.

CHAPTER TWO

I made my way home as quickly as possible, as if a phantom wind carried me, beads of sweat cresting my brow as I reached our mailbox. My hand shook uncontrollably as I fumbled for the latch of the worn wood. Dad and I had built this mailbox, something I'd suggested we do in an attempt to get him out of the house after we'd lost Mom. My hands had been so small, I'd barely been able to hold the hammer. The laugh I'd heard from him as I attempted to hit the nail had been the first in close to a year.

Reaching inside, I grabbed the few envelopes I found there. *Junk, junk, a letter from Aunt Addie, junk.* There was nothing. The dream I'd built for myself on the walk back evaporated as quickly as the dew on the grass. I shouldn't have been surprised; humans were seldom invited. Every few years, someone from Escalia receives an invitation. Soon after, it would always be determined that they possessed Fae heritage, no matter how far back.

I closed the box and made my way along the dirt path to the door. Our front door, famous in the neighborhood for its large crack through its center, was open as I approached. *I locked this.* Pushing lightly, the door squeaked as I saw a clearer picture of what was inside.

The opening of cupboards sounded from the kitchen as a petite brown-haired woman reached for a mug. "Hey, Bri."

Flora, Kadian's sister, had made it a habit to stop by every day. It was a small comfort, something I could find a bit of peace in. "Hey, Flo."

As I was beginning to take my coat off, I heard Flora from the kitchen murmur, "I wouldn't do that if I were you. I would turn around and head right to Kadian's. I made a pit stop at his place on the way here. He apparently has some news that he can '*only share once I've told Brida.*'" Flora rolled her eyes.

Glancing at the clock that hung on the wall, I made a note. "I won't be more than an hour," I said.

Turning back from the door, I reached into my pocket, retrieving the packets of herbs. "Would you mind putting this in the kitchen? Vager stopped by this morning."

"Will do!"

Kadian's family had always been close to mine, our mothers having been friends. Even though Flora was a few years older than Kadian and me and had been away at school for the last few years, she'd been a wonderful help to me in the past month.

"I won't be long."

"Just go, Brida. Happy to help!"

I thanked her silently as I closed the door behind me. Kadian's was a ten-minute walk along the outskirts of town. He and I had finished university this past week. I'd taken the few moments of free time we'd had over the past months to plan our annual trip, but instead of a few days away somewhere, we'd decided to take a longer trip to celebrate. Then, well, our lives were supposed to have begun.

After climbing the narrow, uneven steps to Kadian's floor, I paused to take in the familiar, worn surroundings. The building seemed like it had been forgotten by time, barely clinging to itself with sagging ceilings and peeling wallpaper that flaked onto the threadbare carpet. The banister wobbled with the slightest touch, and I swore the entire structure creaked under its own weight, like an old man groaning with every movement.

When I finally reached his door, I raised my hand and knocked as loudly as I could, the sound echoing down the quiet hall. The door had been patched so many times it was more patchwork than wood, and I could feel the rattle of the frame beneath my knuckles.

Ruffling through my bag, I searched for the key he'd given me. The apartment didn't have wards on the doors, just plain old-fashioned keys. Most of Escalia embraced this simplicity, with most of its residents being human.

"There you are," I muttered. It had made its way into my book, my favorite book, *The Trials of Thale*. I'd always been a reader, thanks to my mother, but Addie had ensured it once Mom was gone.

The door creaked as I pushed it open, turning to close it and remove the key from the hole. I was surprised when I heard laughing from behind me.

Sitting on a worn leather chair in his living room by the window sat my best friend, half-naked—thankfully the top half. Following his gaze, I found him staring at a piece of parchment in his hands.

"You summoned me," I jested, tossing my bag onto the hardwood floor. It was surprisingly visible this morning.

Sitting across from him, I took in the furrowed brow and the tight set of his jaw. Gone was the easy smile, replaced by a stern gaze that bore into the paper. The lines on his face seemed etched deeper, his eyes more focused, and the once carefree air around him had given way to a palpable sense of purpose.

"*Ahem*," I finally said. Kadian, to my surprise, looked shocked when he lifted his eyes to me.

"Bri, when did you get here?"

"Are you serious?" I scoffed. "I just about broke down your door, spoke to you as I came in just now, sat in front of you, and you had no idea? Did you have an *eventful* night?" I looked around the room to see if any evidence remained of a party or a guest. To my shock, I found none.

"Sorry," he whispered. "I got lost in this."

Kadian rose and made his way toward me, handing me the parchment as he loomed above me.

My fingers traced the edges of the blood-red seal. Immediately, my eyes shot to Kadian. "How?"

"Read it."

Dear Citizen,
We are pleased to announce the commencement of this year's Courting. This annual event marks the opportunity for new candidates to vie for a place among the four esteemed Courts of Azmeer. On the tenth day of the sixth month at the eleventh bell, please proceed to your nearest designated transportation point, listed below. Wind Walkers will be present to assist you, though you are welcome to arrange your own travel if preferred.
Upon arrival, you will be presented with the first task.
We look forward to welcoming you to Azmeer.

"Say something, Brida," Kadian said.

I couldn't speak, breath caught in my throat. An invitation. He'd received an invitation to the Courting.

"It was hand delivered this morning by a Walker. He mentioned that more than one person had been selected from Escalia this year..." Pausing, his eyes rose to meet mine. "I was hoping the other person was you."

The lump in my throat only continued to grow as the tightness in my chest felt that it would cause me to cease breathing.

Placing the parchment down next to me, I rubbed my sweaty palms along my thighs. *Gods, don't do it.* The earnest look in his eyes made my heart twist. *Don't be foolish.* The words clawed their way up my throat, and before I knew it, I was speaking.

"I got one too!" I blurted out. My stomach churned. I'd never lied before, and the thought of doing it again made me want to be sick.

"You got one too? I knew it!" Kadian beamed, his smile lighting up the room like the sun cresting the horizon.

Of course, I didn't get one; I'm human.

"Sure did!" There. I had just done it again. *What's wrong with me? Stop lying to him.*

"This is going to be amazing, Bri! The Courting, I can't believe it."

"I can't either." I forced a smile, feeling the lie settle uncomfortably in my chest.

"Hey, are you sure you're okay? You're looking a bit ashen."

I was sure I was. Although I'm not sure how much fairer my pale complexion could be. "I'm fine," I smiled. Grabbing the paper, I read the note again.

Within seconds, I felt the cushion sink deeper. "Do you know what this means, Bri?" Kadian said, wrapping his arm around me. "It means that we're finally getting out of here." His constant grinning told me just how excited he was by the prospect.

Kadian had been my only true friend growing up, the one person I could always count on. We promised each other that whenever one of us left, we'd go together. I never planned to hold him to that promise, but now, as the moment approached, I couldn't imagine a future without him by my side.

"A *Courting,* Kad," I whispered as if the peeling white paint on the walls could hear us. Kadian had hated this room at first, but months of saving had allowed him to decorate it with the chair and couch we managed to get for nearly half the vendor's original price. The vendor had mistaken us for a newlywed couple, and Kadian hadn't corrected him, not wanting to lose the deal, though it was the furthest thing from the truth. Now, all this furniture, our possessions, would be left behind. I hadn't realized what was happening until Kadian wiped the tears from my cheek. Turning my face towards him, our eyes locked. "I'm scared," I admitted.

I am scared. Scared of losing my best friend and leaving my father behind, but most of all, I was terrified of failing to secure an invitation of my own. Little was known about the Courting beyond what we had learned in seminars. "*The courts are what make our world thrive. All law and magic stem from them. Even the king is often beholden to their will.*"

To shape how the world is run, to organize and influence its structure, to rise to a position of power and wield magic—magic that could potentially save Dad. *I need to get an invitation.*

"You'll be fine, Brida." Kadian leaned toward me. The familiar aroma of fresh earth and pine needles brought a calm that eased the tightness in my chest. Kadian had always been my safe place, my home.

"Vale is going to be so excited for you," Kadian squeezed my hand as if he could read my thoughts. "We'll make sure he's taken care of, Bri. I can ask Flora to stay with him while we're gone."

"That's a big ask, Kadian."

"Nah, she loves Vale. She'd be happy to do it. She may have already offered when I showed her my invitation and proclaimed that I knew you'd gotten one, too."

Well, she lied to me this morning. Apparently, everyone is doing it today.

The pain from the cracking of my heart seared through me, a sharp, raw ache that felt like it was slicing through my chest. It was as if each beat was reminding me of what I could lose, the hurt spreading through me with every thump. I could hardly catch my breath.

"I'm going to read up on everything," I said, wiping the dampness from my eyes. My voice was steady, but my determination was even firmer. "I'm going to try to learn everything there is to know about these courts before our arrival."

Lately, my nights had been consumed with research. After my father had fallen asleep, I would sit by the flickering light of a single candle, poring over texts and scrolls. My focus was on herbs and their properties—each leaf, root, and flower seemed to hold a universe of secrets. I studied the nuances of their effects, how they could be combined, and the intricate process of brewing teas that might offer remedies.

Reading was my sanctuary, a haven where the chaos of my daily life melted away. In our small-town library, the musty smell of old books was a comfort, and the rustling pages were my escape. Every book I read was a step closer to mastering the knowledge I needed. Even in the limited spare time I had, I devoured every scrap of information, driven by a thirst for understanding.

Kadian laughed. "I'd expect nothing less from you. Gives you something to do in the few weeks until we leave." *Gods he's right. It's only a few weeks away.*

Kadian rose and knelt in front of me, "This is an amazing opportunity. Can you imagine? To be chosen by one of the four courts, to have a say in how the world is organized, how it's run, to have..." He paused.

"*Magic,*" I said. His grin grew feral.

"Yes, Brida. Magic. Of course, we likely won't know what any of that is, regardless of how much you intend to read up on it. Mom says they've always been tight-lipped about that stuff."

He was right. From my research, I knew that the courts were notoriously secretive about what they allowed the public to know. Beyond the laws and regulations that were openly shared with the realm, their true secrets were carefully guarded within the walls of Azmeer and the inner sanctums of the courts themselves.

"Do you think Elana will hope you're placed in the Eternal Court?" Kadian's mother's Fae heritage was so diluted that she appeared human, just like Kadian and the majority of the Fae in Escalia. He looked like a true Escalian, with light brown hair and green eyes. It had made things easier for him as a kid. Easier than it had been for me.

"I'm sure she'd be happiest with that. Keeping familial ties alive, you know, honor and all that bullshit." He ran a hand through his hair. It was getting longer, coming just below his eyes; it suited him. "What are the names of the other courts anyway?"

"Someone didn't pay attention in his History of Azmeer course." I laughed. I'd had to drag Kadian to every lecture our first semester. The look on his face all but confirmed he'd forgotten this had been a topic the course covered. "The four courts are"—I cleared my throat for dramatic effect—"The Court of Reflection, The Eternal Court, The Court of Whispers, and The Court of Shadows."

The names of the courts were irrelevant. The only thing that mattered was securing an invitation. *This is going to work,* I thought to myself. *I will make this work.*

"Let's go get a drink to celebrate!" Kadian said, pulling me up from the couch, wrapping his arms around me. "Come, let's go."

As Kadian grabbed a shirt and ushered me out the door, I couldn't help but look back to the parchment resting on the counter. The letter that would change our destinities.

CHAPTER THREE

I stood in the light of my room, clutching the letter that had been my obsession for weeks, my heart a chaotic mess of fear and determination. Every night after I'd read to my father and seen him to bed, Flora would sit by his side, giving Kadian and me precious moments to study for Azmeer. Our stolen hours were filled with scraps of information, fragments of past Courting trials we could glean.

"It says here that typically one thousand to twelve hundred citizens are invited annually to participate in the Courting," I pointed to a line on the page, "and that number is whittled down to approximately two hundred to two hundred and fifty after the first challenge. We must get past the first task." But the first trials varied so wildly—sometimes purely physical, sometimes a brutal mix of mental games and strength that I couldn't find any pattern.

"I likely won't get through if it's entirely physical," I murmured to Kadian one evening, the weight of doubt pressing down on me.

"*I'll drag you through it if I have to,*" he winked, his voice light but his eyes serious. And I knew he would, but my gut told me this would be a solitary endeavor. Even if we were close, we'd still be apart.

After many late nights, when he'd fallen asleep, I pored over every detail of the original invitation. The flourishes of the cursive, the texture of the parchment, the subtle nuances of the ink—I'd memorized them all. My hands ached from hours of practice, trying to mimic the elegant script just right. Between my check-ins on Dad, lessons with Kadian, and running—something I'd started doing since I'd found out about Dad's illness—I scoured every store in town and spoke to librarians at the university until I found parchment nearly identical to the original. After countless attempts, I finally succeeded in forging a convincing copy. I'd done my best. There was no guarantee of my success, but I knew I had to try.

Rumors circulated throughout Escalia that, in addition to Kadian and me, one other Escalian had been invited. Talia, the baker's daughter, had always left me alone despite others often wishing to drive me from the area. The decision to forge the invitation instead of stealing one had come easily; I couldn't bear the thought of jeopardizing someone else's chance at the Courting. So, I made my own, hoping no one would notice the difference. Yet, even as I held the forged letter in my hands, a tightness in my chest wove a web of anxiety through me.

Despite my best efforts, the worry never left me. I felt hollow as I stood in the center of my room, staring at the place that had once been mine. Memories flooded me. Reading before bed, sitting at my desk cramming for an exam, crying when I learned about Mom, staring at the cracks on my walls, imagining what worlds possibly lived inside them. As I took one final look around my room, a pang of doubt struck me. Would all my careful planning be in vain? The thought of being caught filled me with dread, but there was no turning back now.

I made my way into my father's room to see he was awake and dressed. I wasn't sure if it was the herbs or his constitution, but he had seemed marginally better these last few days. It had been a relief to know that if I was leaving, potentially for an unforeseen amount of time, that at least he was faring better.

"I'm ready." My father said as he reached for his sweater.

My brows furrowed together as a slight smirk pulled at my lips, "Come again?"

"There will be no argument about this, Brida. It's not every day your kid gets invited to the Courting."

Gods. I'd hated lying to him these past weeks. Dad had been incredibly supportive and excited when I told him the news. The initial shock and panic on his face eased when I told him that Kadian would be going as well. *Well, Kadian was the only one technically going.* But I'd kept that part to myself. My father and I had always had an open relationship. He'd played the role of both parents for a time, and as much as the darkness had tried to consume him, consume us, we hadn't let it win.

"Dad, I'm not just going into town. Lesalia is the meeting spot, and no one will be with you to bring you back."

"Flora has already agreed to meet us there. I won't argue with you about this." He smiled, "Do you have everything you need?"

I knew this was an argument I wasn't going to win, especially if Flo had already given her clearance. Nodding, I gestured to the small bags I'd packed if I somehow managed to get away with this and, beyond that, make it past the first task.

Taking a few steps toward me, Dad rested his hand on my cheek, "Let's go."

The sun was shining as we stepped outside, but the air remained crisp. Reaching the street, I turned back, gazing at the house that had been my home for the past twenty-five years. I looked at my father; the sadness etched on his face deepened the lines around his mouth and eyes, revealing the weight of years and unspoken worries.

His purplish-blue eyes met mine. I never knew where my father got his eyes from, never having known his family, and in that moment, the unspoken bond between us felt more palpable than ever, a silent understanding of the shared burdens we both carried.

Dad reached for my hand, tethering me. "This will always be your home."

"I'm supposed to be the one comforting you right now," I managed to croak out, my voice thick with emotion.

With a playful wink, he replied, "You don't have to be strong for me, my beautiful girl. Not today."

I nodded, letting his words settle into my heart. I resigned myself to the belief that someday—hopefully not too soon—I would be back here. The same house, filled with love and laughter and a father who was healed.

"I'm ready."

Not wanting our last moments to be spent in silence, he filled our walk with conversation. "How was it last night?"

"The bar was busier than ever. Everyone preparing for Azmeer was there. I've never seen the staff more disgruntled," I laughed, remembering the chaos. Kadian had insisted we go for a final drink, in order to send us off. What had remained one drink for me turned into several for Kadian and resulted in him singing the Escalian anthem. I wasn't sure how many towns had anthems, but Kadian wanted to ensure everyone knew we did.

Many of those invited from the West had chosen to spend the night in Escalia before making their way to Lesalia in the morning. Our prices were far more reasonable, and besides, Lesalia was only a forty-five-minute walk away.

As I recounted the night's events, the weight of our impending goodbye felt a little lighter, the warmth of our connection wrapping around us like a comforting embrace.

"How's Kadian feeling about things?" Dad asked, his limp noticeable as he leaned slightly against the wall for support. I couldn't help but watch him, the way his face tightened with each step, a faint sheen of sweat glistening on his brow. It was painful to see, like a knife twisting in my chest.

How much longer could he push himself like this? I felt the familiar knot of worry tighten in my stomach. I tried to shake it off, to focus on the moment instead of the inevitable. But the truth was lurking just beneath the surface—he was unwell, and no amount of bravado could change that.

"Are you sure you're okay?" I asked, my voice softer than I intended, almost a whisper.

He flashed me a reassuring smile, but I saw the flicker of pain behind it. "Just a little tired, that's all. Nothing I can't handle," he said, but the tremor in his voice betrayed him. I wanted to believe him, to hold onto that hope, but each time he pushed himself, I couldn't help but wonder what price he would pay later.

As we moved forward, I held onto his hand a little tighter, anchoring both of us. I wished I could take his burdens, to lighten the load he carried, even just a little. But for now, all I could do was be here with him, even as the shadows of uncertainty loomed larger with each labored step.

"To answer your question, Kadian is eager." I sighed. "Arguably more eager than me." In the few weeks since the invitation had arrived, Kadian hadn't been able to talk about anything else. *"Have you read that only members from the Court of Whispers can access the peaks of the Tactras Mountains?"* Or *"Did you know that the Court of Shadows has shadow and fire magic? Weird, it has both!"* It was the most Kadian had read in his life. It'd been a nice change to have a study partner.

"It's good that you'll have him there," Dad said as if he was reassuring himself rather than me. "Will he be meeting you in line?"

"No, his parents hired their own transportation. I'll find him once I get there." They'd offered to take me with them, but I didn't want to risk it. I didn't want to risk Kadian seeing my lie crumble.

The remainder of our walk was filled with chatter about what Flora had been reading to Dad and him pretending to complain about the "concoction" I'd been giving him. "The color really is hideous, but I will say, it doesn't taste too shabby."

As we approached Lesalia's weathered stone gate, we saw Flora making her way toward us. I sighed in relief.

"This is where I leave you," he said as he held my gaze.

He took a step, wrapping his arms around me so tightly that I could barely breathe. "I love you, kiddo," he whispered. Tears streaked down my cheeks as guilt for leaving him washed over me. We'd never been apart for more than a couple of weeks, and now I didn't know when I would see him again. He cupped my face. "You look so much like her."

I'd heard it for years—the comments about how I looked just like her. After we lost Mom, it felt like a curse, a constant reminder of the love that had been torn from us. But now, I understood it as the truest form of admiration Dad could offer.

Placing my hands over his, I smiled, "I promise I'll write when I can."

He nodded. Before I could move, he pulled me in for one final embrace, "I love you so much. Gods, I remember the day you were born, such a feisty thing. You couldn't wait to get into the world," he laughed. "We always knew you would go on to do something incredible, Bri, and you will."

I was on the verge of becoming a blubbering mess. This was the speech I'd anticipated him giving me at graduation, not when I was hoping to bluff my way into the Courting. "Remember, Brida, you're allowed to have some fun." He winked as he turned, making his way with Flora, who waved back.

Don't follow him. I tried not to succumb to every nerve in my body telling me to go back home with him and make him breakfast.

I have to do this.

Watching my father and Flora fade into the distance, I was reminded of my resolve. *This is what I can offer him.* Forcing myself to pick up my bags, I made my way to the line.

Shopkeepers emerged from their stores, everyone was curious as to what was happening at the inn. It was still early, but already a line had formed on the porch and wrapped around the veranda, down the stairs, and onto the street.

I knew I wouldn't see any familiar faces, Talia claiming her family had opted for their own transportation. I was the sole

Escalian here, standing amidst a sea of strangers. The crowd around me was a vibrant tapestry of diversity, each person exuding an aura of mystery and uniqueness. It was clear that some were Fae; their elongated, delicate ears marked them. Their otherworldly beauty and grace set them apart, moving through the crowd with effortless elegance.

Among them were those who were a mix, nymphs. Their features blending the ethereal qualities of the Fae with the solid earthiness of humans. These individuals possessed a unique charm, their hybrid nature evident in the slight point of their ears or the unusual hue of their eyes. They carried an air of both worlds, straddling the line between the mystical and the mundane.

As I looked around, the sense of isolation grew, yet it was tempered by a burgeoning curiosity about these new faces and the stories they carried. The anticipation of meeting Kadian in Azmeer and the uncertainty of what lay ahead filled me with excitement and trepidation as I took in the sight of the gathered assembly, each person a potential ally or adversary in the unfolding journey.

Not paying attention to my feet as I'd been consumed with watching those around me, I tripped, falling flat on my face. *Off to a great start, Brida. Definitely going to make an impression.*

"Here," a soft voice said.

Looking up, I saw one of the most beautiful people I'd ever seen. She stood taller than me, which wasn't difficult, had shiny blond hair and aquamarine eyes that shone with curiosity and delight. I grabbed the hand she'd extended and dusted off my pants.

"Are you okay?" She studied me.

Nodding and sighing, I said, "I'm fine. Nothing is hurt, save for my pride!"

She smiled as she waved at two figures in the distance. "Told them I'd be fine on my own, but they insisted on tagging along." Her laugh was sultry, inviting, warmer than most. "Your folks hanging around here somewhere?"

“My father left already.” I pushed my hair behind my ears, wondering if she’d notice the shape.

“Hopefully not too far of a trip home!” She smiled, ignoring them. “Where are you from?” We took a few steps forward as the line continued to move.

“Escalia,” I said with a faint smile.

“Oh,” she said. “Your hair is unusual for these parts. I would’ve guessed somewhere further east. The red in it is lovely.”

“Thank you,” I replied, my voice barely above a whisper. Compliments about my hair usually came from Kadian or family, so hearing it from someone else felt unsettling. My mother’s hair had been a brilliant, fiery red that lit up a room. In contrast, mine was nearly black, with just the faintest hints of red threaded through it like her fire had dimmed when it reached me. It felt like I was living in her shadow, a ghost of what she had been.

Suddenly, the air felt thick, and my heart raced. I hated how quickly my thoughts spiraled back to her. *Stop thinking about Mom. You’re stressed enough as it is.* I forced a smile, but it felt brittle, like glass about to shatter. “Where are you from?” I blurted out, desperate to steer the conversation away from the weight of her memory pressing down on me.

“Here,” she smiled. “You sure you’re okay?” the girl asked. It was no doubt easier to appear calm when you had actually been invited to the Courting. While Kadian had spent the last few weeks anticipating all the things we would see and experience, my studies had also included breathing techniques—an attempt to manage my anxiety. Thus far, I was failing miserably.

“Yes, sorry.” I smiled.

“What’s your name?” A smirk graced her lips, “I’m Lil, well Lilianna technically, but I’m loath to have anyone call me that.”

“Name and place of origin,” came a stern voice. I looked up, locking eyes with a figure clad in a red and black formal uniform, his posture radiating authority. The king's insignia gleamed ominously on his chest, a stark reminder of the gravity of my deception. "Have your invitation out and ready."

My fingers fumbled with the forged letter, the paper feeling foreign and heavy in my grasp. A cold sweat broke out along my spine, and my heart pounded so hard it felt like it might leap out of my chest. My breath hitched, the world narrowing to the space between my trembling hands and the guard's expectant gaze. Every instinct screamed at me to run, to abandon this reckless plan before it consumed me. *What had I been thinking? How had I convinced myself that I could pull this off?*

I drew a shaky breath, forcing myself to remain still, to face the consequences of my choices head-on. My father's illness plagued me, and the unspoken bond we shared remained my motivator. This wasn't about me; it was for him.

"Brida Larrow, Escalia," I managed to say, my voice barely more than a whisper, quivering with the weight of the lie. I handed over the letter, my hands shaking visibly. The guard's eyes bore into me, scrutinizing the parchment with a meticulousness that made my stomach twist into tighter knots. Every second felt like an eternity as he looked me up and down, his gaze lingering just long enough to stir the cold dread pooling in my gut.

"This looks..." he began, his brow furrowing as he examined the letter more closely. My pulse quickened, a rush of panic threatening to overtake me. I was on the brink of being exposed, of being cast out as a fraud. My vision blurred, and I struggled to keep my expression neutral, to hide the fear threatening to consume me.

Before the guard could finish, a figure stepped forward, his presence commanding immediate respect. "Is there a problem here?" he asked, his voice smooth yet authoritative, cutting through the tension like a knife. The newcomer exuded a quiet power, his hair nearly white with delicate hints of violet shimmering in the light. His eyes, a striking shade of amethyst, met mine with a piercing intensity that left me feeling exposed, yet there was no judgment in his gaze, only a calm, unreadable assessment.

The guard straightened. "Just verifying the authenticity of this letter," he replied, his tone now more deferential. My heart skipped a beat, and I bit down hard on the inside of my cheek to keep from trembling.

The man cast a brief glance at the letter, then looked back at me, his expression inscrutable. For a moment, the world seemed to hold its breath. "I'm sure it's all in order," he said firmly, his voice carrying a quiet assurance that left no room for doubt.

The guard hesitated, his uncertainty palpable, then reluctantly nodded. "Very well. Proceed," he said, handing the letter back to me. I held my composure, giving a curt nod of thanks. My legs felt like they might give out beneath me, but I forced myself to move forward, each step feeling like a victory against the rising tide of fear and anxiety.

Relief washed over me, but I couldn't shake the unease. The man turned to me, his expression softening slightly. "Brida Larrow, was it? Come with me."

I turned back and smiled at Lil, who mouthed "good luck" as we walked away from the guard.

The man spoke in a lower voice. "Every year, people try to sneak in. The guards are cautious. You handled that well."

"Thank you," I managed to say, my voice still shaky. "I didn't expect... I mean, I thought..."

He smiled slightly. "It's alright. Just stay close to me."

Standing at least six feet tall with broad shoulders, he had slicked-back hair that brushed just above his ears, smooth enough to run your fingers through if you felt inclined. His handsome features were only enhanced when he smiled, sending a warm flush to my cheeks.

He continued walking with me, leading me to a quiet spot away from the crowd. "I'm your escort to Azmeer," he said, his tone more relaxed. "Have you ever traveled with a Walker before?"

Placing my bags down, I shook my head, dreading it already.

"Well, it can be...disorienting for those who aren't used to it. So, for my sake and yours, I hope you didn't have a full breakfast this morning." He chuckled.

My stomach churned. "Should I grab my bags?"

"No, they will be waiting for you in Azmeer, in the inductees' quarters. No need to worry."

"Okay," I fidgeted with my hands, fear creeping in.

"Now, Brida, wrap your hands around my waist here." He lifted my arms and wrapped them around him. "And if it's alright with you, I'm going to place my arms around you here," he adjusted our stances. "This will be over in seconds. And remember, if you feel unwell, please hold it in until we arrive. This is a new jacket." He winked.

Before I could respond, we were gone. It felt like being torn apart and thrown through space while simultaneously standing still. I closed my eyes, trying to block out the sensation, pressing myself further into him. I heard a low rumble coming from his chest. *He's laughing. Just breathe and relax.* I'd only just met this man, and here I was, pressed against him. It felt intimate. My mind wandered, taking in the feel of his muscles under the suit. *Who wears a suit for this? Bet he'd look good without it... Get it together, Brida. This isn't what we're going to Azmeer for.*

"You can open your eyes now," he whispered. I held tight, unsure if I wanted to let go.

Warm air caressed my face like a summer breeze. Opening one eye at a time, I was delighted to see we stood on solid ground. The palace, built from limestone, revealed hues of blush and tan marbled together. As I moved, the colors shifted and danced, creating a living tapestry.

"Everything you expected?" he asked with a grin.

"It's nothing like I expected," I marveled.

"You can take a few moments. Afterward, go straight here," he pointed. "Then, take a right at the olive trees. You'll see an entryway."

“Thank you,” I whispered. “The trip wasn’t terrible." I attempted a smile.

“Anytime, Brida,” he said, his smirk widening as he slid his hands into his pockets. “You know, I don’t recall there being a Larrow on the list. Must be my mistake.” With a final enigmatic glance, he vanished. A shiver rippled through me, my heart thudding in my ears.

I stood frozen, the grandeur of the palace towering above me, its cold beauty contrasting with the sweat pooling at my back. The weight of my forged invitation pressed heavily against my chest, each breath a struggle. For my father, I had to move forward, even as doubt gnawed at the edges of my resolve.

CHAPTER FOUR

I took a few moments to admire what lay before me. The path wasn't like the dirt roads of Escalia but rather a polished cobble walkway that wound through a garden before reaching the glistening building.

I stood amidst untamed blossoms mingled with elegant roses alongside trees and bushes of all sizes. The breeze carried a symphony of scents that enveloped me, wrapping me in its embrace, hinting at the capital's opulence. Pausing, I drank in the swirling palette of colors, lost in their beauty. *How tall is this?* I tilted my head back, my eyes tracing the palace's endless ascent. Towers and spires rose to different heights, each one piercing the sky. The intricate design, with sections spiraling upward, suggested an otherworldly craftsmanship that defied the limits of ordinary construction. No building in Escalia was taller than three stories. The palace was several hundred feet high.

Pay attention. Look where your feet are going. Not accustomed to walking on cobblestone, I slipped a few times, catching myself before anyone noticed.

The smell of the olive grove reached me prior to turning the corner. Its trees lined the two hundred yards or so of walkway that led to the massive entrance where palatial guards stood dutifully. Carvings ran up the sides of the doorway and building. Even though I couldn't make them out, I could see that they were detailed and intricate.

"Nice, isn't it?" A familiar voice interrupted my thoughts. I turned around to see Lil walking towards me. "Have a good flight?"

"It's something I can now say I've done and will be fine if I never do again," I replied, smiling at her.

"Yeah, it isn't fun. At least you got to hug that... I don't even want to call him a man as few men I've ever encountered looked like that," she said with a grin. "What's his name?"

The Walker—it took everything in me not to blush. "I never got it," I said as she made her way next to me.

Other arrivals braved what lay ahead as they made their way toward the open doors. *I can do this.*

Don't panic.

I am more than my fear; I am the story I choose to write.

Sensing my trepidation, she wrapped her arm under mine, pulling me close. "Well, best we get to it then. Need to find out that man's name after all, *don't we?"* She gave me a grin. "Brida Larrow, ready for our lives to begin?"

Despite the unease twisting in my gut, I went along with Lil. Azmeer would have to be my fresh start—a place to shed the past and become someone...more. Someone who belonged here. Someone who could let herself be led by the arm of a stranger, confident and fearless.

The guards paid us no attention as we entered through heavy wooden doors. "It's stunning," I remarked. The entryway was several hundred feet tall with mosaic tiles from the floor to the ceiling, depicting scenes of the emergence of each court and how the ruling family came to Azmeer. The images showed each court in its location.

"That's the Court of Reflection," Lil pointed toward a collection of blue and green tiles mixed with ivory to construct the court that sat on the edge of the Hydratas Sea. "It takes your breath away no matter how many times you see it." She sighed.

From my reading, I recognized the Court of Whispers, symbolized by the array of purples that formed a formidable fortress seated amongst the clouds. Tactical in its position, the Tactras Mountains reigned as the tallest in the world. The Eternal Court mosaic stood no less impressive, yet everything remained shrouded by the onyx tiles, holding the mysteries of the Court of Shadows. Something about the way the light glinted on the black and red made me pause.

"Over there," Lil interrupted, pointing forward. Ahead were tables with people waiting to check us in. "If we're lucky, maybe we'll stay together," Lil leaned in. "It'll be nice to know someone."

I smiled, remembering I already knew someone here: Kadian. I was relieved knowing that if he hadn't arrived yet, he would soon. I looked around the cavernous space in the hopes I'd catch a glimpse of him.

"Looking for *someone*?" Lil laughed as she whispered into my ear.

"It's not like that. I'm not looking for the Walker." The hall continued to fill with people, but Kadian was nowhere to be seen.

"Why not? I sure am."

"It's my friend from home. I'm supposed to meet him here." I said.

"*Oh*. Well, that explains it," Lil chuckled.

"It's not like that," I said again, looking at her. "I've known him my whole life. His mother was best friends with my mother. We grew up together, and when my mom died..." I paused. "Well, she became a surrogate mother to me. We've always been close."

The words barely left my lips before I felt the sting of self-consciousness settling in. This was the most I'd ever spoken to a stranger in one go, and the tension building in my chest now clawed its way up my throat. My heart raced, each beat echoing the internal command I gave myself: *Relax, Brida. Breathe.*

But the command did little to ease the familiar discomfort

creeping over me. I'd always been more comfortable blending into the background, letting others take the lead in conversations. Even as a child, I was the one who preferred the quiet corners of the room, burying my nose in a book or watching from the sidelines as others chatted away with ease. Kadian had been the exception—the one person who could coax me out of my shell, who knew how to draw me into the world with his easy smiles and gentle nudges.

"You're lucky you'll have that slice of home here with you. I was the only one from Lesalia, so it's just me!" Despite her bright smile and upbeat chatter, her eyes betrayed a fleeting shadow of melancholy. When she laughed, it didn't quite reach the corners of her eyes, which lingered on a distant thought.

"Well, you'll love Kadian. He's charming and clever." I bumped her hip in a poor attempt to cheer her up. *Gods, Brida.*

"I can't wait to meet him!" She forced a smile.

The women at the table radiated intensity. Their dark brown hair, streaked with blonde, was tied back, and their sun-kissed skin bore battle marks. Amber eyes cut through the room with a fierce gaze. Clad in worn brown leathers, their movements were sharp and deliberate, their beauty edged with a commanding presence that identified them as members of the Eternal Court.

"Lilianna Towler," Lil said.

I swallowed hard, trying to steady my nerves. "Brida Larrow," I said, lowering my face to stare at my shoes as if they held the answers to my anxiety. I could only hope they didn't notice the slight tremor in my voice.

The woman paused, just for a fraction of a second, but it was enough to send a jolt of fear through me. I forced myself to remain still, resisting the urge to fidget under her scrutiny.

"Your names have been registered. Make your way through the colonnade into the courtyard. Good luck with the first task."

As we walked away, my heart pounded in my chest. I couldn't shake the feeling that the woman's gaze lingered on me, as if she had sensed something off, something that didn't quite fit. The forged invitation felt like a lead weight, dragging me down with every step I took. One wrong move, one misstep, and everything could come crashing down.

Columns that seemed to rise several hundred feet high, each carved with the lore of the Primals in addition to the trials of King Elidas, cascaded toward the ceiling. The pale limestone offered a beautiful contrast to the landscape that lay just beyond.

As we walked through the colonnade, the grandeur became clearer. It loomed in the distance, beyond a vast expanse of lush gardens and sprawling courtyards. The path ahead stretched out, lined with flowers and trees, leading to the true palace. My heart sank a little as I realized that what I had thought was the palace was merely an elaborate entrance hall, a gateway to the magnificence that lay beyond.

Lil squeezed my arm, sensing my disappointment. “It’s still a long way to go,” she whispered with a smile. “But we’re getting closer.”

I nodded, feeling the weight of the journey ahead. The real challenge was just beginning.

CHAPTER FIVE

Lil's chatter was a distant murmur, barely registering over the pounding of my heart. My eyes flicked past the vibrant flowers and grand trees, struggling to take in the lush surroundings. Instead, my gaze was fixed on the horizon, where groups of people were gathering, tiny figures from our vantage point.

As we crested the hill, the imposing walls of Azmeer came into view, rising above the swarm of people. They enclosed a breathtaking limestone palace that seemed to pierce the sky with its soaring spires and intricate carvings, far surpassing anything I'd seen before.

"Have you ever left Lesalia?" I asked Lil.

"Gods, yes," she replied, her voice softer, more reflective. "My father's family still resides in the Court of Reflection. The Hydratas Sea is one of the most beautiful places. The sea is like a mirror when you stare at it, a perfect reflection." Her eyes softened as if seeing those tranquil waters once more.

"I haven't been there for several years. My family's hope is that the Court of Reflection will notice me here, and then I'll receive my placement. I hope I get to travel between here and the Court of Reflection—I haven't explored Azmeer."

Just as we were about to step into the crowd, a familiar voice broke through the murmur of voices. "There you are!" In an instant, I was lifted off the ground, Kad's laughter ringing out as he held me. His eyes sparkled with excitement, his tousled hair and warm, mischievous smile put me at ease.

"You won't be seeing me for much longer if you keep that up. You'll grind me to dust," I suppressed a smile.

He laughed, setting me down before placing his hands on my shoulders. "I've been looking for you." His eyes, a captivating mix of green with golden flecks sparkled. Turning to Lil, he asked, "And who might you be?"

"I'm Lil," she answered, meeting his gaze with confidence. "And despite what you might hear, not Lilianna."

He studied her for a moment, a playful smile tugging at his lips. "Duly noted, Lil."

"Lil, this is Kadian. The friend I was telling you about," I said, feeling the warmth of our reunion spread through me.

"You were telling her about me?" Kad's eyebrows shot up, a mock expression of surprise on his face. His eyes flicked down before sighing and shaking his head. "You are far too kind," he teased.

"You can't be sure that what I said was kind or sweet," I shot back, giving his shoulder a light tap.

He leaned in close, his voice dropping to a conspiratorial whisper. "Ah, yes, but I can hope." Grinning, he extended a hand to Lil. "Good to meet you. Despite what she may...or may not have said about me."

Lil shook his hand, her smile widening. "The pleasure's mine. And don't worry, she's only said good things. So far."

As we stepped into the crowd, the playful banter eased some of the tension, but my attention was overwhelmed by the scene around us. My gaze swept over the throngs of Fae and nymphs, drawn to the towering gates that led to the labyrinthine courtyard of Azmeer.

Each gate bore the insignia of one of the four courts: The Court of Shadows, The Court of Reflection, The Court of Whispers, and the Eternal Court. They loomed like ancient guardians, their presence heavy with unspoken power. The limestone palace behind them stood tall and intimidating, a reflection of the complex and formidable world we were stepping into.

The crowd was a roiling sea of hopefuls and onlookers, the air buzzing with excited chatter and hushed whispers. Spectators had gathered on the tops of the walls, their eyes like hawks, scanning the mass of contestants below. The pressure of so many eyes, the anticipation in the air—it all pressed in on me, making my breath come faster. Lil groaned beside me, catching my attention.

"Oh, look at them," she muttered, nodding toward the entrance.

Three Fae men stepped onto the top of the wall, and the entire crowd seemed to draw a collective breath. An immediate hush fell over the courtyard, a ripple of gasps and murmurs following. The men moved with a fluid grace, their every step drawing the eyes of all present. The atmosphere grew denser, as if the very air had shifted with their arrival.

"Who are they?" Kadian edged closer to Lil, his curiosity piqued.

Lil raised an eyebrow. "Don't you know who the princes are?"

Kadian gave her a roguish grin. "I might. But I may just want to hear your voice."

The roll of Lil's eyes drew a chuckle from me and a deeper smirk from Kadian. He never was one to stand down from a challenge.

She gestured toward the tallest one. "That's Alvar. He's the eldest—charming, but ruthless. To his left is Rai. And trust me, you don't want to know what he is." Her gaze shifted. "And the one to the right is Dainan. All dangerous in their own way, so you'd better keep a lookout for them. Always."

My gaze locked onto Dainan, and a flush of warmth spread through me. "He's beautiful," I murmured, captivated by the dark-haired prince's presence.

Kadian snickered beside me. “Get your head out of the gutter. You’ve got a job to do.” He nudged me, teasing.

“My head is in its appropriate place, focusing on the task at hand. Thank you.” I grumbled.

“You’ve always had a type.” Kadian leaned in and winked as a laugh escaped him.

Lil turned to me, her expression serious. “If any of them approach you, stay sharp and keep your distance. Especially Dainan—he’s known for taking a special interest in new women at court. If you’re not careful, you might give the impression that you’re here for titles, like princess or queen, rather than focusing on earning your place in the courts. Keep a safe distance.”

I nodded, trying to hide the embarrassment heating my face. My throat felt tight, and I swallowed hard, forcing myself to focus.

“How old are they?” Kadian murmured, following my gaze.

“I’m not sure how old Alvar is, but Rai and Dainan are around the same age. Close to three hundred years.”

“Did I just hear you correctly?” Kadian’s voice began to fade from my mind as my gaze solidified itself on the brothers.

From where we stood, Rai seemed the smallest of the brothers, just under six feet tall. All three had broad shoulders and dark hair that glinted with red highlights in the sunlight, like living flames. We knew of King Elidas back home, his strifes, his journey to claim the throne, but little had been known about his sons. No one knew what they looked like.

Now, standing before them, I couldn't help but feel a rush of unease coiled in my stomach. They were nothing like what I’d imagined, but just as terrifying. Alvar’s hair fell to his shoulders in a sleek cascade, Rai's was shorter but not quite cropped, and Dainan’s had a slight wave, falling to his chin. Their faces were symmetrical, with features too perfect to belong to anyone I’d ever known. Each sported a slender nose, a strong jawline, and fathomless dark eyes—eyes that carried the weight of a thousand secrets.

Their physiques spoke of rigorous training, muscles taut under their clothes, their disciplined stances reminding me of hunters sizing up their prey. Alvar exuded an air of elegance and control, his movements fluid, precise. Rai, despite being the smallest, radiated an intensity that made my pulse quicken. Dainan's wild waves of hair and the glint in his dark eyes unsettled me more than I wanted to admit. His gaze cut through the crowd, and I felt it land on me, sending a tremor down my spine, my chest tightening.

I looked away, my hands trembling. I didn't want him to see—didn't want anyone to see the mess swirling inside me. My palms were slick with sweat, and I rubbed them against my thighs, trying to stay calm. This wasn't the time to fall apart. The weight of my lie—the secret that I didn't belong here—pressed harder on my chest with every second.

Lil nudged me, her eyes bright with excitement, but I couldn't return the smile. What would she think if she knew the truth? Would she turn her back on me like everyone else would if they discovered I'd cheated my way in? My breath hitched, and I forced myself to take slow, measured breaths. A mantra started looping through my head—*just stay calm, just get through this, just don't let them see*—but it was getting harder to believe it.

The crowd shifted around us, a living, breathing mass of nerves and awe. The atmosphere grew thick with anticipation, the air suffocating. The sea of contestants felt like it was closing in on me, threatening to drown me in the reality of what was coming. I pressed a hand to my chest, willing my heart to slow down, but it kept hammering as figures in robes began to appear above each gate, signaling the start of the Trials.

As the tension in the courtyard grew, figures in distinct robes began to appear above each of the gates, representing the four courts. Their attire mirrored the essence of their respective domains: shadows danced around the members of the Court of Shadows, the members of the Court of Whispers were shrouded in ethereal silks, the Court of Reflection members adorned themselves with fabrics that looked like walking waves when they moved, and the Eternal

Court's representatives exuded an aura of timeless elegance. The crowd murmured in awe, the weight of the moment settling over everyone like a heavy cloak.

I averted my gaze, focusing on the figure who had just stepped forward—a tall, gaunt man with eyes like polished obsidian. He moved with eerie grace, as if he could slip away at any moment and vanish into thin air. His form seemed almost translucent, flickering in and out of focus. He wasn't real in the way we were. The Master of Trials. A living archive, the keeper of all the knowledge and rules of the Courting.

The unease in my gut twisted tighter, and I could feel the sweat trickling down my spine. I wasn't ready for this. I wasn't ready for any of it.

But I had no choice.

CHAPTER SIX

"Welcome to the Courting," the Master of Trials intoned, his voice weaving through the thrumming crowd like a vibrant melody. "You stand upon the threshold of an ancient and sacred tradition. This annual gathering is more than mere opportunity; it is a rare invitation, a beacon beckoning the brightest, the most ambitious, and the most deserving among our citizens. Each of you has been chosen to contend for a cherished place within the hallowed halls of one of the four courts of Azmeer—the pinnacle of honor to which one can aspire."

Kadian's gaze found me, his eyes begging the question as to why he had received an invitation. But I knew Kadian deserved to be here.

"The courts are not mere seats of power or symbols of prestige; they are the sacred legacy gifted to us by the Primals themselves. In their infinite wisdom, the Primals forged these courts to uphold the delicate balance, peace, and prosperity of our realm," he proclaimed, his voice resonating with unwavering conviction. "Each court embodies a vital essence of this world."

I struggled against the creeping unease that threatened to overtake me, my gaze drawn to the restless fidgeting of those surrounding me, but I anchored my focus back to him.

"Every trial you face, every challenge you conquer, is a reflection of your worthiness to uphold the legacy of the courts and the will of the Primals."

With a commanding grace, he ascended the dais that had materialized, taking two measured steps toward its summit. "Prepare yourselves. The path ahead is fraught with trials, yet for those who prevail, the rewards transcend measure. You are not merely competing for a place among the courts; you are vying for your legacy in the annals of history." His voice rang out with authority as he declared, "Your first task is to solve a puzzle. The first two hundred and fifty contestants to unravel its mysteries will be granted passage into Azmeer and the chance to claim their place within one of the courts. Fail, and you will be cast aside."

As the Master of Trials finished speaking, a hush rippled through the crowd, swallowing even the smallest murmur. The air buzzed with anticipation so thick it seemed to settle on my skin. My stomach twisted in knots, a tight coil of anxiety that pressed against my ribs, threatening to spill over. A bead of sweat rolled down the back of my neck, but I forced myself to stand straighter, to keep my hands from trembling. We were all herded into a line like cattle, and though I tried to breathe, my pulse betrayed me—too fast, too loud.

Beside me, an amber-skinned man, bald with a wide, toothy grin, turned toward me as if this was the most casual outing imaginable. "Good luck," he said, his voice low and warm, with a softness that clashed with the raw tension pulsing around us.

My lips curled into what might pass as a smile. "You too." My voice shakier than I'd hoped.

To my right, Lil caught Kadian's eye, and the two of them exchanged a small smile, a brief flicker of warmth that cut through the mounting pressure. My chest tightened as I watched them, a wave of longing mixing with my fear. I wanted us all to make it through, but a cold voice in the back of my mind whispered that this puzzle might tear us apart. Not everyone would make it. Kadian then turned to me, bringing his forehead to mine. We took a moment to pause, to breathe, to just be. "I'm with you, Bri. Until the end."

"Until the end," I whispered as we pulled apart.

The Master of Trials raised his hand, and with a sweeping motion, the ground beneath us trembled. A massive maze began to rise, walls stretching high with intricate mechanisms carved into stone, shimmering runes glowing faintly between cracks. My heart slammed against my ribs. This wasn't just a test of wit or skill. This was a gauntlet meant to devour those who weren't fast enough, sharp enough—strong enough. I glanced toward Kadian, needing just one more look. His green eyes found mine, and he gave me the smallest nod.

A horn sounded, and we surged forward. The walls of the maze closed in around me, symbols and diagrams twisting and shifting, mocking my every step. The pressure to succeed was suffocating, the maze itself a living, breathing entity designed to confound and confuse. My chest constricted. I clenched my fists, nails digging into my palms, a small attempt to steady the shaking in my limbs.

The walls loomed in every direction, a maze of jagged stone and flickering shadows. The light here seemed wrong, casting twisted shapes that moved as if alive. I swallowed hard, my throat dry, my heart already pounding. The center of the room held the source of it all—a deep red orb shrouded in heavy, metallic armor, its surface pulsing with a sinister glow. It hovered in the air, watching, or at least it felt that way. Shadows inside the orb writhed, curling in slow, menacing spirals. The cold, almost mocking judgment it projected sent an icy wave down my back.

The ground beneath my feet shook as a colossal timepiece emerged from the floor, its hands spinning wildly. My heart leaped into my throat as huge metal rings mirroring the action of the timepiece simultaneously appeared on the back wall. My stomach clenched as I watched them, my hands shaking. They moved too fast, out of sync, spinning in chaotic, unpredictable patterns.

Sweat poured down my brow, stinging my eyes as I squinted at the spinning rings. The timepiece before me seemed to tick louder with each second, its mechanical hands moving in strange, erratic motions as if mocking my confusion. I blinked, trying to steady my breathing, but my chest felt too tight, my thoughts too scattered to focus.

Making my way to the wall, the rings spun in all directions—some slow, others faster than I could track. They blurred together, shifting constantly, as if alive with their own chaotic energy. My head ached trying to follow their paths, but the symbols on them—small, faint markings—were too unclear to decipher. Were they stars? Celestial signs? I couldn't tell.

"Focus, Brida," I muttered, dragging a shaky hand across my forehead. The room felt too warm, the pressure of time closing in around me. I stared at the rings, trying to find something—anything—that would make sense.

Minutes passed. Or was it only seconds? My pulse was thundering too loudly for me to focus.

Then, out of the corner of my eye, I caught something on the wall behind them. A faint, almost imperceptible pattern etched into the stone—a constellation. I turned, my eyes scanning the intricate design. It matched the symbols on the rings.

"That's it," I whispered, my hands trembling. "I just need to align them..."

But the rings spun relentlessly, faster now, as if they sensed I was getting close. The symbols blurred again, and I cursed under my breath, wracking my brain, trying to remember anything—any scrap of knowledge about celestial alignments and ancient mechanisms. I knew this. I had studied it, but in this moment of frantic panic, it was slipping through my grasp.

The timepiece behind me groaned, its ticking intensifying, and a wave of dread washed over me. I was running out of time.

I clenched my fists to steady the shaking and stared at the rings again. The timing required proficiency. Match the constellation—line them up—just like the diagram on the wall.

Think, Brida, think!

I took a deep breath, trying to recall the movements, the rotations, and the spacing. Slowly, painstakingly, I moved the rings, one by one, trying to match them to the celestial pattern behind me. My heart raced, each movement feeling like a gamble.

One ring slipped out of place.

"No, no, no!" My voice came out more desperate than I intended, panic rising in my throat. I readjusted it, squinting to keep the symbols in view. Another wrong move, and I'd have to start over.

After what felt like an eternity, the symbols clicked into place, aligning perfectly with the constellation. I exhaled, my whole body sagging with momentary relief. The celestial alignment shimmered before me, casting a soft, ethereal glow. I wiped my sweaty palms on my tunic, my chest tight.

But it wasn't over. The timepiece.

I spun back to it, my mind racing. How was I supposed to match the timepiece to this alignment? I fumbled with the hands, trying to make sense of it, but the symbols on the clock face weren't anything familiar. I closed my eyes, fighting the growing panic, and tried to recall the connection between celestial movements and time...

Stars and time...they were intertwined. I gritted my teeth, trying to remember how my mother had explained it to me when I was little, but the memory was hazy.

Then, it hit me.

I forced my trembling fingers to adjust the hands of the timepiece, aligning them not to hours but to phases, matching them to the stars in the alignment. It was maddening, each tick of the clock like a knife to my nerves, but I kept moving the hands, praying I was right.

With a soft click, the timepiece locked into place. A low rumble echoed through the chamber, and the orb groaned as its armor began to fall away, exposing its glowing red core. I let out an exasperated breath, not believing I had done it.

But before I could dwell on it, the walls of the chamber changed again, revealing a dark, narrow corridor.

I stepped forward, my legs unsteady, my heart still pounding in my chest. The walls were lined with ancient parchment, the faded writing difficult to decipher, but it called to me. The corridor stretched on, endless and shadowed, the air thick with tension.

As I passed the parchments, faint voices called out, as if reading the words aloud.

"I see you, Brida Larrow."

"You do not belong here."

I paused as a warm breeze brushed against my cheek, sending a shiver down my spine, trying to determine if voices were speaking to me or if it was the last vestige of my resolve. I froze, glancing around the empty corridor. The air was still again, silent—but then, I heard it.

Keep going.

"Keep going," I repeated to myself, half convinced I'd imagined the voice.

But even as I pressed on, the words lingered in the back of my mind, urging me forward.

Reaching the end of the corridor, I faced a massive mosaic on the floor. The stones beneath me were cold, biting into my knees as I knelt down to inspect the fragmented tiles. My hands shook, both from exhaustion and the weight of knowing what was expected of me. The pieces lay scattered, each one representing a moment in Azmeer's long and bloody history—the rise and fall of empires, the forging of alliances, the betrayals that had shaped the courts.

I had studied this. Countless nights spent with Kadian, poring over old texts and diagrams, had led me here. My mind raced, trying to pull the right memories to the surface. But my hands wouldn't stop trembling, making the pieces fumble between my fingers as I began to arrange them.

Each click of a tile felt like a countdown. The orb's shadowy tendrils pulsed, their movements in sync with the rhythm of the puzzle, growing stronger with every correct placement. I swallowed hard, feeling the pressure closing in on me. The faint hum of the orb filled the room, its red glow casting eerie, distorted shadows on the walls as if it was reacting to my every move.

Focus, Brida. Piece by piece.

The history of the Courts stretched out before me, an intricate web of power struggles and long-forgotten betrayals. I knew where each piece fit, but my mind was clouded by panic. What if I missed something? What if I wasn't fast enough?

I pressed harder, trying to block out the fear. My fingers traced over a tile depicting a pivotal alliance, one I had memorized with Kadian. It fit with a soft click, and the orb pulsed again, its tendrils curling tighter, almost impatient.

The last tile slid into place. I let out a shaky breath, leaning back to take in the completed mosaic. The orb's armor began to fall away, piece by piece, until it stood bare—a glowing, pulsing heart of red light, suspended by threads of silver. The air around it hummed with a strange, almost musical vibration, like a song just out of reach.

I didn't know why, but I felt compelled to touch it.

I hesitated for only a moment before placing my trembling hands on the orb's surface. The vibrations coursed through me like tiny shocks running up my arms, and the shadows within the orb shifted, twisting and dancing in a chaotic ballet of light and dark. The room seemed to fall away as a vision enveloped me, pulling me into its depths.

Sunlight broke over a vast, endless void. It was calm at first, serene, but then chaos. A rush of creation, violent and overwhelming, as if the entire world was being born and torn apart. I felt it all: the raw power of beginnings and endings, of order fighting to emerge from chaos.

Faces flickered within the vision, one after another as if drawn from my very soul. My mother's face, full of warmth and hope. My dad, his worn eyes heavy with sorrow. Kadian, his steady presence always grounding me. Lil, fierce and unyielding. And then Dainan—his dark, commanding gaze burning through the vision, unsettling me in ways I didn't understand.

Each image brought a fresh wave of emotion crashing over me, but I shook my head, trying to focus. The orb pulsed again beneath my hands, the shadows shifting once more, swirling faster.

What do I do? I wanted to scream, to demand answers, but all that came out was a whisper. The orb shifted in my hands, the vision swirling into something else. Chaos, order. Beginnings, endings. It all blurred together, making my mind spin. I closed my eyes, struggling to make sense of it, struggling to find the clarity I needed.

"Please," I whispered. "Show me a way out of here."

The shadows inside the orb stilled for a moment, and then they began to shift, forming shapes—tendrils of darkness curling into a path. The tendrils stretched out before me, twisting through the air and carving a way forward, leading toward the exit. The path glowed in the darkness, a vision of light cutting through the void.

I followed it, my breath coming in shallow gasps, each step forward feeling like a battle against the panic tightening in my chest. The whispers of doubt still lingered, clawing at the edges of my mind, but I pushed them aside, focusing on the light.

Each footstep echoed through the chamber, a reminder of how alone I was in this moment. The way forward twisted and turned, and with every step, I felt the weight of my decisions—the lies, the risks, the hope that maybe I could still make it through. I wasn't sure if I was walking toward redemption or something far worse.

As I reached the final stretch of the path, the orb pulsed one last time in my hands, and the vision around me began to fade. The darkness lifted, leaving me standing at the exit.

With the final challenge behind me, I stumbled out of the dark passage into the sunlit courtyard, blinking hard against the brightness. The sudden flood of light felt harsh and disorienting, as if I had been thrown from one world into another. My legs wobbled beneath me and the air felt too thin, too real after the oppressive, shadowy maze. I blinked again, trying to steady my breath, but all I could think was: *I made it.*

A hush fell over the courtyard as people turned to look at me. Their murmurs seemed distant, like the soft hum of bees. I could feel their eyes on me, weighing me, judging me. My head was spinning, my heart still hammering in my chest. I was here—I had survived the first challenge—but where was Kadian?

"Brida!"

I jolted at the sound of my name, my heart leaping into my throat. Lil appeared from the crowd, her face bright and relieved. "I'm so glad to see you. I was worried you might not make it."

I tried to smile, but it came out weak, my limbs still trembling from the exertion. "Yeah," I croaked, swallowing the tightness in my throat. "Me too."

Before I could catch my breath, the Master of Trials strode forward, his dark eyes locking onto mine with unsettling precision. "Brida Larrow," he announced, his voice cold and commanding. "You have completed the puzzle. You are the one hundred and twentieth to do so."

Not first. Not last. Somewhere in between. It should have brought relief, but all I could feel was panic. *Where is Kadian?*

My thoughts were racing, careening wildly, too fast to catch hold of. I tried to steady my breathing, but it felt like the air was being sucked out of my lungs. My eyes scanned the courtyard, darting from one face to another, searching for him. But he wasn't there. The longer I waited, the more the panic wound inside me, constricting like a vice around my chest.

What if he doesn't come out? What if something happened to him in there? The thought struck me like a hammer, and I felt a cold sweat break out across my skin. My heart raced faster, the pounding in my chest becoming deafening. *Please... please let him make it.*

The crowd was watching me, but I couldn't stop my hands from trembling. I felt nauseous, dizzy, like I was balancing on the edge of a cliff. Every minute dragged by, each one a fresh spike of panic. My mind kept flickering back to the maze, to the red orb and the puzzle, and then back to Kadian. *He's strong. He's smart. He's fine.* But the mantra didn't help. It felt hollow. My breaths were coming in short gasps now, my vision blurring at the edges.

I wrapped my arms around myself, trying to hold it together, but the fear was gnawing at me, pulling me under. *Why is it taking so long?*

Lil's voice floated toward me, gentle but worried. "Brida? You okay?"

I barely heard her. The world around me felt distant, muffled and far away. My body felt too heavy, too disconnected from the ground. *I can't do this. I can't do this without him.*

I squeezed my eyes shut, trying to breathe through the panic, but my thoughts kept spiraling. *I'm going to pass out. I'm going to faint right here in front of everyone. I'm going to—*

After what felt like an eternity, a figure staggered through the archway. I blinked, my breath catching in my throat. Kadian.

He's okay. Relief surged through me so fast that my knees buckled, and for a split second, I thought I might collapse.

"Kadian!" I shouted, my voice trembling as I ran to him, my legs wavering beneath me. Lil followed close behind.

Kadian looked up, his face pale but determined, his hair damp with sweat. A tired but triumphant smile spread across his face as our eyes met. "I told you we'd both make it."

I threw my arms around him, holding on as hard as I could, feeling his warmth, his presence, the solidity of him grounding me in the moment. "You *not* making it would've been worse than the red orb," I said with a shaky laugh, my voice muffled against his shoulder.

He chuckled, the sound strained. "Red orb?"

I pulled back, wiping my forehead with the back of my hand, the adrenaline still coursing through me.

But the moment of relief was short-lived.

From the edge of the crowd, a sharp glare caught my eye. A Fae woman with bright red hair was staring at me, her expression cold and unreadable. Her gaze was like a dagger, piercing through the haze of exhaustion that clouded my mind. I tried to shake it off, but a chill ran down my spine. Something about her stare unsettled me, and I couldn't shake the feeling that her scrutiny was far from friendly.

I turned away, focusing back on Kadian and Lil. The enormity of what lay ahead began to sink in—the trial we'd passed was just the beginning. The true tests were yet to come. But for now, we had this moment of victory, this fragile, fleeting moment of relief.

I let out a long breath, trying to steady myself, trying to push the fear and doubt back into the corners of my mind where they wouldn't suffocate me. With one final glance at the courtyard, as shadows began to lengthen across the stones, I squared my shoulders.

This was only the beginning.

CHAPTER SEVEN

I followed the contestants through a labyrinth of corridors, each turn revealing new wonders of the palace's grandeur. When we entered the central hall, I was rendered speechless. The stairwell before us rose like a monument of ivory marble. My breath caught in my throat. "Gods, this place is massive," I whispered, my heart pounding with awe and anxiety. My entire house could have fit into this entryway at least ten times over.

A commanding voice boomed as we were led into an antechamber, "Everyone, please proceed through these doors. We are about to begin." Stepping into the next room, a wave of heat hit me, a sharp contrast to the lingering chill on my skin. The warmth was almost stifling, adding to the unease building inside me. Taking my seat among the contestants, I found my gaze drifting around the room. The limestone walls, though unadorned, seemed to glow with the light streaming through the three large windows opposite us. Its beauty only marred by the dark, swirling shadows clinging to the three princes standing on a blood-red stage that dominated the room. The shadows moved like living ink, undulating around them as a reminder of their connection to the Court of Shadows. The oppressive weight of darkness in the room was almost palpable, an invisible shroud that heightened my unease. I tried to focus, steadying my breath, but then I felt it—Dainan's gaze, steady and searching. For a brief moment, everything else faded, and I was simply there, held captive by him. His brow furrowed as his eyes narrowed, an intensity in his gaze that sent heat across my skin. It was a sharp, dissecting look, as though he were measuring every part of me, deciding if I was worth his attention—a curiosity, or perhaps something more. Tension coiled in the space between us, an unspoken question hanging in the air. Was I just another newcomer, a fleeting intrigue to be toyed with, or someone worth pursuing—a challenge he couldn't ignore?

I turned my attention to Lil and Kadian, their lighthearted conversation a welcome distraction from the nervous energy thrumming through me.

Moments later, a tall, slender woman with waist-length black hair took center stage. Her presence was commanding, her black armor gleaming with a fierce elegance. "Welcome," she said, her voice slicing through the murmur of the audience.

An unmistakable tension settled over the room as she continued. "Welcome to Azmeer." A collective murmur of anticipation rippled through the crowd.

"Asana," Lil whispered. "She's the Speaker for the House of Shadows." The name was familiar from my studies. Asana's honey-colored skin shimmered with a golden sheen, her ruby-studded armor a symbol of her formidable power and authority.

The heat of the room grew almost unbearable, and I found myself fanning my flushed face. Lil's concern was evident as she leaned closer. "Are you okay?" she asked.

I nodded, though my distress was evident.

"Congratulations on completing the first task. As the Master of Trials made clear, receiving an invitation to a Courting is a privilege." Asana's gaze swept over us with measured intensity, making my pulse race. "Contestants are allowed only one chance to compete. This will be your sole opportunity."

The room held its breath, the resonance of her words wrapping around us like an iron grip. "To be chosen by one of the four courts is to enter a realm unlike anything you've ever known. This is your chance to shape the very fabric of our world, to stand among those who dictate the laws that govern us all."

Her gaze cut through the air, piercing deep into the hearts of everyone present. "The Houses that represent the courts form the Center Court here in Azmeer, where the most critical decisions are forged. To be granted a seat at that table is not just to have a voice in the governance of our realm; it is to wield the raw, untamed magic bestowed by the Primals themselves."

This elusive magic of the courts—we had only glimpsed fragments of it that afternoon. Despite the endless hours I'd spent searching for even a hint of its true power, I had yet to find anything that detailed the extents of what court magic could do. It was like trying to catch smoke in my hands; the knowledge was always just out of reach, hidden in riddles and whispers, never quite revealing itself.

"If you are chosen," Asana said, her voice steady yet charged with an undercurrent of intensity, "you will step into a life beyond your wildest dreams. A life brimming with power, influence, and a connection to the ancient forces that guide us all. This marks the beginning of a journey that could transform everything—if you can endure the challenges ahead."

She paused, allowing the weight of her words to settle over us. "Your education will commence tomorrow. For now, you will be escorted to the inductees' wing, where your quarters await. Your belongings have already been delivered. Use this time wisely to prepare yourselves. Dinner will be served at the sixth bell this evening. Good luck."

The crowd erupted into applause, but the sound felt distant, hollow. I stared around the room at those who had earned their place, been granted an invitation to Azmeer. *I'm here for Dad.* A tight knot of guilt twisted in my chest, and I forced myself to take a slow, unsteady breath. *I'm here for Dad,* I reminded myself, repeating it like a mantra. *You did this for him. You had no other choice.*

But even as I told myself that, the tremor in my fingers persisted, a subtle reminder of the lie I was living. I stared down at my hands, willing the shaking to stop, but it wouldn't. The crowd's approval, their cheers, all of it felt wrong.

Clasping my hands together, I exchanged an exhausted glance with Lil and Kadian, the weight of the day settling on our shoulders. Asana left the stage, brushing past the princes. Her gesture toward Alvar caught my eye, and I wondered about the significance of that brief contact.

"What a day," Kadian murmured. "Thank the Gods she mentioned dinner. I'm starving,"

"Hopefully our rooms will be near each other. If not, I'm sure we can bribe someone," Lil added with a wink.

I turned back to the stage where the princes had vanished into the shadows. "Shadow stepping," Lil explained, squeezing my hand. "It's a rare gift, limited to members of the Court of Shadows. Dainan and Asana both possess it." The ability to move through shadows...

What world have I found myself in?

CHAPTER
EIGHT

The hours after our dismissal flew by as I unpacked, marveling at the opulence of my new room. Every detail, from the crack-free walls and elegant carvings on the furniture to the luxurious bath with its endlessly warm water—something that was scarce at home—felt like a dream. I savored each moment, knowing how far I was from the world I knew.

There was a knock at the door. "One second," I called, grabbing the first thing I saw on the bed. I selected, without realizing it, a long-sleeved black dress. Made of a light material, it was more form-fitting than anything I was accustomed to wearing. A slit on the left side ran from the ankle up past the knee. I would have to change again before leaving; there was no way I could go out in this.

"Come in." I tucked my bags away in the closet, taking note of the abundance of clothes waiting to be worn. I'd never had so many options. A familiar face poked around the door before entering the room.

"All settled in?" Lil asked.

I nodded.

She had managed to grab the room next door after threatening someone who tried to claim it. “Somebody changed.” A small chuckle left her. Looking down at the slit, I felt my cheeks begin to warm.

“You look great. Don’t change a thing.” She said as I settled into a seat at the desk while she wandered around.

“What a view, right? I thought we’d be in some shit rooms. I’ve never been happier to be wrong in my life!” She made her way towards the desk. “Wow. Is that your mother?” She picked up the miniature I’d brought with me placed next to my favorite books, *The Trials of Thale* and *Vietta*.

“She was beautiful.” Lil set the frame back on the desk. “You look just like her.”

The words hit me with a quiet ache, a pang that was somehow both sweet and raw. *You look just like her.* I didn’t know whether to feel comforted or exposed, as if Lil could see right into the softest parts of me I kept hidden. It was odd hearing it from a stranger’s lips, someone who never knew her yet could see her in me. I tried to swallow the feeling down, but it lingered, pressing against my heart—heavy, proud, and aching all at once.

Lil cleared her throat, moving to sit on the bed. Sunlight poured through the window, catching in her hair and turning it to spun gold. “So,” she said.

“So,” I replied.

She sat in silence a moment longer. “What’s the deal with you and Kadian?” She asked.

I laughed. It seemed Kadian's antics from earlier had done the trick.

“What’s so funny?”

I rubbed my temples as I chuckled.

“I’m not trying to pry,” she said as she fiddled with my bedspread.

“No, no.” I stood and walked over to her, my hands fidgeting as I tried to shake off the awkwardness. “I don’t mind you asking. There’s nothing going on between Kad and me—not like you think.”

She raised an eyebrow, a teasing grin tugging at her lips. "I like to know what kind of situation I'm walking into... or avoiding."

I shifted on my feet, unsure of myself. *How do I explain that Kadian's the only real friend I've ever had?* That's not something you just throw out there, not when you're trying to start fresh. But this was new. I had to embrace it, even if it felt awkward. I smiled, trying to sound more confident. "We're just friends. He's a brother to me. Nothing more."

Lil raised an eyebrow, unconvinced.

I exhaled, the words a little clumsy as I pushed forward. "We know each other too well for it to be anything else. It's all emotional, not physical. Trust me, the thought of anything more... we'd both be repulsed."

Lil's expression softened. "Uh huh," she said. "He seems great from what I've seen. He's just two doors down from me, so I guess we got lucky."

I smiled, opening my mouth to reply when my stomach growled. I looked down at my midsection and laughed. "Well, looks like even though I'm not prepared for dinner, my stomach is." I stood and smoothed out my dress.

"I'm so sorry," Lil said. "I interrupted you while you were getting ready. I'll go. Take your time, and I'll meet you outside." She paused. "I'm glad I decided to speak to you today, Brida. Oh, and one other thing," she said. "Don't you dare change out of that dress." With that, she opened the door and was gone.

Today was the first time I'd spoken to someone in line and made a friend. The feeling was strange, but in a way, I appreciated it more than I expected. For a moment, I almost felt like I belonged—like I wasn't just an outsider watching everyone else. The thought lingered as I moved through the motions of getting ready.

I chose to put more effort into my appearance than was typical. Following Lil's lead, I wore my hair down. *Gods, it's getting long.* It was nearing the middle of my back, even with a wave to it. I washed my face and darkened my eyes. *Here we go.*

Stepping into the hall, I found Lil waiting for me. "Have you been to this part of the palace before?" I asked, closing my door behind me.

"No, we used to stay in the guest quarters, which are the royal quarters. It's a bit tighter than one might expect, especially based on the size of these rooms." Turning to Lil, I found her staring at three men who walked by us, each looking at her as they made their way toward the exit. "We could always find someone to show us around," a massive grin emerged on her face.

"You're incorrigible," I laughed as I referenced the map that had been left on the desk in my room. *This place is huge.* I stared at the map. There were wings in addition to the houses, Center Court, refectory, gym, and countless other locations. *Dinner is in thirty minutes, and I have no idea where I'm going.*

A frenetic energy filled the corridor. Groups of people went in and out of their rooms, some forgetting their maps, others looking for people they knew from home or searching for those they'd just met. I was lost in possibilities when I heard a voice behind me.

"Thank the Gods," Kadian said, "I'm starving. Let's go." He put his arm around my shoulder, gesturing toward the exit.

"Brida has a map," Lil pointed to the one in my hands.

We're North...

"The day I start trusting Brida with directions, even when she has a map, is the day I've lost my mind."

"We can't all be navigators, Kad," I said with a slight irritation in my voice.

"No, but don't worry, I'm happy to lead." He winked.

I rolled my eyes, but he was a natural compass. He always knew where to go and how to get us there. I would come up with the idea, and Kad put its execution into place.

"It's this way," he laughed, "I mapped it out earlier."

Saves me from doing it and getting us lost.

His eyes found Lil. "You look nice," he said as he eyed her up and down in slow motion.

"I always like to make the best impression." She let out a playful laugh, blush rising to her cheeks.

The grandeur of the room itself was breathtaking—one of the largest I'd ever seen. Endless champagne flutes circulated by wait-staff, complementing tables piled high with salads, sandwiches, meats, cheeses, and fruits. A vaulted ceiling soared above, supported by imposing stone columns that lined the dining hall like silent sentinels. Despite their weathered appearance, as though they'd endured millennia, the columns stood strong, giving the impression they'd remain standing through the end of time. The last sunlight of the day filtered through the large windows, casting a warm glow on the polished floors beneath us, where our reflections shimmered.

The air buzzed with flurries of conversation and the clinking of glasses. My constant gazing around the glimmering room was interrupted when I heard Lil say, "I plan to try one of everything."

"Already on it." Kadian leaned toward a server and grabbed three champagne flutes. "Before we begin," he said, handing the glasses to Lil and me, "a toast to new friendships."

"A toast to new friends," Lil echoed, her smile contagious.

Kadian made friends wherever we went—a talent I'd long envied. He slipped effortlessly into conversations, while I'd always struggled to connect. But here, in Azmeer, I resolved to do my best to emulate him, to make it look like I belonged, like I deserved to be here. When I raised my glass and clinked it with Lil's, I felt a spark of happiness—an evanescent sense that, maybe, I could fit into this new life. I took a small sip, savoring the taste, though I was never much of a drinker.

As I scanned the room, the Walker's pale hair caught my eye from across the crowd. He lifted his champagne glass and smiled at me, a subtle but clear acknowledgment. A blush crept up my cheeks, and I looked away, feeling the heat rise.

Lil and Kadian were off to the food table, chatting and stacking their plates high. I glanced around, trying to memorize faces. Almost everyone had freshened up for the evening, and I felt relieved that I had, too. My eyes darted across the room, noticing the unspoken language of discomfort—groups clustered on the fringes, arms crossed, fingers twisting, all masking their nerves.

Act as if you belong here. Be brave.

Despite the breeze wafting in through the windows offering a reprieve from the stifling heat, I found myself succumbing to it. *Why is it so hot in here?*

Staring around the room, I spotted a table adorned with glasses of water, one of the few scattered throughout the vast hall. As I made my way toward it, I couldn't help but admire those who already appeared at home in Azmeer. Their laughter echoed like music, and I wondered if their familiarity with this place lent them that ease or if it was a boisterous confidence that came naturally to some. I felt like an outsider in a realm of glittering connections and easy camaraderie.

The table was lined with a delicate pale tablecloth with small golden flecks that caught the light in mesmerizing waves as I moved my head. It was unlike anything I had ever seen—soft yet ethereal as if woven from the whispers of stars themselves. My fingers brushed against its surface, and I felt a fleeting moment of peace, a connection to something beautiful and timeless. But just as I reached for a glass, I froze, my hand colliding with another.

"Oh, I'm so sorry!" I exclaimed, looking up to meet the gaze of Prince Dainan. His dark eyes locked onto mine, and in that instant, the bustling room fell away, the noise becoming a distant hum. A spark of amusement danced within those depths, brightening the shadows of the hall. For a heartbeat, it was just the two of us, the world narrowing to this unexpected connection.

Without uttering a word, Dainan's lips curled into a small, knowing smile, a gesture that felt charged with unspoken understanding. I felt my heart race, a confusing mix of emotions swirling inside me. Was it intrigue? Attraction? Or something else entirely? I was acutely aware of the significance of this moment, yet I found myself grappling with the enormity of it. *Why is he alone?* My mind raced with questions. I had little experience with royalty, but I had assumed he would be flanked by guards or courtiers, a sentinel of propriety.

Dainan raised a glass, his gaze fixed on me with an intensity that turned the simple gesture into something far more loaded. It was as if, in that small tilt of his wrist, he was toasting more than just my presence—acknowledging a private understanding that hummed between us. His lips brushed the rim of his glass, and he held my gaze, unblinking, over the edge. As he sipped, the flame-like hues in his auburn hair flickered under the low light, giving him an almost ethereal aura, a strange mix of danger and elegance. For a long beat, his eyes lingered on me, smoldering, as if he were memorizing me in that precise moment. And then, with a final, unreadable look, he set the glass down, turned, and walked away, leaving a trail of mystery in his wake, like smoke drifting into the night.

The room snapped back into focus, the laughter and chatter flooding my senses once more. My heart hammered against my ribcage, the brief encounter leaving an indelible mark on my consciousness, a moment etched into my memory that felt both exhilarating and terrifying. *Gods, I hope no one saw that.*

I grabbed a glass of water, my hand trembling as I lifted it to my lips, trying to steady the storm brewing inside me. The coolness of the glass was a stark contrast to the heat of my cheeks, but it did little to quell the confusion swirling in my mind. I took a sip, hoping to wash away the sensation of his gaze still resting on me, but instead, the taste of the water turned bittersweet as I wrestled with my thoughts, unsure of what this encounter meant for me and my journey in Azmeer.

"It just seems weird," Kadian said as he and Lil returned, pulling me from my haze.

"Hey, don't knock it until you try it. It goes great with champagne," Lil said, handing me a plate. "We got there just in time. I snagged the last sandwich for you, and if you don't eat it, I will." She laughed a deep, sultry laugh. It was a sound that echoed happiness, contentment. *What must it be like to feel that comfortable here?*

"Thanks," I smiled, trying to shake off the encounter with Dainan.

"Did you hear," Kadian asked as a piece of food tumbled from his mouth, "that the Courting isn't just a political term but a physical thing?"

"What do you mean?" I looked at him as I wiped my mouth with a napkin, trying to send him a hint.

"It seems," he said while taking another bite, ignoring me, "that when you join a court, your appearance will *change* to align with that court."

"Of course," Lil nodded, taking a sip of champagne. "Each court has its basic descriptors." She pointed at a girl with bright red hair, stunning in a black sequined gown. "Red hair like that is associated with the Court of Shadows. Fire is essential to their court, after all. If you see the princes up close, you'll notice they all have auburn hues, similar to you." She smiled at me.

I turned toward the girl Lil had indicated. As she moved, her gaze briefly met mine, and I felt a flicker of recognition. It was the same girl who had glared at me after the first task.

"Bri has no ties to the Court of Shadows," Kadian cut in, his voice steady. Growing up, he'd spent years making sure everyone knew I had no court connections, despite how I might look. It was ironic. Kadian was the one with Fae heritage, the one who asked the most questions about it. Yet, somehow, he was never the one made to feel like an outsider.

"Oh, I know, but they might find her hair color intriguing. My blonde hair and aquamarine eyes align with the Court of Reflection. Violet eyes are for the Court of Whispers, and green, brown, or amber for the Eternal Court."

"What about the Court of Shadows?" I asked, intrigued.

"Their eye color changes later, sometimes years after joining, making them hard to identify," Lil said. "Each court has unique gifts, but the Court of Shadows is particularly secretive. Even their House of Shadows here at the Center Court is shrouded in mystery."

I glanced back and saw the redhead speaking with Prince Dainan.

"Seems like she's not wasting any time," Lil whispered, nodding toward them. "Good, he'll be distracted." I glanced at Dainan, trying to decipher his expression, but it remained inscrutable.

"I'm going to get seconds!" Kadian bellowed.

"We can't let him get them all!" Lil called out, racing after Kadian.

With a sigh and a reluctant smile, I followed.

As we wove through the crowd, I overheard two court officials deep in conversation. "The landscape is shifting," one said. "Faster than anyone thought."

"He's not doing well—far worse than he's letting on," the other replied, voice low. "Only a handful know, but the news won't stay hidden for long."

The words lingered, intriguing me, but Lil's voice pulled me back to the present. "Come on, Kadian's over here," she said with a grin.

As the night unfolded, laughter and chatter filled the room. Lil and Kadian navigated the crowd like seasoned players, debating over which dishes were best, making friends with everyone they met. I drifted toward a small group of other inductees, a bit hesitant but curious. I found myself next to a quiet girl named Emia, who seemed to listen with intent rather than speak.

I could tell she was observing everything, maybe even feeling a little out of place, like I was. Taking a deep breath, I decided to break the silence. "First night, huh?" I said, offering a smile. She returned one, and nodded. Somehow, the small connection made the crowded room feel a little less daunting.

After dinner, we made our way back to our rooms. "Goodnight," I said as we parted in the hall, smiling at Lil and Kadian. I was grateful they were here to share this experience with me.

☽✳☾

"Bri, come on, open the door!" The thunderous crash of Kadian's fist against my door reverberated through the stillness of my room, jolting me from my thoughts.

After everything we'd been through today, all I had wanted was to sink into a warm bath and then curl up in bed, letting the world fade away for a while. I had already penned a letter to Dad, sharing my first impressions of Azmeer—the towering spires, the vibrant colors, the atmosphere that seemed to hum with energy. I knew he would love it here. He had always dreamed of traveling, of exploring the vast landscapes of Eldara with Mom. They had managed a few trips together, but nothing extensive, always waiting for the right moment, the right time when I would be old enough to join them on grand adventures. But, it never came to pass.

Kadian's persistent knocking and the urgency in his voice broke the spell of my reverie. "Hold on a second," I called out, reaching for a cover to pull over my head as if it could shield me from his enthusiasm.

Kadian was leaning casually against the frame as I opened the door, a grin spreading across his face.

"You look pleased," I remarked, pushing my hair back from my face, trying to shake off the remnants of my daydream.

"Yes! I was getting ready for bed, but Lil decided the night shouldn't end here. She's organized a round of cards in her room. Let's go!" His excitement was palpable, infectious, even.

I rubbed my eyes, fighting the allure of sleep that tugged at my mind, tempting me to melt into the comforting embrace of my mattress. "I was just getting ready for bed, Kad." I gestured back into my room, emphasizing my bare legs peeking out from under the cover.

"As attractive as this look is for you, it's time to get redressed and head next door." He stepped back, his grin widening, a mischievous glint in his eyes. "Better yet, come as you are. It'll make for interesting conversation and might even help you meet someone."

A low chuckle escaped me, unable to resist the growing smirk on his face. "I'm not here to meet anyone. We're here for one purpose only. And after everything that happened today, I am desperate for sleep." I attempted a scolding look, but I had never been able to hold one against Kadian for long.

"Who's to say we can't have some fun along the way?" He winked, his eyes dancing with mischief.

I recalled my father's words, whispered with warmth: *Remember, Brida, you're allowed to have some fun.* It felt like a gentle nudge from the past, a reminder I desperately needed.

"Fine," I muttered, retreating back into the room to grab the closest pair of pants, the soft fabric comforting against my skin.

"You know, it was pretty brazen of you to open the door like that. It could have been anyone on the other side. Maybe Azmeer is already having an effect on you." Kadian tapped against the limestone, his tone lighter now.

"I knew it was you, Kad. I always know when it's you," I replied, the corner of my mouth lifting in a smile. *Not only because you have the insistence of an earthquake.*

As I turned toward the door, Kadian caught me, his hands firm yet gentle on my shoulders. "If you'd rather, I can close the door, and you can slip off to bed. Or we could sit on the balcony, counting stars until you tire of my company."

The idea sang to me, the soft pull of night's embrace, the unspoken stories in the constellations. But the earnest gleam in Kadian's eyes spoke louder, nudging me beyond the familiar.

"Let's go next door." A smile found its way to my lips, and Kadian's face brightened, a spark catching in his eyes.

"How did I get so lucky to have you in my life, Brida Larrow?" he murmured, the words soft, steeped in sincerity.

I squeezed his hands, feeling warmth blossom in my chest. "It's just the way the story was written, Kad." The sentence carried a quiet gravity, a nod to the fate we both shared and defied.

As he draped his arm around me, we stepped out, closing the door behind us. The voices of our new friends, light and full of life, bubbled through the hallway. "You okay?" he asked, stopping in front of Lil's room as the sounds wove into the silence between us.

I am more than my fear; I am the story I choose to write.

"Bri?" Kadian's voice broke through, anchoring me to the present. I met his gaze, nodded, and together we stepped inside.

CHAPTER NINE

We stood amongst the two hundred and fifty candidates in the meeting hall, waiting to be given instructions. The contestants were divided up by floor, "The easiest way to go about it," the officials had said. I was relieved when I realized I would be with Lil and Kadian.

"I'm glad I didn't have to kick anyone's ass to make sure the three of us were together," Lil laughed, though I couldn't help but believe there was some truth behind her teasing tone.

As I glanced around, I saw Emia and waved before my eyes landed on someone familiar—a man threading his way through the crowd. Before I could process where I knew him from, he was in front of me, pulling me into a hug. I froze.

"Good to see you again," he said, his voice warm and full of ease. "Glad you made it through."

Kadian's brows shot up, and Lil let out a laugh. "Who's this?"

I stammered, my mind spinning as I searched for a name. "Uh..."

The man released me with a chuckle. "It's Osforth," he said, then added with a grin, "but just call me Oz. Trust me, I hate the full name just as much as you probably would."

Lil raised an eyebrow, still smiling. "Oz, huh? Nice to meet you." She gave me a sidelong look, amused by the situation.

Kadian smirked, crossing his arms. "So, how do you know Bri?"

I opened my mouth, still flustered, but Oz saved me, nodding toward the room. "I wished her luck during the first task, didn't think we'd end up on the same floor. Looks like luck's still on our side."

I laughed, feeling some of the awkwardness lift. "Looks like it."

Lil grinned mischievously. "Well, now that we've got the introductions out of the way, let's hope your luck sticks with us, Oz."

Oz winked. "You can count on it."

His muscular build was hard to miss, complemented by a tattoo of intricate, swirling patterns snaking up from his left wrist to his shoulder.

At twenty-five, he was the first person my age I'd ever met without hair. "Shaved it off before we got here," he joked, "didn't want to deal with it in this heat." He was a charmer, similar in height to Kadian but with a bigger build. His amber skin and pale green eyes were striking—I couldn't help staring at them. Noticing my gaze, he pointed to his eyes and said, "I think they'll change. If I end up in the Eternal Court, I suspect they'll go brown or amber like my mom and dad."

"They're both members then?" Kadian asked, though his gaze was fixed on Lil.

"They were both here for the Courting two hundred and seventy years ago," Oz said, his eyes reflecting a mix of nostalgia and frustration. "Mom's family is in the Court of Whispers, so when she was picked by the Eternal Court, it caused a rift. She hasn't spoken to them since."

Kadian blinked. "So, you have this whole family in another court?"

"Yeah," Oz said with a wry smile. "Mom had to sort of adopt my dad's family. I think she misses hers sometimes, though. It's like being thrown into a new family where you're supposed to fit in, but part of you is always somewhere else."

I felt a tightness in my chest. The thought of Kadian and me ending up in different courts made my stomach churn. What would happen to us? Could our friendship survive the separation? The idea of facing that kind of divide was almost too much to bear.

"Wait," I managed, my voice faltering. "Did you say two hundred and seventy years ago?" My shock was evident.

"Yeah," he said, raising an eyebrow before a flicker of recognition crossed his face. "I'm sure this is all new to you, being human." His smile softened, and for a moment, I felt a strange sense of relief. At least he didn't see me as an outsider; he seemed...curious.

"My parents are still young for Fae standards. They waited a while to have me and my sister. She's around here somewhere."

Lil smirked. "Luck must have been on your side. For both of you to have been invited the same year."

Oz chuckled. "I told you," he added with a smile.

I absorbed the weight of what he was saying, feeling the quiet ache of my sheltered existence. Centuries to learn, to study, to read, to be with those you love—it felt like such a precious, enviable gift. Our human lives, so often fraught with pain, suffering, and fleeting moments, seemed almost insignificant in comparison. Over in the blink of an eye.

"Are we scaring you?" Lil's voice cut through my thoughts, her eyes gleaming with amusement.

"A little," I admitted, my mind racing with the implications.

Oz noticed my distraction and gave me a reassuring grin. "You'll get used to it. We'll meet all kinds of people around here." He pointed across the room. "There's my sister. I'll catch up with her and see you later?"

"Yeah," Kadian said. "We'll see you later."

Oz patted him on the shoulder as he left. "Seems nice. Friendly." Kadian grinned at me as Oz approached his sister. They were the spitting image of each other, save for her dark, beautiful curly hair. *She's tall,* I thought as I looked at her. She looked like a natural born fighter. Ready to take her place in the Eternal Court.

"Good morning, and welcome to the Center Court," a voice said. I peered around a group of girls and saw a man of medium build. He had no distinguishable traits about him. His hair was a dull color that I couldn't even identify, and his skin a bit lifeless.

He must be the least colorful thing in Azmeer.

"My name is Magister Illerium. Today, we'll start with a tour of the palace grounds and the Center Court. I remember when I first arrived here, it all felt..." he paused, searching for the word, "daunting." He clasped his hands together, satisfied.

Kadian, Lil, and I exchanged glances. *This is going to be thrilling.*

"We understand that for many of you, this will be the first time away from home, except perhaps for your studies, which I assume most of you completed last year." Nods rippled through the group. University had been a high point for me and Kadian. We attended the local college, close enough to Dad that I could visit on a regular basis.

"First days are best for acclimatizing to new surroundings," Illerium said. "So, we'll start with a tour. Follow me and my assistant," he gestured to a figure walking into the room.

"Isn't that..." Lil whispered, nudging me.

"This is Marsh from the Court of Whispers," Illerium introduced with a smirk.

Lil grinned, "Gods. Glad we now know his name." She murmured.

She wasn't wrong. Marsh's violet-streaked hair caught the light, and his amethyst-like eyes held a mesmerizing glimmer. I couldn't help but stare.

"Marsh will provide detailed information as we go. Try to keep up in speed and intellect," Illerium added, irony heavy in his voice. I smirked at Kadian, "Do try to keep up." I whispered.

He rolled his eyes back at me.

As we moved through the corridors, Illerium explained, "The true Courts are not in Azmeer but are rooted where each Primal resided." We turned into a passage lined with deep green stone, like malachite, a stark contrast to the tan limestone that made up the majority of the palace.

"The Center Court is neutral ground for the Courts to convene," Illerium continued, stopping before an ancient-looking doorway. "This is the entrance to the Eternal House," he said, nodding to Marsh.

The moment seemed to pause as my gaze swept across the entrance, tracing the intricate carvings that wove tales of time and power into the very stone. I stood in awe, scarcely able to grasp that I was here, among legends and stories that once felt so distant, so impossible. The air was thick with whispers of history, and the magnitude of it pressed into my chest, a strange mix of exhilaration and disbelief coursing through me. The journey that brought me here felt fragile, as if one touch might shatter the illusion and send me spiraling back to reality.

Marsh stepped forward, his eyes briefly meeting mine, a smile playing on his lips. "When we join a Court, our *skills* are tied to it. Being away from your Court can weaken your magic or abilities. Therefore, Houses were built in Azmeer, using materials from each Court's homeland," he explained, placing his hand on the stone. "This rock is from Hadash, home of the Eternal Court."

"Well said, Marsh," Illerium praised. "Each Court has a House in Azmeer. Some of you will experience one during your placements, but for now, let's move on."

"We'll pass conference rooms, ambassador quarters, and the library before reaching the gymnasium," Marsh continued.

It was hard to stay focused with everything around me, and Kadian and Lil's whispers didn't help.

"So the entire Court refuses to eat fish?" Kadian asked.

"Yes," she replied. "When you're linked to water, fish-eating is frowned upon. My mom freaked out when I told her I tried flounder. Was completely worth it."

Marsh's voice brought me back as we reached the library. "This is the largest archive in Eldara, holding sacred documents from each Court. The treaty binding the Courts required each to leave something valuable here," he said, his eyes locking onto mine. A shiver coursed through me, delicate and fleeting, as though a feather had traced a path along my back at the sight of their pale purple hue. "Scribes preserve knowledge and maintain peace. They aren't pledged to any Court." He added, leading us inside.

My breath hitched in my throat as I stepped into the library. The walls were made of the same pale limestone as the rest of the palace, yet here, the stone shone with a life of its own, bathed in light from the magnificent stained glass window overhead. Soft pastels—every color of the rainbow—danced across the marble floor, shifting as if the light itself were alive. The window, impossibly high, stretched almost to the ceiling, which seemed a hundred feet above me. It was a breathtaking display of craftsmanship, but my eyes were drawn to the books.

Intricately carved stairwells spiraled upward and around, twisting with grace as they led to multiple levels of shelves, each filled with volumes—books upon books, waiting to be read.

My heart raced with excitement, the researcher's instinct in me already sparking to life. The sheer number of texts held the promise of knowledge, and I couldn't help but wonder if the answer to helping my father lay hidden somewhere within these pages. I could spend days—weeks, even—combing through this treasure trove. The thought gave me a strange sense of hope, something that had felt elusive since I left him behind.

"Not a bad place to be," Kadian whispered to me.

I could spend a lifetime here, and it would never be enough.

"No," I said, "not at all."

In the distance, I saw a group of people dressed in tan robes that were brought together at the waist with rope. I made eye contact with one of them. She beamed when she saw me and mouthed *later.*

I could barely contain my excitement. It had been years since I'd seen Addie. *What is she doing here?*

"Is that..." Kadian leaned in to whisper to me. I nodded with excitement.

"We'll pause here and resume our tour in two bells. Feel free to explore the library, but remember, this is a place of quiet study," Illerium continued before gesturing for Marsh to follow him. They left, leaving the rest of us to disperse.

Lil sighed, leaning against a wall. "I don't know if I can handle more of this this afternoon," she muttered, then brightened. "Want to grab some lunch? If we go now, we'll get the best selection."

"Yes, I'm in." Kadian's agreement was instantaneous.

"I'll catch up later. I want to look around a bit," I told them.

Placing a hand on my shoulder, Kadian nodded and smiled at me before he and Lil proceeded to make their way from the library, turning left as they exited. I wandered through the shelves, trailing my fingers along the spines of old books. The scent of worn leather and aged paper was intoxicating.

Rounding a corner, I heard a familiar voice, "This is the sole volume we could find, Your Majesty. I reviewed it myself and believe it will answer your questions." Addie stood there, handing a book to none other than Prince Dainan. My heart skipped a beat as they both turned to see me. Addie's face radiated joy, while Dainan's remained impassive.

"If you have any other questions, please don't hesitate to find me." My aunt Addie bowed her head as a sign of respect.

As Dainan strode past, I couldn't tear my gaze from him. His sleeveless black shirt revealed a lean, muscular build, and his eyes—shifting colors beneath dark lashes—hinted at hidden depths I couldn't quite grasp. His bronze skin and striking features made it impossible to look away, his presence magnetic. For a brief moment, his eyes met mine, and a subtle, intoxicating scent hung between us, leaving my pulse racing.

"Brida?" Addie's voice snapped me back to reality.

"Addie!" I squealed, rushing to hug her.

"What are you doing here! Oh, it has been far too long." She wrapped her arms around me as hard as she could. "Gods, you look so much like her."

"I missed you too," I couldn't help but laugh. I had. We'd seen Addie less since Mom died, but she had always made a point of staying in touch and coming to visit when she could.

"You didn't answer my question." She pulled back, hands on my shoulders. "Wait, you didn't get an invitation to the Courting, did you?"

Here we go. "I did! I was just as surprised as you..."

"That's rare. Only a few humans each year are offered an invitation..."

Before she could continue, I cut her off. "What are you doing here? Last we heard, you were in Haliar." She'd been working as a librarian there for the past several years.

"I started working here not long ago and sent you a letter, but I guess it got lost in the shuffle," she said, placing a hand on my cheek.

My heart sank a little, remembering the letter I never opened. I'd been too consumed in readying myself for coming here.

"Are you settling in okay?" she asked, leading me to the main desk.

"The rooms are more than I imagined." *I'm also terrified of being here, that someone will discover my secret, the repercussions of what that would mean for me...for dad. But that's a conversation for another time.*

She offered a warm smile. "But are you really settling in? Being away from home can be hard." She lifted my chin.

"I'm lucky Kadian's here," I gestured towards the exit.

"I thought that was him," she chuckled. "He's grown into a fine-looking young man."

"Gods, not you too. It's not like that."

She laughed, raising her hands. "Just an observation."

My eyes drifted back to the doorway, "Does..." I began to ask and forced myself to stop.

"*Does?*" She rifled through books. Addie was a multitasker, "*I need to keep busy!*" is what she'd always said.

After a moment of less-than-amiable silence, I asked, "Does Prince Dainan often visit the library?"

She nodded, scratching something off her list, "He's often here. Despite what people may say about him, he's devoted to his studies."

"And what do people say about him?" I asked, trying to sound as nonchalant as possible.

She lifted her eyes to meet mine, a serious glint replacing her usual lightheartedness. "Do I need to remind you to be careful?" Her brow knit, an expression I wasn't used to seeing on her face. Addie had always been the carefree spirit in the family. Not that there was much of a family to speak of.

"No, no, you do not." I shook my head for emphasis.

"Good," she made her way behind the desk and leaned on it. "Well," her hands slapped the top, "you need to go get some lunch," her demeanor and tone grew softer, "come see me whenever you need a break, okay? Maybe I can pull a few strings and your placement will be here." Her smile was so genuine, and warm. It could melt ice even on the coldest days.

"I could only be so lucky," I continued to look around the room. In another lifetime, this would have been my dream. It had been my plan following university to work in a library. Being a herald of stories, a protector of history. I looked back at Addie, who had lost herself in receipts. I grabbed her hand as my way of saying thanks. "I'll come visit soon."

"You better," she picked up a stylus and returned to a list that she had no doubt been working on earlier. My heart felt light as I turned on my heels and made for the exit.

Left or...Right. Ah, yes.

The hallway buzzed with activity, a whirlwind of movement as lunchtime drew most of Azmeer toward the dining hall. The crowd made it nearly impossible to navigate, compounded by the captivating decor—reliefs, tapestries, mosaics. My gaze lingered on a floor mosaic of migrating birds when—shit—I collided with someone. "Sorry," I blurted out.

“Someone isn’t paying attention.”

Freeing myself from the arms I landed in, I glanced upwards. Staring at me with an expression of curiosity was Prince Dainan.

CHAPTER TEN

Yesterday, Lil warned me to stay away from the princes. I now found myself in the arms of one.

Off to a great start, Brida. I stood in absolute silence.

What is wrong with you? Say something... Anything will do. Well, maybe not anything. His eyes traced me from head to toe. His expression left me questioning if he liked what he saw or if he'd been merely assessing me.

My gaze dropped to my midriff—bare, as per the Court of Reflection's fashion, an outfit choice Lil had insisted I wear this morning. Regret washed over me as I crossed my arms, hoping to shield myself.

He finally spoke, his voice low, with a hint of amusement that played at the corner of his mouth. "Do you often walk around without looking where you're going?" The question wasn't unkind, but the slight arch of his brow made me feel like I'd been caught doing something embarrassing. *Thankfully not caught for anything else.* I could see his mouth curve into a smile as he awaited my answer.

My throat tightened, and I forced out words that felt clumsy on my tongue. “I’m not great with directions.”

He stepped closer, the hint of a smile still playing on his face, and I felt my breath catch. I’d seen him at dinner, but I hadn’t noticed the shadows shifting in his red and gold eyes—something no doubt tied to the Court of Shadows. Despite that eerie movement, a spark of amusement made it clear he was enjoying this far more than I was.

A haze of smoke and citrus wrapped around me, rich and intoxicating. I leaned in on instinct, the desire to take in his scent overwhelming. But reality snapped back as I noticed the small distance between us, and a wave of heat rushed to my cheeks.

The faint quirk at his mouth deepened into a full, satisfied smile, his eyes gleaming with a knowing glint of triumph, and I silently berated myself for being so transparent.

This is mortifying. I had never wished to disappear more in my life. He tilted his head, studying me with an unreadable expression, a blend of curiosity and quiet calculation. It was as if he were dissecting the pieces of me, trying to understand the whole—and I wasn't sure I wanted to know what he might uncover.

His tone was laced with humor, and his eyes still held that glimmer of amusement. “Do you know Scriba Velin?”

Scriba Velin? What had he asked? My mind, distracted by him and the way his hair caught the light, appearing like living flames, scrambled for an answer. “Scriba Velin?” I echoed, trying to stall, though I knew I was failing miserably.

His lips pressed together as he stepped closer again, his grip firm as he caught my wrist, guiding me toward the doorway of the library. I gazed down at where his hand touched me, and followed, too stunned to resist.

“Oh,” I breathed, understanding as I glanced into the library. “Addie.” I let out a small sigh. “Yes, I know her.”

His grip loosened, his expression shifting as though my answer had surprised him. “Addie,” he repeated, as if tasting the name. His eyes searched mine, as if looking for something I couldn't quite place. "You must know her well to be on a first-name basis."

His skepticism was evident in the way his brow arched, but there was a hint of something else, too—curiosity, maybe. I smiled at Addie. "I've known her all my life."

His smirk returned, softer this time. "Have you now," he said, his tone lighter, though his eyes still held that look of calculation. He was a puzzle, a mix of contradictions that left me more confused than before.

Lil's warning echoed in my mind. Keep a safe distance. But the space between us had all but vanished. I needed to move, to put some space between us, but my feet remained rooted to the spot.

"I should be going," I mumbled, taking a half step back.

His gaze held steady, almost playful, but his eyes betrayed a sharper interest. 'What's your name?

Gods, he's tall. I eyed him from head to toe. "I'm nobody important," I murmured, the words feeling small and inadequate.

His lips quirked into a half-smile. "That's not true," he said, his voice dropping to a whisper. "Everyone here is someone important. Or important to someone."

Everyone here. Here, the place I wasn't meant to be.

There was something in his tone, a softness that made me feel both seen and exposed at the same time. His voice wrapped around me, warm and dangerous, and I knew I needed to get out of here.

"Brida," a voice called, breaking the spell, tightness coiling in my gut. A large figure appeared at my side, his violet eyes kind and familiar.

"Your Highness," Marsh said, bowing his head with a grace that spoke of years spent in such company.

The prince's expression hardened, his lips pressing into a thin line as he stepped back, though his eyes never left mine. The amusement was gone, replaced by something colder, more guarded. The golden hues had all but vanished, onyx eyes with living shadows were all that met me now.

Turning to me, Marsh said, "I noticed you weren't with the group and thought you might have gotten turned around." His tone was light, but his eyes flicked between me and the prince. "The dining hall is this way." He gestured left, and I cursed myself for turning right earlier.

I can't be trusted to navigate this place.

The tension between Marsh and the prince was palpable, a silent standoff that made the air thick with unspoken words. I glanced between them, curiosity gnawing at me. What history lay buried beneath those sharp looks? Marsh's expression was guarded, but there was a storm simmering behind his eyes. And Dainan—his features, though calm, seemed to flicker with some deeper, restrained emotion. Had they been allies once? Rivals? The kind of relationship that spoke in the language of betrayal or brotherhood? The questions swirled in my mind, each one more unsettling than the last.

"Yes. We wouldn't want the two of you to be late," the prince said, his voice icy.

I nodded, eager to escape. "Your Grace," I managed, though my voice came out far too small. Marsh turned on his heel, striding down the hall, and I moved to follow, my steps hurried and uneven.

But before I could take more than a few strides, the prince's grip tightened around my wrist, halting me. His gaze found mine, sharp and unrelenting, and the intensity there stole the air from my lungs. For a heartbeat, something flickered in his eyes—an emotion I couldn't quite place, something raw and magnetic that sent a shiver racing down my spine.

"It was good to meet you, Brida," he murmured. His voice was low, rich, and unhurried, each syllable settling over me like an unspoken promise. My throat tightened, and I swallowed hard, unsure if I wanted to hold his gaze or tear myself away.

I turned and followed Marsh, but the urge to look back tugged at me, relentless and insistent. I gave in, glancing over my shoulder. The prince was already walking away, his shoulders broad and steady, the book Addie had given him clutched in his hand. Something about the sight lingered, like the echo of a song I couldn't stop hearing.

☽⁎☾

"So, are you personally responsible for ensuring we all eat three balanced meals a day?" I asked, breaking the silence as we strolled down the hall.

Marsh slipped his hands casually into the pockets of his dark purple suit, the fabric catching the dim light with an understated elegance. He let out a warm, low, easy laugh.

I couldn't help but smile back, caught in the infectiousness of his amusement. "Not everyone," he replied, his grin lopsided and teasing. "Only those I have a vested interest in."

What does that mean? I studied him, unsure how to respond. I opened my mouth to ask but thought better of it, opting for a safer topic. "Marsh...is that your first name?"

He raised an eyebrow. "An odd question."

"Sorry," I said, "it's just...Marsh sounds more like a family name. At least where I'm from."

"Ah, yes. Escalia." His eyes found mine, and I saw a spark of recognition. "An odd place," he mused, his brow furrowing.

You have no idea. "Yes," I sighed. "You could say that."

"You're right, though," he said, "it's a family name. We were from marshlands, but that was close to twenty thousand years ago." He gestured for us to turn a corner. "The Magister finds it amusing, as my family wasn't courted or selected by either the Court of Reflection or the Eternal Court. The Court of Whispers has nothing to do with marshlands, so he insists on calling me that. He may be the only one who finds it funny," he added, pushing open the door to the dining hall for me.

The room had changed since last night's dinner—six long, dark mahogany tables now filled the space, their weathered surfaces beautiful despite the years. The chairs had been replaced by benches that looked as uncomfortable as they were long. To my right, an incredible spread of food awaited, tempting me with the scent of fresh bread.

"Do you like people calling you Marsh, then?" I asked, trying to keep things light.

"I've gotten used to it," he said with a smile. "But if you wish, you can call me Reed." His tone was casual, but there was a challenge in his eyes.

I tried not to laugh but ended up coughing instead, failing to cover up my reaction. "Your full name is Reed Marsh?" I asked, my voice still choked with amusement.

"The irony is lost on few," he said, looking down at me, his expression jovial. "I'm still unsure why my parents chose it." He scratched the back of his head, his eyes narrowing as if debating the mystery all over again.

He leaned in closer, his breath warming my skin. "I believe your friends are over there," he whispered, nodding toward the main table where Lil and Kad were seated. They looked up as Marsh and I approached, their faces lighting up when they spotted me. I flashed Marsh a quick, grateful smile.

"Thanks, Reed, for escorting me to lunch," I said, trying out the name. It felt strange on my tongue, like trying to call a wolf by its given name. "I believe it's clear that I wouldn't have found my way here and would have died of starvation as a result."

"That would've been a tragedy," his lips curled upwards.

"Brida Larrow, she lived, she loved, she starved."

He gave me a small chuckle, his eyes lingering on mine for a moment longer than necessary before he turned to leave.

Does he know? The thought gnawed at me as I watched him walk away. *And if he does, why hasn't he said anything?*

Kad waved me over, a grin plastered on his face as he motioned to the seat beside him. "You're late," he teased. "We thought you got lost."

I forced a smile, slipping into the spot next to him. "I took the scenic route," I said, glancing over at Lil, who was already mid-bite.

She raised an eyebrow but didn't comment, offering me a look indicating she'd want details later.

"Scenic, huh?" Kad's grin widened as he took another bite. "And what pray tell did you see?"

"Oh you know...this and that." I reached for a roll, hoping to shift the conversation. But as I tore it open, I couldn't help but replay the encounter with Dainan in my mind. His eyes, the way he'd looked at me like he was peeling back layers...

"Brida?" Kad asked, and I blinked, realizing I'd been staring at the roll in my hands for far too long.

"I'm okay," I said, flashing a smile that no doubt looked as forced as it felt. "Just...thinking."

"About what?" he pressed, his tone light but concern danced in his eyes.

I hesitated. *About the prince who I cannot seem to avoid? About Marsh knowing more than he lets on? About Dad...*"Just...the Courting," I said, picking the safest option. "It's a lot to take in."

He nodded, accepting my response without pushing for more, though his expression hinted that he saw through my lie. "Yeah, it is," he agreed, his gaze wandering over the room's familiar contours. "But we'll get through it. Together."

Lil chimed in, her voice casual as she reached for another dish. "Just remember, we're all in the same boat. Everyone here is just as nervous as you are." She winked, though I wasn't convinced she believed it.

I tore off another piece of the roll as I watched Marsh across the room. *Is he waiting for the right moment, or is he...protecting me?* The thought was as unsettling as it was reassuring. I'd have to be more careful around him—and Dainan, for that matter.

"Brida," Lil's voice cut through my thoughts, pulling me back to the table. "You sure you're good?"

"Yeah," I said, forcing another smile. "Just, you know, the scenic route."

Kad chuckled, nudging me with his elbow. "Well, next time, stick with us. It's safer that way."

"Right," I agreed.

I caught Marsh's eye from across the room. His expression was a mask crafted of tranquility, yet I couldn't shake the nagging feeling that beneath that calm facade, he was concealing something—just as I was.

CHAPTER ELEVEN

Illerium's voice was a monotonous hum that penetrated my thoughts. I couldn't tell if it was fatigue or if the Magister loathed his position, but he possessed a tendency to fade mid-sentence, much to Kadian's amusement. I struggled to focus, my mind flitting between the gnawing anxiety of what tomorrow might bring and the rising dread that someone might pierce through the cracks in my façade.

We weren't even headed toward the other House entrances; instead, Illerium guided us to the gym and sparring area, noting our training would begin in the morning. My stomach twisted at the thought. I had seen the others—muscles taut beneath their clothes, their confident strides radiating the certainty of those who knew they belonged. The Eternal Court would take one look at me tomorrow and scoff, dismissing me as an interloper in their world.

"We knew this was coming," Kadian tried to reassure me over dinner, but his voice was drowned out by the laughter and chatter of the other candidates.

"Not exactly looking forward to it," I muttered, my voice low. My eyes drifted around the room, taking in the broad shoulders and confident smiles. They were ready. Me? I wasn't so sure.

Kadian leaned closer. "It's not just about strength or speed. You've got more going for you than you think."

Oz, who had been quiet while eating across from us, watching a few girls who sat further down the table, piped up, "My dad said the same thing when he first started. Useless at the physical stuff, but with training, he found his footing. You never know."

I forced a smile, but my gaze slipped past Oz to Lil. She was watching me with that knowing look in her eyes, the one that said she was about to say something I wouldn't like.

"Well," she began, a smirk playing on her lips, "no matter how you do, Marsh will definitely be paying attention."

I could feel the heat rising from my neck to my cheeks. "I shouldn't have told you he came to get me," I said, focusing hard on my plate.

"Too late now," Lil teased, nudging me with her elbow. "But really, Brida, you're going to kick ass tomorrow, and you know it."

Kadian chuckled beside me, his laughter light and teasing, but I could barely muster a response. The room felt too loud, too bright. I just wanted to get through tomorrow without making a fool of myself.

"Can we talk about something else, please?" I asked, desperate to change the subject.

Kadian sighed, but his smile softened. "How's Addie?"

Gratitude surged through me, and I latched onto the lifeline. "She's great. Looks just the same as the last time I saw her."

"Who's Addie?" Oz asked, curiosity in his tone.

"Only Brida's favorite person," Kadian answered before I could, a grin spreading across his face. "Except me, of course."

I couldn't help but smile. "He's not lying. Addie's my aunt. She's a scribe here in Azmeer."

"I thought your family didn't have any ties to Azmeer?" Lil's question hung in the air.

"She's more of a freelancer," I replied, keeping my tone light.

"Started working here a few months ago on a project for the royal archives. They liked her work and offered her a job."

The conversation drifted into lighter topics, but my mind stayed on edge. I didn't mention Dainan. Didn't bring up the library or the strange tension between Marsh and him. What was there to say, anyway? *He was in the library, he wanted a book. Where does one go to get a book? The library.*

As we made our way back to our rooms, I watched Lil and Kadian walking close together, their laughter bouncing off the corridor walls. Kadian had been in plenty of relationships during our university years, but they were always fleeting—none of them ever made him smile the way Lil did.

Looking at him now, it struck me how many women had thought flirting alone would be enough to win him over. But to truly know him, to have him, you had to make him laugh. A soft smile tugged at my lips as I thought about it. They're in for an interesting year.

Oz said his goodbyes first, slapping Kadian on the shoulder, then pulled Lil and me in for an embrace before heading to his room. Lil followed soon after, her eyes lingering on Kadian. As she disappeared into her room, Kadian's shoulders slumped, and he shook his head.

"Someone's in trouble," I teased, trying to push aside my worries.

He laughed, but it sounded a bit forced. "Tell me about it."

Kadian wrapped an arm around my shoulder, guiding me to my room. "Try not to get too caught up in your head tomorrow, okay? It won't be as bad as you think."

But I could hear the uncertainty in his voice. "You don't really believe that, do you?" I asked, unable to keep the fear from creeping into my tone.

"No," he admitted, pressing a kiss to my cheek. "But I don't want you to worry."

After we parted ways, I made a beeline for the bath, hoping the warm water would calm my nerves. But even as the jasmine and vanilla-scented steam curled around me, my thoughts refused to settle. Dainan, Addie, Marsh, the Eternal House—they all spun around in my mind, refusing to let me rest.

By the time I crawled into bed, my skin wrinkled from the bath, I felt no closer to peace. I *love this bed,* I thought as I pulled up the covers, but even that comfort couldn't stop the faint smell of smoke from seeping into my dreams.

☽✳☾

"Attention, inductees," Illerium announced. "In six weeks, the next trial begins—a decisive elimination round. One hundred of you will be sent home. Each Court will present a challenge, a reflection of its domain."

The room seemed to hold its breath as he continued. "The Eternal Court's challenge will test your strength against a formidable rock wall. The Court of Reflection will immerse you in a pool where truth and perception become indistinguishable. The Court of Shadows will challenge your mind with a riddle. And for the Court of Whispers, you will face a treacherous course high above the ground, where the wind is your adversary. Your time on each trial will be added together. Only those with the best overall time will continue in Azmeer. However," his eyes glinted, "finish one trial with the fastest time, and you'll secure your spot in the next round."

Illerium's gaze swept over the room, unreadable, before he added, "The details will come in due time. For now, prepare. Perseverance, adaptability, and a sharp mind are your best tools."

Illerium's announcement had barely settled amongst the crowd before I felt the dread begin to rise. Six weeks to prepare for the trials. I should have felt relieved—it was time to train, to strategize—but all I could think about was that one trial. The Court of Whispers.

I hated heights. My knees buckled just thinking about it.

Around me, the gymnasium hummed with excitement and tension. Emia's arm brushed against mine, her bright eyes wide with anticipation. "I'm going to the pool," she said, bouncing on her toes. "You coming?"

The pool—the Court of Reflection's trial. Calm, serene water. No wind, no dizzying drops. My mind screamed for me to follow her, to avoid the trial that haunted me, but my heart knew the truth.

If I didn't face this fear, none of the other trials would matter.

I shook my head, forcing a smile that didn't quite reach my eyes. "No, I'm heading to the ladders. I need to work on the heights."

Her smile faltered for a moment, but she nodded in understanding. "Good luck. If anyone can conquer those heights, it's you."

I wished I believed her.

I glanced over at Kadian, who shot me a wink, before gathering his things to head toward the rock wall with Lil and Oz—the Eternal Court's trial. The one I should've been starting with. I could already picture Kadian scaling it with ease, the others cheering him on. A pang of guilt hit me. I should be with them, but no. This was something I had to do alone.

It was better this way. No one to see me fail. No one to watch as I faltered or froze.

As I made my way to the trial area, my heart pounded, my palms already clammy despite the cool air. The chalcedony ladders loomed in the distance, rising like skeletal fingers grasping for the sky.

I paused at the base of the first ladder, staring up at it. The wind whistled through the gaps between the rungs, tugging at my clothes and sending my hair whipping around my face. It felt alive, a force determined to push me back. My breath caught in my throat, and for a moment, I couldn't move.

I can't do this.

Illerium's words echoed in my mind—one hundred of us would be sent home. The thought made my stomach lurch. If I didn't master this trial, I might be one of them. And my father—What would become of him if I couldn't secure the resources Azmeer promised?

I gripped the rung of the ladder, the smooth stone cold against my hands. I had to do this. There was no other option.

The climb was harder than I'd imagined. The wind howled in my ears, a constant, brutal reminder of how high I was climbing. My hands, already sore from gripping the rungs too tightly, began to throb with each pull. My feet slipped more than once, my boots struggling to find purchase on the slick, narrow rungs. The higher I went, the worse it got.

I looked down once, just once, and regretted it. The ground below was nothing more than a blur of brown and gray, the trees looking like tiny specks of dust, and the people—there were no people. Just emptiness. The world stretched out beneath me like a vast, indifferent void, and I was dangling over it, entirely at its mercy.

My head swam. I swallowed hard, trying to force down the nausea creeping up my throat. My breath came in ragged gasps, the cold air stinging my lungs. Each time I inhaled, it felt like knives cutting through my chest, sharp and unrelenting. I wanted to stop, to retreat, but the thought of failure was worse than the fear itself.

After what felt like an eternity, I reached the top. My legs wobbled as I stepped onto the platform, the wind slapping me across the face, almost as if it were mocking me for making it this far. I staggered forward, trying to steady myself, but the sight of the rope bridges ahead made my stomach drop all over again.

Eight houses, as if supported by the air itself, awaited me. Connected by treacherous rope bridges, each one swaying in the wind. From this height, I could see the chipped purple paint with sharp detail, the faded hue clinging to the wooden slats in uneven patches. How had they survived the relentless gales? The thatched roofs, somehow still intact, seemed like they were holding their breath, waiting for the wind to tear them apart.

I took a step toward the first bridge. It groaned under my weight, the ropes creaking as if warning me to turn back. I gripped the sides, my knuckles white, and forced myself to move. My ears ached from the cold, the high-altitude wind cutting through me like shards of ice. I could barely see; my eyes stung from the wind, making them water. Every step was a battle, each gust threatening to rip me from the bridge and toss me into the abyss below.

I focused on the first house. The door was ajar, and I pushed it open with trembling hands. Inside, the air was still, the walls bare save for a single parchment lying on a wooden table. I picked it up, squinting at the strange symbol drawn in dark ink—a twisting, jagged shape that looked almost like a broken spiral. It was light, almost weightless, and the parchment felt rough against my fingertips like it had been left out in the wind for too long.

I tucked it into my pocket and stepped back out onto the bridge, my legs shaking as I made my way to the second house. The wind was worse now, screaming in my ears, and my cheeks burned from the cold. My fingers were numb, stiff, and uncooperative as I tried to grip the ropes.

The second house was colder, the wind seeping through the cracks in the walls. The room was empty, save for another piece of parchment on the floor. This one had a different symbol—sharp, angular lines crossing in a star-like pattern. My fingers fumbled as I reached for it, the cold making it hard to hold onto anything. The parchment slipped from my grasp, and I had to chase it across the floor, the wind howling through the open door.

I stumbled back out, fighting the urge to cry as the panic surged in my chest. I had only made it a quarter through, and already, the wind was breaking me down, picking at my resolve with every gust. The next bridge stretched ahead of me, swaying violently. I could scarcely make out the third house, the wind and cold blurring my vision.

But as I crossed the bridge, the world tilted beneath my feet. My knees buckled, and I clung to the ropes, my breath coming in shallow, painful gasps. I couldn't focus. Couldn't breathe. The panic was taking over, pulling me down. I had to turn back.

I forced myself to retreat, step by agonizing step, back across the bridges and down the ladder. My body was shaking, my hands raw and blistered.

By the time I reached the ground, my legs ached, struggling to keep me up. Marsh was there, his familiar smirk in place as he caught me by the elbow. "Not bad," he said, his voice annoyingly cheerful. "It takes a few tries. Twenty, in my case."

I gave him a weak smile, my legs trembling beneath me. "Twenty times?" I echoed, my voice hoarse.

"Yeah," he shrugged, "It's a nasty one. But you'll get it, trust me. Just keep at it."

Despite myself, I blurted, "Is there a reason you keep being so nice to me?"

The words slipped out before I could stop them, my tone more vulnerable than I intended. Marsh didn't seem fazed, though. He casually slipped his hands into his pockets, the deep purple of his suit catching the light as it fluttered around him like a storm about to descend. That suit—he wore it as effortlessly as he wore his smile. It was hard to figure him out.

"Would you prefer me not to be?" he asked, his gaze soft but probing.

I hesitated, tucking my hair behind my ears as if that simple motion could mask the sudden unease building in me. "I'm just not used to strangers being so kind," I admitted, the words tasting strange as they left my mouth.

Marsh's eyes flickered with something, but it was too quick to catch. "Not everywhere is Escalia, Brida," he said, his voice laced with something deeper, something knowing. "Seems like it was a good thing you got an invitation to a place where you belong."

His remark hit me harder than I expected. *A place where I belong*. The words sank into me, filling all the spaces I tried to keep hidden—the places where doubt festered, where fear of being discovered gnawed at me, constantly threatening to undo everything. But underneath that fear, beneath all my defenses, there was a whisper of something I hadn't let myself feel in a long time.

Hope.

Despite everything—despite the lies I'd told, the weight of my father's illness, the constant dread that I wasn't good enough to survive here—Azmeer had been the first place where people looked at me without judgment. The first place where strangers spoke to me with kindness, without assuming I didn't belong. For so long, I had fought to blend into the backdrop of Escalia, to go unnoticed. But maybe Marsh was right. Maybe here, I didn't have to be invisible.

"Thanks, Marsh," I said, my voice softer. I took a step toward him, feeling a strange pull as though he had chipped away at some of the walls I'd built. "You know, I come for a run in the evenings, and I plan on starting in the mornings too... Going to need to if I have any chance at surviving this next round."

He smiled then, a genuine smile that lit up his face in a way that made something flutter in my chest. "Running is good. Keeps you quick."

"Yes, but..." I hesitated, feeling my palms grow damp. "You know," I said, "I've found it's a much more enjoyable activity when I have a partner."

Marsh raised an eyebrow, his smirk returning, though softer this time. "Is that so?"

"It is," I nodded, trying to keep my voice steady despite the sudden wave of nervousness washing over me. I wasn't sure where this courage was coming from, but the words were out now, and there was no taking them back.

He studied me for a moment, his eyes searching mine as if trying to read the layers beneath my words. Then, he smiled again, a warm, almost mischievous grin. "Well, it's a good thing I just happen to love running, then, isn't it?"

I felt my heart skip, a mix of relief and excitement swirling inside me. I hadn't expected this—hadn't expected *him* to be so...open. He gestured toward the building, and without another word, we walked side by side, the wind still cold but less biting, the weight of my earlier fear somehow lighter.

We made our way back inside, where we were greeted to an unexpected silence. My gaze fell on the center of the room, where a circle had formed, and within it, Princes Dainan and Rai were engaged in a fierce sparring match.

"What's going on?" I whispered, curiosity piqued.

Lil gestured us over, her eyes fixed on the mat. "Started about fifteen minutes ago. They do this regularly—sometimes Alvar joins too, but not today." She pointed to the side where Asana and Alvar stood, watching with evident amusement.

"Who's better?" I asked.

"Dainan," Marsh replied in a hushed voice.

It was impossible not to be captivated. The brothers moved with a deadly grace, their strikes and counters fluid and precise. Their bare chests glistened with sweat, every muscle taut and defined. It was a display of skill and power that was both mesmerizing and intimidating.

I glanced up at Marsh, noticing his similar build to the princes. He had a confidence about him, one that made me feel more at ease despite the chaotic scene before us.

"Dainan likes to take them down and pin them there," Marsh murmured, leaning closer. "He's a strong fighter."

The room seemed to hold its breath as the brothers circled each other. Dainan made a move that took him to the far side of the mat. I caught his eyes, and for a fleeting moment, it felt like he was looking straight at me.

Rai took advantage, lunging at Dainan and pinning him to the floor. The sudden shift in the fight brought a cheer from Alvar and Asana, and soon, the entire gym erupted in applause.

"Well," Lil said with an unsatisfied nod, "that's that."

"Why the celebration?" I asked Marsh, who wore a smug smile.

"Dainan hasn't lost in a very long time," Marsh said, his tone hinting at admiration.

On the mat, Rai extended a hand to Dainan, who took it reluctantly. Dainan's gaze flickered between Marsh and me as he placed a hand to his chest, catching his breath. Before I could blink, he vanished in a swirl of shadow.

CHAPTER TWELVE

"I'm sure you've all been enjoying yourselves these past few weeks," Illerium's voice grated against the thick tension in the room, his words heavy with a kind of bitterness that seemed to press down on the air itself. He shuffled to the podium, his figure hunched like the weight of the centuries he spoke of was pressing down on his bones, his entire demeanor exhausted.

The slight smirk that flickered across his lips didn't match the resentment in his voice. "From what I've heard, some of you have garnered attention—though not always for the right reasons."

His sharp gaze locked onto a boy seated a few rows ahead. I recognized him as the poor kid who'd fallen off the rock wall before, struggling to make it halfway up before he crashed to the ground. My heart twinged with secondhand embarrassment for him, remembering the awkward thud when he hit the ground. The boy's face flushed red under Illerium's scrutiny, his head ducking lower as if to hide from the weight of the room's collective gaze.

Illerium's voice droned on, detailing the values of the Courts—the need for strength, stamina, and physical prowess. His eyes swept over us, intense and expectant, like he demanded full attention from everyone. "You might wonder why you must endure such displays—why we value strength over wit, your bodies over your minds, when in reality, we should be seeking the sharpness of intellect, your skill, your cunning."

A timid voice broke the tension, a girl from the second row; her hand half-raised as if unsure if she should even speak. "Do you mean war, sir?"

Illerium scoffed, rolling his eyes with the disdain of someone who thought the question was beneath him. "What else would I mean?" he snapped, his irritation crackling through the room like a whip.

Kadian leaned over, his breath warm on my ear as he whispered, "He isn't suited for this, is he?" I had to bite my lip to keep from laughing, imagining Illerium losing his cool at even the slightest provocation. His face was already turning an alarming shade of red.

Illerium launched into a tirade about past wars—the violent rise of Elidas, the tyrant Kavriel, and the bloody battles that had carved the history of the Courts. His words painted a grim picture of a world where intellect alone wouldn't save us on the battlefield. But as he spoke, I found my mind drifting, wondering about his past. Had he fought in those wars? Had time and the weight of history worn him down, made him bitter and frayed around the edges?

Snapping his fingers, a stack of papers materialized before each of us. "Your task is to fill out this questionnaire. You will share this with the group, and we will compare your answers with the correct ones. You have thirty minutes. Begin."

I stared at the paper, trying to focus on the task at hand, but my thoughts kept slipping away—drifting back to my father and the research I'd been doing. In the past few weeks, I had spent hours poring over ancient tomes, chasing any lead, no matter how faint, that might ease his suffering. One plant in particular had captured my attention—*Larrea tridentata*. It wasn't much to look at, a resilient shrub with yellow flowers, but its healing properties were renowned. It was said to soothe skin ailments, reduce inflammation, and ease pain. A small part of me clung to the hope that it could help, that somewhere in Azmeer's gardens, this plant could offer some relief for him.

I forced myself to focus, trying to push the worries about my father to the back of my mind. The past three weeks had been a blur of training, studying, and grappling with my fears. Every morning, I ran with Marsh—something that had become the one part of the day I looked forward to. Despite its absurdity, Kadian had spent the first week lingering at the edge of the track, watching. He never made a big deal of it, always pretending to be there "just in case" or "just watching" but I knew better. This was his way—quietly protective, always keeping an eye on me without making it obvious. On the tenth day, he finally left me to it, giving me the space he knew I needed.

On our runs, I learned that Marsh was an only child like me. But unlike me, he had been in Azmeer for over a century, working with Illerium. It boggled my mind every time I thought about it. He didn't look a day over twenty-five, yet he spoke of things long before I was born. And in those weeks of running together, his easygoing nature had become a comfort, a strange anchor in this place that still felt foreign.

Evenings were spent at the gym with Emia, sometimes with Lil, pushing my body in ways I hadn't thought possible. Slow and painful, but I was beginning to master my fear of heights.

Marsh had offered advice, telling me of his experiences with the Zenith. Kadian, too, was my constant source of encouragement; his pep talks somehow made the impossible seem...bearable.

Oz and Tamra, Oz's twin sister, had been more present as well, their quiet support helping in ways I hadn't expected. Oz had taken to meeting me at my door each morning, telling me stories of what it was like to grow up Fae as we made our way to breakfast.

"Here," Oz said, handing me a small jar.

I turned it over in my hands, curious. "What's this?"

"Jam," he replied, grinning. "Wolfberry, specifically. It's the best flavor."

I raised an eyebrow, holding the jar up to my face for a closer look. "What exactly is it...?"

Oz turned toward me, his expression one of exaggerated disbelief. "Are you telling me you don't know what jam is?" He set his plate down and approached, resting his hands on my shoulders. "Oh, sweet Brida. What kind of sheltered life have you been living that you've never had wolfberry jam—or any jam, for that matter?"

Before I could respond, he pulled me into a warm, overdone hug. "Don't worry," he whispered with mock solemnity. "We'll get you sorted. Just remember—wolfberry is the best flavor."

The next half hour was filled with playful debate between Oz, who insisted I could eat the jam straight from the jar, and Lil, who insisted it had to go on toast. Eventually, I tried it both ways and instantly, wolfberry jam became my new favorite thing. Its rich, sweet-tart taste melted across my tongue like a revelation.

From that morning on, Lil or Oz always ensured a jar was waiting for me. In between discovering all the varieties of jam Oz had encountered in his travels, I learned more about him, too. His family wasn't so different from mine—marked by loss, with his grandmother having passed just a few years ago, despite living for nearly two thousand years. Oz had seen much of the continent, accompanying his father on journeys for the Eternal Court, his stories carrying the quiet weight of their histories.

"It's not just that my family are members, the Eternal Court is my top choice," he would tell me. I hoped it would come to pass.

With every free second I had, I tried to see Addie, even if it was just fleeting moments between training and studying. On the days when I couldn't find her, I buried myself in the library, scouring every book I could find on Azmeer's plants and remedies, anything that might help my father. Every day was a race against time, and I could feel the urgency building in my chest, a constant pressure I couldn't shake.

Illerium's voice snapped me back to the present, my eyes refocusing on the questionnaire in front of me. There was no time to dwell on what-ifs. I had to keep going—had to keep trying. For my father. For me.

☽✳☾

"I think I'm going to go stir-crazy if they don't let us out of this fortress soon," Lil muttered, rifling through the clothes in my closet. Emia sat cross-legged on the bed, her soft smile a quiet contrast to Lil's frenetic energy. The Fae girl's brown hair streaked with gold caught the light, a reminder of the first time I saw her during the feast on our first evening. She'd been so reserved then, but she had slowly begun to open up over the past weeks. She was shy but kind, and something about her reminded me of myself.

"You know, I heard there's a place in the Vameer district," Lil continued, pulling out a green dress and holding it up to the light. "Supposed to be the best spot for drinks, music, and dancing. We're going when they finally let us out."

I raised an eyebrow, amused by her enthusiasm. "And who exactly told you this?"

"Iona, that redhead from the first night. Well, I overheard her," Lil admitted, placing the dress on the bed beside Emia.

I knew Iona. The look of disdain she gave me after our first trial had never faded, lingering between us despite the fact that we'd never exchanged a single word. It was as if my very presence offended her, and yet, neither of us moved to bridge the silence.

"Her family lives here, so she knows all the good spots."

Emia looked up, her eyes bright with interest. "I'd love to go out. It's been so long since I've been in Azmeer. I barely remember the city."

"Well then, it's settled," Lil declared, twirling around with a flourish. "As soon as they give us the okay, we're going. And you, Brida, are wearing this dress. No arguments."

I laughed, shaking my head. "If you insist."

The banter flowed easily between the three of us, the camaraderie almost startling in its suddenness. A few weeks ago, I wouldn't have imagined having friends here—real friends who made this whole experience feel a little less overwhelming. It was odd, like finding something you didn't know you needed.

As the evening crept on, we sat on the bed and talked for hours, losing track of time. Lil, of course, was in her element, spinning tales and jokes with reckless abandon; I don't think I'd known her to be quiet for more than a few seconds. Emia chimed in now and then, her soft voice weaving its way into the conversation.

"I'm telling you," Lil said, standing up to stretch, "Illerium is going to drop dead of boredom. It's only a matter of time." She opened the door, ready to head back to her room, when she froze. Her gaze locked onto something down the hall.

Following her line of sight, I spotted Kadian cornered by one of the girls, Shay. She'd been eyeing him at the gym, and judging by the way she had him almost pinned to the wall, she'd decided to make her move. Kadian's eyes flicked towards us, and the moment he saw Lil's expression, he extricated himself from Shay's grasp.

"Missed you tonight," I called out to him with a grin.

"I'm going to take off. Night!" Emia said, excusing herself from whatever was about to unfold.

His face was tight, tension radiating off him. "Yeah, well, I was preoccupied." His gaze shifted back to Lil, who had gone rigid, her smile replaced by a predatory stare.

A smile crept onto his face but didn't reach his eyes. "Did you guys hear?" he asked, his attention still fixed on Lil. "We aren't allowed out for the month. They're preparing for the Festival of Giaxia."

Lil's breath caught, her expression flickering with something close to panic.

"But," he continued, as if sensing her distress, "they've already said we'll be allowed out after the festival. Just a bit longer to wait."

Lil relaxed, snapping out of her trance.

"Well, looks like you made someone's night," I teased. "Who told you this?"

"Marsh sent notice on the wind to the dining hall, wondered if he had sent it here as well," Kadian replied as if it were the most natural thing in the world.

"Of course he did," I muttered, shaking my head. The Fae's abilities still caught me off guard sometimes, even after these weeks of witnessing them. Wind Walkers appearing out of nowhere, the odd member of the Court of Shadows melting into darkness—Azmeer was a place of wonders, and every day, there was something new to marvel at.

"It was so weird the first time I heard it," Lil admitted, "but they use it all the time here. It's how we got our wake-up calls."

"Yeah, it scared the shit out of me too," Kadian said. "But I guess we better get used to it."

I patted them both on the arm and said my goodnights. Whatever had happened between Kadian and Lil, they could figure it out on their own. I wasn't about to get in the middle of it.

Closing my door behind me, I began to undress as I made my way to the bathing chamber. The wooden shutters that covered my window were slightly open. The breeze felt incredible. Even though the air was warm, I treated myself to a scalding hot bath. I lowered myself into the steaming water, not realizing how much my muscles had been aching until my legs were submerged.

My mind wandered as the pains and aches began to relieve themselves. Allowing me to fall into a deeper state of relaxation as time passed. My eyelids grew heavier as my fatigue won out. I was just on the precipice of sleep when I felt a slight tingling sensation on my neck that nestled just below my ear.

"Brida," a voice whispered.

My eyes snapped open, and I scanned the room in a panic.

The air around me felt charged, like a secret waiting to be shared. My breath caught in my throat as a voice, soft and intimate, brushed against my ear, the kind of whisper that sends shivers down your spine. I sat up straighter, the breeze teasing my cheek from the open shutters, drawing me into a game I hadn't anticipated playing.

"It can be strange the first time you hear it," the voice murmured, amusement lacing the words. "Don't worry, it can't hurt you."

This has to be some kind of wind whispering—different from the vague, impersonal message Kadian had mentioned. This felt personal as if someone was leaning in close, their breath tickling the edge of my ear.

I hesitated, unsure how to respond, and the silence stretched, my heart pounding in the quiet. The voice coaxed me, "Just speak. It will carry it back to me." It was muffled, but it was familiar, with a playful edge. "Do you plan on going for a run this evening?"

The way the air caressed my ear sent a warm flutter through me, like a secret touch in a crowded room. I cleared my throat, suddenly hyper-aware of the water lapping around me. "Uh..." was all I managed before another chuckle echoed in my mind.

"Can you hear me?" I asked, my eyes scanning the room for any sign of the source, half-expecting to see someone materialize.

"Not typically, but I made sure you could answer back," the voice cooed, closer now, almost too close.

I sank lower into the water, my cheeks flushing despite myself. "You...you can't see me, can you?" I hated how hopeful I sounded, praying that the answer was no.

The laugh deepened, teasing. "No. Only a few in the Court of Reflection can do that, and even then, it's rare."

I nodded to myself, trying to calm my racing thoughts.

"You didn't answer me. Do you plan on going to the gym this evening?"

Emia and I had frequented the gym most nights, working on each trial as best I could. The limited time we had in the morning wouldn't be enough if I were to make it to the next round. I was getting better, but I still hadn't made it through the Zenith.

I shook my head, trying to focus. “No, I was just about to fall asleep.” It wasn’t true; sleep felt a million miles away now.

“That's a shame,” the voice whispered, like a breath against my skin as I stood and wrapped a towel around myself. “I could help you practice.”

“I’m sorry to disappoint you,” I replied, feeling the pull of his words as I dressed. “But I need to save my energy for the daylight hours when court officials are watching. As much fun as it might be, I’ll have to pass tonight.”

“If you change your mind, I’ll be here for the next hour.”

I slipped into bed, the voice lingering in the air, a tempting echo in the quiet. “Goodnight,” I whispered, and a final chuckle filled the room.

CHAPTER THIRTEEN

I walked into the gym, surprised to see Tamra and Oz already in the midst of their morning workout. "I guess you're in for a harder workout today," Tamra teased, her eyes sparkling with mischief.

Oz grinned, his arm around his sister's shoulders in a gesture of camaraderie. "And what makes you say that?"

"You'll have to work harder to keep pace with me," Tamra retorted as the two took off. Of our group, Tamra was the most accomplished with each of the tasks, having mastered three of the four thus far.

As most inductees scattered to their preferred trials, I noticed a cluster of girls lingering in the back of the gym, their voices buzzing with excitement. Curiosity got the better of me, and I drifted closer.

"My money's on Dainan," one of the girls said. "His loss last time was just a fluke."

"Not a chance," her friend disagreed, eyeing a towering figure across the room. "Alvar is massive. Look at him!"

Alvar stood out among the crowd with his imposing presence and sharp features. His shoulder-length hair pulled back to reveal a face etched with determination. In contrast, Dainan's waves of hair fell into his eyes, giving him a more disheveled yet charismatic look. Their fiery hair seemed to dance with their movements, mesmerizing in its own way.

Deciding I didn't need to witness the outcome of them circling each other on the mat, I headed towards the track area. As I stepped through the glass doorway, a familiar devilish grin greeted me.

"Morning, Brida," Marsh said, his smile broadening as he saw me.

As much as I'd questioned Marsh and feared his intentions the first few weeks, he'd become a confidant, a friend.

"Marsh," I replied, feeling a rush of warmth spread across my cheeks.

"How'd you sleep?" he asked, casually stretching, his sleeveless leathers accentuating every defined muscle. My gaze traced the lines of his physique as I thought of the wind whispering from last night... *Focus.*

"Are those..." Marsh's eyes lingered on my outfit, his expression both amused and intrigued.

"They are," I responded with a grin. "I thought my running partner might appreciate a little court representation." I'd chosen to wear my Court of Whispers leathers, which, though black, shimmered with a violet hue at the neckline and cuffs.

Marsh stepped closer, his fingers grazing the edge of my neckline. The brief touch sent a tingle racing down my spine. His eyes, stormy and intense, held a flicker of warmth that drew me in, as if daring me to step closer.

"Purple suits you," he said softly, stepping back to prepare for our run.

"Maybe it will become my favorite color," I replied as I took my place beside him and took off.

As we ran together, conversation flowed. We'd settled into a rhythm—knowing when to push and when to ease off. Our pace shifted, but we never slowed. Each lap made me feel stronger, more in tune with my body.

On our eleventh lap, I gasped, "What's the deal with the Giaxia festival?"

"What do you mean?" Marsh's breath came in controlled bursts, sweat slicking his brow.

"Is it like the festivals in villages? Simple stuff. I figured it might be more elaborate here." I nodded around the track, trying to catch my breath.

"Giaxia is the Primal of the Eternal Court. They handle the festival planning. It's not as grand as in Hadash. Here, they'll have a feast, light candles outside the Eternal House, and everyone makes their offering. Then, they get the afternoon off."

"And in Hadash?" I pressed as our speed increased.

"There's a crater five miles west of the court; the mountains around it are stunning. They hold a huge feast in front of the caves."

"Have you ever seen the caves?"

"I have," he said, glancing at me with a smile that made my stomach tighten. "They're beautiful, but not the most beautiful thing I've seen." He flashed a dimpled grin.

I refocused and quickened my pace. "Stop being such a flirt," I teased and pushed ahead.

As we finished our run, I wiped sweat from my brow and caught my breath. "I'm meeting Emia at the Zenith next," I said, "I'm getting closer to finishing it."

Marsh's smile was reassuring. "I'm sure you'll get it done soon. And you're still working on the other tasks?"

Nodding, I said, "Yes. I've gone to the pool a few times after dinner with Lil, and Kadian has dragged me to the wall a few times. Not going to worry about the Court of Shadows just yet."

Marsh raised an eyebrow, a curious expression resting across his face.

"I appreciate your confidence." We laughed before I made my way towards the next obstacle.

As I walked away, I thought about how Marsh had stepped in to help me with my invitation. Without his help, I wouldn't be here. I wasn't sure if he knew how much that meant to me. For now, I focused on the next challenge.

☽✳☾

"I think we may have it tomorrow," Emia said as we reached the last rung of the ladder. Of the papers for the clues we'd manage to each gather, we were one short before the wind knocked everything from us. The magic in the Zenith only permitted one attempt per day.

"If we're lucky!" I said as I wiped the sweat from my brow. "Lil's over there." I saw the jovial blonde waving in the distance.

"Tell her hi from me. I'm going to head over to the track." My gaze found its way to the track, where I saw a tall, dark-haired Fae aimlessly wandering around.

I laughed as my gaze returned to Emia. Derek and Emia were from the same town, Retia, not too far from Azmeer. My eyes locked back to Derek. He was handsome, shy like Emia, and soft-spoken from the few words I'd heard him utter.

"Stop making it so obvious!" Emia snapped her fingers in my face, bringing me back to attention.

"Alright, alright. Go, tell Derek hi from me, and we'll see you at dinner... Maybe." I grinned as I made my way towards Lil.

"How was the pool?" I asked.

"It was illuminating," she said, linking arms with me and leading us towards the gym. "Turns out the king is unwell and in worse shape than they're letting on. They think he has a year, but it might only be months."

I thought back to our first evening in Azmeer, "*He is not doing well—far worse than he's been letting on.*" "*Only a handful know, but the news won't stay hidden for long.*"

They must have been discussing the king. *Gods, a possible coronation, and a Courting.*

"Certain ordinances need the king's approval, and those who

don't want to wait for the next king are pushing their agendas." Lil opened the gym door for me.

"I think," Lil said, her eyes lighting up, "it's time to clean up and grab some lunch. What do you think?"

"Even if I said no, I don't think I'd have much choice," I laughed as we headed toward the exit.

"That's true, but I'm glad you think you have a say when it comes to food."

"Please," I said, "I know better than to get between you and Kadian where meals are concerned."

Lil grinned. "I'm hoping there's more than just salad for lunch..."

Just as we were about to exit, a voice rang out, "Hey, Lil."

We turned to see Prince Alvar approaching, with Prince Dainan trailing behind. Lil's grip on my arm tightened as she pulled me closer, placing herself in front of me. Her relaxed demeanor shifted into something more guarded.

"Alvar," she said, her tone flat.

"Oh, come now, don't act like you're too upset to see me. It isn't my fault I kicked your ass at cards the last time I saw you." Alvar said with a smirk. He had a rough charm, the kind that only added to his allure.

"You only won because you're an absolute cheat, Alvar. And you know it." Lil shot back.

I found myself stunned into silence at the way Lil spoke to them. *She knows them. Better than she let on.*

Alvar's laugh was warm, his voice deeper than Dainan's. It carried a kind of easy warmth that made it hard to stay annoyed with him. "Rai's around here somewhere. I'm sure he'd be happy to see you." Alvar said as he pulled his rolled sleeves down.

"I'm sure he would, but alas, I'm very busy," Lil said, gesturing to me.

"Ah yes, and who is your friend?" Alvar asked, stepping closer.

"Brida," Dainan said. I'd nearly forgotten he was there, so quiet and still. Lil's gaze flicked to me, a mix of irritation and anxiety.

Shit. So much for keeping our encounter to myself. I found my eyes continuing to drift between the three of them, unsure who to focus on next.

"Is that so? How do you know her, Brother?" Alvar turned to Dainan, who remained composed.

"We met at the library," Dainan said, his gaze fixed on something distant as if he were done with this conversation.

Lil's eyes narrowed, disapproving.

Alvar turned to me, "If you spend any regular amount of time in the library, you will no doubt run into this one." He looked back to his brother, "The only thing he loves more than kicking my ass is reading," his smile became wicked. Dainan's expression didn't change.

"We need to go," Lil said, her arm tightening around mine as she led me away.

"I'll let Rai know you're here. We should get together soon. You can even bring Brida," Alvar called after us, his laugh trailing behind. Dainan stayed silent, his expression unchanged.

"I doubt it," Lil said, glancing back at them.

As we rounded the corner, I couldn't help but look back despite Lil's firm grip on my arm. I could sense the tension in her, something unresolved.

Lil's demeanor suggested that whatever history she had with them, it wasn't pleasant.

Her gaze fixed on me, her eyes sharp. "You have some explaining to do."

CHAPTER
FOURTEEN

"Do you want to tell me why Dainan knows your name?" Lil demanded.

He did remember my name.

"Dainan," I said, trying to ease the tension a bit, "first name basis, how very informal of you, Lil."

"No," she stopped, pointing her finger in my face, "don't you try to deflect. Last I heard, you saw him in the gym, same as me, and that was the only time you've seen him."

The hurt in her eyes sliced through me. What had happened between her and those brothers? I fiddled with my fingers, trying to calm the nervous energy buzzing in my veins. "It was like he said," I sighed. "I saw him in the library while visiting Addie. She gave him a book, and when I got lost trying to leave—because, of course, I did—and then I walked into him, as one does. Marsh found me afterward."

Lil raised an eyebrow, arms crossing in a defensive stance. "You accidentally walked into him?"

"Yes, I don't exactly make a habit of colliding with people," I replied, my words tripping over themselves. A bit like my feet had been lately. "He asked my name. I didn't give it to him—I had your voice in my head, telling me to keep a safe distance. But then Marsh showed up, called my name, and...well, Dainan remembered it."

Lil studied me, her silence a heavier burden than any accusation. I clasped her hands, the coldness of her fingers grounding me. "I'm sorry I didn't tell you. I just...after what you said that first day about having personal experience with them, I didn't want to stir anything up for you."

She sighed, her resolve softening. "I do have personal experience with Rai, not Dainan." She hesitated, then slipped her arm through mine, guiding us down the corridor. "A couple of years ago, we visited during the Autumn celebrations. Our families were close, so Rai and I spent a lot of time together. I was here when his mother died. It was awful."

I opened the door to our hall.

"The night Alvar mentioned... That's when things changed between Rai and me. I don't want you caught in a similar situation. Especially..."

"Especially?" I pressed.

"Especially because you're human, Bri. I can mess up, and it won't ruin my life. But you...you're different. You have an opportunity here. I don't want you to lose it."

Her sincerity twisted something deep in my chest. "Thank you," I whispered, pulling her into a hug. "I wasn't trying to get close to him, I swear."

"I believe you," she murmured, her smile faint but genuine. "And even if something does happen, I've got your back. We're stuck together now."

Lil's attempt to smile faltered, the pain in her eyes resurfacing. "Did you and Rai talk after that?"

She shook her head, a distant look shadowing her face. "He tried, but...no. I've seen him around, but I've avoided him. I was hoping Dainan would knock him out during that sparring match. It's the only time I've seen Dainan lose. For a bookworm, he sure can fight."

Her expression tightened, lost in whatever memory was haunting her. I placed a hand on her arm, offering silent support. "If you ever want to talk about it..."

Lil managed a weak smile, the storm in her eyes clearing. "I'm fine. And before you ask, yes, the sex was great with Rai, but only because I'm fucking incredible." She winked and disappeared into her room.

I stood there, staring at her closed door, a sinking feeling in my gut. I wanted to believe she was okay, but the lingering unease told me otherwise.

☽✳☾

I knocked on Emia's door, anticipation buzzing under my skin.

"Just a second!" she called from inside. Over the past weeks, we'd all paired off—Lil and Kadian at the pool and rock wall, Oz and Tamra tackling every obstacle. Emia and I had been inseparable, her calm presence grounding me through the Zenith and every grueling climb.

The door opened, revealing Emia in her Court of Shadows fighting leathers, black with red shimmering along the cuffs and neckline.

"Projecting?" I teased.

"Oh, hush," she shot back with a grin. I knew Derek's family had ties to the Court of Shadows, though Emia kept the details vague.

"Ready?" I asked. She nodded and we made our way towards the gym.

As we walked, Emia talked about her family—two sisters, four brothers. "It's rare for Fae to have so many kids. By the time they had me, I think they just expected it."

"I can't imagine having six siblings—or any, really," I said.

"You and Kadian are close?"

"I don't remember a time without him," I admitted, hoping there would never be one. "He and Dad, they're my family. I love Addie, but she wasn't around as much as I would've liked. We kept in touch, though."

Every night, I wrote to Dad, telling him how much I missed him and I couldn't believe I was still here. I'd received a few responses and some letters from Flora. I sent instructions to her for some teas she could make and some herbs that I'd found around Azmeer, well, those that were in the accessible areas.

These weeks had been the most eye-opening of my life. With the trial just days away, I was determined to be among those who continued.

The rock wall loomed before us, two hundred feet of daunting height. Sweat dotted my brow before I even moved.

"Ready?" Emia whispered beside me.

"Why are you whispering?" I asked.

"It feels like the rock can hear us."

We were alone, the gym eerily quiet. Whether others were more confident in their ability or we were just paranoid, I couldn't say. I checked the clock, took a deep breath and stepped to the wall. As soon as my fingers touched the stone, a strange thrumming vibrated through them, the magic of Hadash's rock urging me upward. Each pulse pushed me higher until time and sound blurred into a soft song.

At the top, I rang the bell and looked down. Emia was only halfway up. She'd have to be faster if she wanted to make it through.

"Way to go, Bri!" she shouted, her voice echoing in the quiet gym.

When Em finished, we proceeded to make our way to the pool. Unsure exactly as to what the task would be, we had practiced most things.

"I'll time you first," Em said as we made our way into the water. "Hold your breath as long as you can, and we'll go from there."

I nodded.

"Go," Em whispered, her voice barely a ripple in the air. I took one last breath, then plunged beneath the surface.

The world above disappeared, replaced by the serene stillness of the water, a silence that wrapped around me like a comforting shroud. Down here, time seemed to stretch and slow, the usual chaos of my thoughts quieted. As foreign as this underwater world felt, it also welcomed me, a strange comfort in the embrace of the water. Em and I had practiced this each night. I knew I could hold my breath for close to eighty clicks. Yet, tonight felt different, as if the water itself was alive with a secret it wanted to share.

Eyes open, I fixed my gaze on the distant wall of the pool. The cool blue seemed to pulse faintly, the light shifting and bending in ways it shouldn't. Then, out of nowhere, a streak of light shot through the water. It was quick, almost like a flash of sunlight breaking through the surface, but there was something unnatural about it. The light twisted and curved, like tendrils of the sun itself, slithering along the walls and floor, creeping closer with every beat of my heart.

I didn't have time to react before darker tendrils appeared, coiling out of the shadows. They twisted together with the light, a dance of opposing forces, and they were heading straight for me. Each click in my head marked their approach, and my heartbeat quickened in response. The tendrils' edges began to morph, taking on shapes that were terrifyingly familiar—hands, reaching out, almost sentient in their intention.

My breath hitched, and without thinking, I kicked hard, shooting up out of the water. I broke the surface with a gasp, the world above rushing back in a chaotic blur.

"Bri, that wasn't long at all. What's wrong?" Em's voice was sharp with concern.

I looked around frantically, but the pool was just as it had always been—calm, ordinary, betraying no hint of the bizarre vision I'd just seen. Em placed a steadying hand on my shoulder, her touch grounding me.

"Brida?" she said softly, trying to pull me back from the edge of my panic. "Take a breath, it's alright."

I greedily sucked in air, my lungs burning as if I'd been under for hours. “Sorry,” I whispered, the word trembling on my lips. “I thought I saw something.”

Em offered to time me again, her voice gentle, but I shook my head. I couldn’t go back under, not tonight. Whatever I had seen—or thought I’d seen—left a lingering fear that the water wasn’t as safe as it seemed.

☽✳☾

The knock came as a whisper, so soft it blended into the morning as light crept shyly through the edges of my curtain.

“Brida, Brida, it's me, open up.”

I groaned, every muscle in my body aching like a rusted hinge. The covers clung to me, but I peeled them back, rising on legs that still trembled from yesterday's trials.

“Come on, you’ll have to be quick,” the voice urged again, now more insistent.

Lil. Of course.

I stumbled to the door, rubbing my eyes, each blink a plea for clarity. When I cracked it open, Lil's grin greeted me, wide and mischievous.

“Good, you’re up. I want to show you something,” she said, barging past before I could protest.

“I wasn’t up,” I mumbled, gesturing helplessly at my wrinkled clothes and tangled hair, a testament to the war I’d waged with sleep and lost.

“Doesn’t matter. Throw on a sweater; no one will see us,” she insisted, rifling through my things while I stood there, still clutching the doorframe, trying to gather my scattered thoughts.

"What time is it?" I rubbed at my eyes again, the blur refusing to lift.

“Brida,” she said, her voice sharp and impatient. “Put on something warm and comfy. You won’t want to miss this.”

Before I could argue, she tossed a sweater at me, and I tugged it over my head, still half-asleep, before she shoved me into the hallway. Her energy was relentless, like a gust of wind sweeping me along.

"We have to go this way," Lil said, leading me down an unfamiliar corridor, the opposite direction from where we normally went.

I blinked, trying to orient myself. "Where are we going? Should we get Kadian? You know I'm useless with directions."

At the mention of Kadian, a grin spread across Lil's face. "Nah, I saw him earlier. Besides, this is something I wanted to show you."

Her words hung in the air, thick with mystery. I followed, heart pounding harder than it should have this early in the morning. When Lil smiled like that, you could never quite tell what she was planning.

We rounded a corner, and Lil paused before a door, its hinges groaning in protest as she nudged it open.

"Get in," she whispered, her eyes darting around like we were breaking into the Eternal Court itself.

"You sure we're okay to be doing this?" My voice was hushed too, caught between the thrill of the unknown and the constant gnaw of anxiety in my gut.

Lil shot me a look. "Yes, yes, Brida. You need to live a little. Be daring!"

If only she knew. Daring had brought me here, hadn't it? Lying, cheating, abandoning the one person I cared about most. I'd been daring enough for a lifetime.

Still, I followed. The stairwell wound upward in a dizzying spiral, each step making my legs burn anew.

"I found this place one of the last times I was here," Lil started, her voice echoing off the narrow walls. "We used to stay in the House of Reflection unless we were trapped in the royal quarters. But I overheard them talking about something—something called a Mirage."

"A Mirage," I repeated, the word hanging between us like a secret.

"Yeah, I thought it was some cheap magician's trick at first." Lil's voice carried a thrill of rebellion. "But then I begged them to show me. Six rounds of cards later, when I'd cleaned them out, I bet everything I had left on one condition—they had to take me to see it."

Her story pushed me up the staircase, faster now. I didn't even notice how many steps we'd climbed, my curiosity outweighing the fatigue. There was something in Lil's tone—like the world was about to crack open, revealing something far more magical than I could imagine.

"Naturally, they thought they would best me, I was just a kid and a girl. *Fucking pricks*." Lil spat the words out as we reached the final step. "But, despite everything, they kept good on their promise, and they showed me this."

We reached the top at last. Lil pushed open a final door, and I stepped onto the flat roof of Azmeer, breath catching in my throat. The city had disappeared.

Before me, an endless ocean seemed to stretch out, shimmering like liquid silver under the early morning light. The desert surrounding Azmeer had dissolved into the mirage, a perfect reflection of the sky.

"What...what is this?" I whispered, moving to the edge and leaning against the cool stone, trying to take it all in.

"It happens once a year," Lil murmured, joining me at the railing. "Some mix of the air currents, they say. But to me, it's the start of summer. My favorite time of year."

The quiet joy in her voice tugged at something deep within me. I turned to face her, a smile creeping onto my lips despite myself. "It's beautiful, Lil."

Her grin softened as she gazed out at the horizon. "Just wait, this isn't even the best part."

For a few moments, we just stood there. Lil filled the silence with stories—her adventures sneaking through Azmeer, stealing moments of freedom from under her mother's watchful eye. But as the sun began to rise, painting the sky in hues of gold and amber, we both fell silent. The mirage shimmered, and for an instant, it looked as though the whole city was engulfed in flames. The sight was so unreal, so majestic, I had to remind myself to breathe.

Lil's voice broke the spell. "I wanted us to have something beautiful to remember Azmeer by, just in case..."

Her words hung heavy in the air. I swallowed the lump forming in my throat, forcing a laugh. "There's no way you won't make it through, Lil. You were born for this."

I turned to face her.

"You know I'm here for you, right?" I always sensed that something chased Lil in the silence, a shadow she could never quite shake —a reason she never let it linger for too long.

She didn't answer right away. Instead, she kept her gaze on the horizon, her face unreadable. "For the first time in a while," she said softly, "I feel like I've got something to fight for."

CHAPTER FIFTEEN

This is it.

In school, tests had been a welcomed challenge. A way to assure that my studying had paid off. This was different. All of the inductees stood in the center of the gym, each being divided into four groups by the Master of Trials.

"Each group will rotate from challenge to challenge." The lithe figure said in a voice that almost seemed to echo.

Kadian, Oz, and Lil were placed into group one, Tamra—the most capable of us—was in group two, and Emia and I were in group four.

"Each group will begin at a different task. Group one proceed to the wall, group two will make their way to the Zenith, group three will enter the chamber, and group four to the pool."

My heart raced as I followed a member of the Court of Reflection to the pool. The mother-of-pearl walls shimmered, a deceptive calmness in their beauty. We were given five minutes to change into our suits, and as I stood on the deck, the officiant's words echoed in my mind.

"In your first task, you will have to face the truth."

Emia and I exchanged a nervous glance. The officiant's blue robes, adorned with white embellishments, reflected the water's surface as she pointed to the stairs descending into the pool. The task would reveal itself once we were in the water, she had said.

"We've got this," Emia mouthed, squeezing my hand. Her confidence did little to quell the anxiety gnawing at my insides. I hadn't come back to the pool in the last few days. I'd have to rely on my wits and whatever calculated efficiency I could muster. My steps were measured as I entered the water, the coolness embracing my skin. Then, without warning, a flurry of bubbles erupted, swirling faster and faster until they coalesced into a larger bubble, enveloping me entirely.

In an instant, I was no longer in the pool. The world around me had shifted, becoming something intimately familiar yet dreamlike in its clarity.

"Hey, kiddo," Dad's voice broke through, and I whirled around. The kitchen—our kitchen—came into view. It wasn't much, but it was home. Dad stood by the stove, the scent of his cooking filling the air.

"Dad!" I cried, rushing forward. My arms wrapped around him, and for a second, I didn't care if this was real or not. He was solid, warm, alive. His sunken cheeks were full again, his eyes bright with life, not the dull fatigue I had become accustomed to.

"What's the matter?" he asked, laughing as he pulled back. "I just saw you five minutes ago. Did you grab the mail?"

I glanced down, noticing the envelopes stuffed in my pocket. "Uh, yeah," I stammered. "Looks like I did."

I clung to him, afraid that if I let go, this moment would slip through my fingers like sand. His hands were gentle as he brushed hair behind my ear. "Are you feeling okay?"

For the first time in what felt like years, I answered honestly. "Yes."

"Good, because I made your favorite." He gestured to the stove, where noodles and broth simmered in a pot. My heart ached. It wasn't really my favorite, but it was his best dish, and I had never had the heart to tell him otherwise.

"Thank you," I whispered, trying to memorize the way he looked, the way he sounded. But my mind was a traitor, already pulling me back to reality.

"What's wrong, honey?" Dad's voice was soft, his hand wiping away a tear I hadn't noticed. I didn't want to cry. I wanted to stay here, in this perfect illusion, where Dad was whole, and everything was as it should be. But the tremors in my limbs reminded me of the truth, the insidious force trying to separate us. "Let's have a seat, and I'll serve you some dinner."

I nodded, allowing him to lead me to the table. The wood creaked under my weight, a familiar sound that only heightened the unreality of it all. This wasn't real. I knew that. But it felt real, so real that I could almost forget.

Almost.

He placed the bowl in front of me, the steam rising in gentle curls. "Here we are," he said, smiling as he took his seat across from me. "Don't just sit there, dig in."

I stared at the bowl, at the ripples in the broth that shouldn't have been there. "Something wrong with the food, kiddo?" Dad took another bite, oblivious.

The ripples grew, distorting the surface until an image flickered within. Azmeer. The reality of where I was, of what I was doing, crashed back into me with a sickening jolt.

"You need to leave, Brida," a voice whispered, curling around my thoughts like smoke. My pulse quickened. I couldn't stay here, no matter how much I wanted to. This wasn't real, wasn't a place I could remain. Azmeer was waiting. I had a mission, and time was slipping away.

I stood, the chair scraping against the floor as I pushed back. Dad's gaze followed me, confusion creasing his brow. "What are you doing, honey? Your food is going to get cold."

I hesitated, my heart pulling in two directions. I could stay. I could live this half-life, bask in the warmth of this illusion if it meant Dad would be okay. But he wouldn't be. Not really. And neither would I. This was just a shadow of the truth, and staying here wouldn't save him.

Walking around the table, I placed a hand on his shoulder, leaned down, and kissed his cheek. "I love you," I whispered, my voice breaking. He looked at me with that same pure love and understanding he always had, and it shattered something deep inside me.

With a deep breath, I turned and walked to the door. My hand trembled as I grasped the knob, and I paused, looking back one last time. Dad was still there, his expression a mixture of confusion and concern. But he didn't stop me. He couldn't. This wasn't real.

I twisted the knob and stepped into the light, leaving him—and the dream—behind.

The world snapped back into focus with a jolt. I gasped, lungs burning as if I had just breached the surface of a deep, dark ocean. My chest heaved, sucking in the air that felt like it had been stolen from me, the cold water clinging to my skin like a second layer. I blinked, and the gymnasium's pool deck shimmered back into view, a hazy mirage against the brightness of the overhead lights. The memory of Dad's warm kitchen dissipated like mist, leaving behind a hollow ache.

My body trembled, muscles taut from the strain of holding onto something that wasn't real. The truth still echoed through my mind, the words from that strange, familiar voice reverberating against the walls of my thoughts. I tried to shake off the lingering sensation of the dream—no, the illusion—but it clung to me like wet clothes, refusing to let go.

I glanced to my left, and there was Emia, her face pale as the mother-of-pearl walls around us. She had surfaced only moments after me, her breathing ragged, her eyes wide and unfocused. Her hand trembled as she wiped the water from her face, the usual spark in her gaze dulled by whatever nightmare she had faced.

"Em, are you okay?" The words tumbled out before I could stop them, concern lacing my voice. I wanted to reach out, to offer some semblance of comfort, but my limbs felt heavy, sluggish.

Em's lips pressed into a thin line, her eyes flickering with something I couldn't quite decipher. "I'll tell you later," she murmured, her voice barely audible. She looked like she wanted to say more, but instead, she turned away, focusing on the task of wringing the water from her hair.

I nodded, though the knot in my stomach tightened. Whatever she had seen, it wasn't something she was ready to share. Not yet.

We were given a few precious minutes to change, and I welcomed the distraction, letting the familiar routine ground me. My fingers worked quickly, stripping away the damp suit and replacing it with my Eternal Court leathers. The leather hugged my skin, a comforting weight, the cool touch of the metal clasps a stark contrast to the lingering frigidity of the water. I took a deep breath, letting the familiar scent of the worn leather fill my senses, anchoring me in the present.

When we were led to the next task—the rock wall that seemed to stretch up into the heavens—I couldn't suppress the shiver that ran down my spine. The wall loomed before us, jagged and unyielding, its surface dotted with handholds that promised both challenge and reward.

The others in our group began their ascent, one by one, their faces set in determined grimaces. I watched them, trying to calm the storm of thoughts swirling in my mind. I was the twentieth in line, but all I could think about was the dream—Dad's laugh, the warmth of his hand on my shoulder, that broth. It had all felt so real, so vivid, that for a moment, I had almost forgotten where I was, what I was doing.

"Next!" The call snapped me out of my reverie, and I realized it was my turn. I shook my head, trying to clear the fog from my mind as I approached the base of the wall.

The cool stone met my hands as I began to climb, the rough texture biting into my fingers. I focused on the sensation, on the strength in my arms and legs, pushing everything else to the back of my mind. I couldn't afford to lose focus now, not when every second counted. I moved with purpose, each grip and foothold calculated, measured, deliberate. The higher I climbed, the more the dream with Dad seemed to fade, replaced by the present, by the urgency of the task.

Above me, someone slipped, their handhold giving way with a sharp gasp. My heart skipped a beat, but I forced myself to keep climbing, to push through the fear. I had to make it to the top. I had to succeed—for Dad, for Kadian, and for me. I'd come here for my father but these past few weeks had shown me that I wanted to be here. In a place where I'd found friendship and acceptance, I could help both my father and myself.

When I reached the top, my breath came in ragged gasps, my muscles burning. I pulled myself up onto the ledge, collapsing onto my back as the adrenaline began to fade, leaving behind exhaustion and a dull ache in my chest.

It wasn't until Emia climbed up, finishing after me, that I allowed myself to exhale. She looked even more drained than before, her face drawn and pale, but she managed a weak smile in my direction.

"We're still in this," I said, though the words felt hollow.

"We are," Emia echoed, her voice strained.

The words between Emia and I hung in the air, an unspoken understanding passing between us. The trials were far from over, and whatever lay ahead would be more grueling than anything we'd faced before.

We had mere minutes to catch our breath before we were ushered to the next task. The ladder wound up and up, the air thinning with every step, until we found ourselves atop the Zenith. The wind relentless as it tore at everything in its path.

I looked at the wooden sign, its weathered surface a stark contrast to the raw power of the wind. The words were barely visible through the gusts: "Solve the riddle." The challenge was here, and as the wind howled around me, I knew this was the moment I'd been dreading.

The real test had begun.

The wind howled around me as I stood atop the Zenith, its icy fingers clawing at my clothes, my hair, my very breath.

I gritted my teeth, narrowing my eyes against the biting wind. I knew from my previous attempts that the answers were hidden somewhere in those precariously perched houses, each connected by a web of rope bridges that swayed with every gust. I hated those bridges—they were flimsy, unpredictable, and now, with the wind, downright dangerous.

But I couldn't waste time. I had to move, had to get to the first house. My heart pounded in my chest as I stepped onto the nearest bridge, the ropes creaking beneath my weight. Every step felt like it could be my last, the ground far below a swirling blur. The wind whipped around me, tugging at my body, and I could feel the bridge sway beneath my feet more violently than before. I was halfway across when a vicious gust hit me, and the bridge buckled.

I screamed, grabbing for the ropes as the ground lurched beneath me. My grip slipped, the world tilting as my feet lost their hold. My heart plummeted, my mind blank with terror, but somehow—miraculously—a gust of wind worked in my favor, thrusting me upward, I was able to catch myself, clinging to the rope with white-knuckled desperation. I dangled there for a heartbeat, the abyss yawning beneath me, before pulling myself up and stumbling forward, gasping for air that the wind stole from my lungs.

I made it to the other side, my body trembling with fear and adrenaline. I couldn't afford to stop, couldn't afford to think about how close I'd come to falling. I burst into the first house, the door slamming shut behind me, cutting off the worst of the wind's fury.

Inside, the house was dark and cold, the wooden floorboards creaking beneath my boots. I searched frantically, throwing open cabinets, overturning furniture until I found it—a scrap of parchment, tucked away in a dusty corner. My fingers trembled as I smoothed it out, my eyes scanning the strange runes scrawled across it. The runes were unfamiliar, their shapes jagged and sharp, like they'd been carved with anger or desperation. I couldn't make sense of them, and that terrified me more than anything else. But I didn't have time to panic. I shoved the paper into my pocket and bolted for the next house, my legs unsteady beneath me.

The second bridge was worse than the first. The wind had picked up, howling like a beast, shaking the bridge with such force that I thought it might snap. I tried to focus, tried to keep my breathing steady, but every step was torture. I was almost across when a shrill scream tore through the air, cutting through the wind like a knife.

I turned just in time to see Emia—her small frame silhouetted against the sky—slip from the bridge ahead of me. My heart stopped, and for a moment, everything else disappeared. "Em!" I screamed, my voice hoarse, barely audible over the wind. I watched in horror as she fell, her body plummeting toward the ground far below.

A moment later, the wind—so fierce and unforgiving—seemed to catch her, cradling her fall, slowing her descent. *Thank the gods. A safety net.* She drifted downward like a leaf, the wind carrying her gently to the ground below. I wanted to cry with relief, but there was no time for that. She was safe, and I needed to keep moving.

The wind howled, growing fiercer with each passing second as if it knew I was running out of time. Each gust slammed against me, nearly knocking me off my feet. I couldn't stay upright any longer. Dropping to my hands and knees, I crawled up the incline, the force of the wind so strong it threatened to toss me over the edge. My fingers dug into the dirt and stone as I dragged myself forward, the cold seeping through my clothes.

The final house was smaller, more dilapidated. The roof groaned under the pressure, leaking rain in thin, relentless streams. The walls shuddered with every gust, as if they might collapse at any moment. I pushed inside, panting and soaked, scanning the room. Everything here was falling apart—the furniture splintered, a mirror cracked and broken. But it was behind that mirror that I found the last scrap of parchment.

The runes on the brittle paper glared back at me, mocking, like a riddle I was never meant to solve. My hands trembled as I laid all the pages out, trying to make sense of the symbols. My mind was racing, but nothing clicked. Frustration bubbled up as I fumbled through the mess of books and debris, searching for something—anything—to help.

A glint caught my eye. There, buried beneath a pile of dusty tomes, I found it—a small, worn decoder. Relief flooded through me, but I wasn't out of danger yet. The runes weren't just a puzzle; they were a fight. I matched the symbols one by one, sweat dripping down my face despite the freezing wind tearing through the cracks in the walls.

The decoder wasn't perfect. Some pieces were missing, leaving gaps in the sequence, I had to guess. I retraced my steps again and again, each wrong combination sending a spike of panic through me. It felt like hours—hands shaking, breaths shallow—until the meaning snapped into focus.

The answer was simple. Too simple. And it filled me with dread.

"*Whisper to the wind your greatest desire and deepest secret.*"

I stared at the words, my heart pounding in my chest. I knew, deep down, that if I didn't speak the truth, if I tried to lie, I would fail. But my deepest secret...? The thought of voicing it, of admitting it aloud, made my throat close up with fear.

The wind howled around me, the walls of the house trembling, as if urging me to speak. I clenched my fists, my mind racing. I wanted to be here, to find answers, to be offered a final placement in a court. But was that my greatest desire? No.

I took a deep breath, closing my eyes, feeling the wind tug at my hair, my clothes. The words came out as a whisper, so soft I couldn't hear them over the storm. "I want to heal my dad. And I hate that I've lied to be here."

The moment the words left my lips, the wind seemed to shift, growing impossibly strong. The walls of the house groaned, the air around me crackling with energy. And then, the sky above me split open.

A portal, swirling with darkness and light, appeared high above, its edges glowing with a strange aura. It called to me, a pull so strong that I didn't resist. I stepped forward, my heart racing, and before I knew it, I was inside, the world around me dissolving into shadow.

When I emerged, I found myself standing in a room made entirely of black obsidian, its polished surfaces reflecting the dim light of the flames that flickered on tripods in each corner. The air was thick, heavy with the scent of smoke and something older, more powerful. My heart pounded in my chest as I took it all in, the oppressive darkness pressing in on me.

I was alone, but I could feel eyes on me, unseen, watching, waiting. The flames crackled, their light casting long, twisted shadows across the floor. I swallowed hard, my breath coming in shallow gasps, as the full weight of where I was—and what I had just done—settled on me.

CHAPTER
SIXTEEN

The black obsidian walls felt like they were closing in on me, the gleam of the stone reflecting the flickering flames from the tripods. The only sounds in the room were the crackling of the fire and my shallow breaths. My mind raced as I replayed what I'd whispered to the wind. *I hate that I've lied to be here.*

What if someone had heard me? What if the wind wasn't as mindless as it seemed? My greatest desire, my deepest secret—out there, carried on the wind for anyone, anything, to hear. A chill ran down my spine. *Had I been careless?* The very thought made my skin prickle with anxiety. The walls seemed to press closer, as if they knew, as if they were waiting for me to slip, to fall into the very trap I feared.

And then, the shadows moved.

At first, it was subtle—a shift in the darkness, a ripple along the floor that seemed almost alive. I froze, my heart hammering in my chest. The shadows hissed, curling and uncurling like smoke, like they had a will of their own. I should have been terrified, but instead, a strange sense of calm washed over me, like the darkness was whispering promises of safety, of protection.

The shadows gathered, swirling in the center of the room, a dark mass that grew larger with each passing second. My breath caught in my throat as the mass began to take shape, coalescing into the figure of a man. No definitive features—just an outline, an impression of a man made entirely of shadow, his face indistinct but unmistakably male.

He stood there, silent and still as if waiting for something. For me.

I didn't know what to expect, but the shadows didn't threaten—they beckoned, drawing me in. The flames in the tripods flared, the fire leaping from its perch and spilling onto the floor like molten gold. It snaked across the obsidian, encircling me, the heat licking at my boots as the circle tightened, shrinking, forcing me closer to the shadow figure.

My heart pounded in my ears, but it wasn't fear driving it. The fire closed in, the ring growing smaller by the second, and I knew what I had to do. The test wasn't just about solving riddles or outsmarting my competitors; it was about something deeper, something primal. Embrace the darkness, or be consumed by it.

The shadowy figure extended an arm, the gesture fluid, inviting. I hesitated, every instinct urging me to flee, to escape the fire's relentless advance. But there was something about the darkness—something that felt familiar, almost comforting, like the embrace of an old friend. The flames licked closer, nearly brushing my legs, leaving me with no real choice.

I looked up at the shadow figure, its presence inexplicably calming the storm that raged within me. Slowly, I reached out and took its hand, the coolness of the darkness seeping into my skin, a stark contrast to the scorching heat. The moment our hands connected, the flames receded, the suffocating heat vanishing as if it had never existed. The room began to shift, the obsidian walls dissolving into nothingness.

Then, in a move that caught me off guard, the shadow leaned in and pressed its lips to mine. The kiss was tender, almost reverent, and I felt a strange sense of peace wash over me, though I couldn't comprehend why. My mind reeled, trying to make sense of the moment, but I found myself unable to resist, unable to pull away. I didn't fight it; the kiss anchored me.

As the shadow figure pulled back, its hand lingered, gently grazing my cheek. The touch was fleeting but electric, sending a familiar shiver down my spine. Then, as swiftly as it had appeared, the figure began to fade, melting into the surrounding darkness. I stood there, breathless and bewildered, with only the memory of that unexpected kiss and the soft brush of its touch remaining as the world around me shifted once more.

When I opened my eyes, the gymnasium's familiar walls greeted me. The oppressive weight of the obsidian room was gone, replaced by the echoes of distant voices and the scent of sweat mingling with something else—citrus and smoke. The air was thick with it, clinging to my senses, grounding me in reality.

I was back, standing in the center of the gym, surrounded by the hum of activity, but something had changed. The calm I felt in the darkness lingered, a quiet strength that settled deep in my bones. Whatever fear I'd felt before was gone, replaced by a strange, new understanding.

As the remnants of the obsidian room faded from my mind, I caught sight of Kadian.

"Thank the Gods, there you are. How do you think you did?" He patted my arms and scanned my body, looking if I'd been harmed during any of the trials.

Peeking around him, I saw Oz, Lil, and Tamra huddled together in the corner. Tamra was animated, her hands gesturing wildly; Lil had her jovial smile, and Oz leaned back, an easy smirk on his face.

They were strong, unshaken by the trial's intensity. But right now, I couldn't bring myself to share in their victories or their camaraderie.

"I'm fine, Kad. I'll be right back."

Kadian's mouth gaped open as I skirted around him. My

thoughts were elsewhere, my feet moving of their own accord as I searched the room for Emia.

I'd begun to panic when Marsh appeared in front of me, blocking my path. His face was somber, his usual lighthearted demeanor absent.

"Brida," he whispered, "if someone fails any part of the trial... they're sent home immediately."

His words hit me like a blow, my breath catching in my throat. The memory of Emia falling, the wind catching her, flashed through my mind.

I forced myself to breathe, to keep the tears at bay. Emia had been my ally, my friend. But I couldn't afford to break down. Not here, not in front of everyone. I had to hold it together, to keep my composure, even as my heart ached with the loss. I didn't even know if I'd done enough to stay, if my time on the Zenith would be enough to secure my place.

But at least I'd completed all the tasks. That had to count for something.

Marsh's hand closed around mine. I couldn't help but stare at it. It was cool but grounding. "You had the best time on the Zenith," he said, his voice pulling me back to the present. "That secured your place. Anyone who comes first in a section automatically moves on to the next round."

I blinked, the words sinking in. I'd done it. I was moving on. But the relief was muted, swallowed by the hollow ache left by Emia's absence.

"Kadian was the fastest on the wall," Marsh added, his tone lightening. "Tamra was right behind him."

He released my hand and reached into his pocket, pulling out a small, folded note. "Emia wanted you to have this," he said softly. "I was the one who caught her...and escorted her out of Azmeer."

My heart twisted, but I nodded, taking the note from him with trembling fingers. I didn't trust myself to open it here, in this crowded room with so many eyes watching. Instead, I slipped it into my pocket and managed a small, grateful smile for Marsh.

He gave me a reassuring nod before stepping back, allowing me to make my way over to Lil, Kadian, Oz, and Tamra. Their excitement was a stark contrast to the turmoil churning inside me.

Before I could say anything, the Master of Trials appeared at the front of the room, his presence commanding immediate silence. He held a list, his eyes scanning the faces in the crowd before he began to read the names of those who would be moving on.

One by one, my friends' names were called. Relief washed over me as their places were secured, but my thoughts remained with Emia, wondering what would become of her now. Would she be okay? Would she find another way back to Azmeer? The uncertainty gnawed at me, even as my own name was called, ensuring my place in the next round.

I went through the motions for the rest of the day, smiling and nodding when appropriate, but my mind was far from the laughter and chatter around me.

When I returned to my room, the weight of the day settled heavily on my shoulders. I'd done what I could. A step closer to helping Dad, to earning my spot. Closing the door behind me, I leaned against it, my hand reaching into my pocket for Emia's note.

The paper was crumpled from being carried all day, but I unfolded it carefully, my heart pounding as I read the single word written in Emia's neat handwriting:

Dawn.

CHAPTER SEVENTEEN

Hey Dad,

Wanted to let you know that I made it through the last round! Much to my dismay, and everyone here, I think, I managed to secure the fastest time in a height challenge of all things. I only came out of it with a few cuts and bruises.

We still haven't been informed what the next trial will be, I am hoping it will be something less physical!

I've been able to spend a bit of time with Addie. It has been so nice to see her again; she looks the same as the last time we saw her but more formal, if you can believe it.

I'm growing used to the weather here, even though the heat was initially stifling. It shocks me each morning that there is a part of the world that becomes this warm. I wish you were here to see it, to feel it. I think you would love it here.

I can't wait to show Azmeer to you.

I've attached some herbs and flowers in this letter; please be sure to give them to Flora to make you some teas.

I'll write as soon as I know more.

Love you, Dad,

Bri

☽✳☾

The following days felt like a blur. I found myself missing Em's quiet presence. With her, it felt like I was okay to blend into the shadows more, we were a united front. I still didn't understand her message and had thought about it endlessly over the past few days.

"Have you written to her?" Kadian whispered to me as the others found themselves embroiled in a conversation about the courts.

"Now that you have withstood the first two trials," Magister Illerium said, "it is time we begin our studying of the Primals." He led us into the library towards a lecture hall, "If you've been paying attention, you'll be aware that the festival for Giaxia is approaching next week."

The smell of old books, leather covers, and worn pages warmed my heart. I took deep breaths every time we entered the library, unable to get enough of it.

We met in the same hall every afternoon. However, today, Illerium opted for something much grander. I stepped into an ancient and beautiful past. Its towering stone columns and intricately carved wooden benches, weathered by time, were enough to give anyone pause. Dust danced in the faint shafts of light filtering through stained glass windows, casting a muted glow over the ancient tapestries adorning the walls. In the center of the room stood a podium. Illerium made his way towards it, beckoning us all to sit.

"Giaxia, thought by some to be the first Primal, was responsible for the foundation of the Eternal Court," he grumbled, taking his final step before letting out a sigh of relief.

"That man is falling apart," Lil whispered.

"Indeed, theories persist regarding the identity of the first Primal," he continued, adopting a more formal tone. "Unfortunately, without their presence, verifying such claims becomes challenging." He continued, "Our understanding of our world's origin remains limited. Speculation suggests that a war erupted among the Primals, though the exact cause remains uncertain. However, given Giaxia's deep connection to the Earth, she bore the weight of every battle, every war that scarred her soil."

I knew bits and pieces about each of the Primals and their festivals; everyone did. However, this was the most information I'd ever received. "Giaxia is believed to have ventured into the depths of Hadash, to the very core where life originated, the Pool of Vitality. Throughout our recorded history, countless have sought its blessings, yet the pool demands a sacrifice in return for its gifts. The nature of Giaxia's offering has long been debated, but with her petition, the Eternal Court and the courts themselves came into existence."

Looking around the room, I knew I wasn't the only one captivated by his tale.

"There must always be balance in the world. Giaxia understood that to establish the courts, she must sacrifice a part of herself. It's speculated that she offered her consciousness, which led her to descend into a profound slumber. Yet, the truth remains shrouded in mystery, leaving us to ponder her fate. With the establishment of the Eternal Court, Giaxia beckoned the other Primals to Hadash." He cleared his throat, "Ollo, Vasenia, and Hild made their way to the Pool of Vitality, each offering a part of themselves. The establishment of the courts marked a significant shift towards stability, offering people clear guidelines and territories to call their own. Each court was governed by its unique regulations and magical practices, ending the era of territorial strife and fostering an era of peace. However, as history shows, peace is often fleeting. But that remains a lesson for another time." He looked to his left, "Marsh, if you would," he gestured him over.

"I wish we knew more about the Primals," I whispered to Lil, who nodded in agreement.

Marsh stood at the podium now; a smile broached his lips when he saw me. "Each year in Azmeer, during Giaxia's festival, it's customary of those living here, regardless of their court to make an offering. A symbolic gesture in recognition of the Eternal Court's creation. Your task is to find something that Giaxia and the Eternal Court deem worthy of offering and for your gift to be accepted. Magister Illerium and I would advise you to do research into what may be a suitable tithe." He looked to Illerium, who nodded in confirmation. "Your gift is expected by the day of the festival, just before the evening feast."

"One more thing," Illerium spoke up, "this shall be your third test in Azmeer. If your gift is not accepted, you will be asked to leave." His eyes grazed the crowd as a murmur rumbled through it. "You're dismissed," Illerium said in his customary goodbye.

"I'll no doubt be fine. It's the Eternal Court." Oz grinned as we exited the lecture hall.

"Didn't you say your mother ended up in a different court from her family?" Lil asked as she arched an eyebrow at him.

"Well..."

"This is not a good look for you, Brother." Tamra added as she walked off.

"It would seem that you may not be as guaranteed of a spot as you might hope," Lil laughed.

Lil and Kadian continued to tease Oz as we wove our way through groups of people towards the dining hall. I didn't partake; I was too wrapped up in my thoughts.

Marsh mentioned research, there must be records.

"Any idea what you're going to offer?" Lil asked as she elbowed my side. I shook my head, but I knew where I would start looking.

The inductees began to fracture and splinter into their groups, my friends insisting it was time to eat.

All of us could be asked to leave. There is no set number for this test that get to move on.

"You okay?" Oz placed a hand on my shoulder. I hadn't realized it, but I'd stopped to admire the setting sun.

In the distance, the sun dipped towards the horizon; its golden rays shone through the ancient stained glass, casting vibrant hues of red, orange, and purple onto the floor and walls. The intricate patterns of the window glass danced with the shifting light, painting the corridor with a kaleidoscope of colors while shadows played across the floor, adding depth to its majesty.

"I don't think I'll ever grow accustomed to the beauty here," I said.

"Me either. I don't want to be forced to leave. Seems like we'll have to find some decent offerings." Oz sighed. We stood next to each other and gazed out towards the fading sun. A silence fell between us as our smiling eyes met. A quiet understanding between friends. Oz wrapped his arm around me, pulling me close. I rested my head on his shoulder as we watched the last vestige of day transform into dusk.

CHAPTER EIGHTEEN

A wave of relief washed over me as I stepped into the library. The familiar scent of parchment and old leather wrapped around me like a comforting embrace. It was a place that always felt like home, a sanctuary where the world outside could melt away, leaving only the quiet hum of knowledge waiting to be discovered. But today, the comfort was tinged with an undercurrent of anxiety.

I was lucky to find Addie behind the desk, engrossed in another list. Seeing her there warmed my heart. She looked up, and her face lit up with a smile that felt like the sun breaking through clouds.

"Hey, kiddo," she greeted, abandoning her papers as she opened her arms to pull me into a hug.

Her hugs were the kind that made you feel safe, loved. As if you were the most important person in the world. I melted into her embrace, wishing I could stay there forever, forgetting about the weight of the task at hand.

"If you keep calling me kiddo and hugging me like this, you're going to stop giving the impression that you're a very serious scriba," I teased, though I leaned into her touch, craving the comfort it brought.

"I can continue to scare others while giving you some needed attention." She released me and moved back behind the desk, her eyes twinkling with affection. "What can I help you with tonight? Or are you just here to see your favorite aunt?"

"You're my only aunt, Addie," I laughed, but it was a weak attempt to hide the knot of worry tightening in my chest.

"Ah, victorious once again," she declared with a triumphant grin.

"I wish this were just a catch-up," I admitted, my voice growing quieter. "But I need your help."

"Tell me what's on your mind," she said, leaning forward.

I took a deep breath, letting the words spill out—Magister Illerium's lesson, the history of the Primals, the significance of Giaxia, and most importantly, the task we'd been given. As I spoke, the anxiety that had been gnawing at me all day surfaced again, more potent than ever.

"I need to know what offerings have been favored in the past," I finished, my voice barely above a whisper. "I need to find the right gift. If I don't, I'm afraid..."

"That you'll be cast out?" she asked.

I nodded, biting my lip to keep the fear at bay. "I need to be here, Addie. The thought of being asked to leave... I don't know what I'd do." I'd informed Addie of how Dad was doing, but had yet to tell her how I'd truly come to Azmeer.

"You know, Kadian's mother, Elana—her great-grandfather was a member of the Eternal Court," Addie said, her tone thoughtful.

I nodded again. "Elana always told Kadian that's where the gold in his eyes came from," I said with a small smile. "These days, though, I think Kad hopes he ends up in the Court of Reflection." I laughed. "But that's a story for another time."

She gave me a curious look but let it go. "I'll fetch those records for you. It might take a few minutes. Feel free to look around while you wait. It's quiet right now, one of the best times to experience it."

I gave her a grateful smile as she disappeared into the back, leaving me alone with my thoughts. The library was a labyrinth of knowledge, each shelf a doorway to another world. The stained glass windows were now dark, the only light coming from the flickering lanterns. Shadows danced on the walls, but instead of feeling eerie, it felt peaceful, like the books themselves were whispering their secrets to me.

I wandered through the stacks, my fingers brushing the spines of the books as I passed. The weight of the task ahead pressed down on me, but beneath it all, there was a flicker of excitement. I loved research, the thrill of diving into the unknown, uncovering truths hidden in the pages of ancient texts. It was a solace I'd found in the darkest time of my life after my mother died.

The memory of her hit me like a tidal wave, overwhelming in its intensity. She had been a beacon of light, of hope, guiding us through life with an unshakeable strength. When she died, it felt like the sun had gone out, leaving us in a world of shadows. My father and I were nearly consumed by despair, drowning in grief. But then I found books—her books. They became my lifeline, a way to stay connected to her, to keep her light alive. They saved me.

As I wandered, I picked up a book without thinking. The cover read *The Seventeen-Year Drought: Surviving in the Alkadian Hills.*

A faint sound pulled me from my thoughts. Whispering, soft and distant but growing louder as I moved through the stacks. Curiosity got the better of me, and I peered around a corner. Two figures stood at the far end of the room, one seated, the other leaning close in conversation. I strained to see them in the dim light, but it was difficult. The lanterns seemed to be growing dimmer by the second, or maybe it was just my imagination.

Then I caught a glint of light reflecting off the hair of the seated figure. I squinted, and my breath caught in my throat. Dainan. And standing before him, her red hair almost glowing in the darkness, was Iona.

I should have looked away, but I couldn't. The way they stood, the way she leaned in—there was something intimate, something flirtatious about it. I felt a pang of something sharp and uncomfortable, but I pushed it aside. It wasn't my place to judge or care.

Just then, the library plunged into darkness. Every light extinguished at once, leaving me in a void. Panic flared in my chest. I threw my arms out, trying to find something to hold onto, but there was nothing but empty air. I was terrible at navigating on the best of days, and now, in the pitch-black, I felt lost.

A sensation brushed against the back of my neck, soft and cold, sending a slithering sensation down my back. I whirled around, but of course, I couldn't see anything. My heart pounded in my chest, and I took a cautious step forward, trying to stay calm.

Then, a smooth, almost silky touch grazed my wrist. A low hissing filled the air, and I felt a surge of fear. "Whatever or whoever is doing that," I said, my voice trembling, "I'd like you to stop. It's rude to touch someone without their consent."

For a moment, there was only silence. Then, a voice, smooth as velvet and laced with amusement, replied, "Has no one informed you that it's impolite to listen to conversations that don't concern you?"

My stomach dropped. Dainan. Of course, it was him.

"I don't know what you're talking about," I said, trying to sound nonchalant, but the tremor in my voice betrayed me. The darkness around me began to lift, dissipating like fog in the morning sun. And there he was, standing before me, arms crossed over his chest, his eyes glowing with something I couldn't quite decipher.

He looked...angry. And yet, there was something else in his gaze, something that made my heart race even faster.

"Nothing to say for yourself, Brida?" His voice was calm, but there was an edge to it, a challenge.

Don't back down. I took a deep breath, steadying myself. "It isn't my fault you two were being loud *in a library*." I retorted, my voice gaining strength. "Anyone would've been intrigued."

"Does Scriba Velin know you're here?" His eyes raked over me, and for a moment, I thought I saw something flicker in his expression—something almost like surprise. But it was gone before I could be sure.

"She's fetching something for me," I replied, trying to match his calm.

"How studious." His tone was light, but there was a tension in the air between us, something unspoken yet undeniable. His stillness, the way he seemed to control the very space around him—it was unnerving and yet...captivating.

Trying to break the tension, I blurted out the first thing that came to mind. "Were you reading?"

He raised an eyebrow, amused. "I was. Were you?" He gestured to the book still clutched in my hands. Before I could respond, he took it from me, his fingers brushing against mine. A spark of heat shot through me, and I pulled my hand back, hoping he didn't notice.

He glanced at the title, and a slow, wicked smile spread across his face. "I didn't think you'd be interested in irrigation, *Brida*."

He took a step toward me, his grin feral, "Are you experiencing a dry spell, *Brida*?" His voice lowered. Not realizing there was little space behind me, I'd backed myself into a shelf lined with ancient tomes. *Any of these would have been better than the one I'd chosen.*

"*Uhm*" was the only thing that came out. I had no idea why, but my brain and my mouth ceased connecting at this very moment.

He took another step and stood directly in front of me. He placed his right arm on the shelves behind me, supporting himself as he lowered his head close to my neck, "I could help you with that, should you need it."

The whisper of his words, his breath on my neck, shivers ricocheted down my spine. I could feel my heart beating, my blood thrumming. His eyes fixated on me, gleaming with a predatory intensity, ablaze with fire and shadow. They were alive with an unmistakable hunger.

"It's not something I've experienced before, no." I weaseled my way out from beneath him as his other hand was making its way towards my hip. "And I'm managing just fine. If you want to keep that," I gestured to the book as I pushed my hair behind my ear, "it would be useful information for a prince. You know how to help keep his kingdom prosperous and fertile."

He adjusted his stance, maintaining a pleased look on his face. *He knows he's making me uncomfortable. Gods, why's it so hot here?*

"You are just full of surprises."

My face heated. "Yes, well," I stammered, at a loss for words. *Gods, why did I pick this book?*

He took a step closer, his presence overwhelming, and leaned in, his voice dropping to a whisper. "I look forward to discovering more of them."

My breath hitched. "That's presumptuous of you," I managed to say, my voice wavering. The air between us crackled with tension, thick enough to choke on. I could feel the heat radiating off him, the subtle scent of smoke and citrus making my head spin.

"Oh?" he asked, his tone teasing, but his gaze was intense, piercing through the walls I had carefully constructed. "We'll see."

He stood up straight, eyes glinting with mischief. I was about to respond, to say something—anything—when Addie reappeared, her footsteps echoing through the library. Dainan stepped back, a playful smirk on his face as he noticed her.

"I should let you get back to your research," he said, his voice smooth as silk. He gave me a knowing look before turning on his heel and disappearing into the shadows.

"Brida?" Addie called out, concern in her voice as she approached. "Are you all right?"

I nodded, forcing a smile. "Yes, just...deep in thought."

She handed me the records, her eyes searching mine for any signs of distress. "Here they are. Be sure to bring them back in a few days."

"Of course," I said, taking the papers from her. "Thank you, Addie."

As I made my way out of the library, I couldn't stop my eyes from flicking back to where Dainan had stood. It felt like his presence still clung to the air, a dark, electric charge that buzzed beneath my skin.

My chest tightened just thinking about the way the world seemed to shrink in on itself when he was near, the way my pulse thundered whenever he looked at me.

I hated how I lost myself around him. How everything I thought I knew, everything I was here for, blurred the second he entered the room. I didn't understand why I reacted like that, why my body betrayed me with every glance, every breath. He unnerved me, intrigued me, made me feel exposed in a way I couldn't quite explain.

I clenched my fists, forcing myself to turn away. I was here for a purpose, and it wasn't him. It wasn't whatever this pull was or the strange heat that lingered between us. I was here for my father. For his life. I couldn't let myself forget that—not now, not ever.

But as I pushed through the doors, my heart still racing, I couldn't deny the truth—the part of me that wanted to know more, that wanted to feel that pull again was stronger than I wanted to admit. And I didn't know if I had the strength to resist it.

CHAPTER NINETEEN

"I'll see you at dinner," I said, turning towards my room, my voice lighter than I felt. Since the second trial, our days had morphed into a quick breakfast, a choice of exercise, and lectures. Illerium had granted us afternoons off, presumably for research. I had a date with the library. Kadian often teased me for my unyielding love for study, something he shared no affinity for. Despite that, he'd always accompanied me when I'd asked or had waited at the library when it was pitch black outside to walk me home. He was always there when I needed him, but this was something I would be doing on my own.

When I entered my room, I saw a sealed envelope lying on the floor. My heart sank a little as I picked it up, recognizing the handwriting. I broke the seal and unfolded the letter.

Brida,

I wanted to write to you to let you know that your father has been quite ill the past few days. I've been following the instructions you sent for the teas and will continue to administer them to him. Vager has come by, and we hope he'll be feeling better soon. It's possible he's just recovering from heat exhaustion.

I caught him gardening a few days ago. When I asked him why, he said,
'The flowers out back are Brida's favorite.'
Enclosed is a pressed flower he wanted you to have.
Tell my brother to write home too. Mom is wondering how he's doing.
I'll write if anything changes. Be safe.
Flora

I pressed the letter to my chest, trying to draw comfort from its words, wishing I could feel closer to home. I sank into the desk chair, placing the flower next to the portrait of my parents. It was my mother's favorite flower, and now, it seemed, my favorite too. I needed to focus.

"Dear Flora..." I began, my pen moving over the paper.

☽✻☾

After dropping the letter at the courier chamber, I made my way to the library, clutching the records from Addie. The quiet here was my refuge. I found a table at the back, bathed in a gentle green light from a stained glass window. It dawned on me that this was where Dainan had sat the night before. I shook my head, trying to banish the memory.

I laid out the records, simple but crucial: names, dates, and gifts. The list was a puzzle, and I was determined to find the pattern.

Jadia Kemer, 124 AC, Blood pearls, Denied
Alister Althorne, 323 AC, Geode, Accepted
Ithanny Traver, 444 AC, Information, Accepted
Donnal Ladier, 444 AC, Gold, Denied

Hours passed with no clear pattern emerging. Just as frustration began to settle in, a thud broke the silence. I looked up to see Marsh, clad in a deep purple suit. "I thought I might find you here," he said, leaning casually against the table.

"Someone dressed up," I said, trying to sound nonchalant. "What brings you here?" My smile was genuine despite my distraction.

"I'm sorry I missed you this morning," he said, setting a book down in front of me. "I wanted to make it up to you."

I had grown accustomed to Marsh's company on our morning runs. On the days he was absent, I found myself missing him more than I cared to admit. The book he'd placed on the table was exquisite: leather-bound with gold gilding.

"What's this?" I asked, picking it up and reading the cover: *The Trials of Thale*. My favorite. My cheeks flushed as I looked at him, realizing he had listened to my ramblings about it.

I brought the book to my nose, savoring its faint, sweet scent. "It's beautiful," I said. "But I can't accept this. It's too much."

"It's yours."

His hand brushed against my hair, tucking a stray strand behind my ear, and I felt a jolt of warmth. I leaned into his touch, the sweetness of his scent enveloping me.

"You're quite forward today, Mr. Reed Marsh," I teased, though my voice was softer than usual.

"I think," he said, his thumb tracing slow circles on my jaw, "if you were opposed, you'd have pulled away by now."

"Well," I leaned in a bit closer, my heart racing, "if you're sticking around..." I placed my hand on the table, creating a soft echo. "You could help me figure out what to give Giaxia so I don't end up blacklisted by the Eternal Court."

His grin widened as he pulled back. "I have no doubt you'll be chosen by the right court."

I rolled my eyes, trying to regain my composure. "Look at these names." I pointed to the records. "It's clear there's some connection to the court or maybe Hadash with the accepted gifts."

His smile turned wicked. "I'm sure you know all about that."

He raised his hands in mock innocence as he laughed. "Now that you've got this information, what's your plan?"

I knew he was teasing, but my thoughts were still tangled in the closeness we'd shared. I forced myself to focus. "Are we allowed to leave the premises?"

He looked at me, puzzled. "You know that's not allowed."

"Yes, but..." I hesitated, then pressed on, "If you accompanied me, would I be allowed to leave?"

His grin grew. "You're trying to charm your way out of here, aren't you?"

I gave him a mischievous smile, feeling a flutter of excitement at the thought of spending more time with him outside these walls.

☽✳☾

I braced myself for the journey ahead. "It won't be as bad as the first time, I promise," Marsh said as we prepared for our night out. We planned to meet at the fountain outside my room, and I had kept my secret from Kad and Lil, knowing their concerns and insistence on joining us would complicate things. I needed to face this on my own.

I selected my long-sleeved Eternal Court fighting leathers, a symbol of our destination. "It can fall below freezing in the evenings," Marsh had reminded me. I slipped an empty vial into my pocket—a small but essential item—and stepped out into the cool night.

Marsh was already at the fountain, his gaze lost in the rippling water. "Grow tired of waiting for me?" I teased.

"Grow tired of waiting for you?" His violet eyes, reminiscent of twilight skies, met mine. "I don't think I could tire of such a thing, Brida Larrow."

I couldn't suppress a smile.

"Are you sure about this?" Marsh asked, his voice low as I approached.

I had wrestled with this decision all week. *Fortune favors the daring,* my father's voice echoed in my mind. I hoped his wisdom would hold true.

"Don't try to talk me out of it now. You helped come up with this plan," I said, attempting to steady my nerves. Success would mean acceptance and standing with the Eternal Court. Failure would have to be dealt with later.

"I'm not," he said, offering his hand. "I just want to make sure this is your choice."

"It is."

"Remember how to do this?" He moved closer, his breath warm against my skin. "Wrap your arms around me, and I will you. If you want to close your eyes, go ahead. It will be a bit longer than last time since Hadash is farther than Escalia, but it shouldn't be as disorienting." I leaned into him, feeling the firm outline of his chest. His breath caught as I moved closer. The effect I had on him made me smile.

Tilting my head up, I murmured, "Ready."

His dimpled smile appeared as he grinned back at me. And then, we were gone.

The sensation of wind-walking was still unnerving, but less so than before. The feeling of being pulled apart by the wind was something I doubted I'd ever get used to. I kept my eyes shut, the low rumble of Marsh's laughter vibrating through me. "Don't you dare laugh at me," I shouted over the wind, to which his laughter only grew. Moments later, I opened my eyes.

"I didn't want to take us directly into the crater in case someone was down there. It'll be a short hike," Marsh said as he released me, his voice quiet in the stillness. The sunlight filtered through the jagged peaks of the distant mountains, casting long, golden rays across the barren landscape. The ground beneath us was cracked and dry, jagged rocks jutting up from the earth like the bones of some long-dead creature. Dust stirred in the faint breeze, swirling lazily around our feet, the only movement in an otherwise silent, lifeless world.

I stood there, captivated by the emptiness. The air was thin, sharp in my lungs, carrying no scent of life—only the dry, metallic tang of stone. There were no animals, no signs of movement at all. Just the stark contrast between the light spilling over the mountains and the cold, unforgiving ground that stretched endlessly before us.

"It's...breathtaking," I whispered, my voice swallowed by the vast, quiet space around us. Despite the desolation, there was a strange beauty to it—the way the landscape stretched out in every direction, untouched and wild. The jagged cliffs on the horizon were bathed in a golden glow as if the sun itself was trying to soften the harsh edges of the world.

Marsh leaned in closer, his warmth grounding me in the middle of the emptiness. For a moment, it felt like we were the only two people left in existence, standing on the edge of something ancient and forgotten.

Marsh's amethyst eyes sparkled with a tender glimmer. "We need to get moving before the light fades." He offered me his hand. "The crater and entrance to the caves are down this path." He gestured ahead. "Don't wander off. I've seen how you are with directions."

"I knew I brought you for a reason. You're not just an easy ride," I teased, patting his shoulder as I walked past.

"Oh, I see," he laughed, matching my pace with a grin.

Descending the mountain was starkly different from my usual hikes with Kad. The vast landscape stretched before us, painted in shades of tan and terracotta, stark and desolate. Only the rocks, dirt, and the tall, handsome figure beside me broke the monotony.

"Have you traveled this far west before?" Marsh asked, guiding me around a steep corner.

"I've done a few shorter trips," I said. "Dad and I used to camp in the Eridian district every summer, and Kadian and I explored nearby towns and villages, but nothing more than a few days away."

"The first time I visited Hadash," Marsh said, guiding me over a boulder, "was for a trial. The Eternal Court resolves disputes at the very heart of where they believe life began."

“Why were you here for that?” I asked.

“Well,” he said, “a member of the Court of Whispers was on trial for espionage. My father wanted me to witness how other courts administer justice. Anyone connected to those Courts may attend.”

“What happened to him?” I asked, trying to maintain my balance.

“He was found guilty. They strung him up in the cave entryway and left him to die. It was horrifying.” We walked in silence until we reached the crater’s base. It stretched wide and deep, the entrance to the cave a simple cutout in the rock face.

“They store lanterns and flint here for the festival. We’ll grab one inside.” Marsh said.

As I made my way to enter, he placed his hand on my arm, stopping me.

“Brida, before we do this, I need to tell you something.” He said, removing his arm from me. His hands began to fidget with each other.

“Marsh, you’re making me nervous.”

He pulled away from me before clapping his hands together, “I know you lied about your invitation.”

My pulse began to quicken. *Gods, did he bring me here to accuse me, like the man from the story?* I started to back up, staring around me to see if anyone or anything was close by. *How am I going to get out of here?*

“Gods, Brida, I’m sorry, I worded this wrong. It’s okay; I know what you did, and it’s okay. It’s more than okay.”

My brow began to furrow as I continued to put some distance between the two of us.

“Brida, please. Shit, I’ve really gone about this the wrong way.” He ran a hand through his violet-streaked hair. “I know you lied, and it’s okay because I lied too.”

I stopped moving. “What do you mean you lied too?”

“The story about the man, he was strung up, right here.” He

pointed to the entryway of the cave. “It left an impression on me. I thought this could not possibly be justice. The man was convicted. It was unjust, we all knew it, and yet nothing was done. No one in a position of power chose to step in and do anything. At that moment, I decided I would never let anything like that happen again, at least, I would do my best to prevent it.”

I folded my arms as I made my way to a rock and sat down, encouraging him to continue his story.

“Year after year, I waited for my invitation. Each passing Courting without being given the opportunity, the chance to prove my worth, until I took matters into my own hands.” He sighed as he made his way over and sat down in front of me.

“My father is a court member, and I asked to accompany him on a trip to Azmeer. I snuck off and made my way into the scribes’quarters. I managed to steal an invitation.”

The pained expression that befell Marsh’s face told me he understood my struggle.

“I waited until the invitations were sent out and revealed mine to my father. He’d never been more proud of me. Well, other than the day I was granted entry to the Court of Whispers.” Marsh looked at me as if yearning for something to hold onto.

“I knew your invitation was a fake, but when I saw you, I thought that maybe you too were doing it for a reason, and I wanted to give you the same chance, the same opportunity, no matter what it was you were fighting for.”

After I reflected on his words, I rose and extended my hand to him. Moments later, he grabbed it, and we found ourselves pressed together.

“Thank you,” I whispered as I pressed a kiss to his cheek. It was cool, like the breeze on a crisp morning.

“I’ll ask you once more, are you sure you want to do this?” Marsh said as his hands began to graze my arms.

“You were right,” I said as I moved in closer to him. “I am here for a reason. For my father." And as I told him everything, a weight that had been suffocating me was lifted. "So yes, I'm sure."

Marsh nodded and I hoped I wasn't making a grave mistake.

At the cave entrance, lanterns of various sizes were scattered around. "You grab a lantern," Marsh said, lighting the flint to start a flame. "Are you okay if I lead?"

"Oh, are you sure?" I teased. "I'm a natural compass."

"If that's what you wish," he said, handing me the lantern. "But I'm happy to lead us."

I smiled and followed him into the cave.

The instant we crossed the cave's threshold, I sensed the unmistakable presence of magic. A soft, humming energy filled the air, surging through my veins with a vitality and potency I hadn't imagined possible, igniting a newfound sense of life and power within me. It was a challenge not to be overwhelmed and swept away by its currents. It felt as though I was being pulled in every direction at once, but Marsh kept us on course.

As all light from the outside faded away, save for the dim glow of our lantern, we found ourselves enveloped in darkness. "Don't worry," Marsh said, "we'll have more light soon." Marsh guided us around several twists and turns before I saw a faint shimmer in the distance.

Rounding the corner, stalagmites rose from the cavern floor like ancient sentinels, their surfaces adorned with crystals that cast a soft, ethereal light. Unlike the barren exterior, the cave was teeming with life. Each step we took was cushioned by lush moss, and the air was filled with the delicate crunch of fungi beneath our feet.

I couldn't help but feel a sense of wonder. In the span of a few months, I'd gone from living a sheltered life to walking in the place where the world was said to be born. My reverence and awe only continued to grow with each tunnel of the cave.

The humming had turned into a soothing melody luring me deeper into the cavern. Percussion and strings echoed in my mind. *What's that song? It's beautiful.*

"Do you hear that?" I asked Marsh.

"Hear what?" He looked back at me.

"It...It sounds like singing," I said. A steady rhythm of melodies began to envelop my senses, and it felt like it was guiding me to the very heart of the cave.

"Sorry, what did you say?" He stopped for a moment and raised his hand to my face. "Be sure to look where you're stepping. It's easy to get distracted while here."

I nodded as he led us down a path lined with purple and green fungi that had the slightest luminescent sheen. "This way," Marsh told me as he continued to hold my hand. I'd never noticed how much larger his hand was than mine. His fingers and hands were soft, not calloused. Something that would have differentiated him from those of the Eternal Court. I hadn't witnessed Marsh fight yet, and while I'd heard he was skilled, it didn't quite match his demeanor. Dainan and his brothers seemed the type to seek physical confrontation, whereas Marsh struck me as more contemplative.

"Not much longer," Marsh said, glancing back at me. Just as he spoke, he missed a root growing out of the moss and tripped, releasing my hand to catch himself. As his grip loosened, I lost my balance and tumbled backward. It hadn't dawned on me that we were standing on a ledge until I was already plummeting. When I hit the ground, my hand bore the brunt of the fall, pain slicing through. *The stalagmites,* I thought. With so little light down here, it was hard to make out anything.

"Shit," Marsh yelled, "shit, are you okay Brida? Please tell me you're okay."

I hadn't hit my head, and no bones felt broken. Other than my hand, somehow, I seemed okay. "I'm fine," I croaked. *Maybe not that fine*.

Groaning, I forced myself to stand, brushing myself off. As I took a step forward, a strange sensation washed over me. My whole body started vibrating. A pulsing shockwave ran through me, starting at my feet, traveling up my spine. It took all my strength to remain standing.

With a sinking feeling, I realized my feet were wet.

It can't be. This can't be it. That would be too easy.

I lowered my hand to the water and halted when I swore I heard it hiss. It took my eyes a minute to readjust without the flame from the lantern, but what I saw was beautiful.

I looked upon a pool of starlight that shimmered with each ripple. An ethereal glow that carried with it whispers of mystery that hinted at the depths of the void from where all life sprang. It was a place of profound tranquility and cosmic resonance, where the boundaries between worlds blurred, and time itself seemed to stand still. My heart stuttered in my chest, and I pulled back. But as I listened closer, I realized it wasn't a hiss at all—more like a soft exhale, like the pool itself was alive, breathing under my touch.

And then I heard it again—music, faint at first but growing in intensity, like the pool itself was humming. The sound wasn't like anything I'd heard before. It was delicate, like the distant chime of crystal bells, but underneath was a steady, deep pulse—almost like a heartbeat, vibrating through my chest. It felt ancient, a sound that had been playing since before the world began. Each note echoed in my bones, making the air around me feel thicker, charged with something I couldn't name.

The longer I listened, the more the melody filled the space around me, weaving into my mind until it was the only thing I could focus on. It wasn't just music anymore—it was emotion, raw and untamed, flowing through the air and into me. Awe. Wonder. Fear. It felt like standing at the edge of the universe and gazing into eternity, knowing I was only a fragment in the grand design but somehow connected to it all.

The pool seemed to call to me, the music swelling as if it were pleading for me to touch it, to dive deeper into its mystery.

I hesitated for only a second before giving in. My fingertips grazed the surface, and the moment they did, the symphony exploded.

A surge of sound and light rushed through me, so powerful it almost knocked me backward. The water hummed beneath my touch, warm and welcoming, but with a pulse that felt alive, like I was touching something sacred. The music swirled around me, no longer distant but inside me, in my veins, pulsing with the rhythm of my heartbeat. Each note was a burst of color in my mind's eye, vibrant and glowing. I felt connected to the very essence of creation, as if time had unraveled, leaving only this moment, this melody, and the weight of the universe pressing into me.

I wasn't just listening anymore—I was a part of it.

"*Your music is beautiful,*" I whispered.

"Holy shit, Bri," Marsh came running around the corner moments later. He froze when he saw me, a look of complete shock upon his face. He came closer, bringing the light with him. As he approached, the pool went dark. "You're bleeding," Marsh reached out to look at my hand. "We need to get this cleaned and wrapped up."

"Not before I get what I came for," I declared, retrieving the vial I'd stowed in my pocket. It remained intact despite my fall. I opened the lid and carefully filled the glass with the water from the pool. After sealing it shut, I turned to Marsh, "Can you get us out of here?"

Rather than answer me, he pulled a cloth from his pocket, wrapping it around my wound. "Better?"

I nodded. Lowering his face to mine, his breath grazed my lips, "Are you ready?"

I held my breath as the gusts of wind enveloped us.

☽✳☾

"Thank you for helping me with my plan," I smiled at Marsh as he walked me back to my room, "I couldn't have done it without you." He'd been quiet since the cave. It was mirrored by the silence of the palace.

We'd been gone several hours and the majority of Azmeer lay sound asleep. "What's wrong?" I asked as we arrived in front of my door. He said nothing until I laid my hand on his arm, "Please tell me."

"For a moment tonight," his voice just above a whisper, "I feared something terrible had happened to you. Parts of that cave system are hundreds of feet deep, and I had no idea because of the lack of light. I should've had a firmer grip on you the entire time." He glanced at my wrapped hand. "I'm sorry."

"It's not your fault that I have poor balance," I smiled at him, "besides, everything turned out okay, and if I have a scar, well," I paused, "it'll serve as a reminder of a great evening."

Marsh's gaze softened, his eyes searching mine as if trying to understand the depths of what I had just shared. He reached out slowly, his cool hand trembling as he cupped my face. "Thank you for sharing that with me, about your father," he murmured, his voice filled with a tenderness that made my heart ache.

For a moment, time seemed to pause. Cool air brushed against my skin, but all I could focus on was Marsh, standing so close that I could feel the heat radiating from his body. His thumb gently stroked my cheek, and I closed my eyes, leaning into his palm.

Before I could find the words to respond, he leaned in, closing the distance between us. His lips met mine in a kiss that was soft and delicate yet brimming with unspoken emotion. It was as though he was pouring all the understanding, the compassion, and the unspoken feelings between us into that single, tender moment. My heart fluttered, and I found myself returning the kiss, a spark of something profound igniting within me, something deep and meaningful that I hadn't expected.

When he pulled back, his forehead rested gently against mine, his breath mingling with my own. "I should go," he whispered, his voice laced with hesitation, as if he, too, was reluctant to break the connection.

I nodded, unable to speak, my heart racing in the quiet aftermath of our kiss. Even as he stepped away, I could still feel the cool touch of his lips on mine, a lingering reminder of the brief but intense moment we had shared.

As I entered my room, I undressed and unwrapped my hand. The cut was clean and not as deep as I'd thought. It would need to be monitored the next few days. After washing and wrapping it once more, I curled up in bed and pulled my covers around me. That night, I dreamt of diamond speckled water and the world's first lullaby.

CHAPTER TWENTY

My hand throbbed when I awoke, a lingering sting from yesterday's adventure. The morning light filtered through the curtains, casting a soft glow on the vial of water from the Pool of Vitality, which sat beside the painting of my parents on the desk. My gaze lingered on the portrait, and I wondered what Dad would think of last night. He'd be a mix of appalled and impressed—his little girl putting herself out there. I owed him a letter, but I decided this latest escapade would remain my secret.

Dressed in shades of brown and tan to honor the Eternal Court, I picked up the vial without a second thought and slipped it into my pocket. Opening the door, Marsh greeted me, his fist poised to knock.

"Marsh," I said, my voice filled with surprise.

"Uh," he mumbled, caught off guard.

"Good morning to you, too," I smiled, stepping out and closing the door behind me. "What brings you here?"

His eyes dropped to my hand, concern etched into his features. "I wanted to see how you were doing."

I laughed, trying to brush off his worry. "It's just a cut, Marsh. I'm fine. Really."

He hesitated before finally returning my smile. "Shall we get some breakfast?"

"Lead the way," I replied, falling into step beside him.

The morning buzzed with unusual energy. Magisters scurried around, more numerous than usual, and the air hummed with whispers of the king's rumored attendance at the feast for Giaxia. As we walked past a group of organizers heading toward the kitchens, Marsh leaned in closer, his breath warm against my skin.

"You know," he began, "there's a story about what Giaxia sacrificed to make her pact with the Pool of Vitality."

I glanced at him curiously. "There are always stories."

He smirked, a playful glint in his eye. "Yes, but this one is still widely believed by most members of the Eternal Court."

I raised an eyebrow, teasing. "Are you going to get in trouble for sharing another court's secrets with me? You've warned me how the Eternal Court deals with those who've wronged them."

His chuckle was low and warm. "I think, with this one," he leaned in even closer, his breath tickling my neck, "I'm willing to take the risk." A shiver ran down my spine, my heart pounding in response. The urge to close the distance between us, to kiss him, surged within me, but I was painfully aware of the people bustling around us.

"They believe," he continued, "that Giaxia gave up her mating bond."

I'd only ever read of the mating bond in *The Trials of Thale*. It wasn't something openly taught or even casually mentioned. If anything, it seemed more like a whispered myth—highly speculative, nothing concrete. Not the kind of thing you'd learn in school or from any of the scholars I'd met. People didn't discuss it, not seriously, anyway. "The mating bond is a highly speculative myth," I countered, trying to refocus on his words. "It's never been confirmed."

"Ah, but Giaxia, according to the Eternal Court," he said with a slight eye roll, "was the first Primal. The second was Ollo, the Primal of the Court of Whispers."

I nodded, my fingers absentmindedly playing with the vial in my pocket. "Rumor has it they hated each other at first, but one day, everything clicked, and they just knew. They were two halves of the same whole."

Marsh's gaze intensified as he spoke. "By that time, other Primals had come into existence."

"Hild and Vasenia, you mean?"

"Among others," he replied. "But they believe there were more than four Primals and that one named Aldur attempted to take Giaxia from Ollo while he was away. When Ollo heard, he hunted Aldur down and killed him."

Marsh's voice wove through the air; his words painted vivid images in my mind—the cold steel of battle, the roar of primal forces clashing, the world teetering on the brink of chaos.

"Aldur's death enraged the other Primals, sparking a war," he continued, his voice low but steady. "The Fae, humans, nymphs—everyone was called upon by their regional Primal to fight. The battles were bloody, ruthless, spanning millennia."

I could see it: armies stretching across blood-soaked fields, primal magic crackling in the air, the land scorched and barren beneath their feet. It wasn't hard to imagine the devastation, the hopelessness that must have filled the hearts of those who fought, knowing the price of their loyalty was often death.

"The final confrontation came down to five Primals: Giaxia, Ollo, Vasenia, Hild, and Andaras—Aldur's brother." His words carried us further down the path as we approached the dining hall. "Ollo and Andaras had their last stand at the base of the Tactras Mountains, where the Court of Whispers now resides."

I could feel the weight of history in those names, the resonance of ancient battles etched into the earth. The thought of standing where gods once bled was unsettling. And yet, his next words shifted something deeper within me.

"Andaras had the larger, better-prepared army. Giaxia knew Ollo was likely to die. So, on the eve of battle, she went to the Pool of Vitality and begged for the fighting to end." He paused, pushing open the door to the dining hall and holding it for me as I stepped through, my mind still caught in the swirl of his story. "But the pool demanded a great sacrifice in return."

I could almost feel the icy, unnatural stillness of that ancient pool, its waters glimmering with silver specks. My breath caught as I braced myself for what came next.

"She offered the only thing she had—her love for Ollo. Not as a physical sacrifice, but she gave up her bond with him. The pool accepted and created the courts in return, each Primal being given their own territory to reign, believing this would satisfy the lust and true motivations behind the fighting."

I stopped in my tracks, the weight of his words hitting me like a blow to the chest. I turned to face him, trying to grasp what that could even mean. "What happened to Andaras?"

"He refused to offer anything of himself to the pool and met his end soon after. No one knows exactly how."

The dining hall loomed behind us, forgotten. Marsh's eyes met mine, shadows flickering in his gaze as the sadness of the tale seeped into the air between us.

"What happened to Giaxia and Ollo?"

"The Eternal Court believes the Pool of Vitality severed their bond. Giaxia recovered because she made the offering. But Ollo...he was never the same. The remnants of the bond drove him to madness. Some say he killed himself, but no one really knows."

The image of a broken Ollo left adrift in a world where his connection to Giaxia no longer existed filled me with an aching sadness I couldn't shake.

"This is one of the saddest stories I've ever heard," I said, my voice thick with the sorrow that laced the tale.

Marsh's gaze softened, the intensity of the myth fading into the present moment. "You don't believe in any of this, though, right?" he asked, his tone teasing, reminding me of our earlier skepticism about such stories.

I hesitated, my thoughts swirling in the depth of Giaxia's sacrifice. "Even if it were true, it would be a terrible fate," I murmured. "Giaxia did nothing wrong, yet she had to sacrifice the thing she loved most."

The quiet between us grew heavy with the weight of her choice. *Her love was not a flaw, and yet she paid the price.*

Marsh's voice broke through my reverie, gentle but firm. "The mating bond is supposed to be unbreakable. If it even exists."

I stared at him, a knot tightening in my chest. The words echoed in my mind. *To break something so deeply tied to the soul...how much power would that take? And how much would it destroy?*

"Do you believe in the mating bond?" I asked, our steps slowing as we neared the food.

"I didn't always, but I might be starting to."

We paused, eyes locking for a moment. I wanted to lean in, to close the space between us, but the bustling hall reminded me of our audience. Marsh's eyes flicked to the side, and I followed his gaze to see Oz, Kadian, and Lil gesturing wildly in conversation.

"I'll see you later," he said, giving me a quick wink before heading toward the group.

"That isn't what I meant, Kad, and you know it!" Lil's voice rang out as I approached the table.

"I see you all are in fighting form this morning," I laughed, sliding into a seat where a plate of food with toast with wolfberry jam awaited me.

"Did you hear what happened last night?" Kadian's face was serious, his tone urgent.

"Good morning to you too, Kadian," I replied, taking a bite of my food. His grave expression didn't waver.

"What do you mean?" I asked, my heart starting to race.

Oz's face was grim. "There was an earthquake in Hadash."

CHAPTER TWENTY-ONE

"An earthquake?" The words felt strange on my tongue as if saying them would make the truth more real. "What happened?"

Oz sighed, rubbing a hand over his face. "It's bad. Magister Kerai was the first to hear this morning. His family lives in Hadash. He said the damage is extensive. Most of the Eternal Court was there, preparing for the festival."

The realization slammed into me. We had been there last night, walking those very paths touching the ancient stones. "How many people...?" My voice cracked, and I quickly swallowed, trying to push down the panic rising in my chest.

"Fifty or so confirmed dead, but they're still searching through the rubble," Oz said quietly. "They think it could be more."

"Fifty?" The word seemed too small to carry the weight of so much loss. My stomach churned, nausea creeping up. "Gods..."

Lil's voice was unusually soft. "Do you think they'll still hold the festival today?"

"It depends. We'll probably know soon. If they cancel, word will spread fast. Otherwise, people will be preparing their offerings," Kadian said.

The table fell silent again, each of us retreating into our thoughts. I barely noticed the food in front of me, my appetite gone.

We finished breakfast in an uneasy quiet, the clatter of dishes and murmurs of other inductees the only sounds around us. Lil and Oz exchanged a glance before rising, Lil offering me a small, reassuring smile that didn't quite reach her eyes. "We should get ready," she said. "They'll expect us to be at our best, no matter what."

As they left, Kadian lingered, his gaze heavy on me. "Where were you last night?"

The question made my heart spike. I had expected it, but not so soon, not with the news of Hadash weighing on us like this. I forced a calm expression though my mind was racing. "Here. You saw me at dinner, remember?" I tucked my hand under the table, hiding the bandage from his view. This wasn't the time to let suspicion grow.

Kadian didn't look convinced. His eyes dropped to my hand, now hidden in my lap. "You didn't have that bandage last night. What happened?"

I bit back a sigh. "I slipped, cut my hand. Nothing major." *Not too big of a lie.*

"Hmm." He didn't look convinced but let it go, nodding. "Just be careful."

"Always," I replied, trying to sound nonchalant.

Kadian excused himself, muttering something about changing into more appropriate attire for the day's events. I knew it was an excuse. His eagerness to impress Lil was obvious to anyone paying attention.

But I had bigger concerns. The news about Hadash had rattled me. It was like a stone lodged in my chest, heavy and cold. And then there was Marsh...I needed to find him. He'd been there with me last night, right by my side, when the ground trembled. Had he noticed it, too? Or was I the only one who felt the earth's warning? *Should I have said something? Could I have stopped this?*

I needed to speak with Marsh. Maybe he had more information as to what was happening and would be able to fill me in.

I saw Magister Illerium walking towards his office, "Magister,"' I said.

He looked towards me, "Yes, Brida. How may I help?" He was looking even worse than usual. He'd always appeared sickly, never having much color in his face, his hair looking like it had been leached of all color.

"I was wondering if you could tell me where I might be able to find Marsh?"

He smiled. "Ah yes, the two of you have been becoming quite close."

Gods. I sighed.

"He's been a great friend to me since arriving. It's been nice to have a companion on my morning run." I replied as curtly and politely as possible.

"Yes," he looked me up and down, his eyes lingering in a way that told me he didn't believe a word I'd uttered.

"Indeed. Unfortunately, Marsh will be preoccupied for the majority of the day. He'll be transporting members of the Eternal Court back and forth from Hadash to assess the level of damage. He should be back for the feast this evening."

So, things are to continue as planned.

"Do..." I began to ask.

"Go on," he prompted me.

"Do you know how bad it is? In Hadash, I mean?"

"The death toll is two hundred and rising. We've never seen anything quite like it. No one is sure what caused it. No warnings were felt in the hours leading up to the event."

"When did it occur, Magister?"

"Around eleven-thirty last night."

An hour after we returned.

"Thank you, Magister," I paused, "I'm sorry if you know anyone in Hadash who has been injured." I meant it. The loss of life was tragic. I knew what it was like to be without a mother. How many children lost a parent last night? How many would lose them in the aftershocks?

"Brida," he paused, "you have a few hours before your offering needs to have been made. If you wish to do so at a time when few others may be there. I would advise you go now."

I nodded as he entered his office.

My offering is from Hadash. Should I still go forward with it? If I didn't, what would I offer? I pulled the vial from my pocket, red swirled in the water. Not quite realizing in the darkness and haze of last night, blood from my wound found its way into the vial. Staring at it, I had an idea.

The halls overflowed with people. I passed groups of inductees who were crying, people vanishing in and out of sight with Walkers attached to them, and sheer panic on the faces of those preparing everything for the evening. The corridor leading to the Eternal House, however, was empty and mostly dark. Candles had been lit and placed in candelabras outside of the entryway.

They came in assorted sizes and shapes, yet all bore the hallmark of longevity, evident in the thick coating of wax firmly attached to each one. In the midst of the candles, an altar made from stone sat there.

The altar loomed before me, ancient stone veined with cracks that seemed to pulse with a life of their own. I hesitated, the vial in my pocket feeling like a lead weight. My offering, my blood, still fresh and mixed with the sacred water. Last night, it had felt like a necessary act, a step toward something greater. But now, with the knowledge of Hadash's fate...it felt like a curse.

"Giaxia," I whispered, my voice trembling. The name echoed in the still air. "I offer you my blood." My hand shook as I placed the vial on the altar, the liquid inside swirling a deep crimson. "From Hadash comes the life of this world, the Pool of Vitality, and from this is the life of my soul. I offer you this as my troth. May it please you."

As soon as the words left my lips, the vial vanished, swallowed by the altar. I exhaled a wavering breath, but the tightness in my chest remained. Was it enough? Was it accepted?

The darkness in the hall seemed to thicken, the air growing heavier, pressing down on me like a physical force. My senses sharpened, catching the faint scent of smoke and something citrusy, like burning oranges.

"Now, who's eavesdropping?" I said, forcing my voice to steady.

A figure stepped out from the shadows, the darkness clinging to him like a second skin. Dainan. His presence was as unsettling as it was alluring, a dangerous mix that made my heart race for all the wrong reasons. "Don't worry, Brida," he murmured, his voice carrying a silky undertone. "I didn't see or hear what you offered. I just arrived to present my gift." He moved with a predatory grace, placing a leather-bound book on the altar. The shadows around him swirled, as if alive, drawn to the ancient stone.

I barely heard him, too focused on the way the shadows seemed to coil and writhe around him. His scowl brought me back to the present. "What happened to your hand?" His voice held an edge, a mix of concern and something darker.

I hid my hand behind my back, trying to appear nonchalant. "I slipped. Cut myself. It's nothing."

Dainan's eyes narrowed as he stepped closer, his gaze intense. "Who did this to you? Was it Marsh?" There was an unmistakable note of anger in his voice, something raw and primal.

"No," I said quickly, pulling my hand further out of his reach. "Why would you even think that?"

His lips curled into a sneer, his voice dropping to a dangerous whisper. "I can smell him on you."

My heart skipped a beat. "I take it that you don't find his scent to be overly appealing?"

His eyes flared, the shadows around him pulsing in response. "I do not."

I fought to keep my voice steady. "Do you make a habit of

sneaking up on people from the shadows, memorizing their scents? It seems rather unbecoming of a prince."

His chuckle was low, almost a growl. "Are you trying to provoke me, Brida?"

"Just making an observation." I took a step back, needing space between us. The air felt too warm, too thick with unspoken tension.

He took a step forward, closing the distance again. His eyes were like burning embers, hot and unyielding. "And what observation is that?"

My words faltered as I met his gaze, the heat in his eyes causing me to momentarily freeze. I could feel the intensity of his gaze, the way it seemed to strip away my defenses, leaving me exposed. Vulnerable.

"I would say I've taken your breath away," he murmured, leaning in close enough that I could feel the warmth of his breath against my ear. "But I must know, Brida... What did you offer Giaxia?"

The shadows seemed to press in around us, dark and suffocating. I forced myself to meet his gaze, to push back against the overwhelming presence he exuded. "What does it matter?" I managed to say, my voice sharper than I felt. "She's not your Primal."

Dainan's chuckle was dark, rich with amusement. "True. But indulge me."

I hesitated, the weight of the moment pressing down on me. "I offered her life," I finally whispered.

"Life?" His brow arched, curiosity piqued.

I nodded, feeling the tension ease as the shadows around us retreated, the air lightening. "Yes, life. My blood."

"Interesting." He tilted his head, studying me with an intensity that made my skin prickle. His gaze dropped to my bandaged hand again, lingering. "Blood. A potent offering. You should've saved it for Vasenia. She would've appreciated the gesture."

"Vasenia?" I frowned, surprised. "I didn't know that the Court of Shadows had an affinity to blood magic," I said.

Why am I continuing this conversation?

His face remained neutral as he made his way to a bench and sat down. “Very few do know, but that wasn’t always the case. Vasenia was said to have beasts that were connected to her through blood magic, but no one has seen them for centuries, nor can anyone attest to the validity of the claim that they bowed to her.”

“What...what sort of beasts?” I had a vague idea, but I wanted confirmation as I’d never heard it spoken by an actual member of the Court of Shadows. It was mentioned in *The Trials of Thale.*

“Wyvern. Dragons proved uncontrollable, yet wyverns exhibited a distinct affinity for blood magic. Given Vasenia’s status as the progenitor of blood magic, it was a natural pairing.” He gestured to the spot on the bench next to him.

I knew better, but I couldn’t help myself; he’d piqued my curiosity. He smiled as I sat down. Not a wide grin, but a small smile. It was endearing. An amiable silence fell between us.

“Did you know anyone in Hadash?” I finally asked.

He nodded. “It’s a terrible thing. And suspicious timing,” he looked straight ahead at the entrance to the Eternal House.

“What do you mean?” I asked him.

“What is it you see in Marsh?” He looked at me, completely ignoring my question.

“That’s rather personal,” I shifted, feeling increasingly uneasy.

“I thought we were in a sharing mood. I’m trying to get to know you better, *Brida.*”

“Stop saying my name like that,” I said, and he laughed. It was deep, sultry, smokey.

“Should I call you something else then?” He looked at me, eyes ablaze with the warmth of a crackling fire on a brisk day. It was unusual and transfixed me the longer I stared at them. I refused to answer. His laugh deepened and echoed from his chest. “You can call me whatever you wish,” he said with a wicked grin on his face.

I could think of several things in this moment that I wanted to call him, but I refused to utter any of them aloud.

"What did *you* give Giaxia?" I found myself asking in a tone that was less than forgiving.

"I thought it was clear that I gave a book," he gestured to the altar.

"Yes, but..." He looked at me with such curiosity. *Why is he looking at me like that*?

"What is the book about?" I finally said.

He crossed his legs, appearing completely at ease, "A book of the history of Hadash. Despite being known as soldiers, the Eternal Court are the keepers of history. It is a gift bestowed upon few of its members, but it is a well regarded post. That book is valuable to them. Given recent events, I thought they would appreciate it."

So, he is considerate.

"You never answered me," he said while turning towards me, "what is it you see in Marsh?"

"What makes you think I see anything in him?" I stood, folding my arms.

"Like I said," Dainan rose to meet me, "*I can smell him on you.*" There was no questioning the disdain in his voice. A tainted history lingered between the two of them. Somehow, I found myself in the middle of it.

"I should be going," I said as I turned to walk away.

"Until next time, *Ilia.*"

"Ilia?" I said, turning back to face him. The waves of his hair had fallen ever so slightly into his face.

"Well, if Brida is no longer allowed, it will have to do."

"What does it mean?" I asked.

"Figure it out," he smirked. Shadows spiraled up from the floor, enveloping him. In the blink of an eye, he vanished.

CHAPTER TWENTY-TWO

After informing Kadian, Oz, and Lil that the festival would be taking place, I decided to return the records to Addie. I no longer needed them, and now I could only hope that my offering had been accepted.

Dainan. I couldn't pinpoint what it was, but each time he approached, it did something to me. It felt like fire in my veins that I couldn't extinguish. As much as I heard Lil's voice in my head, *keep a safe distance*, I found myself unable to walk away.

As I made my way to the library, it was evident that the mayhem within Azmeer had only increased. Inductees, desperate and frantic, were scrambling to come up with last-minute offerings, resorting to bribery and pleading for information.

Kadian, Lil, Oz, and I had decided to keep our gifts a secret from each other, a game of sorts and one that I was more than happy to play. We hadn't discussed the possibility of any offerings being rejected. Despite my offers to assist and share the records list, they insisted on maintaining the solitary nature of the task in the spirit of competition. I feared any of us being sent home, but I maintained hope that we'd all be here come morning.

The library offered a serene quietude, a welcomed sanctuary amidst the chaos. "What brings you here today?" Addie greeted me as I approached her desk. I lifted the folder and pointed to it. "Ah, did it give you any ideas?"

"It did," I said while pulling the papers from the folder and handing them to her. "Thank you, I think I may still stand a chance."

"And is that something you really want?" She asked while taking the paper from me and placing it on the side of her desk.

"Yes." I paused. As fearful as I'd been when I'd arrived, not only at the prospect of being discovered but by the sheer size of Azmeer itself, I found myself desiring to be selected by a court. What had begun as a quest solely focused on my father had become something I was now striving for, for me. Marsh was right. Being here presents an opportunity to change things, and I could.

Addie smiled, "Just making sure. There's nothing wrong with changing your mind." She placed a hand on mine as her eyes returned to a list.

"Did you know anyone in Hadash?"

Her response came with a slow nod, her gaze distant. "I worked with a man named Kadrata from Hadash. He helped get me this posting." She lifted her head just slightly, meeting my eyes. A flicker of sadness passed through her expression, a subtle shift in her carefully controlled demeanor.

I knew Addie was reigning it in, keeping that tight grip on her emotions, just like she always did. She hadn't cried when Mom died. Even then, I'd understood it wasn't because she didn't care. Addie's way of dealing with loss was to lock everything inside, fortify her walls so nothing could slip through. I admired her for it in a strange way, even though it left me wondering how much pain she carried behind that stoic mask.

"I'm sorry," I murmured, the words inadequate but necessary.

She met my gaze, and there was something fragile beneath her calm exterior, though it remained buried. "Me too."

The heaviness of her simple reply hung in the air, thickening the quiet between us. I felt the urge to lift the mood, to ease us both out of the melancholic depths we were skirting.

I cleared my throat, forcing a lighter tone into my voice. "Hey, have you heard this theory that there were more than four Primals?"

Her eyebrow quirked slightly. I knew Addie well enough to understand that humor wasn't her way of coping, but distraction? That, she would entertain.

"That's an odd thing to remark on," she stood straighter.

"Marsh mentioned something about Giaxia forsaking her mating bond, which, who knew, and that there was a war with other Primals. It's a wild story."

She smiled at the mentioning of Marsh's name, "Like something from your *The Trials of Thale.*"

Of course, she remembered. Addie was the one who'd suggested the book to my father. "*Remember that life will always throw trials your way. You're strong enough to tackle them head on. Never forget how capable you are and who you are inside.*" I've reread that note inside the cover more times than I could count.

"We know very little about the Primals," Addie began, her tone thoughtful. "Some even doubt they ever existed." She leaned toward that belief, aligning with the growing Primal Dissent movement—a philosophical school of thought that had gained traction in academic circles over the years. With no recorded sightings of the Primals for millennia, these theories were seen as plausible by many, particularly among humans.

My stance on the matter remained conflicted. Since arriving in Azmeer and witnessing magic firsthand, my relationship with the Primals had only grown more complex. And then, there was the Pool of Vitality. My memory of the pool, its surface resembling a canvas of night adorned with twinkling stars, was etched into my mind, likely to stay with me for the rest of my life. Such breathtaking beauty seemed almost too divine for mortal eyes to behold.

I wonder if the Eternal House, or Giaxia if she exists, will know what it is I truly offered. The water had been so diluted with blood that it might be too difficult to discern its true nature.

I shook my head, snapping back to the present moment. "Do you not believe that Giaxia and Ollo were mates?" I leaned on the desk, giving her a wry smirk.

Addie's stance on relationships and love remained crystal clear, "a waste of time," she'd often declare with a grin. "Who needs all that when you could be happily married to your work?"

Her words carried a playful undertone of sarcasm, and as she glanced up at me with that mischievous grin, I found myself unable to stop laughing. She looked down at her watch and organized the papers on her desk, "It's time for us to make our way to the throne room."

Addie wrapped her arm around me as we made our way from the library. "Now let us speak on the importance of education rather than the tradition of marriage."

☽✻☾

I'd never been to this part of the palace before. Addie informed me during our walk that the use of the throne room was reserved for issuing royal decrees, Primal holidays, and promotions. As no new decrees had been issued nor promotions given in the last few years, this was a rare occasion. I didn't know what to expect. I remembered Lil's comments about it being ostentatious. Of course, that was not how she'd said it, "*it looks fucking horrendous. I'd never want to sit on that thing,*" had been her exact words.

"*I bet I know what she does want to sit on,*" Oz had whispered to me, his smile wicked as I smacked him.

The framed doorway to the throne room had been lined with guards, each wearing their Court of Shadows leathers, distinguishable by the red threading and embroidery along the neck and edges.

"I'll see you later," Addie hugged me goodbye, making her way over to the scribes. I took a seat in the middle of the room.

In stark contrast to the sand-colored limestone prevalent throughout much of the palace, this room boasted walls crafted entirely from aged wood. The ceiling soared overhead, supported by vaulted beams of rich, dark mahogany that spanned the entirety of the space. The stained glass windows that adorned this room were all dark in their coloration, unlike the one in the library which had more pastels. Shades of ultraviolet, deep reds, oranges, and green depicted scenes of the king winning his crown and the period of stability that followed.

What stories used to be in those panes before King Elidas? Maybe a story of the courts or even the Primals. The throne itself sat in the center of an elevated stage with three stairs to climb to its top. Witnessing it, I didn't think Lil had been entirely incorrect with her assessment. The throne's fabric was the color of a deep blood red that looked to have the texture of velvet. But it was the structure itself that gave me pause. Instead of wood, the arms, legs, and back bore an uncanny resemblance to bone, the pale off-white hue tinged with hints of aged yellow. Curves and indentations suggested a skeletal form.

Gods, I hope that isn't real.

Banners flanked the back wall sitting behind the throne. They didn't represent the courts but bore the royal sigil, a circle with red edging, filled with darkness, and a large ruby with an onyx embedded into its core. Not every royal lineage boasted membership in the Court of Shadows, yet King Elidas made certain that everyone was well aware of his family's allegiance to the court.

I looked to the doorway and saw that Lil had arrived, Kadian and Oz not far behind her, talking to a group of girls from the third floor. As usual, Lil was one of the best dressed in the room. Having worn a jade dress with slits at its sides to highlight her curves, I could see Kadian watching her with every step she took.

I waved them over, having saved a few of the seats beside me. The chairs were sturdy, also covered in velvet, and much more plush than the ones we'd been forced to sit in on the day of our arrival.

“Did you have a good afternoon?” I asked Lil as she sat next to me. Kadian chose to sit next to her, and Oz placed himself at the end.

“I spent most of it getting ready,” she smiled at me, batting her eyelashes.

“I see that,” Unable to hold in my laugh, “You look beautiful.”

“She does,” Kadian said firmly without looking at us.

Ignoring him, Lil whispered in my ear, “He’s been in a mood. Not sure why.”

I shrugged at her. *I’ll check in with him later.*

“I don’t see Marsh anywhere,” Lil remarked, knowing she was baiting me.

“He’s been moving people between Hadash and Azmeer. At least according to Illerium.”

Illerium said that Marsh would be back by this point, and Lil was right, I didn’t see him anywhere.

“He’ll be exhausted by the end of the day. You’ll just have to energize him, Bri,” she gave me a wink.

I couldn’t help but groan audibly in response. “I don’t know why I tell you anything.”

We spoke amongst ourselves for the next several minutes as the remaining members of the Courts funneled into the room. Silence fell when a tall individual who I hadn’t seen before entered. He possessed a complexion of smooth chestnut, his bald head gleaming in the light. He was dressed in flowing brown robes accented with intricate gold patterns and exuded an air of elegance. With each step, he carried himself with a dignified bearing, his gilded staff in hand, crowned by a striking piece of stalagmite.

That must be from the cave. I wonder if anything happened to the Pool of Vitality.

Following him were the princes. Rai wore a small smirk on his face, while Alvar and Dainan appeared somber. The last to enter was the king, my only indication being the crown that sat atop his head. His appearance defied the depictions I’d encountered in paintings adorning the walls of Azmeer and the likenesses portrayed in the books I'd studied before arriving at the palace. He'd been shown with dark hair, sun-kissed skin, and glowing but fierce eyes. The face of a killer, the face of a ruler. You would never have known him to be this man.

The once lustrous black of Elidas' hair had faded, a mere echo of its former self, interspersed with strands of salt and pepper. His eyes bore a melancholic gaze devoid of the vigor depicted in his portraits. But it was his pallid complexion that caught my attention. His skin, drained of its natural color, bore a sickly shade of greenish-gray. The undeniable truth loomed—he was dying, his mortality laid bare for all of us to see.

The king clung to the arm of the woman who stood beside him, "That's his new wife, Dainan's mother," Lil whispered in my ear. Despite not being separated by many years of age, Dainan and his siblings didn't share the same mother. The king had taken many lovers and had legitimized his three children. The affairs had supposedly stopped when he met Indara. The rumor was that they were a love match. I believed it by how she looked at him.

He moved slow, taking each step carefully as all moved aside, waiting for him to guide their way. Throughout their journey, Indara's gaze remained fixed on the king. She allowed her husband to hold onto her as though she were his beacon in the darkness. In that moment, it didn't matter if his image as a strong leader was at risk of being shattered. This was a king who was unafraid to declare his wife as his source of strength. It left me wondering if such a trait would be evident in his successor.

The princes stood on the stage, and I noticed that the darkness I had once thought to surround each of them only clung to Dainan. I wanted to ask Lil if she knew anything about it, but after our last conversation regarding him and the princes in general, I chose to hold off.

Everyone remained standing until the king took his seat on his throne. The queen stood beside him, his personal sentry.

"Good afternoon," the robed gentleman said, everyone returned to their seats. “We welcome you to the Eternia, the annual festival honoring our Primal Giaxia.” It took me a moment, but I realized that this man was Qurasa, head of the Eternal Court. “We are saddened that our most sacred day has been overshadowed by the recent tragedy in Giaxia’s own lands of Hadash. We’re grateful to His Majesty the king for extending aid to us in our time of need.” He turned towards Elidas, bowing his head as the audience erupted into polite applause.

“In light of recent events, we will honor those who lost their lives. I will now read their names. Please observe a moment of silence for each name. When I have finished, we shall proceed to the offerings.”

We stood in solemn silence for the next several hours as the names were read, each one a painful reminder of the lives lost. The death toll had risen since my conversation with Illerium, with hundreds more added to the tragic count. I glanced at Oz and couldn’t help but notice the tears that streaked his cheeks. He had no doubt known some of those people. I only hoped that his family remained safe.

As the list of names came to an end, Qurasa bowed his head. "We offer these names to you, Giaxia, with the hope that you will guide them into the Eternities. May they find light, may they find peace, may they find You." The room remained hushed as Qurasa spoke further.

“Now, let us begin.”

Qurasa walked over to the side of the stage where the Master of Trials appeared. He handed Qurasa a scroll and with that, vanished. My breath caught in my throat as the scroll unfurled, the parchment crackling with the weight of countless hopes and fears.

“Understand that Giaxia's favor can be capricious, her preferences varying from year to year. Yet, I can assure you that many have pleased her this year, and a few have caught our attention." Qurasa's voice, steady and unyielding, filled the silent room as he began to unroll the scroll.

"If your name is read, it means that your offering has been deemed worthy, and you shall continue in the Courting. If you do not hear your name, you will be removed from Azmeer."

The room had fallen so quiet and still that you could practically hear the trembling of hands in the audience. Every breath felt heavy, every heartbeat like thunder in my ears. The tension in the room was suffocating, a palpable force that pressed down on all of us. Each of us, standing on the edge of a precipice, unsure if we would fall or fly.

"Selaria Fowry, Humza Abduah, Stiora Ziggursted," Qurasa began.

Each name echoed in the chamber, a drumbeat of fate that reverberated through my chest. The sound of it seemed to stretch time, each second dragging on like an eternity. My hands were clammy, my heart pounding so hard it felt as though it might burst from my chest. With each name that wasn't mine, the knot in my stomach twisted tighter, winding itself into something unbearable. What will happen if I am forced to leave? The thought hit me like a hammer. If Kadian, Lil, or Oz stay, would they tell Marsh? Would they be able to send herbs to me? Kadian would want to help Dad. The questions swirled in my mind, each one more desperate than the last.

"Lilianna Towler, Iona Vorren, Izbetta Thali."

I glanced at Lil, squeezing her arm as if to ground myself in this unbearable moment. She looked back at me, her eyes wide with relief. One down, but how many more to go?

Qurasa's voice continued, each name falling like a drop of cold water on a fraying nerve.

The room was filled with the soft rustle of people shifting nervously, but I could hardly hear it over the pounding in my head. How many hopes and aspirations would be shattered in mere moments?

"Osforth Kadem, Tamra Kadem, Jehana Stoller."

Two more, two more to go. My breath was shallow, my vision tunneling as I looked around Lil to see Kadian, his face as pale as mine felt. His eyes were fixed forward, his expression tense, his hands clenched into fists. *There are still plenty of names; it will be fine. It has to be fine.*

But with each passing second, each name that wasn't mine or Kadian's, the certainty that had once been there began to crumble. The room felt like it was closing in on me, the walls pressing closer, the air growing thicker. I tried to steady myself, to breathe, but my chest was tight, the panic clawing at my throat. *Breathe, just breathe.* I forced myself to think of the music from the pool, that beautiful, enchanting song weaving its notes through me. *I wonder how many before me have heard it?* How many had stood where I stood now, on the edge of ruin or glory. The memory wrapped around me like a thin veil, not enough to shield me from the fear but enough to keep me from collapsing under its weight.

I realized then that my eyes had locked onto the stage, onto the brothers. Dainan's gaze met mine, sharp and intense. The shadows around him were moving, swirling in a way that wasn't normal, even for him. They pulsed and writhed, more active, more agitated than ever before, as if they were reacting to something unseen, something just beneath the surface. They seemed almost alive, tendrils of darkness reaching out, probing the space between us, as though they could sense my fear, as though they were feeding on it.

My pulse quickened further, my heart hammering against my ribs. *Why are they doing that? Why is he looking at me like that?* I wanted to look away, to break the connection, but I couldn't. It was like staring into a storm, mesmerizing and terrifying all at once.

Qurasa was nearing the end of the scroll, his voice steady but relentless. The closer he got to the final names, the more my panic grew. I could feel the tears pricking at the corners of my eyes, the desperation clawing at my insides. *I need to be here. I want to be here.* I squeezed my eyes shut as if that could freeze the moment, stop the reality of failure from engulfing me, keeping the spark of hope alive just for a second longer.

"Ezalia Hyler, Brida Larrow, Kadian Taldot."

Relief crashed over me like a wave, my knees nearly buckling under its force. I turned to Kadian, who was already smiling, his hand clasped by Lil's in shared relief. My smile was shaky, my hands trembling as I reached out to steady myself. The world around me came back into focus, but my heart was still pounding, my chest still tight. I glanced back at the stage, back at Dainan, and saw that the shadows around him had calmed, retreating to their usual subtle movements.

Qurasa finished reading the names and rolled the scroll back up, his expression unreadable. "To the one hundred and twenty of you who shall be continuing, well done. Those of you whose names have not been spoken, we wish you well. Please proceed to your quarters and collect your things."

Qurasa nodded to the king then took a step back as Alvar strode forward to the center of the platform. "Those of you continuing on, please proceed to the dining hall. Dinner will begin in thirty minutes." He nodded to Qurasa, bowed to his father, and returned to his brothers.

My pulse had yet to return to normal. *We made it through. Thank the gods, we made it through.*

Before exiting the room, I hugged each of my friends, the relief oozing from every pore of me. "I don't know if I could have stayed without you," Kadian whispered as we embraced each other, his presence grounding me in the midst of my frayed nerves.

"I would insist on it," I said.

"I told you, where you go, I go," he smiled, the warmth in his voice breaking through the lingering chill in my bones.

As we exited the throne room, I couldn't resist stealing a glance back at the king. There he sat, his queen kneeling beside him, her hand gently resting on his.

CHAPTER TWENTY-THREE

The dinner was similar to that of our first evening. The long tables had been replaced by circular ones, while the tables with the piles of food on them were lined against the back wall. From where I stood, I could see the different roasts of meats, venison, lamb, pork, chicken, in addition to plates of vegetables and pies. Never before had I beheld such a spread of food. The sheer abundance left me overwhelmed; I didn't know where to start. Lil and Kadian were already at the table, each trying to put more on their plate than the other.

"I'll get you some," Lil told me as they bolted over there.

I don't doubt it.

The king made a fleeting appearance, strolling through the room with his wife by his side, engaging with court officials. His sons trailed behind him for a time before breaking off. I wasn't sure where Rai and Alvar had gone off to, no doubt somewhere in the room, but Dainan had shadow-stepped. Perhaps he felt he had fulfilled his social obligations for the evening.

Ilia.

"Here," Lil said, shoving a plate into my chest.

I gave her a sideways glance while raising an eyebrow at her, "Is there a problem?"

"Kad got the last pudding, despite me saying I wanted it," she took a bite of a slice of poultry, rolling her eyes.

"It's not my fault you moved too slow. It'll teach you better for next time. You go for what you want the most first, the rest can wait." He grinned as he took a bite of the pudding.

A noticeable groan escaped her lips, prompting a chuckle from him. With a smile, he offered her the remainder of whatever he was eating. The genuine pleasure that lit up her face spoke volumes.

"So," Lil looked between the two of us, "who's going to ask the question first?" I raised an eyebrow, glancing at Kadian as if he held the answer. He returned a blank stare, just as clueless as I was.

"What did you end up offering?" She sighed while looking at the server passing by with a tray full of drinks.

Lil grabbed a couple of glasses of what looked to be white wine and handed them to each of us before taking one for herself. I took a sip and confirmed that it was, in fact, a dry white. It had earthy tones to it, which made sense given the holiday we were in the midst of celebrating.

The minor details and decorations that had been seen were all in honor of the Eternal Court. Large smoky quartz crystals had been placed around the room, and the color of the plates, linens, and tableware were all varying earth tones.

"I'm not going to be the first to say," Kadian responded, taking another bite. While they began to engage in a debate I continued to survey the room and its occupants.

Qurasa was mingling, or rather enduring small talk, with a cluster of Court of Whispers officials, offering the obligatory thanks for their aid. His face betrayed his distaste for the conversation, the thin veil of civility barely masking his discomfort. I watched him from afar, wondering how much we truly understood the intricate web of courtly dynamics. We were becoming more accustomed to life in Azmeer, but none of us were privy to its deeper currents.

Over the past few weeks, the lectures have been filled with the formalities of court life—when to bow, when to nod, when to extend a handshake. We'd learned how to greet every official from every court, each subtle gesture loaded with significance. Yet, the topic that gripped me most was the Well of Eternity and the Seers who guarded it. There was so much magic in this world, and I hadn't begun to brush against its surface. My fascination felt like an ache inside me, a longing to know more, to see more.

The evening's festivities unfolded around me as I continued to glance across the room, surveying the scene. Despite the devastation in Hadash less than a day before, it seemed forgotten here. The guests were immaculately dressed, women draped in gowns of deep green and earthy browns, while the men donned sleek charcoal suits. Their polished appearances seemed to say, "We are untouched by tragedy." I tugged at the hem of my dress—olive green, snug against my waist with soft lines cascading down from the hips, the fabric silken and smooth. The capped sleeves fell off my shoulders, framing my collarbones. It highlighted the reds in my hair and accented the curves of my chest and upper body.

I liked to imagine that Giaxia would have chosen something like this to wear—a subtle, timeless elegance, powerful without being overstated. That thought made me stand a little taller.

"People are noticing you," Oz whispered into my ear as he approached us. I put down my plate and pulled him into an embrace.

"I'm so sorry about today," I placed my hands on his arms while holding his gaze. "Is your family..."

"Tamra heard from them this morning," his voice heavy with sorrow. "Most are safe."

"Most?" Kadian placed his hand on Oz's shoulder.

"One of my uncles was killed this morning. In an aftershock."

Before I could move, Kadian embraced him, "I'm sorry. If there's anything we can do, let us know." Kad whispered to him. Oz nodded in return.

"Have you had any food?" Lil asked.

"A little," his voice was meek.

"I'm on it," she grabbed a plate for him and filled it with untouched food from ours. "Here," she said, handing it to him and squeezing his hand. "You'll need your strength."

He nodded as a sign of thanks and took a small bite of one of the pies.

"Well," he said as he found my eyes once more, "like I said, people are noticing you." A slight smile appeared on his lips.

"Don't be crazy; they're looking at those two." I gestured with my head over to Kadian and Lil, who'd begun debating which of the pies had been best. Kadian's vote was the spinach and cheese pie, while Lil's was the fish pie. A pie that Kadian reminded her she shouldn't have eaten if the Court of Reflection was watching.

"This is a festival for Giaxia; she wouldn't care if I ate fish. Besides, it was delicious." Lil said, a massive grin painted on her face.

"No," Oz said, returning our focus to each other, "I distinctly heard people talking about the woman with the black hair, woven with red, in the green dress," he looked me up and down, "and that is most certainly you. And why shouldn't it be? You've earned your place to be here, twice over now. About time you look the part. "

Heat rushed to my cheeks as I lifted my hand. As much effort as I had put into my appearance this evening, there was no way to make a wrapped hand look formal. "They were likely curious about this."

He cocked an eyebrow as if assessing the truth in my words before scanning the crowd. His eyes locked onto something, and after a moment, I followed his gaze to see him staring at his sister and a girl with dark, almost black, curly hair.

"Who's that with Tamra?" I asked, taking another sip of my drink.

"Isidra," Oz said while keeping his stare locked on them.

"Do we not like Isidra?" I made my way closer to him, peering over his shoulder.

He relaxed a bit, "She's alright. I just...I don't love the way she treats Tamra. They started up *something* before we came here and

Isidra has been unclear as to what the parameters of their relationship are. Tamra found her getting close with someone on the 5th floor from Petrias a week or so ago. I had to console her for hours." He sighed, "It's their relationship and their business, but if she hurts Tamra, I'm going to have a hard time keeping my feelings in check." I nodded in understanding. Kadian and I had always been protective of each other's relationships. It was an unspoken agreement—we never wanted to see the other get hurt. Placing my hand on Oz's shoulder, I gave it a squeeze before he drifted off to speak with a few members from the Eternal Court.

Despite the exhaustion from last night and today weighing on me, an inexplicable restlessness stirred inside. I needed to move. Lil and Kadian were deep in an animated debate over which type of carrot was superior, their voices rising and falling, the topic strangely passionate between them, I took the moment to slip away unnoticed.

The room was packed to the brim, the symphony of voices drowning out even the sound of my own shoes tapping against the marble floor, a sensation I found comforting.

The glow of the sun started to wane, and the flames from the candles took center stage. Their flickering dance casting a soft, ethereal gleam upon every surface. I couldn't help but be mesmerized by the gentle, shimmering light they emitted.

At the far end of the hall, a raised dais had been installed for the evening. Upon it were plush cushions, lounging chairs, and rugs. It almost looked similar to the interior of the pleasure den Kadian had taken me to that one time in Asteros. *That had been an experience.* Thinking about that night brought a smile to my face. Lost in my thoughts, I made my way through the messes of people and took a step up.

Few had seized the chance to lounge, perhaps wary of showing weakness in front of Qurasa. However, feeling sore and weary, I couldn't resist the temptation to rest, even if just for a few minutes.

I chose a chair with no arms and a curved back. I rubbed the velvet with my uninjured hand as I sat down. Its texture was rougher than I would have anticipated.

"How'd that happen?" I looked up to a voice that I didn't recognize. My gut instinct told me to leave, but I knew that would be ill-received.

Frozen in place, I met his gaze, "I fell," the words hanging between us in the tense silence.

His face was handsome, even more so this close. *It's no wonder Lil...well whatever it was the two of them had done or shared.*

"May I sit?" Prince Rai asked, gesturing to the chair next to me.

"It's not for me to deny you the chance to sit," I murmured, inclining my head in a gentle sway of acknowledgment.

"I'm told you're Brida," he said as he sat down, facing me. His eyes were a mesmerizing kaleidoscope of reds, browns, and onyx, their unique hues both unusual and captivating. His angular cheekbones were similar to those of Dainan and Alvar, but his face was more classically beautiful than his brothers.

"I am," I replied, eyes darting around the room to check if Lil and Kadian had noticed my absence. Lil's arms were flailing, gesturing wildly. I couldn't help but smirk—they had probably moved on to arguing about potatoes or some other root vegetable, fully absorbed in their debate.

"How have you found your time in Azmeer?" Leaning back into the chair, he folded his hands over his waist. He seemed at ease, which was unsurprising given that this was his home, and perhaps, he would ascend to the throne in a matter of months.

I made an effort not to dwell on that thought.

"It's been more than I anticipated and expected," I replied.

He smiled, a seductive dimple emerging on his left cheek. It was easy to see how Lil could have been swayed by him. His ease, his charm, his beauty.

"I'm sure that's the case. But, have you *enjoyed* yourself here, Brida?" He asked, leaning forward, inching closer to me.

“As much as one can while one is being educated on court life and attempting to survive trials.”

He scoffed, “Court life. Tedious, isn't it? Look at this,” he gestured around the room, his arm sweeping to encompass the entire dining hall, “isn't this all meaningless? No one has seen or heard from Giaxia in millennia, and yet, we continue to make offerings to her each year, hoping they'll be accepted. It's nonsensical,” he concluded, his arm falling back to the armrest of the wingback chair.

I cocked an eyebrow at him. *That’s not what I expected.* “Are you a believer in Primal Dissent then?” I turned to face him more directly now.

“Is that a common terminology amongst the inductees?” He asked, a hint of amusement on his face.

“If you know where to look,” I returned my gaze back to the crowd as I heard him chuckle.

“Are you an ardent of Primal Dissent, Brida?” He asked, curiosity in his voice. A voice that was so similar and yet so different to Dainan’s. Although Dainan himself was not warm, there was a certain resonance in the cadence of his voice that stirred something within me. I couldn't pinpoint when I began to feel this way about him. It had only been a few hours since he had been getting under my skin. And yet...

"Brida?"

“I’m sorry,” I looked back at him, “what was the question?” His entire face lit up, and the joy on it was infectious. I couldn’t help but smile in return.

“I asked where you stood on the debate of the Primals, that is if you even believe there is a debate to be had,” he turned his attention to the wrappings on my hand.

I stilled for a moment before responding, “There are valid arguments on both sides. I value academic discourse and believe that debates can enrich our understanding. I'm uncertain where I stand on the issue. Prior to coming here, I might have been more inclined to share your opinion.

However, everything I've witnessed since my arrival has given me pause." I hoped that my lengthy response would ensure that his focus returned to my face and would not continue to linger on my hand.

"Indeed." He said as his eyes flickered back up to mine. "Would you say that your time here has been educational?"

"Do you believe that I would have been able to maintain a cordial and proper conversation with you without said education, *Your Highness*?"

He laughed, "I do indeed. I suppose that answers my own question. Which Magister have they given you?"

"Illerium," I replied as my gaze drifted back towards the guests in the room. There was beauty in the evening. Not just from the manner in which people were dressed, or how their hair was done, but in the grander sense. In the face of tragedy, life does carry on.

"He's an odd man, even at the best of times." Rai snickered.

Before I could respond, he continued. "Illerium, overall, is a good man. Not overly patient, but who would be when you have held the same post for a millennia."

No wonder he seems to hate his job.

"Well, Brida," he said, rising upwards, "this was...*enlightening*." He started to move forward, halting abruptly before pivoting back towards me. He lowered himself until his face stood mere inches from mine, "I know you're friends with Lil. Please inform her that I wish to see her, and that I want *it* back." His tone changed, devoid of any curiosity or playfulness. His words seemed to reverberate down my spine, compelling me to sit straighter, reminiscent of when Asana had addressed us. Undoubtedly another gift from the Court of Shadows.

I blinked at him, caught off guard. "I have no idea what you're speaking of."

"Oh, of that, I have no doubt," he said, glancing back at Lil before refocusing on me. "But she does, and I want it returned to me." With that, he straightened to his full height. "Enjoy the remainder of your evening, Brida," he said as he began to walk away.

"Oh," he paused, "and I would take care of that hand if I were you. We wouldn't want it to leave a scar."

As he exited the dais, greeting those in the crowd down below, I remained paralyzed. *What did Lil take from him?* I stood and smoothed my dress. *Act naturally*, I thought. I slowly stepped from the dais so as to not trip on the bottom of my gown and began to navigate my way through the crowd.

The room was a bustle with activity. The clanking of glasses, conversation, those celebrating creating a dance floor. *I need to get out of here.*

Lil and Kadian remained in the spot I'd left them, but Oz was nowhere to be seen. My mind raced. *Why would she steal something from Rai? What if it was found out? What if we're all found out?* I paused to catch my breath, the temperature of the room increasing to the height of a midsummer day.

"Are you alright?" The voice startled me, snapping me out of my spiraling thoughts.

"I—pardon me," I stammered, looking up. He had black hair and dark eyes, his features sharp and otherworldly. He was Fae, with that ethereal beauty and agelessness that made it hard to guess his age. "My apologies for blocking the path." I tried to sidestep him, eager to escape the conversation and the unsettling feelings that clung to me.

Before I could get away, I felt his hand on my arm, firm but not unkind. "Aela? What are you doing here?" he whispered, the words hanging in the air like ghosts.

I froze. *What did he just call me?*

"I'm sorry. What did you call me?" I asked, trying to keep my voice steady but failing miserably.

"My apologies," he said, releasing his grip. "I mistook you for someone else."

My heart pounded in my chest as I remained while I watched him walk away, the noise of the room fading to a dull roar. *How does he know that name?*

I rubbed my temple, trying to make sense of it all, but the

thoughts just tangled further. I turned around, desperate for some semblance of normalcy, and that's when I saw Marsh. He looked ashen, his usual calm demeanor replaced with something bordering on dread. Magister Illerium and Qurasa were with him, Qurasa's hand resting on Marsh's shoulder in what seemed like a comforting gesture.

Before I could move, before I could find my voice to call out to him, they were gone, exiting the room together. Whatever I wanted to say would have to wait. Everything would have to wait. And the longer I stood there, the more I felt like the walls were closing in.

"It's going to be so much fun; I'm so excited. I want to take you guys to the Spice Quarter before we visit the bar, though. It's amazing and has the best kebabs I've ever had." Lil said as she and Kadian found me.

Feeling the need to leave, I informed them that Qurasa had left, meaning we were free to follow suit. I remained silent on the way back to our rooms, listening to Lil and Kadian discuss their offerings. Kadian offered a hand-drawn copy of his family tree to inform Giaxia of his ties to the Eternal Court, while Lil offered sand from the Hydratas Sea she had brought with her. "It's earth-based, so I thought it may work," she shrugged as she explained. They forgot to ask me what I had offered and I had never been happier to not truly be part of a conversation.

My room was dark when I entered. I lit the candles that stood atop my desk and bedside tables. I let out an audible sigh, a mix of relief and panic washing over me.

Glancing at my window, I felt a slight breeze across my cheek.

"*Are you alright?*" I heard the wind whisper.

"*I have so many questions,*" I began to say, "*but they will have to wait for now.*"

"*Yes, but are you alright?*" It asked once more.

"*I will be.*"

As I was about to crawl into bed, exhaustion pulling at every limb, a soft knock sounded from the door. My body tensed, the fatigue melting into something more jagged—anxiety, maybe. Who would be visiting this late?

"Just a second," I muttered, my voice just loud enough to carry. I fumbled my way to the chair, my fingers trembling as I grabbed the cover and wrapped it around my shoulders. The familiar, quiet creak of the hinges met my ears as I opened the door, the dim light from the hall casting shadows across Kadian's face. His hands were shoved deep in his pockets, his expression somber.

"Hey, Bri," he whispered.

I didn't hesitate. No matter the time, no matter how drained or broken I felt, I'd never deny Kadian entry. Our parents used to joke when we were kids, spinning tales of invisible portals that connected our rooms. They'd always find us huddled together in the middle of the night, hidden under blankets, sharing secrets or giggling over some silly thing that had happened during the day.

"You okay?" I asked, closing the door behind him, my words more of a reflex than genuine inquiry. I crossed the room and perched on the edge of the bed, motioning for him to join me. The chill of the floor seeped into my feet, grounding me in the moment.

A flicker of a smile tugged at the corner of his lips, but it didn't quite reach his eyes. "I'm actually here to ask you that. Felt like a pretty close call today." His strides were slow, deliberate, as he crossed the room in three easy steps. It struck me then—how much he'd grown. Not just in height or muscle, though that too, but into himself. The scrawny boy I grew up with had become a man while I wasn't looking.

I let out a breath I hadn't realized I'd been holding. "It did feel close. I swear, it felt like I was holding soup in my hands—the way my palms were sweating." I managed a weak chuckle, hoping to lighten the heaviness hanging in the air between us.

Kadian nodded, his eyes soft but sharp, always seeing too much. "Yeah. I don't know what I would've done if they'd called my name and not yours." He hesitated as if weighing his next words. "Well, that's not true. I know exactly what I would've done."

I turned to face him, my stomach tightening. "And what would that be?"

His gaze held mine, unflinching. "I would've told the whole lot of them to fuck right off."

I barked out a laugh, relief washing over me like a tide. "Do you remember when you did that to Tayo Mindalas? I swear, I've never seen a person turn such a deep shade of red."

His grin broke through, wide and easy, as if we were back in those simpler times. "Scarlet. Damn near scarlet, Bri." He clasped his hand over mine, and the sudden warmth of it stilled the restless energy buzzing under my skin. His laugh quieted, his voice dipping lower. "But in all seriousness, Bri, this...all of this...it means nothing if we're not here for each other."

The weight of his words settled into the spaces between us, heavy but comforting. I leaned into him without thinking, my body folding into the familiar curve of his as he wrapped an arm around me. I could feel the steady rhythm of his breathing, the rise and fall of his chest. I didn't realize how much I needed that—something steady, something real.

"How did I get so lucky to have you in my life, Brida Larrow?" He whispered.

My grip tightened, "It's just the way the story was written, Kad."

I smiled up at my best friend, the one person in this world who knew me possibly better than I knew myself, the one who had seen me at my lowest low and I hoped would be there until the end.

"And what a story it is," I said.

CHAPTER
TWENTY-FOUR

The hallway felt eerily silent, the kind of quiet that settles after too much revelry. The echoes of last night's laughter and clinking glasses were long gone, replaced by the occasional muffled groan or the shuffling of feet and the internal fear I felt over what had been said to me last night.

I'd woken more than once, disturbed by the thuds of people staggering back to their rooms, some even fumbling at my door, too drunk to remember which one was theirs. The air still held the faint scent of spilled wine and sweat, a lingering reminder of the night's excess.

When I knocked on Lil's door, my knuckles brushed against the worn wood twice before I realized that she wouldn't be answering. Sighing, I lowered my hand, understanding that this conversation would have to wait until we could speak freely, away from prying eyes and ears, and made my way to breakfast.

The dining hall, now restored to its usual order, was a far cry from the chaotic scene it had been during the feast. The six long tables were neatly aligned, and the stones and crystals that symbolized the Eternal Court's power had been put away. The vibrant tapestries, depicting the king's grand conquests and peace treaties, hung proudly on the walls again as if nothing had disturbed their solemnity.

Lil sat near the back, her face pale but composed, a cup of something warm clasped between her hands as if it were the only thing anchoring her to reality. As I approached, she offered me a small, tired smile, one that didn't quite reach her eyes. "I got you some wolfberry," she said, gesturing to the plate across from her. It was a simple gesture, but I knew it was her way of showing love, a quiet, steady kind of affection that asked for nothing in return. I returned her smile, feeling a warmth in my chest despite the unease lingering in the air.

She took a sip, the steam curling around her face like a protective veil. "I started drinking some coffee and water earlier this morning. I thought I might need the help after last night," she said, her voice a little too steady, a little too controlled. She was holding herself together, but just barely.

"A good idea. I wonder how Kadian and Oz will be feeling this morning." I raised my eyebrows as I brought my cup to my mouth.

Watching Lil, I noticed the way her shoulders slumped ever so slightly and how her fingers trembled as she gripped the mug.

"Did something happen that I don't know about?" I asked, wondering if Rai may have spoken to her too last night.

She shrugged, her movements slow and deliberate. "Kad and Oz insisted we try a few more glasses of wine to make sure it was all the same kind. Who was I to say no?" She forced a laugh, but it was hollow, a mere echo of her usual self. She took another sip of coffee, the steam rising to obscure her face again. "How come you don't feel like this?" she asked as she rested her head on her arms.

I chuckled, though it felt out of place, almost disrespectful to the mood hanging over us. "Because I was the sole responsible adult last night." Lil nodded, the hint of a smile tugging at her lips before disappearing entirely.

A few minutes later, I glanced toward the entrance and saw

Kadian, his face drawn and pale, rubbing his temple as if trying to massage away the remnants of last night. He smacked his cheeks, attempting to wake himself up as he made his way over.

"Well, good morning," I said as he dropped into a seat, his movements sluggish, his usual energy absent.

Kadian's scowl deepened as he met my gaze, then shifted to Lil, who ignored him. Pointing at her, he raised an eyebrow, questioning. "She'll be fine," I said, leaning forward. "Can you believe we're all still here?"

"Obviously, I can. Who would ever deny this?" He gestured to himself, but the arrogance in his voice was muted, his usual bravado dulled by the hangover clinging to him.

"I'd be willing to argue several people, based on the state of you right now," I said, unable to resist teasing him. He looked worse for wear, his hair a mess, his eyes bloodshot.

"We've decided," I continued, glancing between him and Lil, "that next time there's a gathering, we'll all stick to one glass of wine."

Kadian grumbled something unintelligible under his breath, looking at his breakfast with more determination than actual hunger. I'd seen him like this before and knew he'd bounce back in a few hours. Lil, on the other hand, looked as though she needed more than time to recover. Her usual vibrancy was absent, replaced by a dullness that made my chest ache.

Without warning, Lil pushed back and stood up. "I'm going to the pool and staying there all morning. I'll see you guys later," she said, her voice flat, her steps unsteady as she left the refectory.

I watched her go, my worry deepening.

Kadian slumped over his plate beside me and hadn't touched much of his food. "Are you not going to eat this morning?" I asked, trying to lighten the mood with a laugh. "That would be a first."

He raised his head slowly, his eyes meeting mine with a sly smile. "It's yours," he said, pushing his plate toward me.

As I prepared myself to tell Kadian of the man who spoke to me last night, he cut me off.

"I'm sorry about yesterday." Kadian sat in silence for a moment, his expression pensive. When he spoke, his voice was low, almost as if he were afraid of what he was about to say. "Something felt... strange the night before last, and it only felt stranger yesterday."

"What do you mean?" I leaned closer, sensing the weight of his words.

He took a deep breath, his eyes darkening with a mix of confusion and fear. "I don't know how to describe it, but when I went to bed a few nights ago, I felt fine. Then, in the middle of the night, I shot up. I'd been in a deep sleep, and suddenly, I was wide awake, sweating like I'd run for days. It felt like...like something snapped inside me," he said, his voice trembling. He picked up a spoon from the table and pretended to snap it in half. "It was like if you were to take a branch and break it. It felt like part of me just...broke."

His words hung in the air, heavy and ominous. I could see the fear in his eyes, the way his muscles tensed as if bracing for another blow. "It took about an hour or so of pacing around my room and then a cold shower to calm down. I fell back asleep and felt alright until the next morning..." He paused again, his hands clenching into fists. "When I saw Lil being approached by those fucking pricks from the sixth floor, I just... Pure rage filled my veins, Bri."

I could see the way his jaw clenched, the anger simmering just beneath the surface. His muscles were coiled tight, ready to snap at any moment. "You know Lil can take care of herself," I said, though a part of me wondered if there was more to Lil than any of us knew.

"I know that," he said, his voice strained. "It's one of the things I like most about her." His gaze dropped back to the table, his fists slowly unclenching.

"Did anything happen between her and those guys?" I asked, my voice was a whisper, not wanting to draw attention to our conversation.

"No, but she was smiling at them in this way that I just..." He trailed off, his hands gripping the edge of the table until his knuckles turned white. I reached out, placing my hand on his upper back, feeling the tension in his muscles as I stroked between his shoulders.

"I just don't know what happened, why I felt that way, and then I hated myself for it. She's not my property, and I would never think of her that way, or any woman that way," he said, his eyes pleading with me for understanding, for some kind of reassurance that he wasn't turning into someone he despised.

"I know that, Kad," I said, and I meant it. He was the most caring person I knew, always treating everyone with respect and kindness. This rage, this possessiveness, it wasn't him.

"I just don't know what came over me, Bri. I didn't know how to apologize to Lil without telling her all of this. I would like to keep it just between us." He bowed his head, ashamed of himself.

"It stays with me," I promised, my hand still on his back, trying to soothe the turmoil I could feel radiating from him.

☽✳☾

I hoped to see Marsh waiting for me on the track that morning, but he wasn't there. In his absence, Kadian decided to run with me, despite my advising him to perhaps do something that wouldn't jostle his stomach. Ignoring me, he took off. We didn't say much to each other over the course of our run, which was okay. We'd always known when to give the other space, and whatever it was Kadian was dealing with, when he had more to say about it, he would let me know.

Oz joined us for the last few laps. When Kadian pressed him to share what it was he had given, Oz chose to stay silent, and I followed suit.

"There's nothing wrong with an air of mystery," I said to him with a wink.

Magister Illerium asked us to meet him near the library and was joined by a figure I didn't recognize. "Good afternoon, everyone.

Before we begin, let me congratulate you on having your offerings accepted, very well done." It was clear that many members of our group were no longer there, including Shay.

"Can't say I'll miss her," Kadian whispered to me.

Illerium bowed his head towards us. "This is Thalius Towler."

"Towler," Kadian said under his breath, looking confused, as if he'd heard the name before. I shot my gaze to Lil. The blood and color drained from her cheeks.

Thalius was tall and lithe, his presence commanding in a way that felt almost unnatural. There was none of Lil's gentle charm in him. Where she exuded warmth, he emanated a cold, calculated energy. His features were sharp, his face a collection of hard angles and lines that spoke of an unyielding resolve. His golden hair caught the light, a stark contrast to his piercing blue eyes that seemed to see through every pretense, leaving only vulnerability in their wake. There was no joy in his expression, no softness to be found—only a rigid control that felt suffocating.

Thalius bowed his head as Illerium introduced him. His smile grew as he locked eyes with the ever-paling Lil.

"Thalius, or Ambassador Towler," Illerium began, bowing his head apologetically, "will be joining us today as he is here on business in Azmeer. I thought it a good opportunity to continue our tour of the grounds and visit the House of Reflection. It has been brought to my attention," he added, glancing toward the leader of the second floor group across the hall, "that my group is the only one that has not yet seen the entrances to each of the Houses."

The lack of tours around the palace hadn't bothered me. Illerium, despite loathing his post, possessed a wealth of knowledge. We were supposed to learn of the light prisons used by the Court of Whispers today; however, it seemed it would have to wait.

"If you don't mind, Magister," Thalius interrupted, "I would like to say a few words to the group before we depart."

Illerium bowed to him once more, moving to the side. "Good afternoon to you all," his smile sent a shiver up my spine. Lil appeared paralyzed. Kadian, sensing her unease, inched closer to her.

"I hope you've found your time in Azmeer to be pleasurable and of great value. For many of you, this is your first exposure to court life; for the rest of you, I hope you've taken this time to further your... *education.*" His eyes finally left Lil as he turned to face the rest of the group. I could have sworn I heard her begin to breathe again.

"The Court of Reflection has a longstanding relationship with His Majesty. It has been our continued honor and privilege to aid him in maintaining peace throughout the continent." His smile was now gone. "If you follow me, we'll make our way towards the House of Reflection. For those of you who have not yet seen it, it can be quite *overwhelming* the first time." He turned and made his way down the corridor.

"Who is he?" I leaned and whispered to Lil.

"My uncle," she sounded hoarse. She looked to me as tears began to well in her eyes, "he's the head of our family." We followed after him.

"For those of you unfamiliar with the history of the Court of Reflection," his voice boomed, "allow me to elucidate." He didn't look at us as he spoke but continued to face forward. "The Court of Reflection was established after the war that had ravaged our lands for one thousand years. Our Primal, Hild, chose not to partake in the final battle, knowing its outcome before anyone had set foot on the battlefield. Her gift of prophecy is one that she seldom grants to members of the Court of Reflection, but those who it is bestowed upon are deemed blessed," he continued as we turned a corner. "Each court has their stories as to what forced the courts into existence, which Primal was first, but to us, it doesn't matter. What does matter," he paused, "is that peace and tranquility remain, for without it, the wars would have been meaningless. It was a chance for the world to be made anew, a rebirth, a cleansing, if you will." He turned back and once again stared at Lil before returning his focus ahead.

As we continued to make our way down the corridor, the sand-colored limestone of the walls began to lighten. When we reached the end of the hall, the tan stone of the majority of the palace was now a beautiful ivory that sparkled as the light from the windows reflected off it.

Thalius stopped us in front of the entrance to the House of Reflection, and it was the most beautiful structure I had ever seen. Columns stood at the entrance, their weathered appearance belying an enduring beauty. Adorned with coral motifs, sea creatures, and graceful nymphs, they effortlessly captured one's attention. In total, there were four columns, each stretching upwards to support a cascading waterfall. The waterfall did not hinder entry; instead, the water flowed to the sides, filling two reflective pools at the columns' base.

"These are the Mirrors of Reflection," Thalius explained. "These pools have been known to drive many to madness, for they can reveal your deepest desires or greatest fears. It's never known what they'll choose to show you, only Hild knows." He paused, his expression serious. "For those brave enough to test their curiosity, you will be permitted to approach if you wish. However," he continued, raising an eyebrow and clasping his hands near his chest, "I would advise against sharing what you see with others. Information is power, and if someone knows your desires or fears," he glanced at Lil, "it can be exploited against you." With that, he stepped aside, allowing those interested to approach the mirrors.

Thalius and Illerium began to speak amongst themselves as members of our group cautiously approached the water. Oz took a step forward, and Kadian followed suit, but only after assessing what Lil would do.

I knew from my research that some believed what you saw in the pools was not just an indicator of what one desired or feared but rather of what would come to pass, connecting it to Hild's gift of prophecy. I wasn't sure I believed in such a thing.

I approached the pool, feeling a strange mix of curiosity and dread tightening in my chest. As I leaned closer, the water seemed to ripple, just slightly, like a pebble had been tossed in—though nothing had touched it. My breath caught in my throat, and I stared, waiting, almost begging for something to emerge from the depths.

Seconds stretched into minutes, and my heartbeat began to echo in my ears, drowning out the muffled sounds of the others around me. I kept waiting, watching the water, expecting...*something*. But there was nothing. No images, no visions—only the reflection of the columns above, the surface of the pool gently vibrating as if taunting me with its silence.

Why is nothing happening? The question screamed in my mind, louder and louder, until it felt like it might tear me apart. The stillness in the water wasn't calming; it was suffocating. It was as if the pool was refusing to show me anything, and that refusal gnawed at me, filling me with a cold, creeping terror.

There is nothing. My own reflection seemed to mock me. *Do I not have a future?* The thought slammed into me with brutal force, and I could feel my composure cracking, the fear seeping through like a dark ink stain on my mind. What if the pool wasn't showing me anything because there was nothing to show? No future, no path, just a vast, empty void waiting for me.

I forced myself to look away, my eyes darting to the other pool where Kad and Oz were still staring, their faces intense, absorbed in whatever they were seeing. They *had* something. Why didn't I?

Panic clawed at my throat, my thoughts racing uncontrollably. I scanned the others—some looked pleased, even blissful, while others were pale, stricken, like they'd seen a ghost. But none of them had the same emptiness in their eyes that I felt in my soul.

I needed to get away from the pool, from the nothingness that threatened to consume me. My legs felt unsteady as I backed away, my heart pounding with the urge to flee. I caught sight of Lil, standing by the windows, her face turned away from the water.

I hurried to her side, desperate to ground myself in something—someone—solid. I placed my hand on her arm, the gesture as much for me as it was for her. *This isn't about me right now. Be here for Lil.* But the fear still clung to me, cold and relentless, whispering doubts I couldn't silence.

"Are you going to look?" I whispered, trying to keep my voice steady, though it wavered with the remnants of panic.

She shook her head, her gaze unwavering as it stayed fixed on the horizon beyond the windows. "I don't need to. I already know what I'll see."

I squeezed her arm, a silent promise that I was here, even as my own fears threatened to drown me. When she finally turned to face me, her eyes were red, glistening with unshed tears.

"I'll see Rai."

CHAPTER TWENTY-FIVE

Despite Thalius speaking throughout the rest of the tour, I didn't hear a single word. My attention remained fixed on Lil. I couldn't tear my eyes from her. Kadian positioned himself close, acting as a barrier between her and Thalius. However, she seemed oblivious to his presence. She wrapped her arms around herself as if they could serve as armor for when she would have to confront her uncle. Her only form of protection. Oz glanced towards me, gesturing toward the two of them while cocking an eyebrow. I didn't know what to say.

The tour ended in front of the library. Illerium dismissed us and made his way towards his office. "Lilianna," Thalius said. We knew she hated that name, perhaps this was why. Lil refused to look at us, continuing to hug herself while she marched towards him.

"Who the *fuck* is that," Kadian growled.

I moved in front of him, attempting to block his view of her, even though he stood a foot taller than me. "Kad, look at me," but his eyes remained unwavering. "Kadian," I said as I placed my hands on his arms and squeezed just slightly. "Look at me *right now.*" Reluctantly his eyes met mine. "That's her uncle. Thalius is the head of her household, and she answers to *him*."

"*Does all of your father's family live at the Court of Reflection*?" I had once asked Lil.

She had nodded, "My uncle and my dad don't really get along, though. It's why my parents chose to live in Lesalia."

Thalius towered several inches above Lil. Despite her tall frame, she shrank in his presence. He gestured for her to follow. She walked beside him with her head bowed, a stark contrast to her usual confident self.

"Maybe you should go lay down before dinner," I suggested, my tone hopeful, desperate for him to heed my advice.

I wanted to go after Lil—she shouldn't have to face this alone. But there was no way I could have Kadian in his current state with me.

A moment later, Oz placed his hand on Kadian's shoulder, causing him to jolt. "Let's go." I watched as Kadian's muscles tensed at the touch. Oz, unsure of what was going on, smiled at me and gently guided Kadian toward our rooms.

Sighing, I readied myself to follow. *They're headed toward the House of Reflection*. Just as I was about to take a step forward, I felt a light tap on my shoulder. I turned around to find Addie standing there.

"You okay?" She was dressed in the familiar robes I had grown accustomed to seeing her in. It felt strange to see Addie looking so plain when outside of Azmeer, she was anything but. Her hair, pulled back into a neat bun, was allowed to run wild with her brown curls during her visits. Addie was known for her colorful, bright clothing and large jewelry, which she described as "a way to express myself without getting too crazy." But here, none of that vibrancy was present. The colors were replaced with beiges and off-whites, and her usual earrings and necklaces were nowhere to be seen. Despite the simplicity in her appearance, she never looked any less beautiful.

"It's been a strange day," I said, rubbing my temple with my fingers. I could feel the muscles in my face and head tightening.

She gestured towards the library, "I'm on break in a few minutes. Do you want to talk about it?" I peered into the inside, it was empty at this time of the day. "Maybe just sitting for a few minutes will help," she wrapped her arm around me and led me inside.

I sat down at one of the chairs along the tables under the window and closed my eyes.

"*Hmm,*" I heard Addie say. I opened my eyes to see a small smile resting on her face.

"Do you hear that?" She said as she looked toward the window.

I closed my eyes and tried to focus. *Hmm indeed.* I smiled. "Rain," I said a few moments later.

"A good thing, too. It hasn't rained in months." Her gaze continued to linger outside.

"I love rain in the summer."

"Your mother did, too. I always thought she was crazy. *Rain,* I would say. How could *rain* be your favorite type of weather?" Addie looked at me, "Do you know what she would say?" I shook my head. "After every storm, it's like the world is made anew." She sighed. "I think of her every time it rains, and I appreciate how the old world is washed away to make room for what's to come." We sat in a comfortable stillness, listening to the rain tapping against the glass panes. It was a beautiful sound.

"You know, some believe—mostly the Court of Reflection," she rolled her eyes, "that it only rains when Hild has seen something so upsetting, so disturbing that it brings her to tears. A bit ludicrous if you ask me," she said, placing her hands in her lap. "They need to do more scientific research," she added with a smile. "Do you want me to stay with you?"

"What do you know of Thalius from the Court of Reflection?"

She rested her arms on the table and clasped her hands together, "I've never met him," she continued, "but I know that he's important within their court. He's known for having a rather...stern reputation."

"Is he here often?"

She shook her head, "I'd heard he would be visiting. We were requested to retrieve some papers for him over the next few days. Can't say for sure, but I don't believe he is here too often."

"Do you have any idea why he's visiting now?" I returned my gaze to the window.

"I don't. Why the curiosity in regards to Thalius?" She put her hand on my shoulder, "Is he what's bothering you?"

"*He's only part of my problem,*" I wanted to say. I needed to speak to Marsh; I was worried about what was happening with Kadian, and my interaction with Rai. Why hadn't I seen anything in those pools? *Aela*. Thalius and Lil were only the most recent crises.

"He's Lil's uncle and seems rather formidable. She barely uttered a word as soon as she caught sight of him. Just curious in regards to his nature." I said, trying not to sound too concerned.

"I'm sure she's used to how he functions," Addie said while raising herself. "You should be going to get ready for dinner." Addie leaned in, "Make sure you eat something," she cupped my face with her hand and made her way back to the desk.

The library's stillness pressed down on me as I stared at Addie, trying to gather my thoughts. I had walked into this conversation with questions, but now that I was here, now that the truth was so close, I wasn't sure I wanted to hear it. My mind was a tangled web of uncertainty and dread, each thread pulling me in a different direction, each one leading back to the same haunting thought: what else hadn't I been told?

"Addie, I need to talk to you about something." The words felt heavy, like stones dropping into a dark, endless well.

She settled back into her chair, arms resting on the table, her eyes holding a softness that both comforted and unnerved me. I wished she would say something first, give me an out, but the silence stretched on, filling the space between us with expectation. I swallowed hard, trying to steady my voice.

"Last night, at the feast following the ceremony, a man approached me and called me Aela." The name felt foreign on my tongue, yet familiar, like an old melody I couldn't quite remember. Addie's reaction was immediate, her face draining of color as if the name itself had the power to reach across time and snatch the breath from her lungs.

Her eyes darted away, and for a moment, I thought she might deny it, might tell me that the man was simply mistaken. But then she looked back at me, her gaze steady but tinged with a sorrow that made my heart ache. "Now, to my knowledge, Mom had never been in Azmeer, so would you like to tell me why it is that a stranger mistook me for her?"

The accusation in my voice surprised me. I hadn't meant to sound so harsh, but the realization that Addie—and my father—had been keeping something from me was like a sharp, twisting knife in my gut. Addie began to rub her face, a gesture I recognized as one of hesitation, of uncertainty. She was stalling, trying to figure out how much to tell me, how much I could handle.

Addie cleared her throat, the sound unnervingly loud in the quiet room. "Your mother," she began, her voice softening, as if she were speaking to a wounded child. "I take it that your father didn't have this conversation with you before you came here?"

I shook my head, unable to speak. The silence that followed was suffocating, wrapping around me like a shroud. Of course, he hadn't. We didn't talk about Mom anymore, not really. The memories were too painful, too raw, and so we had let them fade into the background, like a book gathering dust on a forgotten shelf.

"Of course not," Addie muttered under her breath, more to herself than to me. She took a deep breath, her expression softening as she reached across the table to place her hand over mine. The warmth of her touch was a small comfort, but it didn't ease the knot of anxiety tightening in my chest.

"Aela, your mom," she said, smiling wistfully, "as you know, was a year younger than me. We were inseparable, everywhere I went, she followed close behind. I never minded because I loved the company. She told the best stories, your mom, and had an imagination that I swear could have filled more books than there are in this room." Her gaze drifted around the library, as if she could see my mother's words etched into the spines of the books that lined the shelves.

I tried to picture it—my mother, young and full of life, chasing after Addie with that same stubborn determination I had inherited. But the image wouldn't come. It was as if the years of silence had blurred the edges of my memories, leaving only a vague outline of the woman who had once been my whole world.

"I was granted a research opportunity during my final year of study to come to Azmeer and work in the library. My dissertation required access to books that cannot leave the premises, and the research was detailed enough that I needed an assistant. I couldn't have chosen anyone better than Aela to accompany me."

I shifted in my seat, the sudden urge to flee almost overwhelming. But I forced myself to meet Addie's gaze, to listen to every word she was saying, even though each one felt like a hammer striking the fragile glass of my reality.

"She came with you?" I asked, the words no more than a whisper. It was a stupid question—of course, she had. But I needed to hear it, needed to know that this wasn't some cruel joke or a misunderstanding.

"Of course she did! You couldn't have stopped her. Gods, she was more excited than I was. She was up first thing that morning, practically had to drag my sorry ass from bed," Addie laughed, the sound warm and nostalgic. I could almost see it now—my mother's determined expression as she yanked the covers off a groggy, wild-haired Addie, chiding her for being late.

The thought brought a bittersweet smile to my lips. Time was a cruel thief, stealing away these precious moments that I would never get to experience, these stories that had been kept from me for so long. The sadness inside me grew, an ever-expanding void that threatened to swallow me whole.

"When we arrived, we were greeted by a man named Yezed. He was Fae and a member of the Court of Shadows; he had been for many, many years." Addie smiled again, but there was a sadness in her eyes that hadn't been there before. "Despite us being here for my research, when Yezed took one look at your mother, it was like I wasn't even there."

"What do you mean?" I asked, my voice trembling.

"I would ask where our rooms were, and he would speak only to Aela. I commented on the palace itself, and he told your mother it was almost as beautiful as she was." She chuckled, but it was a hollow sound as if she were trying to laugh off the pain that still lingered after all these years. "It's funny when I think back on it. He was unmarried, and gods if he did not want to make your mother his wife. Over the course of the year we spent here, they became very close. Every decade or so, the House of Shadows holds a ball. We were invited that year at the behest of Yezed, who at the time served as a personal advisor to the king. Being the only humans in attendance, we felt very special."

My chest tightened as the story unfolded, each detail a sharp sting against my already raw emotions. Yezed had wanted to marry her. My mother had been loved by someone else, someone who wasn't my father. The thought was almost too much to bear, and I felt a wave of nausea roll through me.

"Despite being a high ranking official, he always made time for Aela. He became better about answering me as time went on, too," she said, her lips curling into a small smile.

"But from the moment he saw her, he loved your mother."

The room seemed to close in around me as her words sank in, heavy and suffocating. My mind raced, trying to process this new information, but it was like trying to catch smoke with my bare hands. My mother, the woman I had always idolized, had a whole other life, a whole other set of experiences that I had known nothing about. How could this be true? How could she have kept this from me?

"Yezed wanted to marry her," Addie continued, oblivious to the storm raging inside me. "But one day, while out wandering the streets of Azmeer, your mother said she stopped to listen to a man she said sang the most beautiful song she'd ever heard. While she stood there listening, she saw a man across from her. She said the moment she saw him, she knew that was it. Not soon after, your mother decided to leave here with your father as it became clear Yezed was not going to give up easily."

"Is...is that why they chose to settle in Escalia?" The idea of my parents running from something, from someone, was a strange and unsettling thought. They had always seemed so strong, so sure of themselves. But now, I wondered if that had all been a façade, a mask to hide the fear that had driven them to Escalia.

Addie nodded, her expression serious. "They feared if they went anywhere with too much magic or a connection to Azmeer, that Yezed would find her and somehow lure her back. They wanted to be somewhere safe. It was a logical choice."

Safe. The word echoed in my mind, hollow and meaningless. Safe from what? From whom? And what did that mean for me, now that I was here, in Azmeer, where all of this had started?

"Whatever happened to Yezed?" I asked though part of me wasn't sure I wanted to know.

"No one's sure," she placed her hands in her lap, "the days following your mother's departure, it was as if he seeped into madness. People claimed to see him pacing the corridors at all hours of the night, asking everyone if they had seen her, and then one day, he just disappeared. No one has any idea of his whereabouts or whether he's still alive. I suspect something might have happened to him. He didn't strike me as someone who could cope in such a state. To my knowledge, no one has seen him since."

"What did he look like?" I found myself asking, the question hanging in the air like a thick fog.

"His actual appearance was typical for members of the Court of Shadows. He had darker hair—auburn. He was tall, broad-shouldered, and undeniably handsome." A small smile played on her lips as she spoke, but it quickly faded, overshadowed by something deeper.

"What do you mean by 'his actual appearance'?" I pressed, feeling a chill creep up my spine.

Addie cleared her throat and shifted in her chair, her gaze growing distant. "It was rumored that he was a Shadow Stalker, which is why he was so close to the king."

"A Shadow Stalker?" The term felt foreign on my tongue, heavy with implications.

"I'm not familiar with that terminology, Addie."

"Likely because it's a rare gift," she explained. "Shadow Stalkers can step into the shadows of those they watch, essentially becoming that person..."

My heart raced as I connected the dots. "You mean they could manipulate their appearance to look like the person they stalked?"

She nodded. "It was a gift that, according to your mother, he seldom used. Only ever doing it at the behest of the king."

The idea of it—someone lurking in the shadows, stepping into my life, my very identity—was horrifying. I imagined it, someone slipping into my skin, my actions, my voice, becoming me. How could anyone trust their own reality? How had my mother known and lived with that knowledge? Did she ever wonder if she was speaking to Yezed or someone else he had copied?

As if sensing my thoughts, Addie replied, "Your mother trusted him. That was all I ever needed to know."

The weight of her words pressed down on me, each sentence peeling back another layer of my reality. Yezed's anguish and desperate search had driven him to madness. And my mother—she had left him behind, moved on to a new life, and never looked back.

A wave of emotions crashed over me, each thought more turbulent than the last. I felt lost in a tangled web of my family's secrets and the ghost of a man who had once meant everything to my mother.

The world felt like it was closing in around me. I could barely process the grief that swirled within me. My mother had a history that now felt like a secret I had been kept from. I struggled to comprehend the magnitude of what Addie had shared, the reality of my mother's life in Azmeer standing in stark contrast to the comforting, static image I had carried with me all these years.

"Why have you never told me this before?" I asked, my voice cracking. The question was a plea, a desperate attempt to understand why I'd been left in the dark about so much of my mother's life.

"I never thought it was my place to say," Addie said, her eyes filled with regret. She cupped my face, her thumb brushing away a tear I hadn't realized had fallen. "I assumed your father would have mentioned it at some point, but it seems his way of coping after she passed was to stop speaking of her. Frankly, it's an insult to your mother. Her praises should be sung daily. She wouldn't have wanted to be forgotten."

"I never forgot her, Addie," I said, the tears now flowing freely down my cheeks. But I'd been so caught up in trying not to disturb my father's grief that I let her memory slip away.

"I know, sweetheart." Addie's voice was the medicine to my wounded heart as she caressed my cheek. "And I'm sorry to tell you this way. I figured she would have shared her stories with you when you were older, but you were robbed of an incredible mother."

I nodded, sniffling as the full weight of her words settled over me. I had never pushed my father to talk about her. I had tried to respect his silence, but now I wondered if, in doing so, I had been complicit in letting her memory fade into obscurity. I had been afraid to confront his pain, but in doing so, I had ignored my own need to know, to understand, to connect with the mother I had lost.

Addie's gaze softened with sympathy. "Do you know if Yezed left any records about the time you and Mom were here?" I asked, my voice trembling with a mix of hope and desperation. The idea of finding something, anything, that could bridge the gap between my fragmented memories and the reality of my mother's past was almost too much to bear.

A small, wistful smile appeared on Addie's face. "I do not. The House of Shadows does not keep records like that in the library." Her words felt like a final blow, the last hope of finding a tangible connection to my mother slipping away.

I rose from the table, my legs trembling as if they might give way beneath me. The weight of the conversation, the revelations, was almost too much to bear. "Thank you for telling me," I said as I struggled to keep my composure.

Addie stood as well, pulling me into a tight embrace. "I'm so sorry, honey." When we parted, she cupped my face, her touch warm and steady, like she thought she could hold me together. "What did this man look like—the one who spoke to you at the ball?"

I swallowed hard, the memory resurfacing in sharp, unwelcome clarity. "He had dark hair, a beautiful face," I choked out, my voice breaking despite the practiced sarcasm I tried to wield as a shield. "Pretty standard for members of the Court of Shadows, it seems."

Addie nodded slowly, her lips pressing into a thoughtful line. "Likely a friend of Yezed's," she said, her voice low and distant, as though the words carried her somewhere far away. "Someone who had been introduced to your mother."

The warmth of her hug was a fleeting comfort, a temporary reprieve for the raw wound that had been opened inside me. I held onto her, trying to steady myself, but as I pulled away and left the library, the story of my mother, my father, and Yezed continued to swirl in my mind.

I wandered through the corridors, my thoughts a chaotic whirlpool of grief and confusion. The walls seemed to close in around me, and before I knew it, darkness had fallen. I found myself in an unfamiliar corridor, the moonlight casting eerie shadows across the floor. The garden beyond was bathed in a silver light, and I laughed as I saw the yellow blooms of the Larrea tridentata plant waiting ahead.

Of course, this would be when I'd find it.

The solitude of the garden was both a refuge and a torment. The moon hung low in the sky, its light reflecting off the still water of a small fountain. I felt drawn to it, as if it might hold the answers I was seeking. However, it rested as still as the mirrors outside of the House of Reflection. *What a day*. I thought as I rubbed my temple.

Before I could do anything else, a voice echoed from deeper under the canopy, "*Hello, Ilia.*"

CHAPTER
TWENTY-SIX

"As thrilling as it is to see you, I'm not sure you're supposed to be here." Dainan emerged from the shadows, his voice smooth as the moonlight that bathed the garden. The silver glow danced across the sharp lines of his features, emphasizing the coppery strands of his hair that shimmered like a flame in the night.

I knew he was right. The weight of Illerium's vague warning hung heavy in the back of my mind: "You never know what spot you might find yourself in, and I, for one, will not come to save you." I should have listened. After what I'd uncovered tonight, every cryptic caution felt less like idle chatter and more like a dire prediction.

"I'm not sure how I got here," I muttered, wrapping my arms around myself as if the gesture could somehow shield me from the uncertainty swirling in my chest. The air was thick with the scent of earth and flowers, but underneath it all, I could still smell the secrets this place seemed to hold.

Dainan took a few more steps forward, his presence both commanding and comforting as if he belonged in this mystical space. The scent of smoke and citrus surrounded him, weaving through the air like a warm embrace. It was oddly familiar, grounding, even as the world around us felt far from steady.

"What are you doing here?" I asked, breaking the silence before he could come too close. My voice sounded smaller than I intended, fragile and filled with an unsteady rhythm.

His brow arched, as if he hadn't expected me to question him. "I often come here," he said, his tone softening as he glanced around the moonlit garden. "It's not far from my quarters. Besides, there is a plant here that has always fascinated me."

"Larrea tridentata," I whispered, not realizing I'd spoken aloud until his gaze snapped back to mine, sharp with intrigue.

His eyes narrowed, the playfulness in them fading. "Now, how would you know about Larrea tridentata? To my knowledge, it only grows in Azmeer, and this, dear Ilia, is your first time visiting."

His words hung between us, a challenge, a subtle threat wrapped in curiosity. He folded his arms, studying me with a mixture of suspicion and something deeper—something that stirred a spark within me.

"How can you be so sure this is my first time in Azmeer?" I asked, raising my chin, trying to regain some sense of control over the strange energy thrumming between us.

Dainan's smile deepened, his eyes glittering with amusement as he stepped closer, the distance between us shrinking to nothing but a whisper of breath. "I would have known otherwise."

His words sent a shiver through me, and I found myself taking a step back, needing space, needing air. "I believe you're overestimating yourself," I retorted, though my voice wavered. I made my way toward a bench beneath a pomegranate tree, its branches heavy with ripening fruit. The leaves whispered secrets in the breeze, and the night air felt cool against my flushed skin.

To my surprise, Dainan laughed—a rich, warm sound that somehow felt out of place in the stillness of the garden. It tugged at something deep within me, something I wasn't sure I wanted to acknowledge, igniting an ember of warmth in my chest.

"And what, may I ask, is so funny?" I demanded, trying to keep my voice steady, but it wavered under the weight of his gaze.

"Your candor," he said, following me with graceful ease, his presence enveloping me like the shadows surrounding us. "It is refreshing to be reminded that I am more than a prince." He sat beside me on the bench, his movements fluid, as if he belonged in this realm of whispers and moonlight. "Do you care to share why you've wandered into my garden, Brida?"

The way he said my name—a lilt of amusement mixed with something almost tender—sent a flutter through my chest. His gaze held mine, a mix of flame and shadow, soothing yet unsettling, igniting a tension that crackled in the space between us.

Why had I wandered here? The question echoed in my mind, a ghostly refrain that refused to quiet. Addie's revelations had torn apart the image I'd held of my mother—of the woman I thought I knew so well. She'd lived two lives, one of which I was only now discovering, and my father had been complicit in keeping it all hidden from me. The weight of their silence pressed down on me, suffocating, leaving me lost in a sea of questions I didn't know how to answer.

"Ilia?" Dainan's voice was gentle, pulling me back from the edge of my thoughts.

"Sorry," I muttered, but the word felt hollow. A tear slipped down my cheek before I could stop it. The grief was sudden, overwhelming—the realization that I would never get the answers I needed from my mother, that soon, my father might be lost to me too, leaving me to navigate these treacherous waters alone.

"Ilia, what's wrong?" Dainan's voice was softer now, more insistent. Before I knew it, he'd closed the space between us again, his arm wrapping around my shoulders, pulling me into his warmth. For a moment, just a moment, I let myself lean into him, let myself feel the steadiness of his breath, the solid comfort of his embrace. The heat radiating from him seeped into my skin, wrapping around my heart like an unexpected balm.

His hand gently cupped my cheek, guiding my gaze back to his. His eyes, so often filled with fire and shadows, now held something gentler, something deeper. "Please, tell me," he whispered, his voice a soft breath against my lips, the intimacy of the moment stretching taut between us, daring to cross the invisible line that separated us.

"She was the light in my world, my beacon, my guiding post. And then, that light was gone. And for a long while, all that remained was darkness." *I am more than my fear; I am the story I choose to write,* I reminded myself. *I am...*

"Who was?" The light caress of Dainan's fingers against my jaw felt as inviting as an evening breeze, warm, tender, and soothing enough for me to rest there.

"My mother," was all I could say. As much as I wanted to talk about her, to share stories of how she'd danced around the kitchen every morning, or how when she was proud of you, you felt like the center of the world, as if you were the only person. Her loss felt like a void, and continues to feel like something is forever missing. Something I can never reclaim.

"I'm certain she was an extraordinary woman," Dainan murmured, his voice so soft it felt like it was meant to wrap around just the two of us. His eyes, dark and steady, lingered on mine, and for once, there was no teasing, no veiled humor—only quiet sincerity. "She would have to have been to have had you as her daughter."

The weight of his words settled into the space between us, tender and unyielding, as though he were stating a truth that had always existed. His hand, warm and steady, brushed the edge of mine, just enough to tether me to the moment.

"For only a woman of immense strength and unshakable fortitude," he continued, his voice dipping lower, almost reverent, "could have brought someone like you into this world."

I felt my chest tighten, an ache blooming where his words had taken root. There was no mockery in his tone, no embellishment. Just him, speaking as if he could see parts of me I hadn't dared to show anyone else.

"She would be so proud of you," he added, his voice laced with a quiet conviction that unraveled something deep within me. "Of everything you've done, everything you've fought for."

Would she? Forging an invitation, lying to be here... *I am more than my fear; I am the story I choose to write.*

"Brida, look at me." Dainan tilted my face towards his and I found myself drawn into the depths of his eyes. The darkness that lingered there mirrored my own, swirling like the shadows that enveloped us.

The intimacy of the moment—his closeness, the tenderness in his touch—made my heart ache. The shadows that usually clung to him now danced around us, less threatening, more like playful spirits in the night, amplifying the electric tension coiling in my gut. His words felt like a gentle caress, softening the sharp edges of my grief, coaxing a warmth I hadn't expected to feel. I tried to blink away the tears welling in my eyes, but the way he looked at me—with such unguarded tenderness—made it impossible to hold them back.

I let out a shaky breath, unable to find the words to match the intimacy of his. But in that moment, it didn't feel like I needed to. Dainan wasn't asking for anything in return; he wasn't trying to fill the silence or pry open the places I kept hidden.

"Today, I realized that the road to the past is one we can never walk again, no matter how much we wish it."

The light touch of Dainan's fingers grazing my cheek sent a shiver through me, a gentle current that I couldn't resist. My body betrayed me as I leaned into his touch, seeking more of the warmth he offered, more of the calm that seemed to radiate from him in a way that made my heart ache. For a moment, the storm inside me quieted, silenced by the tenderness of his gesture.

"You do not have to fight your battles alone, Brida," he murmured, his voice low and steady, a quiet promise that wrapped around me. His thumb brushed against my skin, a motion so deliberate and intimate it felt as though he could read the fractures in my soul. "There are those who will travel those peaks and valleys with you."

Without thinking, I reached for his hand, curling my fingers around his. His thumb traced a gentle circle over my skin, a silent reassurance, and I felt the lump in my throat dissolve just enough to whisper, "Thank you."

He tilted his head, an exasperated chuckle escaping him, an inviting warmth that made me want to stay. "And what exactly are you thanking me for?"

"For offering me a moment of peace when I needed it," I said, my voice soft as I glanced at him. My pulse quickened at the proximity of our bodies, a sensation that both thrilled and unnerved me. Rising slowly, I put a little distance between us, the space a necessary shield against the pull I felt toward him.

I kept my hands at my sides, fingers curling into my palms, grounding myself. His gaze lingered, heavy and unreadable, and for a moment, I swore he knew—knew how my resolve threatened to crumble under the weight of his presence. I swallowed hard, my breath uneven, as though the air had thickened around us. "I should go," I said, though the words felt hollow. I turned before I could see his reaction, afraid of what I might find—or worse, what I might not.

Before I could take another step, his voice stopped me. "What do you know about Larrea tridentata?" he asked, his tone curious but careful.

I turned back to the blooms, their yellow petals glowing in the moonlight. "It's a healer," I whispered, my fingers brushing one of the blossoms, a thrill sparking at the contact. "Used to treat respiratory issues, inflammation, skin problems...but only in small doses. It's potent, powerful."

Dainan's shadows shifted around him, swirling in the air like a low, soft hum. He stepped closer, plucking a few blooms and handing one to me, his fingers brushing mine, igniting a spark that traveled up my arm. "A token to remember our evening," he said, "or perhaps a reminder of what you aren't saying."

I took the bloom, tucking it carefully into my pocket, my mind heavy with the weight of everything left unspoken. "Thank you, Dainan," I whispered, my heart pulling me in two directions as I turned to leave.

CHAPTER
TWENTY-SEVEN

Hey Dad,
Not sure if the news has reached Escalia yet but there was a massive earthquake in Hadash. It happened just around the festival for Giaxia. Did you manage to go into town for the celebrations?
The feast here was unlike any we ever saw in Escalia, but they were never one to go all out for celebrations or much of anything!
It is a horrific event, and it has been terrible to hear about all of those affected. We're hoping the region will be able to recover as best they can. One of my friends here, yes friends, lost family members. We've been trying to comfort him as best we can.
Kadian has been keeping me company as always, and I've managed to make friends with a half-nymph, half-Fae girl that I met in line in Lesalia named Lil and twins from the Western Ridge named Oz and Tamra.
Azmeer has opened my eyes in ways I couldn't imagine. I wish I could share it with you.
Please be sure to continue with your teas, and keep me updated as to how you are feeling.
I'll write more soon.
Love you,

Bri

☽✳☾

The next few days passed in a bit of a blur. Marsh had sent me a letter explaining that he'd been summoned back to Hadash by Qurasa himself. There was no room for refusal. As I read his words, a pang of loneliness settled in my chest. I missed him—his steady presence, his understanding, the way I could be myself around him. He was the only one who knew the truth about why I was here and how I had come to be in this place. The only person who had seen beyond the mask I wore. Now, that connection felt distant, almost unreachable, leaving me adrift in a sea of uncertainty.

Illerium's lectures, however, offered a welcome distraction. They captivated me, each story more enthralling than the last. He spoke of the arrival of the Fae in Azmeer, painting a picture of a time long past when the world was new and raw. The reign of their first king, Loran, was a tale of glory and tragedy, of power struggles and wars. Humans, caught in the crossfire, established their own settlements, while nymphs and sirens retreated to the secluded corners of the continent. It took a millennium of negotiations, treaties, and fragile peace for us to stand here now, participating in the Courting.

When I asked Illerium about Lil, he told me that Thalius had requested her help with a special assignment, and while she would return when they were finished, there was no telling when that would be. Her absence left a noticeable void, most noticeable in Kadian, whose moods swung wildly. He had taken to retreating to his room after quick, solitary meals, avoiding Oz and me altogether. It was painful to watch, and the constant worry gnawed at me. Kadian, who had always been the steady one, the anchor for our little group, now seemed as adrift as I felt. The only thing that seemed to lift the fog around him was the thought of exploring Azmeer. He clung to the idea like a lifeline, hoping Lil would join us.

She had been the most enthusiastic about it from the start, and I couldn't help but hope for her return.

"If she isn't back, are you still wanting to go?" Oz asked over breakfast that morning; his voice tinged with concern as he glanced at Kadian's dark, sullen eyes. The weight of sleepless nights and restless thoughts had begun to show on him. He had taken up running at night, a way to burn off the frustration he felt building up inside. It wasn't like him, and it made my anxiety worse, the worry twisting tighter with every day that passed.

"I think getting out of here may do you some good," I said softly, placing my hand on Kadian's forearm, where it rested on the table. He barely acknowledged the touch, his gaze distant.

"Let's aim to leave around six," Oz suggested, "we can eat dinner here or find something when we're out. Tamra said she'll meet us at the bar. Iona's been saying there will be music tonight."

Music. I couldn't remember the last time we'd gone out just to listen to music. It felt like a lifetime ago.

As the day wore on and Lil remained absent, we agreed to meet in the atrium before heading out. Oz, Kadian, and I would grab dinner somewhere in the city. I chose not to wear a dress, opting instead for black high-waisted pants that flared at the bottom and a dark crimson long-sleeve shirt that accentuated my curves. The outfit was bold, something I never would have worn before coming to Azmeer, but I was becoming more comfortable in my own skin. I left my hair down, savoring the way it moved in the evening breeze that teased the city.

The excitement was palpable in the atrium. We had all valued the opportunity to participate in the Courting, but the chance to explore Azmeer itself had been a much-anticipated event. The city was an ancient enigma, steeped in secrets and mystery. Illerium had told us that Azmeer was called the First City, constructed after the establishment of the courts. Its origins dated back to a time when the world bore little resemblance to what we knew, a time when the Primals were said to have roamed.

As we descended the stairwell, I couldn't help but notice how the darkness of the courtyard gave way to the warm, inviting torchlight guiding our path through the gardens to the city gates. It was like stepping into another world. The city itself was alive, buzzing with energy as we entered the swarm of people beyond the palace walls.

"Where's everyone going?" Kadian asked, his voice tinged with curiosity, the first sign of life I'd heard from him in days.

"Likely a night market," Oz replied, glancing around, "we have them in Thredian."

"I didn't know Thredian was large enough for anything like this," I said, surprised.

"It's a bigger city. The largest in the West," he smiled, a touch of pride in his voice. "But we should move out of the middle of the street," he added, gesturing for us to follow him to the side.

"A night market sounds like a good place to grab some dinner," I suggested, feeling the pangs of hunger grow stronger.

Oz laughed, the sound deep and warm. "Definitely, and based on the amount of smoke in the air," he pointed east, "I'd venture a guess that it's that way."

"I'll let you lead," I said, falling into step behind him.

Kadian's face lit up with a smile, the most genuine one I'd seen in a week. It was as if the weight of his worries had lifted, even if just for a moment. I breathed a sigh of relief, thankful that this little adventure was doing him some good.

The streets of Azmeer were unlike anything I had ever seen before. The buildings were taller than those in Escalia, their terra-cotta and pale clay exteriors designed to combat the intense summer heat. The roofs were tiled, curving like the waves of the sea if you squinted just right. It was enchanting, each corner of the city revealing something new, something I had never experienced before.

Vendors lined the streets, selling everything from beautiful colored glass lanterns to fine woven rugs. Even though this was a place of commerce, it felt more like a gathering of friends. Vendors greeted each other with kisses on the cheeks, shook hands, and picked up the babies of their patrons. There was a warmth here, a connection that made my heart swell.

The smells were intoxicating—roasted meats, pastries, and a rich, smoky aroma that made me wish I had more room in my stomach. "What're we in the mood for?" Oz asked.

"Anything," Kadian replied, his grin wide and genuine. There he was—my friend, coming back to life.

"That's my vote," I pointed across the square to a stall that seemed to offer fried food and roasted meat on a spit.

"Done," Kadian said with a grin, taking off towards it.

Melodies filled the square as street musicians set up their instruments and rugs, creating a symphony of sound that blended with the laughter and chatter of the crowd. I couldn't help but sway to the music as we sat on a bench, enjoying our dinner. In that moment, I was absorbed in the scene around me, and for the first time in months, my mind was quiet and at peace.

I savored every single bite, the flavors dancing on my tongue, each morsel a revelation of Azmeer's culinary delights. I even went as far as to lick my fingers, unable to resist the lingering traces of the savory feast. When I looked over at my friends, I saw that their faces mirrored my own contentment.

As the last remnants of our meal were devoured, I stood up, drawn irresistibly by the sound of music that drifted through the air. My feet carried me towards a man sitting on a deep red, orange, and crimson rug, strumming a guitar and singing with a soul-deep passion. His voice wove a spell, pulling me into the heart of the melody:

In a realm where the stars meet the sea
The Goddess weeps, her sorrow free
In tears she mourns, a love so rare
A bond that shook the world, beyond compare

Lost in the lyrics, I watched as he played, his eyes closed, immersed in his performance. The guitar strings seemed to echo the very pain and longing described in the song:

Through realms of time, her cries resound,
A love so pure, now underground
The heavens weep, the earth below
For love's departure brings endless woe

In shadows cast by love's cruel flight,
The goddess mourns throughout the night.
From depths of grief, a glimmer gleams,
Love's lost embrace, now in her dreams.

As the song neared its end, the singer opened his eyes and locked his gaze with the crowd. His eyes, a captivating blend of yellow and brown, held a story of their own. He sang with a fervor that seemed to resonate with the very core of our beings:

Through endless cycles, the world reborn
The goddess finds her love, no longer torn
In fiery light, their souls entwine
The Mates reunion, an eternal sign

The crowd erupted into applause and cheers as the performer took a bow, placing his right hand over his heart. He set his hat near his feet, and people began to drop coins into it, many of them moving forward to express their appreciation. I stepped up and tossed a few silver coins into the hat, feeling compelled to reward such a beautiful performance.

"Did you like it?" I heard his smooth voice ask as I approached.

"It was enchanting," I replied, a smile brushing my lips. "I've never heard anything quite like it."

He took a seat on his stool, his eyebrow quirked in curiosity. "You've not heard that song before? It's a tale as old as time, a tale older than Azmeer itself," he said as he put down his guitar. "And yet, you have not heard it?"

I shook my head, slipping my hands into my pockets. "No, I haven't."

"Where are you from?" he asked, his accent unfamiliar but intriguing.

"Escalia," I answered.

"Ah," he clicked his tongue. "It's no wonder then that you've not heard that song." He bent down to pick up a glass of water.

"You're familiar with Escalia?" I was surprised; few people had even heard of it.

He smirked. "I've been there once or twice." His eyes remained fixed on mine, their gaze warm and knowing. "What did you like about the song?"

I hesitated. "I...I'm not sure," I admitted.

"It clearly evoked some emotion from you, my dear," he said, pointing to my cheek.

I touched my cheeks and realized they were damp. I had been crying without even realizing it.

"It's a song that can bring out the deepest of emotions, well, for anyone who has known and suffered a great loss." His eyes held a shared understanding.

I nodded, wiping away a stray tear. "Is the song about Giaxia?"

A hint of amusement danced across his face. "Of course not," he leaned in closer. "It's about Vasenia." He set down his glass and picked up his guitar once more. "Should you have any more questions or wish to hear more tales, do find me again," he said, his voice warm as he began to play once more.

They say she was the herald of light
A Dawn awaiting her Dusk...

The crowd gathered around him again, swept up by the allure of the music. I found myself pushed by the flow of the masses, so I retreated to where Oz and Kadian were standing.

"You okay?" they asked as I approached.

"I'm fine," I said with a smile. "It was just a beautiful song." I glanced at them both. "Speaking of music," I said, weaving my arms through theirs, "shall we go listen to some more and maybe get a few drinks?"

"You?" Kadian raised an eyebrow. "A few? If that's the case, prepare yourself, Oz. We're in for quite a night."

"I'm not making any promises," I teased back.

Their voices became a distant murmur as my mind wandered. Why had the singer invited me to speak with him again? Why had he visited Escalia? And why was the song that seemed to tell the story of Giaxia and Ollo not about them at all, but about Vasenia?

My thoughts drifted away as we entered the bar, a vibrant, crowded place that promised the excitement we craved. It was nothing like the quaint local pub Kadian and I frequented. This bar had a rustic charm but with a touch of refinement. I left the boys at a standing table and made my way through the sticky floor to the bar.

It was peaceful. The most peaceful the night was going to get.

CHAPTER
TWENTY-EIGHT

The light flickering from the lanterns inside was dim, further adding to the atmosphere. It felt as if this was a place that had withstood the tests of time, all the while maintaining a mysteriousness and charm.

Musicians were set off to the back left side of the room, while on the right side, there was a dance floor. A few couples and friends were dancing to an upbeat song while the rest of the crowd stood at tabletops or barrels used as tables for the night. I didn't recognize the song being played, but I was tapping my foot along to the rhythm.

The crowd was alive, full of the hopefuls from Azmeer in addition to the locals of the town surrounding the blush stone gates. I found myself entranced by them. Never had I seen such an array of people, outside of the palace itself. While university had been a change, it had been made up of locals, humans, and the only times I'd ventured from the library had been when Kadian dragged me out.

"Your drinks, miss." I thanked the barkeep and brought the drinks back to Oz and Kadian.

"Here's to..." Oz paused, "*feeling good,*" he elongated his words, and I couldn't help but smile. Kadian's complexion appeared healthier than it had in a week as he took a sip. A hint of color graced his cheeks, though it was difficult to determine if that was from the ale or the crowd growing inside.

Over the next couple of hours, we shared stories. We learned of when Oz and Tamra got separated from their parents in Samina, a town near Hadash while visiting the Eternal Court.

"I didn't think they were ever going to find us. One second, we were in the middle of this market," I knew he was starting to feel the effects of his drink because his gestures had become bigger with each story he told. "And then all of a sudden, this sheet was pulled back from the cart, and there they were! It was crazy."

"It wasn't that crazy," Tamra said as she arrived and put her hand on her brother's shoulder. "Somebody thought it would be funny to try to get our parents' attention by making them think that they lost us when in reality, we hid in a merchant cart next to where they were standing," she raised her eyebrows at her brother, "not one of your better ideas."

"I didn't hear you offering anything better at the time," he looked back at her as if she had ruined the story.

"Well, how about I offer something now, a round on me?" She smiled at us. The guys cheered, and I mouthed to her that I was good with the one I had.

The noise continued to escalate, with the music adopting a more sensual tone to complement the flow of conversation. All while smoke billowed from the corners of the room, adding to the haziness of the atmosphere.

"It's pucchia," Tamra told us when she arrived with our drinks. Her arrival without Isidra didn't go unnoticed by anyone. When prodded about it, her response was curt. "I didn't ask her, nor is it any of your business, Osforth."

"You wound me, sister," he exclaimed, placing his hand over his heart, feigning a dramatic fall.

"What's pucchia?" I asked, trying to switch the conversation from Tamra.

"It's a plant that grows just outside the walls of Azmeer; it helps...*relax* you." She smiled.

"Have you tried it before?"

She nodded and made her way closer to me while the boys compared notes on which of the ales they liked best thus far. "I've found it helpful during trying times in my life. Not to say that my parents haven't always been supportive, because they have, but..." she took a sip of her drink, "sometimes we're hardest on ourselves."

I laid my hand over hers and gave it a squeeze. Her eyes found mine, and for a moment, we understood each other.

Tamra and I became swept up in stories of where we grew up. I loved getting to know her more. Despite her and Oz being twins, the two of them couldn't have been more different. It wasn't that Oz wasn't thoughtful and well-meaning, he was. He was also offbeat and charming. Tamra was more grounded, a bit more serious, but still warm.

By the time the boys had gone on to their fifth round of drinks, they'd forgotten about my earlier statement as I continued to sip my very first one. Despite only having one drink, I was feeling lighter and warm. I couldn't tell if it was due to the number of people that had found themselves inside, if it was the drink I had been sipping on, or something else, but I was beginning to feel flushed.

"I'm going to get another drink," I said to the group. Their faces appeared pleased at this notion. However, they didn't know that I intended to ask for shaved ice in an attempt to cool down. I made my way to the bar, hearing snippets of conversations along the way.

"It's all those kids from up at the palace. Seems like they let them out," a man grumbled to a woman that I assumed was his date.

"I invited him, but who knows if he'll show," I thought I heard Iona say as one of her friends handed her some pucchia. She'd glared at me when I entered, but I pretended not to notice. Whatever her issue with me was, I had no desire to uncover it. It was easier, safer, to keep my distance.

The song changed, the tempo more upbeat, this was one Kadian and I were familiar with. Locking eyes across the room, I inclined my head toward the dance floor. He flashed a tight-lipped smile, persuading Oz and Tamra to join us and ushered them toward the back of the room.

I finished my drink, and twirled myself, arms in the air as I walked to join them. Gods, it felt so good to just get lost in rhythm and feeling. Nothing mattered but the beat of the song and how we all came together to enjoy the music. The first song, we all danced together. Everyone clasping hands at one point or another, spinning the other, immersing themselves in the experience. It felt as if a smile had permanently etched itself on my face. Laughing filled my ears, and for a moment, I thought of Lil and how much she would have loved this.

By the third song, the musicians had continued to play with an upbeat tempo but had encouraged everyone to find a partner. Tamra was joined by a slender woman with black hair who had been watching her from the bar.

"It's time to determine once and for all which of the ales is superior." Kadian smacked Oz on the back as they exited the floor.

I chose to stay by myself, continuing to sway to the music. The haze of smoke made it rather difficult to see, and to the majority of the people in the room, it looked as if I'd found someone to join me. I knew this ballad and the beat of the drums had always been one of my favorites. It would be soft for a three-count and then crescendo. When with a partner, it was the perfect song to time the movement of one's hips and just get lost in the feel of the song and each other.

I closed my eyes and allowed myself to be transported. The bar smelled of ale when we arrived but it now smelled of smoke with cinnamon. With each breath I took, it felt as if the stressors of the past few days had begun to erase themselves from my mind.

Gods, I felt like I was floating in the middle of the room.

The lights grew dimmer as the evening progressed, and with the smoke and the ever-growing crowd, it had become dark inside. You could hardly make out someone's face unless they were close enough to stand within arm's reach. I savored this time alone, relishing the rare chance to feel free.

I saw Tamra and the woman she'd been dancing with exit the dance floor. She was leading Tamra to one of the back corners. It was only then I noticed it seemed that the darkness was moving, it was not steady or solid. Moments later, it appeared as if it began to slither and creep along floorboards before stopping at my feet.

Shadows swirled and rose around me, as if following the cadence of the song. I leaned out and touched it, drawn to it in a way I couldn't explain. I could've sworn I heard the shadows laugh. The thrumming in my body only grew as the smell of smoke permeated my senses. I continued to spin in circles, letting the music consume me, captivated by its melody so much that I didn't care when I became encircled in darkness.

I stood still for a moment in my cocoon of shadow. It was an odd sensation, but I was unafraid, knowing it wouldn't harm me. It was silent. I somehow managed to forget that mere feet from me, music continued to blare, and I was surrounded by blissfully drunk dancing fools. None of that mattered; all that mattered was what had enshrouded itself around me.

As if from nowhere, two glimmering eyes appeared in the darkness, reminding me of the shadow figure during the trial. They looked me up and down before a man emerged from the shadow. Dainan. I wondered if he'd been watching me from the shadows in the corner and, if so, for how long. *Was he the one Iona had invited? Was that why he was here?*

"Do you often dance alone?" His voice was sultry, like molten honey, as if every word dripped directly into my ear, teasing my senses. His arms folded across his chest, and I was acutely aware of every line and ripple of muscle beneath his sleeveless tunic. It was as if he had been sculpted by the gods themselves, a masterpiece of strength and beauty. The space between us seemed to shrink with every heartbeat.

His scent—smoke and citrus—overwhelmed any rational

thought. My body responded without hesitation, a silent hum of anticipation buzzing through my veins. I wanted to move closer, to close the inches that separated us, and feel the press of his skin against mine. Words barely formed on my lips as I fought the pull of his gaze, but it was futile. I couldn't resist.

"Not always," I managed, my voice a breathy whisper, taking a step toward him. The air between us crackled with tension, our bodies nearly touching.

A flicker of surprise lit his eyes, his body going rigid for a moment before softening into something more primal—curiosity, excitement, desire. His gaze traveled the length of me as if considering how far I'd take this.

I reached out, placing my hand on his chest, feeling the steady rhythm of his heart beneath my fingers. My palm slid down his torso, tracing the hard planes of his stomach before halting just above the waistband of his pants. "Do you dance, Lord of Shadows?" My voice was bold, dripping with challenge, despite the storm of emotion building inside me.

His grin turned wicked, a predator's smile. In one swift movement, he was behind me, his breath hot against my neck, lips grazing the sensitive skin there. "Only when I find a worthy partner," he purred, his words vibrating through me, igniting a fire deep within my core. His hands slid around my waist, pulling me closer until there was no space left between us, his body pressing against mine.

"Will you dance with me, Ilia?" His voice, so close, sent shivers down my spine as his fingers brushed the curve of my abdomen, teasing, waiting for my permission.

"Yes," the word left my lips in a moan, my body arching into him, already pliant, already surrendering to the sensation of his touch. His right hand tightened its grip around my waist, his strength palpable, while his left hand explored the lines of my body with slow, deliberate strokes as if savoring every inch.

The shadows fell away from us, revealing other dancers lost in the rhythm of the music, but they were nothing more than a blur in my peripheral vision. All that existed was him. His hips moved with mine, grinding, swaying in perfect harmony. We fit together effortlessly, our bodies speaking a language more ancient than words.

Dainan's breath was at my neck again, his lips grazing the tender spot below my ear. Each exhale sent electric waves through me. *Gods,* I thought, the warmth of him unbearable, the need overwhelming.

"Is this how you like it, Ilia?" His question was a tease, his lips moving against my skin, leaving me breathless.

I couldn't answer, couldn't think beyond the feel of his hands on my body. My hand pressed against his, guiding it lower, urging him on, and when he let his fingers brush the top of my pants, I gasped, arching into his touch, craving more.

I slid down his body as the tempo of the music slowed, the feel of him hard and unyielding against my back. As I rose again, my hips pressed into him, dragging slowly upward, I stole a glance over my shoulder. His expression was predatory, eyes dark and heavy with want.

"If you do that again, Ilia," he growled, his voice rough, "I can't promise I'll behave."

"No one's asking you to," I whispered, heat surging through me as I lost myself in the rhythm again, my body moving with his. Every thought, every worry melted away, leaving only the sensation of him behind me, his hands on my skin, the music wrapping around us.

I turned to face him, the space between us vanishing. My hand slipped behind his neck, pulling his face closer to mine. His touch was fire, each brush of his fingers down my spine sending sparks through my veins, igniting something primal. His control was slipping, I could feel it in the way his eyes blazed red and gold, like a fire barely contained.

"Stop toying with me," I murmured, my breath mingling with his, lips so close I could almost taste him.

His gaze locked onto mine, dark, intense. "How am I toying with *you?*"

"You know very well, my prince," I whispered, my voice thick with need as I guided his hand lower. He grabbed me, pulling me hard against him, and I gasped at the feel of his body pressed to mine, every inch of him taut with restraint.

Our mouths hovered, lips brushing as if testing the limit of self-control. I felt his breath on my lips, my heart pounding in my chest. He was holding back, but I could feel his desire in every line of his body.

His lips were so close, a hair's breadth away from mine, and the tension between us was unbearable. Every breath we shared felt like a spark, and my heart pounded in my chest, each beat echoing my need for him.

"Bring the shadows up," I whispered, my voice thick with desire, but he didn't move. Instead, he studied me, his eyes burning with restraint.

"Brida..." His voice was low, rough with need. He wanted this as much as I did—I could feel it in the way his body tensed, the way his grip on me tightened—but still, he held back.

I couldn't wait any longer.

In one swift motion, I closed the space between us, pressing my lips to his, igniting the fire that had been simmering between us all night. The kiss was explosive, a clash of need and hunger. He pulled me against him as his mouth moved against mine, fierce and unrelenting.

It wasn't soft, it wasn't tentative— we had been holding back for far too long, and now, neither of us could stop. His lips devoured mine, hot and fevered, and I responded with equal fervor, pouring all of my want into the kiss.

I felt his hand slide into my hair, his fingers tangling in it as he tilted my head, deepening the kiss. His other hand gripped my waist, holding me against him as if he couldn't bear for there to be any space between us.

The feel of him, the taste of him—salt, smoke, and something wild—sent a shiver down my spine, and I pressed myself even closer, desperate for more. My hands roamed over his chest, feeling his hard muscles, and a soft moan escaped my lips, swallowed by the heat of his kiss.

His mouth was everywhere—my lips, my jaw, the sensitive spot on my neck—and each touch ignited me further. I could feel his breath, ragged and shallow, against my skin, and it only fueled my desire. I kissed him back with an urgency I had never known, giving in completely to the moment, to him.

"Gods," I whispered against his lips, my voice breathless, my heart racing.

Dainan growled low in his throat, the sound vibrating through me, and before I could react, he spun me around and slammed me against the wall. His hands were on either side of me, caging me in, and I was completely at his mercy.

His lips moved down my neck, and I gasped, my body arching into him as his mouth left a trail of heat along my skin. His shadows danced around us, curling and swirling in time with the frenzy of our kiss, sealing us off from the rest of the world.

There was nothing else but him. Nothing else but this moment.

I cupped his face, bringing his lips back to mine, the kiss now slower, more deliberate, but still filled with the same urgency. Every movement was a promise, a wordless declaration of desire.

"I want you," I whispered against his lips, my voice trembling with need.

His eyes, dark and filled with longing, met mine for a brief second before his lips crashed back down, sealing my words with another kiss that left me dizzy and breathless.

"Fuck," he hissed as I moved against him, the friction between us exquisite, unbearable. His control was hanging by a thread, and the sound of his groan made me smile, knowing I was driving him to the edge.

"This is not what you want, Ilia," I heard him say in a pained voice.

He's out of his mind; this is the only thing I want.

"This is exactly what I want. What I *need*," I breathed, leaning in to lick the nape of his neck, tasting salt and smoke on his skin. The sound that escaped him was a low, guttural groan, raw with pleasure.

But then, his voice cut through the haze. "Ilia, as much as I wish to believe that you want this, want me," he gestured between us, his voice steadying. "It's the pucchia. It's making you feel this way."

The pucchia? I blinked, the fog in my mind clearing just a little. *What?* Tamra had mentioned it, but...I hadn't been smoking. I hadn't touched the stuff.

But the smoke.

It hit me all at once. The smoke in the room, the heat of the dancing, the drinks. My head swam, and suddenly, I was stumbling, the weight of the realization crashing down on me.

A flash of horror crossed my face. I hadn't been thinking straight. Everything I had been feeling—the overwhelming desire, the need to touch him, to claim him—the pucchia had amplified it. And he had known.

Oh gods.

"When you decide you do want me," he said, his voice low and full of that same wicked charm, "and you *will*," he pulled me just a little closer, his eyes gleaming with mischief. "I want you to be in your right mind. And not be concerned with...another."

With another? My heart sank. Marsh.

My mind raced. I pulled my hand from his, feeling the heat drain from my body. The dance floor was empty now, just the two of us alone in the fading shadows.

As we stepped back into the light, my eyes fell on them—Kadian, Oz, both staring, mouths open. And there, by the bar.

Marsh.

My stomach dropped. *Oh gods. What is he doing here? What had he seen?* His eyes were locked on me, dark, angry, seething with something that cut through the air between us like a blade.

I felt the blood drain from my face. How much had he seen? The kiss? Me licking Dainan's neck? Had I done that?

Before I could move, before I could even breathe, Dainan's arm wrapped around me again, pulling me close. "Take a breath," he whispered, his voice smooth, dangerous. And then, darkness. Shadows wrapped around us, suffocating me in their grip. I tried to speak, to pull away, but I couldn't. It was like being swallowed whole, every sense dulled by the swirling blackness.

When the world reappeared, I was coughing, doubled over in front of my bedroom door.

"Did you just—" I sputtered between coughs. "Did you *shadow-step* us here?"

"I did," he said as if it was the most normal thing in the world.

The anger hit me like a bolt of lightning, sudden and blinding. "Why did you do that?"

"We had a nice time," he said, his voice laced with amusement. "I only thought it appropriate to see you home." His lips curled into that infuriatingly calm smile.

"That's a lie," I growled, stepping toward him, my hands trembling with fury. "You did it because you saw Marsh. You didn't want him taking me home. What kind of game is this to you?"

His expression darkened, his voice dropping low. "This is no game."

I could barely comprehend the words. "You're *angry*? After what you just did?" I laughed, but it was hollow, full of disbelief.

"I didn't do anything, Ilia," he snapped, his voice sharper. "If anything, I was the one with *self-control*." He paused, his eyes raking over me. "It's a good thing, too, because you would have done anything I asked of you on that dance floor."

"You felt threatened because of Marsh? What are you, some kind of animal, claiming territory?"

Dainan's smirk returned. "Pucchia doesn't lie, Ilia. It reveals what's already there. Your desires. Your *true* desires, Ilia. I could smell those desires on you tonight."

His words cut deep, a mixture of truth and cruelty that made my blood boil.

"Don't call me that," It angered me that he was right. I'd wanted him, and somehow, he'd been able to smell it on me. *Betrayed by my own body. Lovely.*

He smirked and closed the distance between us with another step. We were inches apart, and the scent of him was just as alluring without the pucchia in the air.

Fuck.

I heard a low chuckle rumble in his chest as if he knew what I was thinking. "I think you may need to spend some time reflecting on what exactly it is *you* want, Ilia. When you're ready, I'll be waiting."

"Why did you come out tonight?" I demanded, but before I knew it, my back was pressed against the wall with Dainan looming over me.

"An intriguing question, indeed," he murmured, pressing his lips to the nape of my neck once more. "As I said, I'll be waiting."

And just like that, the shadows enshrouded him once more, and he vanished.

CHAPTER TWENTY-NINE

The night had been restless, with me tossing and turning, drifting in and out of dreams where I found myself with Marsh, then Dainan. In each dream, just as I attempted to speak to Marsh, I would awaken, feeling more exhausted than before.

Was it just the night before I was walking through the streets of Azmeer, eating one of the best meals of my life? I never got the musician's name. Not that it mattered. The likelihood of my seeing him again was non-existent.

I sat down at one of the long tables, sighing as I took a sip of my coffee. The steam rushed up to meet my face.

"You've looked better," Tamra smirked, sitting across from me.

"I've felt better," I lifted my eyes to meet hers, a beautiful amber with onyx.

"*So,*" she took a bite of her oatmeal, "did you have fun last night?"

"For a while."

She grinned, "Color me surprised when I returned to dance with Amera, and I see you, surrounded by shadows. Dancing as if your life depended on it," she laughed.

I shuffled as if the bench beneath me were on fire. I hadn't thought of how it appeared to anyone other than Marsh. Everyone there who was from the palace would have seen us.

If you're not careful, you might give the impression that you're here for titles, like princess or queen, rather than focusing on earning your place in the courts. Keep a safe distance. Lil had tried to warn me, and I'd been foolish not to listen.

I tried to sink lower to hide myself, but there was no point.

"Even though he's not my type, I can see the appeal." Tamra chuckled.

Gods, she's as bad as Lil.

"I have no idea what you are talking about," was all I could muster while taking another bite of toast.

"As much as I'd love to believe that, a word of advice," she leaned in closer, "stay clear of Iona. I overheard her on the walk back. She invited Dainan to the bar last night, and when she saw the two of you," Tamra grimaced, "well, let's just say that she was *pretty* pissed. So, best to avoid her for now."

"How's it my fault? It's not as if I told him to come use his shadows around me and force me into dancing with him."

Tamra was trying not to laugh, "*Oh,* is *that* what happened?"

"Ugh," I groaned as I slammed my head into my arms on the table to hide myself from the world. "No. That's not what happened." As much as I wanted to blame someone other than myself, I was at fault. I'd approached Dainan on the dance floor, encouraged him, and kissed him. *Gods, that kiss.*

"Thank you," I muttered, "if I see her, I'll walk the other way."

"Good girl." Tamra patted my arm, all the while stealing one of my pieces of toast.

"Remind me," I lifted my head to look at her, "if we're ever in a place where pucchia is in the air again, to get out."

She laughed now, "Don't get too down on yourself for having a good time. Everyone deserves to let loose every now and then.

Besides, they say pucchia just encourages you to do things you'd already consider doing."

"So I've been told," I muttered under my breath.

"Did you end up seeing the Wind Walker again last night?" She asked, leaning on the table.

I shook my head. "I hoped he would've stopped by or sent me a message, but I've heard nothing. It was a good thing; I had no idea what I would say to him." I owed him an explanation, an apology, something.

"You seemed to have quite the time last night," I said, attempting to steer the conversation in a different direction.

Tamra sighed, "You know what? I really did."

We continued to chat over the remainder of our breakfast until the boys showed up, and Tamra decided she couldn't bear listening to their arguments over who felt worse. "Suits you both right for trying to drink the bar dry," she rose to leave.

"See you later," I told her, and she nodded back.

Despite how I was feeling, I chose to run while the boys strolled around the track. Marsh didn't join me, nor was he anywhere to be seen.

As the hour was coming to a close, Oz decided to go find Tamra, and I slowed to talk with Kadian.

"How are you feeling today?" His color had left him again.

"I'm doing okay," he forced a smile at me, arms dangling by his sides. He looked weaker somehow despite still appearing muscular and fit. I couldn't put my finger on it.

"I never got a chance to ask you," he began to say. "What did you see in the Mirrors of Reflection the other day?" A look of genuine curiosity furrowed his brow. "Or are you keeping that secret too, like what you offered Giaxia?"

"It's not a terrible thing for a lady to have a few secrets."

"You and I both know that you don't consider yourself a *lady*," he laughed, "as a matter of fact," he put his arm around my shoulders, "I recall you refusing to attend the annual tea because you deemed it sexist that men weren't invited."

"It was sexist. Who's to say who can enjoy tea? I mean, I don't really like tea, but that's beside the point," I said while smiling at him. "Fine," I sighed, chuckling all the while. "If you must know what I saw, prepare to be disappointed."

He looked confused.

"I saw nothing," I stopped walking and faced him.

"Nothing?"

I nodded as I folded my arms across my chest. I'd tried not to think about it much. Every time I did, I found myself fearing what it meant. "I stood there for several minutes, and it looked at one point as if the water was beginning to ripple and that an image may appear, but all I saw was the reflection of the columns by the doorway."

"I thought it either had to show you what you feared or desired and based on last night," he folded his arms back at me and raised an eyebrow, "it definitely seems like there is someone you desire. Maybe someones, if we're counting the blonde, that is."

"I'm not having *that* conversation right now." I started walking once more

"Why do you think it chose not to show you anything?" He caught up, walking beside me.

"I'm not sure. Maybe because...I don't know what it is I fear or desire right now? I know I'm happy to be here despite being nervous at the beginning."

He had no idea just how nervous.

"All I know is that I want this." And I did. I knew I wanted to be here, not only for my father but for me. I'd found a place, people who mattered to me, and I them, despite the confusion surrounding my feelings, I knew Azmeer is where I wanted, needed to be.

“Still, it’s strange that you saw nothing.” He didn’t say anything else about it, and we walked the next few laps in silence.

“What did you see?” I asked.

“Lil,” was all he said as we made our way inside.

CHAPTER THIRTY

"Over the course of the next week, each of you will be informed of your placements for where you will work while in Azmeer." Illerium said, "Some of you have been requested, while others I have placed in the houses where I believe you will have the best chance of success. If one or more courts have expressed interest in you, you'll be informed. You're required to tell me of your final decision by the end of the week. In addition to the Houses, the library may offer you a placement. Often, the scribes pull from the candidates."

Marsh hadn't been with Illerium this afternoon. It seemed as if he was avoiding me, and I couldn't blame him. I would have kept my distance if I had been in his position. I felt terrible and found myself missing him.

"Can we request a specific placement if we feel we would do best there, Magister Illerium?" A boy named Thoren asked.

"You may not." He turned his back to us and, with that, dismissed us for the day.

"Any idea how we're to be informed over said *placements*?" Oz asked, looking between Kadian and I as if we would know.

I hoped it would arrive in the form of a letter and not something more dubious and mysterious.

That evening, I decided to go to the pool on the off chance that I might spot Lil. I didn't think Thalius was a lounge-by-the-pool kind of man, but my understanding was that members of the Court of Reflection wanted or needed to be in water every so often. It was possible he was going at off hours to avoid having to speak to those he deemed lesser, which, if my assessment of him was correct, was everyone.

I sat my towel down on one of the chairs and made my way to the stairs that lowered into the temperate water.

I'd never been a great swimmer but decided that I wanted to give it an honest attempt. Submerging myself in the water, I pushed off the bottom, propelling myself forward, slicing through the water with determined strokes. My legs were kicking behind me, forming small splashes. I was making a decent pace.

I soon found I had tuned out the sounds of those chatting; there was an echo and loud reverberation within these walls. I focused on my heartbeat and my breath. *This is just as meditative as running.* No one stopped or spoke to me for the hour or so that I swam. I became lost in my thoughts, what I would say to Marsh, to Lil, Kadian, and the placement I hoped for.

After my cooldown, I decided to go sit in the smallest pool for a few minutes. Closing my eyes, I was brought out of my haze when the splashing of a man joining me grazed my skin.

"You've been here before?" A golden-haired man asked, sitting down. His blue eyes shone as the light hit them. It was like staring into the sea. They were breathtaking.

"A few times," I nodded, but my voice felt hollow like it was slipping out of my control.

His gaze slid over me, too casual for the weight of the question that came next. "I take it you're not familiar with the Court of Reflection?" He rested his arms on the edge of the pool, leaning his head back as if we were talking about something trivial.

I shifted, the water lapping against my skin. "What makes you say that?" My voice was steadier than I felt. I sat up straighter like I could somehow hide my nerves behind perfect posture.

"Your hair, your eyes, your ears." He smiled, a knowing curl at the edge of his lips. "My intuition is telling me you're human, and if there's any part of you that's not, it's tied to the Court of Shadows. Your hair stands out in a place like this." His hand gestured to the room around us.

I wanted to laugh it off, but a coil of tension twisted in my stomach. *Why was he paying so much attention to me?* "You're right, I'm human." The words felt like an admission I didn't want to make. "I don't know much about the Court of Reflection, but I was hoping to run into a friend of mine here. I haven't seen her in a while."

"A lover?" His eyebrows raised, his tone light.

I couldn't help the laugh that escaped me, but even as it bubbled up, it felt wrong, out of place.

"No, just a good friend."

He closed his eyes, a soft sigh escaping his lips. "Pity."

The silence between us stretched thin, and I fought the urge to fill it with meaningless words. I wasn't sure why, but I could feel my skin prickling like there was something unsaid beneath his questions, something I wasn't catching. Before I could piece it together, he asked, "What's their name? Perhaps I know where they are."

"Lil," I said. "Lil Towler."

He mouthed the name to himself, not quite speaking. The sight of it made my chest tighten. *Why did this feel so wrong?* "Do you mean Lilianna Towler? Niece of Thalius Towler?" His head turned slightly toward me, the sudden shift in his demeanor making my pulse quicken.

"Yes, but she hates Lilianna. We call her Lil." I could feel my heart thudding in my chest now, louder than the soft echo of water around us.

He laughed, but it wasn't comforting. "Yes, I know her. Feisty little thing. Always has been. What would you expect from those bloodlines? Her mother is something else. You'd never guess she is a water nymph." He leaned back again, more relaxed, but I couldn't follow his lead. "Last I heard, she was working with her uncle on a deal between His Majesty and the Court of Reflection."

My chest tightened. *A deal? With the royal family?* A knot of dread settled low in my stomach. *Was she working with Rai?* The question pushed its way through my mind, uninvited and unrelenting.

"Do you know if she's working with the king?" I asked, trying to keep my voice even though the effort made my throat ache.

"Don't be daft," he said, the sharpness of his words cutting through my fragile composure. "The king? Have you seen him? He's barely clinging to life, let alone making deals. He looks as poor as the lands just beyond Azmeer; he's dying and in no state to mediate an arrangement between anyone."

"Is Azmeer not thriving?" I began, considering what we had witnessed in the night market. But how much did we know about Azmeer? We'd seen what we had been permitted to see.

He inched himself closer to me, "Azmeer is dying," he said almost in a whisper.

"Dying..." I found myself repeating

He nodded. "Few are aware of the severity of the situation, but it is growing more dire by the day. It's not just the king who is dying, but many think there is a connection."

"What's happening? To the land, I mean. What does it look like?" I asked, my voice shaken.

"Well," he sat upright once more, "it looks much like the king and some of the magistrates you may have seen wandering around the palace. It looks devoid of color as if life has been sucked," he pulled his arm back to mimic his words, "right from the soil itself. The food has already started to taint, and the water has begun to vanish. Those living in Azmeer thus far have remained protected, but those outside its walls," he clicked his tongue, "a misery worse than death awaits that sorry lot."

"And no one's doing anything about this? To stop it?" I found myself saying without thinking. It was as if the connection between my mouth and brain had been severed. I didn't know this man, nor why he was telling me this.

"There are a few that are making inquiries; some are trying to use this to their advantage. Some believe," he ran his hand through his hair, "that when the courts stopped intermingling, meaning when the courts forbade marrying someone in a differing court, that magic began to change. You see, the courts infuse magic into the land. It's a give and take; magic always requires a balance."

Always requires a balance. Wait, did he say courts weren't allowed to intermarry?

"This is, of course, just conjecture but a deeply held belief by some. Now," he tilted his head towards me, "someone like Thalius, for example," he raised an eyebrow, glancing around to check for eavesdroppers, "is a staunch believer in this ideology. And with a new ruler ascending the throne, what better time to try to mend what is possibly broken by uniting the courts through marriage."

I thought I was going to be sick. "He's trying to marry Lil to one of the princes..." I began to say.

He nodded.

"Do you..." I paused, despite already knowing the answer to my question, but I felt compelled to ask, "Do you know which prince?"

"Rai," he said, moving further back from me once more.

I felt a hollow pit in my stomach.

"Thalius is brokering an arranged marriage between Lil and Rai. Without the king's consent?" I asked as the rage began to fill my voice. I couldn't tell if the heat from the pool or my anger was making me feel hotter.

He nodded once more.

"Who's authorizing this?"

"That I don't know. What is most interesting though, my dear, is that many believe it's not Rai that will ascend the throne but his brother."

"Which brother?" I asked.

"Ah, now that is a conversation for another day. I must be going," he rose from the pool, climbing the stairs. "If I were you, I would keep what we have discussed between us, and I would not seek out Lilianna again. Especially not while Thalius is around."

"What's your name?" I found myself standing. He'd told me so much, and I had no idea who he was.

"You may call me Thetius, Brida."

He began to walk away from me, "How do you know my name?"

"We've been watching." He didn't look back as he exited.

☽✳☾

When I arrived back at my room that night, I opened the door and found a black envelope lying on the floor. I bent down to pick it up and saw that it was closed with two wax seals. I broke them and retrieved the paper,

Brida Larrow,
You have been offered placement at the Library of Azmeer under the tutelage and guidance of Adriana Velin.
You have been offered placement at The House of Shadows at the request of Fayma Aliz.
Please inform your magister of your final decision.

I wondered if my invitation to the Court of Shadows was at the behest of Dainan, but told myself not to care. I was lucky in that I had a choice, one being a much safer option than the other. However, if the Court of Shadows was where I was offered my final placement, it wouldn't matter in the end.

I finished my letter to Dad, letting him know this bit of news and to tell him I would write once I'd made my final decision.

I crawled into bed that night and blew out the candles on my bedside tables, once again hoping to hear anything on the evening breeze.

Nothing came.

CHAPTER
THIRTY-ONE

Hey Dad,
There is so much I want to talk to you about; however, it cannot be discussed in a letter.
In the meantime, I wanted to let you know that I will begin my placement soon. I think I am close to making a decision, but haven't decided yet. When I do, I'll let you know.
Addie says to say hello and that she hopes to see you soon, as do I.
I miss you.
Give Flora my love.
Love you,
Bri

☽✳☾

The House of Shadows does not keep records like that in the library. My conversation with Addie concerning Yezed had been on loop in my mind following the placement notices.

Most of us received two offers, except Oz, who had only been offered the Eternal Court. "It makes sense, and besides, it's the one I was hoping for, so I'm glad for it," he took a bite of a tart. Tamra had been offered a placement in the Eternal Court and Court of Shadows, which we all thought was somewhat surprising.

"I'm very dark and mysterious," Tamra said, attempting to make her face look even more serious than usual.

"Dark, yes, *mysterious*?" Oz shook his head, "I don't buy it." Tamra smacked him in the arm, we all laughed. Well, all of us except Tamra.

"What about you?" Tamra pointed her fork at Kadian, who had only taken a few bites of his dinner.

"Eternal Court and Court of Reflection," he said almost in a whisper.

My mind drifted back to events the day following the notices of our placements. When a fellow inductee had asked Illerium which traits each of the courts look for, he had said, "The courts like to keep that information to themselves. However, it's speculated that each court does value specific things."

He paused for a moment, considering how much to reveal. "The Eternal Court," he continued, "of course, values strength and bravery. They are often the first to a battlefield, but not all of their members are fighters. There are some who carry the gift of history. These keepers of the past hold the stories of our world, though it's a gift seldom given. The Eternal Court admires those who are keen on studying the past. So if you have an eye for ancient texts or unraveling forgotten mysteries, you might find a place among them."

Illerium's eyes flickered as he spoke about the Court of Reflection. "The Court of Reflection is different. Strength means very little to them. What they value is adaptability. Agility of the mind and body—being able to change, to reflect, and to act with clarity and precision. They admire an even temperament and quick thinking. You must be able to navigate their world with fluidity, a calm mind ready to react without hesitation."

The conversation shifted, and his voice dropped when he spoke of the Court of Whispers. "Cunning," he said, his lips curling into a smirk. "They value those with sharp wits, a mind for diplomacy and politics. They don't care about brute force. They need people who can move unseen, speak with precision, and use their words as weapons. It's a court where alliances can shift in a heartbeat, and only the most clever survive."

His expression hardened. "The Court of Shadows is for those who exude power. They look for strength, yes, but it's more than that. It's about presence—commanding a room, bending others to your will. A willingness to lead and take control, even if it means stepping over others to do so. They don't need followers; they want rulers."

I had to assume Dainan had been the source behind my invitation. Based on Illerium's descriptions, it was not where I belonged.

The House of Shadows does not keep records like that in the library.

After that day's lesson, I made up my mind and headed to Magister Illerium's office. As I approached, I spotted him outside, deep in a heated discussion with Marsh, who stood with his back to me in a sharp black suit. I lingered off to the side, waiting for their conversation to end.

My heart ached. I hadn't seen or heard from Marsh in weeks, despite having written to him to apologize, to share my side of what he had seen. Despite having written him five letters, I'd received nothing.

I'd never heard Marsh raise his voice before. It seemed odd that he would be doing so to his direct superior. Illerium opened his office door and closed it on Marsh's face. When he turned around to find me standing there, he shook his head and vanished. I remained uncertain if I was angry with myself, the situation, Dainan, or Marsh. I had to think that Marsh would know that pucchia lingered in the air that night and the effects it could have.

Pucchia is said to just...encourage you to do things that you would already do.

I didn't have the time or energy to think about that now. I knocked on Illerium's door.

"Marsh, if that's you, don't bother. I'll summon you when I'm ready." His voice boomed from inside. I didn't think him capable of speaking that loud.

"Magister Illerium," I muttered, almost apologetically, "It's Brida Larrow."

There was silence. "Yes, fine, come in."

I'd never been in his office before. If Addie was disorganized, well, it was as if a storm had come through here. Nothing appeared to be in order. The room had shelves from floor to ceiling that contained scrolls, books of all shapes and sizes, notes that had been scribbled, all scattered about. I saw a deep bronze astrolabe, a gilded birdcage that was empty, along with countless knickknacks. Atop his desk sat a stack of books, at least twelve. You could barely see him behind them.

"Yes?" he asked with reluctance.

"I wanted to inform you of my decision, Magister...in regards to my placement."

"Ugh, that, yes, well, I'm to inform you that you have also been offered a position at the Court of Whispers."

"The Court of Whispers?" I replied, "They weren't mentioned in the letter I was given."

"Yes, well, they exceeded the deadline, but you have been offered a placement."

"Did Marsh ask for this?"

Magister Illerium rose, placing his hands on his desk, "Why yes, yes he did, Ms. Larrow," his tone grew angrier, "you may not have noticed, Ms. Larrow, that I'm a busy man, and you may not know that I do not like being interrupted. I have now been interrupted twice in a single afternoon. Now, it may not have occurred to either of you but it is not my job to play matchmaker, whomever you choose to see on your own ti—"

"Magister," I interjected, "I had nothing to do with Marsh making that request of you and only came to inform you of my decision, as you indicated."

He nodded, "Very well. Does this news alter your decision?"

"It does not," I said.

"What is your final decision?"

"Please inform Fayma Aliz that I appreciate her offer and accept." I knew Addie would be supportive of my decision. This was my opportunity, not only to help Dad, but to find out more about Mom.

He nodded, sitting back down. I turned and attempted to navigate my way to the door, trying not to step on something that could be hiding or alive.

"Ms. Larrow," his voice called, staring down at the document he'd been working on, "you're sure with this decision?"

"I am, Magister," he nodded once more. I closed the door behind me.

Why had Marsh requested a placement for me and then refused to speak to me?

Oz's voice cut through my memories, bringing me back to the present. "So none of us got Court of Whispers?" He asked, looking around at each of us.

I'd chosen to keep the incident outside of Marsh's office to myself.

"Unsurprising, none of us is cunning enough. Well, maybe Lil would have been."

Kadian shot up at the mention of Lil's name. I placed my hand over his, reminding him we were among friends, giving it a slight squeeze.

"Which one will you choose?" Oz looked over to Kadian, who just sat there staring at his plate.

"I'm leaning towards the Court of Reflection," he said and I knew why. He was missing Lil more than the rest of us. He couldn't quite explain it, and I hadn't had it in me to tell him what Thetius had shared with me in the pool.

"Maybe take a day or two to think about what will be best for *you,*" I said. He didn't bother to look at me. It didn't matter what I or anyone else said; there was no way he was choosing anything other than the Court of Reflection.

His eyes found mine, and all I saw was despair. I didn't know how to help him. We'd all tried. I had taken him to the medic on multiple occasions, but they had dismissed his condition as a poor adjustment to the climate—a diagnosis that gnawed at me, leaving a bitter taste of doubt.

Determined to find answers, I spent countless hours in the library, poring over texts, searching for anything that might help him. I scoured ancient tomes and dusty scrolls, desperate to uncover a remedy for both my father's ailment and Kadian's struggles. Yet every lead I followed led to dead ends or vague references that offered no real solutions.

Most mornings, I found myself dragging Kadian from bed, trying to motivate him to train or to engage in his coursework, but it was clear that my efforts weren't enough. I had even taken to writing his essays, believing that if I could at least ease his burden, he might find his footing again.

Oz, Tamra, and I spent the remainder of our dinner talking while Kadian sat silent, acknowledging us every so often. We speculated what tasks each court would have us working on. Oz hoped his spy skills would be put to work and he would be allowed to look over classified documents. I reminded him for that type of thing, he would have been better suited in the library.

We all played a few rounds of cards that night. Oz taught us a game called Crescendia, named for the mythical king, Crescend.

"You're cheating," Tamra said, folding her hand, glaring at Oz.

"I would never!" His grin grew bigger. Tamra had been spending more time with us. It felt if Lil and Emia were here that our group would be complete. I'd remained unsure what Emia had meant by her note. Despite my research in the library, the sole thing I could discover for Dawn had been the time of day. I'd written to her but hadn't heard anything in return.

I looked to Kadian, who hadn't said anything for the past twenty minutes. "I'm going to head to bed," I said while looking at the twins. "Kadian?" His eyes found mine. "Care to walk with me?" He nodded and rose, mumbling what I could only have assumed to be goodnight, but none of us could make it out. I shrugged to them, "See you in the morning."

He said nothing until we made it to his door, "Thanks for walking with me. I...I think I need some sleep."

I placed my hand on his arm, "Let's get you inside," I pushed open his door.

Kadian froze as he walked into the room. We saw a tall woman with golden blonde hair standing with her back to us, staring out the window. "Lil?" I said.

The woman turned around, and it looked as if Kadian's heart had been ripped from his chest. It wasn't her. A tear ran down his cheek.

"She told you to call her Lil, did she," she walked over to the bed and sat down. "No, I'm not Lil. I think that much is obvious," she said, gesturing to the chair in front of the desk. I walked Kadian over and sat him down while closing the door behind me. "I do appreciate you thinking I was her, though; good to know I'm still not quite looking my age," the woman said with a smirk.

"Who the fuck are you?" Kadian growled, color coming back to his cheeks.

"Easy," she said, holding up her hands, "I'm only the messenger."

"You're a messenger?" I asked, "Whose messenger?"

"My daughter's, of course."

CHAPTER THIRTY-TWO

Kadian's tension was palpable, like a storm brewing beneath his skin. His words, sharp and brittle, shattered the fragile calm we were trying to maintain.

"Where is she?" he demanded, his voice raw and jagged.

The woman—tall, poised, and unsettlingly familiar—cocked her head, her turquoise eyes gleaming with quiet amusement as they flitted toward me. "Is he always like this?" Her lips curled into a faint smirk.

"Not usually." I sighed, rubbing my temple. "He's...not quite himself lately."

Gods, why am I even explaining? There were bigger things to focus on. Lil. I needed to stay sharp. "Lil sent you?" I asked, my voice steadier than I felt.

"She did." Her gaze swept over me, dissecting me with every blink. She looked so much like Lil; it was almost painful. The curve of her lips, the confident tilt of her head—it was all there, only older, more refined, more dangerous. Her sleeveless dress clung to her, teal like the depths of an ocean, and her golden heels looked sharp enough to puncture a heart. I shuddered.

Kadian, on the other hand, was losing his patience. His fists clenched, his voice dripping with rage. "Where. Is. She."

"Tell your pet to settle down," she said, her voice light but laced with venom.

"If you speak like that again, I will rip out your fucking throat," Kadian snarled, his voice trembling with rage.

"Kadian!" My voice shot through the tension like an arrow. "This is Lil's mother."

He didn't flinch. He didn't even acknowledge me. She begun laughing, a cruel, lilting sound that seemed to echo off the walls.

"Gods, this is exhausting," she muttered, rising from the bed with fluid grace, smoothing her dress as if to dismiss us altogether. "I assume you're Brida," she said, casting a dismissive glance over me, "and I know from your little outburst that you're Kadian. Yes, Lil mentioned you—both of you," her turquoise eyes bore into me as she spoke, her words dripping with an edge I couldn't quite place.

The air in the room felt thicker with every passing second. She ran a finger along the desk, inspecting the dust with a raised brow, her expression settling into something cold, almost disdainful. "Lil wanted me to let you know she's okay. She also wanted me to tell you to stay away from her."

"What?" Kadian's voice broke, confusion and disbelief rippling through it. "Why would she say that?"

Her sigh was deep, exasperated, as though we were children asking the most mundane questions. "Because of Thalius. You've met him, haven't you?" Her eyes flashed with something dark. "Does he strike you as the kind of man you'd want to cross?"

I froze. Thalius. His name sent a chill through me, one I couldn't suppress.

"He's dangerous," she continued, her voice softening but losing none of its edge. "A powerful man. There's not much anyone can do to defy him. Do not interfere." Her eyes locked on Kadian, unyielding. "Do you understand?"

Kadian's fists were still shaking; his jaw clenched so tight I thought he might snap his teeth. He didn't answer, didn't move.

"Do you understand?" she repeated, stepping closer, her heels clicking against the stone floor. She was taller than I expected, practically meeting Kadian's gaze head-on. Her voice was low, dangerous.

When he remained silent, she turned her attention to me. "Can I trust you to handle this?"

I swallowed the lump in my throat and nodded. Whatever this was, whatever web Lil had gotten herself entangled in, we weren't prepared. Not for this.

Lil's mother nodded, a thin smile playing on her lips. "Good." She turned to leave, her eyes drifting over the room one last time. "Do clean up." And then she was gone, her footsteps fading into the corridor.

I stood frozen, unsure of what had just transpired. The room felt heavier, darker. I turned back to Kadian, who hadn't moved an inch. His fists still clenched, his knuckles white.

"Stay here," I whispered, gesturing to the chair. My heart pounded as I bolted after her.

"Mrs. Towler," I called louder than I intended. Her steps slowed, and she turned, exasperation written across her face.

"For Gods' sake, girl, call me Nayla. If you keep that up, people will think I'm much older than I am."

"Nayla," I started, my voice tight, "do you know what happened between Rai and Lil? He's been demanding something back from her."

Her lips pressed into a thin line. "And what do you know about that?"

"Rai approached me during the festival. He made some veiled threats and mentioned something about wanting something back. I don't know what it is, and I haven't had the chance to ask Lil before Thalius swept her away."

A long silence stretched between us before she finally spoke. "It's a ring. His mother's, to be exact. That's all I can tell you for now."

A ring. I wasn't sure what I expected, but it didn't feel like enough. She took a step closer, her voice softening. "Brida, let us handle this. There's far more at stake than you can understand."

Her words stung, but I nodded. What else could I do?

"And your friend," she added, nodding back toward Kadian's room, "he's going to have to get a handle on himself. This won't be easy if he doesn't."

"Do you know what is going on with him?" I asked, hopeful that she may have some sort of answer.

Nayla's smile was thin and knowing like she had answers I couldn't even begin to fathom. "Ask yourself why he's so defensive of her. Then you might start to understand."

With that, she left, her heels clicking down the hall, leaving me with more questions than answers. My temple throbbed, and I rubbed it as I made my way back to Kadian's room.

"Kadian?" I whispered as I opened the door.

He was sitting on the floor, his arms wrapped around his legs, his body trembling as he cried.

Gods.

I rushed to him, wrapping my arms around him. "Shh," I whispered into his hair, trying to soothe him. "It's going to be okay."

He rocked in my arms, his sobs muffled against my chest. "I thought it was her."

☽✳☾

I stayed by Kadian's side until his breathing evened out into the steady rhythm of sleep. I had coaxed him into bed, draping the blanket over him with a gentle touch, my fingers combing through his hair in a futile attempt to ease his restless mind.

I needed to escape—to shed the weight of the past weeks like a heavy cloak that clung too tight. The shower seemed like the only sanctuary where I might find a moment of peace, even if it was fleeting.

I slid out of bed with careful precision, avoiding any creaks in the floor that might betray my movements. The darkness of the hallway seemed to pulse with its own quiet intensity. As I made my way to my room, the sight of him—Marsh—stopped me cold. He was pacing, the tension in his body evident in every measured step he took. When our eyes met, his were searching, pleading, as if they might find answers in mine.

"Now is not a good time, Marsh," I said, my voice a whisper as I tried to brush past him, heading towards my door.

"Just tell me why," he demanded, his voice rising with a mix of frustration and desperation that clashed with my exhaustion.

"I'm not in the mood for riddles. It's been a long evening, night, morning—whatever fucking time it is," I snapped, running a hand through my disheveled hair, hoping it might somehow calm the storm within me.

Marsh's eyebrows shot up in surprise at my sharpness. It was a new side of me, born out of the countless frustrations and disappointments accumulated over recent days.

"Why didn't you accept the placement?" His question cut through the air like a blade, sharp and unyielding.

I sighed, a sound that seemed to carry all the weight of my fatigue. "Can this not wait until morning? I need to shower."

"Tell me," he said, reaching out for my arm. His touch was an electric shock of unwanted intensity. I jerked away, feeling a surge of anger that I couldn't ignore.

"Where have you been for the past several weeks?" I demanded, my voice cracking under the strain of my pent-up emotions.

He took a step back, confusion flashing across his face. "What do you mean?"

"You know exactly what I mean, Marsh," I said, my anger burning bright in my eyes.

"You know where I've been. I've been shuttling court members between Azmeer and Hadash," he responded, but his words felt hollow, inadequate.

"That's not what I mean, and you know it." My exhaustion and frustration mingled into a potent cocktail of rage. All I wanted was a moment of peace, a chance to clear my mind, but instead, I was caught in this exhausting confrontation.

"I...I didn't know how to act or what to say after I saw you and Dainan at the bar. I thought it would be best to give you some space."

"Some space! Five unanswered letters," I shouted, the sound echoing down the hallway. I was so tired of the endless game of miscommunication and misunderstanding. "I didn't know what pucchia could do to me. I didn't know that merely being in its presence could influence me. I would never have willingly done what I did, not after what happened between us." My words felt like they were tearing through the tension in the air.

Marsh's face hardened. "Dainan is dangerous, Brida," he said, taking another step closer, but I retreated, my head pounding with the weight of his words. "I can't say more than that, but he is dangerous. It's not safe for you to be around him. He's playing with you, trying to make a point. This is a fucking game to him," he said, frustration evident as he began to pace.

"Do you hear yourself right now?" My head throbbed with every word he spoke.

"I was hoping if you accepted the placement, we could talk and sort things out. I missed the deadline because I was in a meeting with Qurasa, and I wasn't sure if you would have accepted."

I would have considered it. The Court of Whispers intrigued me, and despite the tension, I liked being around Marsh. But rage clouded my judgment, overtaking my thoughts.

"You should have come and spoken with me, maybe not that night but the next day. Or when you saw me outside of Illerium's office."

"I was in no state to speak with you," he retorted, his voice tinged with frustration.

"You mean like me right now," I muttered under my breath.

"Brida," he said, reaching out once more. I stepped back, his touch a painful reminder of our unresolved issues. "I just heard tonight that you accepted the placement with him." His eyes were hard, a mix of anger and something else I couldn't quite place.

"It isn't with him, Marsh. Did it ever occur to you that I might have chosen them for other reasons?" I shot back, feeling a pang of disappointment.

His face fell into an expression of frustration. "Please just be careful, Brida. He isn't safe." He shoved his hands into the pockets of his black suit and turned to leave.

My energy was drained. I felt as if I had nothing left to give. I knew I missed him, but I was in no state to continue this conversation. He walked away, his footsteps echoing down the corridor.

☽✳☾

Tamra's gaze flicked up from her plate as I sat down, her eyes widening in surprise. "Saved you a bite," she said. "Gods, what happened to you?"

"It was a long night," I mumbled, wrapping my fingers around the warm coffee cup. The steam was almost soothing, threatening to lull me back into sleep.

"Did Kadian fair okay?" she asked, her voice laced with genuine concern.

I shook my head, too weary to articulate the depth of my worries. "Have you seen him this morning?"

"He and Oz were here earlier," Tamra said, offering a small smile.

I nodded, too tired to muster more than a brief acknowledgment.

"I made a decision, you know," Tamra said, her tone shifting to one of barely contained excitement.

I perked up, curiosity overriding my fatigue. "Oh?"

"Looks like we'll be playing in the shadows together," she smirked, her eyes twinkling.

The news was a rare ray of light. "What made you decide?"

Tamra glanced over her shoulder, pointing discreetly to the back of the room. There sat Amera, the woman from the bar, radiating a quiet confidence. "Turns out she's a court member and she's mighty good at convincing," Tamra said with a laugh that was both relieved and amused.

"I'm happy for you," I said, managing a weak smile. "But you do realize you'll have to introduce her to us eventually, right?"

"Ha, I plan to hold off on that as long as possible," Tamra said, chuckling. "Oz has a knack for scaring off anyone I might be interested in. His protectiveness can be a bit overwhelming."

"He loves you," I said with a shrug.

"Yeah, well, sometimes I wish he'd love me less," she said with a soft laugh. "Any word from your suitors?" Her mocking grin was hard to miss.

I grimaced. "I haven't heard anything from Dainan, but I'm just waiting. He seems to have a knack for appearing at the most inconvenient moments." I paused. "Marsh was waiting for me outside my room last night."

"Was he now?" Tamra's eyebrow arched in interest.

"I have no idea how long he'd been waiting. All I know is that I was exhausted and needed a shower. He just kept pushing."

"Well..." Tamra leaned in, her curiosity piqued. "What did he say?"

"He questioned why I accepted the placement with the Court of Shadows. He warned me to stay away from Dainan. There's something ongoing between them, and I'm caught in the middle of their game." I took a sip of my coffee, trying to steady my emotions. "Lil warned me about all three brothers when we arrived here. I should have listened. Instead, I'm now entangled with two protective alpha males. Not my best look."

"No, I'd argue this," Tamra said, gesturing at me with a teasing smile, "is your best look."

"Congratulations, you made a joke," I managed a smirk.

"What are you going to do?" she asked, leaning against the table.

"Do what everyone else here is doing," I said, staring into my coffee. "Keep my head down, do the jobs they assign me, and hope that at the end of this, I find somewhere to land."

Tamra raised her mug in a small toast. "To somewhere to land."

"Somewhere to land," I echoed, clinking my mug against hers.

When I arrived at the gym, Kadian and Oz were scaling the rock wall. Despite whatever struggles Kadian faced, his physical prowess remained intact. The gym was more crowded than usual.

I sighed as I surveyed the room. I wasn't up to running. Instead, I planned to observe the boys as they competed. As I turned towards the rock wall, two figures approached me.

"Ah, Brida," a voice said, and I looked up to see Prince Alvar standing before me.

"Prince Alvar," I bowed, trying to appear more composed than I felt.

Dainan stood beside him, his indifference as palpable as ever. The scent of smoke and citrus clung to him, pulling me into a foggy haze of exhaustion.

"We're pleased to see that you accepted the placement in the Court of Shadows," Alvar said with a warm smile. Among the brothers, his expression was the most genuine, inviting trust.

"I'm honored to have received the offer," I said, bowing my head again, though my gratitude was tinged with uncertainty.

"Are you acquainted with the others joining you?" Alvar asked.

"Yes. I'm friends with one." I replied.

"Oh?" Alvar's curiosity was evident.

"Tamra Kadem."

"Ah yes, Amera's girl," he looked back at Dainan, whose expression still showed nothing. Dainan stood with his arms crossed, wearing a deep crimson shirt today that stretched all the way down his arms. I could still see the ripples of his muscles, each indent, each perfectly sculpted... Alvar coughed. Dainan raised one of his eyebrows.

"I'm sorry," I uttered, "did you say something?"

I could tell that Alvar was trying not to laugh. "I asked if you had given any thought as to whom you might work alongside."

"I didn't know we're offered a choice," I said while trying to avoid staring at Dainan. That was only going to get me in further trouble.

"Yes," Alvar nodded. "If you have a preference, I'll be happy to see that it comes to pass."

I gave him a meek smile.

"I do know that you are on great terms with Scriba Velin, and are an avid reader and excellent researcher."

"That's kind of you to say," I meant it. He didn't have to be so free with his words.

"I've never known anyone to consume more literature than my brother here," he looked over to Dainan, "it's possible he could make a great pa—"

I cut him off, "I'd like to work with *you,* Prince Alvar."

Alvar's eyes flickered between Dainan and me, his curiosity piqued. I stood firm, not flinching.

"With me?" Alvar's smile widened. "I'm flattered, though I'm not sure if I'd be the best fit..."

Gods, Brida. I needed to learn to keep my mouth shut in these type of situations. But I was exhausted. I had no choice but to commit to what I'd started.

"I believe working with those who share my interests, as well as those who don't, is crucial," I said. "I think we could become fast friends." I hoped he saw the attempt at sincerity in my words.

Alvar stood a bit straighter, bringing his hands behind his back. "Very well," he said, his voice steady. "I'll find you on Monday, and we'll begin. Until then, Brida." His lips quirked up and he turned to leave.

Dainan lingered, his gaze fixed on me with an unsettling intensity. "Afraid to be too close to me, Ilia?" he took a step forward.

"Yes," I wanted to say, but I settled on, "hardly."

"My brother is a stickler for punctuality. Be sure to be on time." He leaned in, his breath warm against my ear. "Oh, and Ilia, should you change your mind about who you want to work with, just let me know. I'd be happy to see that you are paired with the correct partner." He smirked as his shadows hissed around him, engulfing him in darkness before he vanished.

CHAPTER THIRTY-THREE

The days passed in a slow crawl, each one the same as the last, except for the note I found slipped under my door in the dead of night. It must've been early morning when it came. I didn't hear it, didn't sense it, just woke to its presence.

Brida,
I wanted to apologize for how I spoke to you the other night. It had been a long day; I had just arrived back from Hadash, where things are still quite dire.
I have so much I would like to say to you, but I do not wish to push you. I will be gone again for the next few days, but when I return, I hope we may talk then.
I hope you know how sorry I am.
I miss you,
Marsh.

His words lingered on the page like ghosts—silent, distant. They didn't pull at my heart the way I thought they might. I wasn't angry anymore. Just...indifferent. The world had shifted beneath my feet in ways even Marsh's absence couldn't explain. My focus wasn't on him; it was on Kadian. The shadows that clung to him had deepened, and I couldn't shake the feeling that something was slipping through my fingers. He was unraveling, and I was helpless to stop it.

That night, as the sun sank behind the palace walls, I found myself standing in Kadian's room. He was already curled up in bed, the light in the room dimming with the fading day.

"Get up," I nudged him gently, my voice soft, though my desperation clung to the words.

"Why?" His voice was muffled, buried in the pillow.

I could feel the weight of his weariness, the heaviness that had settled deep into his bones. "We haven't gone to see the entrance to the Court of Whispers yet. It's time for us to embrace adventure. Let's go explore."

He didn't move, didn't even open his eyes. I hated to press him, to drag him out of whatever darkness was swallowing him, but I was afraid of what would happen if I didn't. "Please, Kad. I need this. I need a distraction. Do this for me."

His sigh filled the space between us, heavy and slow. He rolled onto his back, his face blotched with the evidence of recent tears. His red eyes searched mine as if looking for a reason to care.

"What do you have planned?"

I tried to lighten the moment, pulling out two pastries I'd swiped from the dining hall. "I brought us snacks."

He stared at them for a beat longer than necessary. He hadn't been eating, and seeing him wasting away broke something in me. But finally, after what felt like an eternity, he sat up, pushing the blankets away. "What's your plan, Brida?"

"Let's go check out the entrance," I said, a hint of excitement bleeding into my voice. "I heard some of the first-floor students talking about it. It sounds...interesting."

"Interesting like the Mirrors of Reflection?"

I grinned, knowing he'd catch my meaning. "One and the same."

He shook his head, but I could see the faintest hint of a smile pulling at the corner of his lips. "Fine," he muttered, and I squealed, unable to contain my joy.

"Let's go."

The palace at night was a different world. The day's golden light, which illuminated the vast corridors and high ceilings, had been replaced by the ethereal glow of moonlight. Silver spilled in through the windows, catching the gold filigree on the limestone walls and turning everything soft and shimmering.

As we walked, I tried to fill the silence. "Addie told me this hallway was one of the first things built in Azmeer," I said, gesturing toward the long corridor lined with iron-wrought windows. The soft moonlight bathed everything in a silvery hue. "It was meant to honor the moon goddess, said to be a daughter of one of the Primals. No one's sure which, though."

Kadian glanced at me, but his eyes were distant, his mind elsewhere. I pressed on, hoping to catch his interest. "Azmeer's built to reflect its natural surroundings. They believed that the magic—the life of the land—came from the moon, not the sun." I stepped closer, placing my hands on his sides and turning him to face the windows. "That's why they built this here. It has the best view of the moon. And on the other side..."

The mirrors.

The entire hallway was awash in silver; the moonlight caught and refracted a thousand times over. The effect was breathtaking, as if the light had become a living thing, breathing around us, filling the space with its soft, radiant glow.

"It's beautiful," Kadian murmured, his voice hushed. "It's like there are gems dancing in the air."

I followed his gaze to the crystal chandeliers above, each catching the light and casting a cascade of shimmering reflections on the walls. For a moment, it was as if we were standing inside a dream.

We stood there in silence, letting the beauty of the place envelop us. Then, I placed my hand on Kadian's back and guided him forward. We walked, our footsteps soft on the limestone floor.

After a while, Kadian broke the silence. "You don't know where you're going, do you?"

I smirked, unwilling to give him a straight answer. "That's part of the adventure, Kadian. Allowing yourself to get lost...learning from the journey, and then finding yourself again."

He laughed, a sound I hadn't heard in weeks. The lightness of it lifted something inside me.

As we continued, he spoke again. "I made my decision, you know." His voice was quiet, but there was a weight to his words.

I stopped, turning to look at him. "What decision?"

"I'm going to the Eternal House."

Relief surged through me. "Are you sure?"

He nodded, though there was something uncertain in his expression. "Yeah. I think...it's what I'm meant to do."

"Why?"

His eyes flickered with something—hesitation, maybe? "I don't know. I have this...feeling about Lil. She's not in the House of Reflection. I can feel it. It's like...we're connected somehow, but it's distant. Faint."

I swallowed, my throat tight. "Why do you think that is?"

He exhaled, running a hand through his hair. "I don't know, Bri. I don't know her. Not really. But ever since I first saw her, it's like...it's like I can't get her out of my head. There's this pull...this need. And it's only getting stronger."

His voice cracked, and I could feel the pain in his words. "Some days, I think I can smell her. It's like she's right there, and it drives me mad. I feel like I'm suffocating without her."

I took Kadian's hand into mine and squeezed it as we walked along in silence. I said nothing as I had no words that would offer him comfort. Only despair.

After several minutes, I halted us as I reached into the back pocket of the billowing pants I was wearing.

"What's that?" He raised a single brow at me.

"A map, of course," I looked at it.

"You've had a map this entire time?" He grabbed it from my hands.

"You should know that despite my wanting to embrace adventure," I said. "That I seldom go on one being unprepared."

He chuckled as his eyes met mine. For a moment, the Kadian I'd always known looked back at me. But as fast as blinking, he was gone.

He studied the map for a moment, "we're here." He pointed to a part of the map that was titled *Astral Observatory.* "And we want to go..." His eyes scanned the map, "here. This way," he gestured his arm forward.

As was commonplace on our adventures, I let him guide the way.

"What've you heard about this entrance?" He folded the map and handed it to me.

"Not much, only that it is shrouded in mystery. Whatever that means," I smiled.

"How intriguing," he wrapped his arm around my shoulders, "thank you for getting me out tonight." He gave a light kiss to the top of my head.

"Anytime." I placed my hand over his and squeezed it.

When we reached the final corridor, the limestone walls darkened to slate gray as we approached the entrance to the Court of Whispers.

"What is that?" Kadian pointed to a pale sheen that began to slither along the floor, moving with an unsettling grace as it raced toward us.

"I think it's mist." The words barely left my lips before the mist reacted, rising like a living thing, its tendrils curling into the air. It swelled, swallowing the end of the hall in a thick, ghostly shroud. The atmosphere grew oppressive, each step forward making the air feel denser, more suffocating. It clung to my skin, cold and damp, a clammy touch that sent shivers racing up my spine.

At first, the pounding of my heart drowned out everything else, but then I heard it—a faint, almost imperceptible sound. As we ventured deeper into the mist, the sound grew clearer: whispers. Faint at first, they caressed the edges of my mind, soft and melodic, like voices from a distant dream. Yet, there was something off about them—something ancient, wrong, like forgotten voices clawing their way back into the world.

You do not belong here.

The words slithered through the air like a serpent, brushing against my skin, cold and intimate, as though the speaker stood mere inches from my cheek. I shivered, my heart hammering. I glanced at Kadian, hoping for reassurance, but his face had gone pale, drained of color, his eyes wide and distant, staring into a void I could not see.

You do not belong here, the voice hissed again, harsher now, a razor-sharp edge to the words.

Before I could react, Kadian bolted, his movements frantic as he disappeared into the mist, swallowed whole by the thick, swirling fog.

"Kadian!" I screamed, chasing after him, but the mist was alive, moving faster than I could comprehend, closing in around me, sealing me off from the world. It pressed in from all sides, suffocating, endless. The whispers morphed into something else—laughter. Low, mocking, a sound that curled in my mind like smoke.

We know who you are, Brida Larrow. You do not belong here.

A cold terror gripped me, sharp and unyielding, tightening around my chest. I pressed my hands to my ears, desperate to shut out the voice, but it was inside me, creeping under my skin, burrowing deep into my thoughts.

"Get out of my head!" My mind screamed the words, but the laughter only grew louder, more vicious, more invasive.

Oh no, dear Brida. You came to us. You have no power here.

My heart raced, panic clawing at the edges of my sanity. I spun in place, disoriented, searching for any sign of Kadian, but the fog was impenetrable, a void that devoured everything. The world had vanished. I was blind, helpless.

"Where's Kadian?" My voice trembled, thick with fear.

Where he is meant to be, the voice hissed, its words dripping with dark amusement.

"What does that mean?" I snarled.

Some who come here are granted information. You will not disturb him.

I grasped at any semblance of control, clinging to the only thing that might help. "Will you grant me information?"

The mist shifted, swirling tighter around me as if considering. Then, the voice responded, low and dangerous. *What will you offer?*

"I've nothing to offer you," I whispered, my voice cracking with fear.

The laughter returned, a soft, chilling purr. *Oh, but you do. So much.*

The mist curled closer, brushing my skin like icy fingers, teasing at my senses, its presence heavy, watching, waiting. Every breath I took was laced with the weight of something ancient and malevolent. It wasn't just mist—it was alive, sentient, and it knew me. It knew my name. My fears.

The whispers grew louder, pressing in from all sides, gnawing at my thoughts. "What do you want?" I asked, though I already knew the answer would be dangerous.

A favor. When the time is right.

My blood ran cold. This was no ordinary magic—it was a pact, a promise that I wasn't sure I could keep. The weight of it pressed down on me, suffocating, as the darkness coiled tighter around my mind. I needed Kadian, needed to find him before this thing consumed us both.

But then Kadian's scream pierced the air—a sound so raw, so full of pain that it ripped through the fog and into my soul.

Panic flared in my chest, my pulse racing. "Yes!" I shouted into the mist. "Yes, we have a deal!"

Silence followed, a heavy, crushing silence. Then, the voice returned, colder than ever. *He is dying.*

My heart stopped, fear flooding my veins like ice. "If you hurt him—" The threat was empty; I knew I had no power here, no leverage. But the words escaped me anyway, trembling with desperation.

He is not dying by our hand but by the bonds.

The words hit me like a blow. Bonds? The mist swirled with cruel laughter, mocking me as if I were a child lost in a game far beyond my understanding.

My mind raced, trying to piece together the impossible. "Bonds? What are they, with whom?" The words felt hollow in my mouth.

Foolish girl. There is much you do not yet know.

The chill deepened, the weight of the unknown pressing harder on my chest. I needed answers, needed to save Kadian before it was too late. "Tell me where to look. Tell me how to help him."

The voice chuckled, a sound full of dark amusement. *The time will come when all shall be revealed to you.*

Frustration and fear warred within me. "How do I help him?" I pleaded, my voice cracking with the force of my desperation.

Both must accept the bond.

The room spun, my heart pounding as the impossible truth settled in.

"How am I supposed to help him if you do not tell me what bonds these are and whom he is bound to? What if they don't find each other?" I asked, my voice barely more than a whisper.

The voice was quieter now, almost contemplative. *We do not belong to the Primal of Death. That is not ours to say. Even still, that is not all that ails him. What is coming will bring a great change.*

A shiver ran down my spine. The Primal of Death? I'd never heard of such a thing. This was magic far older, far darker than anything I'd encountered.

There is much you do not yet know.

And just as quickly as the mist had consumed the world, it began to dissipate, peeling away like smoke in the wind. The hallway emerged once more, and at the end of it, Kadian knelt on the cold stone, trembling, his hands covering his face.

I ran to him, my heart in my throat. "Kadian?"

He was cold to the touch, his body slumped and frail. When he looked up at me, his eyes were hollow, haunted by something I couldn't see.

"They're waking up," he whispered before collapsing into my arms.

CHAPTER THIRTY-FOUR

Kadian lay on the floor, unmoving.

Please, please be okay.

I lowered my head onto his chest, feeling the hard stone beneath us, and counted the beats, slow and steady. The relief was so sharp it hurt. But he wouldn't wake up. His eyes wouldn't open, no matter how much I whispered his name or shook him. The mist had done something to him, something I couldn't fix.

What is that? The doorway to the House of Whispers. The pale hues of dusk had vanished, leaving behind a storm—dark and violent. The blacks and grays twisting like angry clouds ready to burst.

I stumbled to my feet, my hands shaking as I pounded on the door, my voice cracking with desperation. "Please! Someone, please open the door!" The sound of my pleading felt too loud in the heavy silence, the words swallowed by the shadows creeping in from the edges.

A sudden crack split the air, and the door groaned open, splitting down the middle like it had been waiting to devour me whole. And there, standing in the doorway, was Marsh.

"Brida?" His voice was soft, but it had a hard edge of confusion. He stepped toward me, eyes narrowing. "What are you...?"

"Please!" I gasped, the words tumbling out before I could stop them, tears spilling hot and unbidden down my cheeks. "Kadian—he won't wake up, and I can't...I can't move him!" I couldn't breathe, the weight of Kadian's limp body behind me pulling me under.

Marsh didn't hesitate. He turned, shouting back through the door, "Xavius!"

"What do you want?" a voice, gruff and irritated, called back.

"Now!" Marsh's tone was sharp, a commander issuing his order. A moment later, Xavius appeared, a towering figure with blonde hair, his eyes hard as he knelt beside Kadian.

Xavius's fingers pressed into Kadian's neck, searching for the same heartbeat I had heard. "What happened?" he muttered, his hands moving over Kadian's body, checking him.

"I don't know," I whispered, my voice small, weak. "He's breathing. I checked." It felt so insignificant, so useless. The knot in my chest tightened, twisting harder.

Without another word, Xavius hoisted Kadian into his arms, his body hanging limp like a child's doll. The sight of Kadian's head lolling to the side made bile rise in my throat.

"Where are you taking him?" My voice was frantic now, edging toward hysteria. I reached out as if I could somehow pull him back, keep him from slipping out of my grasp.

Xavius didn't even look at me. "Infirmary. He needs immediate attention."

"I have to go with him," I insisted, my feet already moving as if I could will them to let me follow. But Marsh stepped in front of me, his warm hands catching my arms, holding me.

"Brida," his voice softened. I wanted to shake him off, run to Kadian, but the way he looked at me made my body still. "He'll be taken care of. Xavius knows what he's doing."

And then they were gone, Xavius and Kadian's limp form

vanishing from sight. The emptiness that swallowed me was immediate, a cold ache settling deep in my chest.

“Wait,” I called out, but the word dissolved in the silence.

“Brida.” Marsh’s hand lifted my chin, forcing my gaze to meet his. His touch was tender, the kind of touch that made me want to crumble right there. “Tell me what happened.”

My voice trembled as the words came out. “We...we just came to see the entryway... Illerium hadn't taken us yet, and Kadian—he’s been locked in his room for days. I just...I just wanted to help him.” The tears came harder now, unstoppable. “I brought him here.” My chest heaved as I sobbed, the guilt suffocating me.

Marsh pulled me close, his warmth wrapping around me like a blanket I didn’t deserve. “Shh...you did nothing wrong, Brida.” His voice was soft in my ear, his hand stroking my hair in gentle, soothing motions. "You did nothing wrong."

I stood there, buried in his chest, the sobs wracking my body until I felt like there was nothing left in me. But he didn’t let go. He held me, whispered those words over and over until I could breathe again, until my body stopped shaking.

I pulled away, wiping at my face, trying to pull myself back together. “Thank you,” I whispered, my voice hoarse. “But I need to check on him. I have to make sure...”

“They won’t let you,” Marsh interrupted, his voice calm but firm. “Not until morning. They’ll examine him, make sure he’s stable, and then he’ll need to rest.”

He was right, of course. But it didn’t make the ache in my chest any less painful, didn’t stop the gnawing fear that something else might happen, that Kadian might be alone and suffering, and I wouldn’t be there.

Marsh reached out again, his hand hovering in the space between us. “Let me take you back,” he said. “Please, Brida.”

“I will be ill if I have to wind walk anywhere,” I muttered, feeling the fatigue deep in my bones.

A low chuckle rumbled in Marsh's chest, and for a fleeting moment, I almost smiled.

"Allow me to walk you, then?" His voice was soft, his eyes searching mine, and I couldn't help but feel the weight of his gaze as if it carried more than words could ever say.

The corridor stretched endlessly before us, though I'd walked it many times. Every step felt heavier than the last. The joy I'd felt earlier—seeing Kadian stir with the faintest hint of life when we left—had long since drained away, leaving me hollow.

Marsh walked beside me, his hands tucked into the pockets of his black suit, the silence between us thick with unspoken thoughts. The soft shuffle of our footsteps echoed through the still air.

"Is..." My voice broke through the quiet, tentative, as though afraid to disturb the fragile space between us. "Is he going to be okay?"

"I'm sure he'll be fine," Marsh continued, offering me a small smile that didn't quite reach his eyes. It was a kind lie, one we both pretended to believe for a moment. The silence swallowed us again, and I found solace in it, too tired to push for more.

As we reached my door, Marsh finally spoke, his voice quiet but insistent. "What happened tonight, Brida?"

I rubbed at my eyes, my mind swirling with too much, too fast. The mist, Kadian's limp body, the weight of it all crashing down on me.

"There was mist," I said, my voice hoarse.

"Mist?" He frowned, the concern deepening in his features. "What kind of mist?"

"The kind that takes everything," I whispered, my fingers trembling as I brushed them against my temple. "The kind that wraps around you until you can't see or move. The kind that..." My voice faltered, words hanging in the air. There was more, so much more, but it felt too dangerous to say aloud.

"What do you know about this mist?" I asked, my eyes searching his, desperate for answers, for anything that would make sense of this nightmare.

"I don't know," Marsh admitted, shaking his head, his expression tight with frustration. "There's never been mist outside the entryway before. Not that I've seen." He sighed, running a hand through his hair, and for a second, the torchlight caught the violet strands, turning them into flickers of light in the dim hall. "Sometimes, there's mist up in the Tactras mountains, but...it's not something tied to the house."

"But the entryway," I pressed, "It's magical, isn't it?"

"The door..." He paused, his lips pressing together as if weighing his words. "The door is said to foretell fortune or misfortune. Clear skies mean good luck, storms... Well, you can guess." He shrugged, a hollow smile on his lips. "But it's just superstition."

Superstition. I wanted to believe it, to cling to the word and let it dissolve the dread creeping under my skin. But the weight of Kadian's collapse hung over me like a shadow, and I couldn't shake the feeling that this was more than just an old tale.

"Thank you for walking me," I murmured, turning away, my hand resting on the cold brass of the doorknob. "And please...thank Xavius for me."

"Brida," Marsh's voice softened, almost pleading. I turned back to him, his face etched with an unspoken need, something he couldn't quite say. "If there's anything else I can do..."

His words trailed off, and I nodded, unable to form the words that sat on the edge of my tongue. He wanted to say more, but we were too far from whatever it was we'd once been able to say to each other.

I slipped into my room, the door closing behind me with a soft thud. Leaning back against it, I slid down, the exhaustion pulling me down to the floor. The silence pressed in, thick and unbearable, but it was the emptiness that undid me. I waited until I heard Marsh's footsteps fade down the hall.

I cried until my eyes burned, until my body shook with the force of it, until there was nothing left but the hollow ache inside.

☽✳☾

"We believe he'll be alright," Magister Thorne said the next morning, his voice steady but lacking the reassurance I needed. I stood by Kadian's bed, staring down at his pale, motionless form. "However, we don't know how long his body and mind will take to recover." He adjusted his spectacles, peering at Kadian as though he could see something I couldn't. "It's possible he may wake in a few hours...weeks...perhaps longer."

My throat tightened, words clawing at the back of it. "But do you believe he'll wake up? Please, tell me you believe he will." My voice trembled, the desperation I tried to hold back spilling into the space between us.

Magister Thorne hesitated, a flicker of something unreadable crossing his face. "At this moment, we can't be sure. But rest assured, we'll be monitoring him. Should anything change, you'll be informed."

He glanced at his watch, and his tone shifted as if we were discussing something far more mundane. "Is today not the first day of placements?"

"It is," I whispered. My eyes drifted back to Kadian. He looked so peaceful, so still, as if he were untouched by the chaos that had consumed the night before. I could only hope that wherever he was, whatever this state was, he was free from pain. That the voice in the mist hadn't followed him here, hadn't sunk its claws into his mind the way it had into mine.

"Well, you better get going," the Magister said, his words a formality, as though this were just another day.

I hesitated, lingering by Kadian's side, unwilling to leave. "Magister," I began, my voice thick with emotion, "Kadian... He's the closest thing I have to a brother."

Magister Thorne gave a small, understanding nod. "We'll take care of him, Ms. Larrow."

"Thank you," I whispered, though the words felt empty. I left the room, but my heart stayed there, tethered to the bedside of the only family I'd ever chosen.

I stood frozen, my mouth hanging open in a silent gasp, grappling with the enormity of what lay before me. Tamra's voice, both familiar and oddly distant, cut through the heavy silence. "I told you," she said, her tone almost amused, as though she were privy to some private joke that eluded me. "I no doubt looked similar when I saw it for the first time." Her words registered as I struggled to comprehend what stretched endlessly before us.

The entry hall to the southern tower loomed above us; its ceiling lost in a shadowed expanse that seemed to go on forever. My gaze was drawn upward, but the ceiling remained hidden in the oppressive blackness. The air was thick with the acrid tang of smoke, remnants of a fire that seemed to linger long after the flames had died out. The familiar scent of Dainan was present, but without its usual citrus and salty undertones, it was more disquieting than comforting.

Amidst the shadows, dimly lit torches were strung up in a way that when you looked, it appeared as if it were a wall of fire.

Columns rose from the floor, swirling towards the ceiling. Sitting between the columns were blazing onyx tripods. The rubies that adorned the sides glinted in the reflection of the flames.

No matter where I looked, I sensed movement. "It feels like we're being watched," I muttered.

"That's because we are," Tamra said.

We stood for a few moments longer before approaching the circular door on the opposite side of the atrium. Like everything else in the room, it too was made from onyx, but in its center rested the largest blood ruby I'd ever seen, and in the heart of the ruby, an ember sparked as we approached.

We heard a faint whisper as we stood outside the door. A voice began to hum until it became clear,

In the realm where flame and shadow meet,
The goddess reigns, her court complete,
We welcome those who dare draw near,
But remember, secrets whispered must disappear
In the shadows dance, and fiery glow
None may share what happens down below

With that, the door opened as more smoke ran free.

Alvar's voice rang out, crisp and warm, as his hands clapped together, pulling my attention away from the knot of nerves in my stomach. "Ah, Brida!" He said my name with an almost playful energy, the flicker of joy unmistakable in his eyes. He made his way toward us with long, purposeful strides, his expression a blend of charm and expectation. The space around us felt charged like it was holding its breath.

"You must be Tamra Kadem," he said, his hand extending toward Tamra as though they were old friends. His fingers curled around hers, offering more than just a handshake—there was a connection there like he already knew more than he was letting on. I saw the slight stiffening in Tamra's posture, her shoulders lifting as if to shield herself from the weight of his words. "Amera has told us quite a bit about you." Alvar's voice dropped into something softer, something more intimate. Tamra's jaw tensed, and for a moment, I thought she might pull away. His laugh followed, light and carefree, diffusing the tension before it had a chance to settle.

"All wonderful things, don't worry." His laugh danced through the air like a melody, pulling her forward as he waved us closer to the group.

I found myself instinctively stepping alongside her, our movements synchronized.

"Now that we're all here," Alvar continued, his tone shifting into something more official, "we may begin." He pressed his hands together in front of him, the gesture simple but holding the weight of centuries of tradition. His voice was smooth, rich, and commanding. "Welcome to the House of Shadows, home to members of the Court of Shadows whilst in Azmeer." He smiled, the edges of his lips curling with genuine excitement.

His eyes scanned the room, lingering just a beat longer on each face as though assessing, appraising. "I believe it goes without saying that this is not where Prince Dainan, myself, or Prince Rai stay, though we do have our own private rooms here." There was a brief glimmer of amusement in his gaze, like he was letting us in on a private joke. "Our official quarters are in the royal residence."

His words flowed over us like a gentle current, and yet I could feel the underlying pulse of it all—the assessment, the weight of their watchful eyes, the gravity of the moment. He seemed almost boyish in his excitement, and yet there was an undeniable tension simmering beneath it, an awareness of something larger than this introduction, larger than us standing there.

"Placement offers a great opportunity for us to further assess if those we have been watching will make a good fit once the Courting is complete." His smile widened, and though his tone was casual, I could feel the precision in his words. "This year, we invited seven of you, and we were pleased that all seven accepted our offer."

Seven. The word hung in the air, solid and heavy. The realization coiled inside me, a tight, twisting knot of disbelief and pride. My eyes flickered to the side, curiosity tugging at me. I wanted to see who the others were—who had made the cut. And then I saw them. Familiar faces.

Derek, Emia's friend, a boy named Finan who I'd never spoken with. I blinked. The rest? Redheads. All of them. Iona stood in the center, her confidence palpable. The others were friends that I had come to associate her with.

Alvar's voice continued to rise and fall, but I was distracted, my mind tracing lines of connection between us, wondering about the threads that had led each of us here. "While you're here, you'll be given the chance to work alongside a member of the Court of Shadows," Alvar explained. His words were inviting, coaxing, and his eyes met mine, a flicker of something unreadable passing between us before moving on. "We're believers in choice," he added, his lips quirking in amusement, "and we wish to provide you with a selection of whom you would like to shadow while you're here." The playful smirk lingered as if daring us to enjoy the pun.

Dainan's gaze burned into me before I even had a chance to react. He could sense it, that flicker of amusement on my lips. His eyes darkened, their intensity sending a shiver up my spine. I forced myself to look away, to pretend that I hadn't noticed.

"In the spirit of fairness, we've placed numbered papers into a bag," Alvar's voice cut through the tension. He stepped forward, hat in hand, the fabric of his sleeve brushing against me. "Please," he said, his voice lower now, more intimate, "place your hand inside and remove one paper, unfold it, and inform us of the number."

I nodded, my throat dry, as I reached in. The cool paper was smooth against my fingertips, and I pulled one out, feeling the edges as if the number was written in some kind of secret code.

Prior to making our selections, shadows shifted around us, and senior members of the court emerged, slipping from the darkness like they were born of it. Asana entered first, her gaze lingering on Alvar.

"This is Fayma," Alvar announced. My eyes were drawn to her—her striking beauty, tall and thin with skin like polished onyx, her eyes glowing like molten amber. A small bow, graceful and deliberate.

"Over here we have Hadiar," Alvar's voice hummed on, and I barely registered the words as I watched her, my breath catching for a moment. She was power and grace, wrapped in elegance.

"And lastly," Alvar's voice was brighter now, teasing, "we have Yasi and Kay, the Court of Shadows' favorite married pair." His laugh echoed through the room.

"That's not all we're known for," Kay chimed in, one eyebrow raised in playful challenge.

Alvar's laughter joined his, warm and familiar. The sound of it made me want to lean in, to fall into the ease of it all.

My eyes shifted, catching Dainan's. His gaze never left me, and my skin tingled with the weight of it, heat flooding my cheeks. But I could hear it, the whispering doubts in my mind. *You mean nothing to him. He's making a point. This is a game.* I couldn't linger on that now. I looked away, finding a distraction in one of Iona's friends as she raised her hand. I saw Dainan suppress a smirk, and my heart thrummed faster.

"Yes, Salea?" Alvar's voice was calm, steady.

"Will Prince Rai be joining us?" Her voice was soft, hopeful, her weight shifting as she tried to peer around the other court members.

"Prince Rai is otherwise occupied," Alvar's answer was smooth, practiced, but not dismissive. "You'll have a chance to meet him during the ball in honor of the goddess of shadows."

The moment was quiet, save for the soft rustle of paper between fingers. My pulse echoed in my ears as I opened my hand. A collective inhale filled the space, everyone teetering between hope and dread, and then, Iona's voice cut through the stillness.

"One," she announced, her tone firm, resolute.

Alvar's hands met with a sharp clap, the sound startling in the charged silence. "Excellent!" His voice brightened the air, the weight of the moment somehow lifting with his easy cheer. "Who would you like to work with?"

Iona didn't hesitate. "Dainan."

Of course. I swallowed the bitterness that rose in my throat, a pitiful thing that had no place in this moment. What did I expect? It made sense. Perfect sense. I should have been indifferent, unaffected, but my skin prickled, burning with the heat of my own gaze as it found Dainan across the room.

To his credit, he remained still, his face a blank canvas. Not a single muscle betrayed him. Not even a flicker of acknowledgment toward Iona's choice. But his eyes—his eyes hadn't left me. My breath hitched, something electric stirring beneath my skin. A thrum, like a pulse of warmth flooding through my veins, making my fingertips buzz.

I forced my attention back to Alvar as his voice resumed, each word pulling us along the inevitable process.

"Three." Tamra's voice was steady, and the corner of her mouth lifted in satisfaction as she secured her match—Asana. Her relief washed over me like a wave, grounding me, and I let out a breath I hadn't realized I'd been holding.

"Four," I said, meeting Alvar's eyes. "And I choose Prince Alvar."

Alvar nodded, his smile brightening just a fraction. There was something in his expression—surprise? Amusement? But it was Dainan's gaze that I felt most. His focus still unwavering, piercing through the small space between us like a physical force.

The selection process continued, a distant hum in the background as I fought to ignore the weight of his attention. Alvar was speaking again, but my focus drifted, snagging on the pulse in my throat and the inexplicable warmth pooling in my stomach.

"You'll be working with us for the next couple of months," Alvar's voice brought me back, steady and direct, "Your mornings are yours. You're no longer obligated to go to training, though we encourage it." A pause. "Your afternoons, however, will be spent here. You're free to leave for dinner, but depending on tasks, we may ask you to return to ensure everything is completed by day's end."

His gaze swept over the group, a mixture of authority and warmth radiating from him. He smiled as though this arrangement were the most exciting thing in the world. "As I've said, use your time wisely."

He stepped toward me, and my heart thudded faster once more. "Brida," he said, his tone softening, "shall we get started?"

Behind me, Tamra stifled a smile, her eyes gleaming as she nodded toward Asana, their conversation already beginning to trail down one of the long corridors.

"What will we be working on?" I asked, my voice steadier than I felt as Alvar moved beside me.

His laugh was low and genuine, the kind of sound that made you forget your nerves for just a second. "I thought we might start with a tour for today. I'll admit," he paused, his eyes twinkling with something close to mischief, "I hadn't planned on pairing with anyone this round. I'm still formulating what it is I'd like you to work on. But I'm open to suggestions." His gaze flicked back to mine, searching.

A suggestion? My mind raced, thoughts slipping like water through my fingers. I tried to focus, but there was something disarming about the way he watched me.

I tilted my head, smiling. "Well, as you know, Prince Alvar..."

"Please," he interrupted, a playful edge in his voice, "drop the honorifics. Alvar is fine. If we're going to be working together, I'd prefer we do so as friends."

I couldn't help the small laugh that escaped. "Very well, Alvar." His name rolled off my tongue, and the casualness of it felt strange, unfamiliar. "As you know, I love to read. I've become a bit of a student of history since arriving in Azmeer, and I was wondering..." I hesitated, then pushed forward, "...if I might go through records of the court. I'd love to dive deeper into the archives, to study its past."

His eyes flickered with interest. "Oh?" he asked, intrigued. "Is there a particular period you're interested in?"

"I'm not sure if you're aware," I said, my voice softening, "but Scriba Velin is my aunt."

He raised an eyebrow, surprise clear in his features. "Is she? I never would've guessed. My interactions with her have never hinted at close family."

I smiled, a small, knowing curve of my lips. "You see a different version of her here. Azmeer changes people."

His gaze softened, and he nodded. "I don't doubt it. She's well respected among our scribes."

"She spent time in Azmeer while studying for her dissertation. I was wondering if there were any records mentioning her. I think it would be fun to surprise her with them." Despite the lightness of my voice, it was a casual lie. While I was interested in records mentioning Addie, I would be searching for those with mention of my mother.

Alvar's smile deepened. "I'm confident we can make time in our schedule to investigate." He extended his arm with a flourish. "But for now, shall we start the tour?"

With a slight nod, I looped my arm through his, and together, we stepped into the shadows.

CHAPTER THIRTY-FIVE

My first day at the House of Shadows passed in a strange blur, a kind of unsettling calm that gnawed at the edges of my mind. Alvar led me through the halls with their fiery veins pulsing in the walls, magic embedded deep, like the heartbeat of the house itself. I should have found it unnerving, but instead, there was something about the quiet that felt safe. The distant sounds of the palace seemed muffled here, far away, like I had stepped into another world. For a moment, it was almost comforting—the way the serenity folded around me. But my thoughts refused to stay still.

Dad, Kadian, Lil, Marsh... Their faces kept creeping back into my head. The ache of Kadian's stillness, Dad's health, the silence from Lil, and Marsh—gods, I wasn't sure what I felt anymore. All I knew was that the weight of it followed me through every step of the house, lingering even as Alvar told me stories of the artifacts in the treasury. A dagger belonging to Vasenia, webs of starlight, a wyvern egg—I barely heard him. My mind was too heavy, spinning with what I couldn't control.

By the end of the tour, I needed to see Kadian. I couldn't bear not knowing if anything had changed.

But when I arrived at the infirmary, nothing had.

In the following days, I found myself drawn back to his bedside every morning. One-sided conversations, endless updates about our lives, about our tasks. I told him about Oz and his reluctant assignments, Tamra becoming more like Asana, and Alvar, who remained unsure what to do with me. I talked, hoping—no, *needing*—Kadian to hear me. But with each passing day, a restlessness clawed at me. I needed to move. To run.

The evening was cool when I headed to the gym, the breeze wrapping itself around me in a soft embrace. I closed my eyes for a second, letting it wash over me, offering a moment of reprieve.

My fingers twisted my hair into a braid, the motions automatic, my mind already reaching forward, desperate for the release I craved. As soon as my shoes hit the track, it happened. That sweet, familiar feeling of everything falling away.

Running was the only time I felt free. The steady rhythm of my feet against the ground was like a heartbeat, syncing with my own, a perfect, wordless harmony. The miles dissolved, and with them, the weight on my chest. For a while, there was nothing but the wind and the stars and the pulse of my own breath. Kadian's stillness, Lil's absence, even Marsh—they all melted away. I could breathe again.

I ran faster, pushing myself harder. I wanted to outrun it all—the fear, the doubt, the anger simmering just below the surface. I don't know when the tears came, but I let them. The night sky blurred around me as I ran, the sound of my own voice tearing from my throat in a scream I hadn't even known was there.

It wasn't enough.

By the time I finished, my chest was heaving, the hollow ache settling back in. The brief, euphoric reprieve from the weight of everything was gone. I wiped at my face and went in search of water, my throat raw, my body craving something I couldn't quite name.

And then, I smelled smoke and citrus.

"What do you want, Dainan?" I turned, finding him standing

with his arms folded across his chest like always. His eyes were darker than usual like he had something weighing on him too.

"That isn't very friendly now, is it?" He smirked, but there was an unease in his expression. He wore a sleeveless black tunic, the top few buttons undone, exposing his chest. I tried to ignore the memory of what it felt like to touch those muscles beneath my fingertips, our dance, that night, the last time we had spoken.

He can smell arousal on you, I scolded myself, trying to hold it together.

"Excuse me—what do you want, *Lord of Shadows*?" I added with a little more bite.

He chuckled a low sound that made my heart skip a beat. "It's been a while since we've spoken. I wanted to see how you were." He took a step closer, unfolding his arms, his eyes softer now, watching me.

"And you chose tonight? Here?" I gestured around me, trying to make sense of the sudden encounter.

"It seemed...pressing." He glanced toward the track.

"Pressing?" I raised an eyebrow.

He hesitated. "I heard you screaming."

My jaw clenched. "I'm fine," I muttered.

"From what I heard, I'd say you're lying to me, Ilia," he said, stepping even closer.

"I'm not in the mood for your games, Dainan," I sighed, starting to walk past him toward the door.

His hand shot out, catching mine. "I told you once—this is no game." His eyes, burning brighter now, held me captive.

I stopped, my heart pounding. "How do your eyes do that?" I blurted out, not aware of what I was saying.

"Do what?"

My heart raced. His eyes were burning, the storm inside them so much like my own. And before I could stop myself, my hand was on his cheek, my fingers tracing the contours of his face like they'd been there a thousand times before. His skin was warm, almost too warm.

"A waltz of flame and shadow dance in your eyes. Rage and darkness fighting for supremacy, an ongoing battle, a fiery storm," I reached up, placing my hand on his cheek. "Why do you live in the shadows, Dainan?" For a moment, I lost myself as if the words I was speaking weren't my own, but despite everything, I'd felt compelled to say them.

He studied me, his gaze piercing. "I'll answer if you do."

I realized then that I was caressing his face and slowly pulled my hand away, my mind racing. "I'm sorry..."

"What are you sorry for?" His eyes didn't leave mine.

"I shouldn't have done that," I whispered, stepping back.

His face darkened. "Did someone hurt you this evening?"

"What makes you think that?"

"I heard you." He sighed, and I could feel his frustration. "And I came. But I saw you were alone."

"I was alone," I confirmed.

He stepped toward me again, his voice low and dangerous. "Did someone hurt you?

I shook my head. "Not in the way you think." Exhaustion settled into my bones. "I need to go, Dainan. It's late."

He walked towards me, I didn't move. "You're safe with me, Ilia." His thumb grazed my cheek as he rubbed soft circles along my jawline.

I longed to surrender to his touch despite knowing it was unwise. In my shattered state, resisting him felt almost impossible. Looking up at him, I saw the shadows in his eyes had vanished, replaced by embers that danced in flames.

"Thank you," I whispered as he brushed away a tear that coursed down my cheek.

"You don't need to thank me," he pulled me in closer to him. His embrace offered me a brief moment of sanctuary. It felt for an instant as if we were suspended in time. Everything around us, fading into obscurity. I wasn't sure if his shadows were cocooning me as they once had or if I had allowed myself to let go.

His scent, his touch, it all soothed me in a way I couldn't explain. I could feel his heart beating, pulsating with an intensity that left me breathless.

The cold kiss of shadows lingered on my skin as Dainan vanished, leaving me in my dimly lit room. The imprint of his body against mine faded slowly, the quiet moments we had shared—without a single word between us—echoed in the silence. He hadn't pushed for more. His restraint wasn't out of politeness, I knew. It was control. And if he had pressed, if he'd tried to pull anything from me, I wouldn't have answered. My walls were still too fragile, my mind too tangled. His fingertips had brushed my hair back from my face, a light touch that sent warmth through me, and his kiss on my cheek had been soft, almost an apology. Then, without a sound, he disappeared into the night.

The stillness swallowed me, but for once, I wasn't restless. Exhaustion wrapped around me like a heavy blanket. I shed my clothes, the weight of the day still clinging to my skin, but my bed offered comfort I hadn't known in days. As I sank into it, sleep claimed me.

Morning came too soon. The remnants of whatever comfort Dainan's presence had given me had long since vanished. Kadian was the same as always when I checked on him.

By the time I made it to the dining hall, my stomach was growling loud enough to announce my presence. The smell of eggs, meats, and bread filled the air, mingling with the scent of summer blooms. Tamra and Oz were already seated, their bickering providing the usual backdrop of noise. They'd prepared a plate for me, as always.

"Eat up," Tamra smiled, pushing the plate across the table. I hadn't realized how hungry I was until I took the first bite. The meat melted on my tongue, the seasoning more vivid than I remembered.

The spices were sharp, alive in a way that made me wonder if I'd been numb all this time.

I glanced up between bites. "You guys don't taste a difference today?" I asked, licking a bit of sauce from my thumb.

Oz shrugged, too wrapped up in whatever argument he and Tamra were having to pay me any real attention. "I thought we were supposed to be learning something useful," he groaned.

Tamra rolled her eyes and smacked him upside the head. "Use this as a chance to see how they handle disasters. According to Asana, the Eternal Court's been lost on how to deal with this. It's their worst mess since the Collapse."

The word lingered in the air, heavy with history I didn't know. My mouth opened, questions forming, but Tamra was already halfway down the hall, off to wherever Amera waited.

Oz sighed, watching his sister's retreating figure. "She's going to have to introduce her to me at some point," he muttered, stabbing a piece of sausage with unnecessary force.

I hid my smirk behind a sip of coffee. "Maybe if you weren't so damn protective, she wouldn't have to worry about it."

His eyes shifted to me, narrowing playfully. "Fae males are territorial by nature. Hard to break something that's in our blood." His tone was casual, but there was a weight to his words that made me pause.

"Territorial?" I snapped my fingers in front of his face when his gaze lingered on Tamra and Amera. "Focus."

He blinked, pulling himself out of his thoughts. "Yes, sorry. It's just how we are."

"What do you mean territorial?"

Oz leaned in closer, an amused glint in his eye. "You really don't know about this?"

I shook my head. "I didn't grow up around the Fae, remember?"

"Kadian's Fae," he shot back as if I'd said something absurd.

"Kadian has Fae blood, sure. But he's more human than anything."

Oz barked out a laugh, choking on his food. “Have you seen the way he looks at Lil? He’s Fae. He might look like a human but I’d argue his blood is pure Fae.”

I didn’t have an answer for that.

“But Tamra’s your sister,” I pointed out, shifting the topic back to safer ground. “How is that the same?”

His face softened, just a touch. “We’re protective of anyone we love. Familial bonds are strong, but it’s different with mates. It’s... primal.”

I narrowed my eyes. “Mates?”

Oz’s grin widened. “While I’m flattered, Brida, I’d say we’re not destined to be mates.”

I groaned, rolling my eyes. “Don’t be an ass.”

His laughter was easy, filling the space between us. “Mates began with the Primals, Giaxia and Ollo. She rejected their bond, and Ollo went mad because of it.”

“What does the Eternal Court have to say about mates and mating bonds?”

He wiped his hands on his napkin, shaking his head. “Some believe the bond spread from the Primals to the Fae. It’s said that when a bond is denied, it can drive a man insane, maybe even kill him.”

I let the silence sit between us for a moment before asking, “How does it kill them?”

Oz’s face darkened. “No one knows. It’s more of a myth than anything, but...” His voice trailed off as he considered me. “Why the sudden interest?”

I chose my words, weighing the truth against my hesitation. “After everything I’ve seen since I got here... I’m not sure what to believe anymore.”

He nodded, his expression thoughtful. “A healthy dose of skepticism is good. Just make sure you leave room for the unknown.” He winked before standing up and leaving the table, his laughter echoing in the empty dining hall.

I cursed under my breath, realizing how much time I had lost. If I didn't move soon, I'd be late.

The halls of the House of Shadows whispered my name as I approached. "Good afternoon, Brida," the shadows purred, their presence brushing against my skin like a lover's caress. I couldn't help but respond, feeling foolish every time I did.

Alvar greeted me as I entered, his formal attire a stark contrast to his usual casual demeanor. "Brida," he smiled. "I'm sorry, but I've been called away."

I tilted my head, taking in his crisp black jacket with red embroidery. He adjusted the collar with a sigh, uncomfortable in the formality.

"Anything you want me to work on while you're gone? I'm happy to work on whatever." I offered, eager for something to occupy my mind.

"Wonderful!" He clapped his hands together after he adjusted his jacket. "I hate wearing these things," he muttered to himself.

"Suits?"

"Any formal wear, really," he sighed.

"Well, it makes you look dashing if that makes you feel any better." I smiled at him, I meant it.

His lips curled upwards, his eyes sparkling, "That's very kind of you, Brida. What's that saying? Flattery will get you everywhere?" He laughed.

"What would you like me to work on while you're gone?" I tried to get him to refocus.

"I've written down a list of books that I would like you to retrieve for me from the library. The list is..." he reached into all of his pockets and snarled. "I thought it was in this jacket, but alas, it's in my other one, which is in my room downstairs."

"If you wish for me to do something else.."

"No, no," he interrupted, "please go into my rooms, retrieve the list; it should be in the right front pocket of the other black jacket, I swear we are only ever given black," he began to stray off topic.

"Are you alright?" I asked, not sure if I was overstepping my bounds.

He raised his eyebrows to me, "Are we friends now, Brida?" His tone was jovial.

"I thought that was your intention for this partnership, *Alvar,*" I replied.

He laughed once more, "I never enjoy going to the Court of Reflection, it's beautiful to be sure, but I don't thrive there." He double checked his pockets.

"You're going to the Court of Reflection today?" My curiosity piqued.

He nodded, "You'll find, Brida, when you're officially a member of a court, when you visit another court, which I will admit is rare," he paused, looking at me, "you feel as if you don't belong there. Your magic is unruly, not truly your own. Now," he said, "please go into my chambers, get that list, find those books, and if you wish, begin reading them. When you've retrieved them all, you may leave them with the librarian or you may leave them in my quarters. While I don't sleep there, the room does come in handy for storage."

He began to stride towards the exit.

"Good luck today," I said.

He winked at me, "And to you."

As he disappeared through the doorway, I turned, making my way down to the prince's rooms. The stairwell was alive, like every part of the House of Shadows.

Smoke and shadow slithered along the floors and walls. The veins of fire that pulsed through the stone gave light and life to everything around it.

The stairs, made of polished volcanic rock, maintained natural grooves along its edges. I needed to pay close attention to each step I took. It was a long way down, and I didn't want to fall.

Each brother had been allotted three adjoining rooms on one of the lower levels. Alvar's was first, then Dainan's, followed by Rai's. I took a step towards Alvar's rooms and saw the door come alive.

Shadows began to swirl as if it were forming a maze, hiding the handle.

I remembered at this moment that Alvar had protected his room with wards, Much of the palace was warded. "*An ancient practice,*" Illerium had noted. I didn't know how I was going to be able to get inside.

With each step closer, it felt as if the shadows hissed in protest. Sensing the subtle warning, I chose not to push my luck any further.

I peered down the hall and saw that the door to Dainan's room was slightly ajar. I walked towards it and knocked, "Dainan?" I asked. "Are you here?" Within a second, a shirtless Dainan stood in front of me.

"Good morning," he said in a smooth voice.

"It's afternoon, Dainan," I smirked, "you do know that we only come here in the afternoons."

"*Mmm,*" was all he replied as he observed what I was wearing.

"Are you just waking up?" I cocked an eyebrow at him as my gaze drifted to the v in the muscles of his lower abdomen.

"I had a late night last night," he smirked. "Have you come to see me because you realized just how much you miss me, Ilia?" He pulled back, "I must say, I'm flattered," he put his palm to his chest in mockery.

"That's not why I'm here," I said through gritted teeth.

"Did you get lost? I've heard that your sense of direction is something of note."

"And who told you that?" I asked him.

"It's no secret that you were lost no less than three times on your second day here. Did Alvar not give you a tour?"

"He did..."

"Would you like another? I can think of several places I'd love to show you." He took a step towards me.

"As a matter of fact," I replied, "there is somewhere I would like you to take me."

His eyes shone with intrigue. He took another step towards me, my blood began humming. "Stop that," I found myself saying.

He cocked an eyebrow at me, "Stop *what*?"

I didn't want to have *that* conversation. "I need you to help me. Do you think you'll be able to do so?"

He was inches from me now. I could feel the heat radiating off of his sun-kissed skin. His hair was unkempt but beautiful with its slight wave. It fell across his face in a way that only brought more attention to his cheekbones and eyes. They were calmer this morning.

"You need *my* help with something?" He purred.

"I do," I found myself beginning to lean into him. His scent was entrancing. It was as if I couldn't get enough air, I just needed more.

"Ask nicely then, Ilia," he lowered his head and whispered, "say *please Dainan.*"

"*Please,*" I said while holding his gaze.

"Ah ah, *please, Dainan*. You must say the whole thing."

I stood for a moment in silence just staring into his eyes. The flames that had been embers were smoldering. His scent of smoke and citrus was now joined by that salty tinge that I sometimes noticed when he was around.

"Fine." I began to say, "*Please, Dai...*"

"*Ahem,*" I turned my head to see Iona standing there, eyes seething at the sight of me.

"Yes?" Dainan snarled at her.

"I was wondering what I should be working on today?" She asked, her eyes lingered on his naked chest.

"The same thing as yesterday," he refused to move his eyes from me.

"If you need anything..." she began to say.

"Then I'll let you know," he growled.

As Iona walked away, I looked back towards him, "Now *that* wasn't particularly friendly."

He rested one of his hands on the doorframe, using the other to rub his eyes, "Is there something *specific* you needed?" His tone back to its velvet melody.

I paused for a moment, "Your brother wanted me to retrieve something from his room; however, I'm unable to get past the wards. I thought perhaps..."

"That I would be able to?" He smiled as his gaze drifted toward my mouth.

"Exactly," I said, swallowing hard.

My mind wandered to last night when he'd held me. I found myself leaning in towards him.

His scent... Gods.

"Ilia?"

"Hm?" I said, trying to refocus.

"Give me a moment," he walked into the room, grabbing a shirt. "We can't have you getting *distracted*," he said to me as he put it on.

I sighed as he accompanied me back to Alvar's door. He placed his palm on a spot that the shadows had cleared for him, as if they recognized him. A moment later, a blood-red door knob appeared, and he opened it. The rooms were pristine, and well organized. Everything that I would have expected from Alvar. I walked in and saw the black jacket hanging off the back of the chair that sat at his desk. It was littered with books.

"You know," Dainan said, leaning against the doorframe, a grin on his face, "Alvar must like you if he asked you to retrieve something from here. He doesn't just allow anyone into his quarters."

"If that's the case, the feeling is mutual," I said, reaching into the right front pocket. "Ah," I held up the paper for Dainan to see. As I attempted to exit, he filled the doorway.

"Are you better this morning?" He whispered.

I looked into his eyes and saw concern reflected in them. I nodded in response. "I am."

He stood for a moment longer, brushing his fingers along my jawline. Slowly stroking my face. The thrumming in my body returned once more, and he knew it. His mouth twitched into a smile as he leaned down and whispered, "*Should you need anything else.*" His breath sent a fiery sensation through me.

I knew I needed to move, but my body refused to listen. "What is it *you* want, *Dainan*?" His grin only grew more wicked as his thumb inched its way closer to my mouth.

The smell of salt was beginning to overtake my senses. I found myself losing the ability to think clearly. *Move around him and get to the library. You have the list, just go.*

"There are many things I want," each of his words dripped with temptation.

Gods. I stared at him for a moment longer before losing all sense of control. "*And what do you need, Dainan?*"

He stiffened, not taking his eyes from my mouth, "I think I've made it clear what it is I *need*, Ilia."

I stepped closer, pressing my body into his. I could feel his need —a pulsing, aching need that I was beginning to feel within myself. I wrapped my hand around his neck, digging my nails in. He moaned at my touch. His fingers intertwined with my hair as he guided my face towards his. Our lips hovered tantalizingly close, the warmth of his breath brushing against mine.

"Do you understand what it is that I need, Ilia?"

I was molten. A low chuckle rumbled deep in his chest, "it appears I'm not the only one with this *need*," he said, leaning in to kiss me.

"Dainan," a voice came from behind him. He didn't flinch or move. "Dainan," the voice was more forceful this time.

"This better be important, Asana," he turned around, blocking me from her view.

"We've been trying to reach you all morning. You're needed."

"I came here to avoid being called upon; I'm exactly where I need to be," he growled.

"This is not a request and is not my order. You need to be ready to leave in minutes." The sound of her footsteps faded as she left.

Dainan remained with his back to me. I could see the tension that had risen within him. Finally, he looked at me, lifting his hand to my cheek. "When I come back, we'll continue this conversation." He stepped into the shadows and was gone.

It took me a few moments to catch my breath and think about what I'd almost just done.

There was no pucchia in the air to blame this time. This had been my own choice, and I had been the one to push him. I closed the door behind me and made my way to the library.

☽✳☾

I said hello to Tura, the librarian, as I entered. She nodded to acknowledge me. Unlike the main library in Azmeer, the library in the House of Shadows possessed no windows. It didn't need one. The fire from the walls and the braziers that lined the stacks made one almost think daylight lived inside this room.

I began to scan the list and retrieve each book Alvar requested. None of the books seemed connected, at least not by their titles. The books ranged from topics on soil in the Alduan region to fire wielders of the past.

Starting with one of the earliest known followers of Vasenia, I delved into an ancient journal among the six novels I'd retrieved. I'd found a stylus and paper to take notes, thinking perhaps Alvar would find it useful.

I continued to read until I saw someone sitting down from me across the table.

"Can I help you with something? I said.

Iona sat there, her expression seething with anger. "What the fuck do you think you're doing?" she asked me, venom dripping from each word.

"Right now?" I asked her, " I think it's clear that I'm reading a book and taking notes. I've never seen you with a book, can I interest you in a story? I know several that would be of particular interest to you."

"Do not play coy with me." Iona had never spoken to me. In the days that we'd been in the House of Shadows, we'd seldom seen each other.

"How can I help you, Iona? If it's not a book that you're after, I'm not sure there is much I can do for you." I asked, putting the book down on the table while noting my place.

She stood, making her way around to face me. She placed the palm of her hand down and leaned in closer, "Stay the fuck away from him." She snarled.

"Dainan."

She nodded. "He's spoken for, stay the fuck away from him, Brida."

I rose to meet her, "I think he's capable of making his own decisions, and I think it's clear, *Iona*, that if he were spoken for, he'd let me know himself."

She laughed, "This was a courtesy. Do yourself a favor and stay where it's safe. You do not want to become tangled with shadows, Brida," she turned her back to me and walked away.

I stood in silence for a few moments longer before sitting back down. Attempting to distract myself, I chose to get lost in the books in front of me.

I only knew that hours had passed when Tura informed me that I was free to go to dinner. She agreed to hold the books for me until tomorrow, understanding that I couldn't leave them in Alvar's room without someone breaking the wards for me again. I found I wasn't very hungry and decided to visit Kadian earlier than planned.

Magister Thorne greeted me as I entered the infirmary, telling me there'd been no changes. He remained stable. I nodded to him in thanks and made my way towards the room they had him in.

I heard the magister mutter something to me as I walked towards Kadian, but was so tired that I didn't process what it was he'd said. I opened the door and, for a moment, was paralyzed. There was a woman with long, flowing golden hair who was sitting on the bed with Kadian's hand in hers.

"I was wondering when you would show up."

CHAPTER
THIRTY-SIX

"Lil!" I shouted as I made my way over to her, embracing her.

I pulled back to look at her; she looked horrible. Pallid and drained of color, "How are you here right now?" I said, holding her hands in mine.

"I don't have long," she said as she rose from the bed.

"When did you get here?" I asked her while looking down at Kadian. He looked the same as he had every other time I'd been to see him.

"I got here about thirty minutes ago," she said as she made her way next to his head. She began to run her hand through his hair. "How long has he been like this?" She asked without taking her eyes off of him.

"Ten days," I whispered, the words catching in my throat like a secret I'd been holding onto for too long. It had been ten long days. Ten days of haunting the House of Shadows, feeling its constant warmth seep into my bones, while the nights slipped away in the library, surrounded by crumbling pages and the dim glow of candlelight. I searched for anything on bonds, some clue or thread of understanding. But every search came up empty.

Ten days of asking, pleading, trying not to sound too desperate as I prodded anyone I could find. "Have you seen her? Lil?" My voice had grown thinner, more strained with each passing day, like a song that had lost its melody. Each time, I received the same response: a shake of the head, a furrowed brow, a distant stare.

"What happened to him?" She continued to stroke his hair and then began to stroke his face.

"Where have you been, Lil?"

She turned her glance to me, "At the Court of Reflection," she said. She pulled her hand back as if she realized what she'd been doing.

"Have you been back here at all? We haven't seen you in months." I was desperate for answers.

"Twice, but I wasn't permitted to go anywhere without my uncle. Did my mother not speak to you? I told her to find you, the both of you." She looked back down at Kadian.

"She did."

"And?" Lil asked, "What did she tell you?"

"Other than the fact that Kadian needed to get his shit together and dust his room, not a whole lot, Lil."

"*To dust*?" Lil questioned under her breath.

"I needed to speak with you after the festival for Giaxia, but your uncle showed up, and then you were gone. A lot has happened, but I need you to know a few things. Rai..."

"Don't get me started about Rai," Lil cut me off, turning to face the window.

Kadian's view overlooked another beautiful garden. There were so many of them here. This particular one was filled with lavender, chamomile, and mint. All known for their healing properties. I had snuck into this particular garden during one of our first weeks in Azmeer. The herbs were available in Escalia, but if there was a chance they were a different variety, or imbued with magic somehow, I had wanted Dad to have them. To have any chance at beating the odds.

"Unfortunately, we have to talk about him. He says you have something of his and wants it back." I took a step towards her. A tear streaked down her face. "What's going on, Lil?" I placed my hand on her arm, squeezing to remind her I was there.

She looked as if she were breaking in front of me. The beautiful, happy, and vivacious girl I'd met on my trip to Azmeer had ceased to exist, replaced by this empty vessel that cracked with the slightest touch.

"I have to go," Lil said, turning towards the door.

"Lil..." pleading in my voice for her to understand that she couldn't leave yet.

"Brida, stop talking," Lil said, panic flaring in her eyes.

"Lil..." I continued to say.

"Bri..."

"There you are."

We both turned to the door and saw Prince Rai entering. "I was wondering where you had made your way off to."

I didn't know if I was stunned or unsurprised.

"Brida," He spoke with firmness yet maintained a royal level of cordiality.

I bowed my head at him, "Prince Rai," I was seething.

Keep it together.

"Have you told her the good news?" He stood by Lil, placing his hand on her lower back. She turned ashen. "Well, did you?" He asked again.

"I hadn't yet," she faked a small smile, looking him in the eye. "Brida was just about to tell me of her placement. I've been out these last weeks, and we haven't been able to keep each other informed."

"You're in the House of Shadows, are you not?" Rai inclined his head towards me.

"I am," I nodded

"Is Alvar keeping you busy?" A smile landed on his face, appearing genuine at first glance, but beneath it lurked a predatory intent.

"He's been a wonderful advisor and teacher thus far. I look forward to continuing to work with him."

"No doubt your work will now include planning," his grin grew wicked.

"Planning?" I looked over to Lil.

"But of course," Rai said, grabbing Lil's hand, raising it to me. Lil wore a rose gold ring adorned with a large black onyx at its center, flanked by three rubies on each side.

"*Uhm,*" I tried to clear my throat.

"Everything was finalized this afternoon." Rai's voice sang victoriously.

This is why Dainan and Alvar were called away. I wondered if either of them had known.

I looked at Lil, she stood still and did not flinch. "Congratulations," I said, shifting my gaze to Rai. I wanted to be sick.

"Thank you," Rai chuckled, pulling Lil in closer to him. "The wedding will take place in a few months, following a ball in our honor."

"Will that be in addition to the ball to honor Vasenia?" I asked.

"It will be in lieu of it," he snarled.

"Lil," he looked to her, "I wish to have a word with Brida in regards to Alvar," he pressed his lips to her cheek. The little remaining color drained from her.

Dark circles marred the skin beneath her eyes, evidence of countless sleepless nights. Her bright eyes now were now dull and lifeless, gazing into the distance with an unfocused stare.

"I'll wait for you outside," she said to Rai.

He watched her leave the room, waiting until she was gone to speak. "A word of advice, Brida," he took a step closer to me as he clasped his hands behind his back. "My marriage wasn't the only thing decided today," he paused, glancing at Kadian, "pity," turning his gaze back to me.

"Be cautious with whom you associate during your placement. The House of Shadows is indeed exclusive, and while we are skilled at keeping secrets, rumors can still circulate," he took a deliberate step closer, "you wouldn't want to upset those who hold sway over your final placement, especially if you aspire to join the Court of Shadows."

"What's this about?" I asked, putting myself between him and Kadian.

"A very many things," he sighed, "despite you ignoring my request when we last spoke, I found a way to reclaim what belonged to me."

"*She's not your property,*" I growled at him.

"No," he laughed, "she's just a nice perk." He turned, making his way to the door, before looking back at me, "Do heed my advice, Brida. It's for your own benefit." He turned the handle and closed the door behind him.

I stood in silence before collapsing in the chair that sat next to the bed. *Lil is to be married. To Rai. What does this mean for her? For the Courting? For Kadian?*

With Kadian's hand in mine, I closed my eyes as the tears began to roll down my cheeks. I sat there until the sun had been swallowed by the evening sky, and I eventually fell asleep.

CHAPTER THIRTY-SEVEN

I opened my eyes. I didn't know where I was. It was nowhere in Azmeer, nowhere I'd been before. I stood beneath a veil of shadow, the night sky stretching overhead, a vast canvas of velvety darkness studded with stars that glimmered like scattered diamonds, a breathtaking midnight tapestry.

"*Brida,*" I thought I heard someone whisper.

Ahead in the distance, moonlight danced upon the still waters of a lake, surrounded by fireflies that assisted in lighting up the night sky.

"*Brida.*" I turned, but I did not see anyone. "*The water, Brida.*"

I was barefoot, standing on dew-covered grass. I wiggled my toes and felt the blades between them. The air was cool and crisp but had a faint hint of salt.

The sound of crickets filled the air as I approached the water. I couldn't recall the last time I'd heard that familiar melody, perhaps during a camping trip with Dad or Kadian. It was a comforting sound, evoking memories of simpler and happier times in my life.

Everything was calm here. Other than the fireflies, there was no movement. No evening breeze like there was in Azmeer. It almost felt as if this place were in stasis. A perfect moment forever frozen in time.

I began to feel a slight tingle in my arms as I neared the edge of the lake. There was no beach, just some marshes along the water.

"*Look down, Brida,*" I heard the voice say, taking my final steps.

For the first few moments, all I saw was the silver light reflecting the moon. Just prior to a full moon, it was a waxing gibbous. A moon in transition.

I saw nothing as I stared into the water.

"*Focus,*" I heard the voice say, "*I need you to picture me, Brida,*" I closed my eyes and tried to hone in on the voice. Where it was possibly coming from, and who it belonged to.

"*Do you hear me, Brida?*"

"Yes," I whispered. I knew that voice, it felt so close, and yet so far. "Lil?" I asked, opening my eyes.

"Finally," she said as she came into focus in the body of water.

"How..." I began to ask.

"We don't have much time. I'm using liquid night. I'm sorry I had to do this to you, but I knew that you would touch Kadian's hand."

"Did you mark him with this?" She nodded her head.

"I stole some from Thalius. Not enough for him to realize it's missing and not enough for us to have a full-length conversation." She began, "I knew Rai would show up while we were talking today, and I'm sorry he spoke to you that way and no doubt threatened you."

"You don't need to apologize to me. You don't need to apologize for any of this. How did this happen?" I asked her, "And how am I here?" I looked around once more. The sound of the crickets had vanished into the everlasting night.

"You know that we can use bodies of water to communicate images. Well, I'm sending myself through the reflection. I will explain more later; however, in the meantime, I need you to know a few things."

I nodded at her.

"As Rai told you earlier today, we're to be married. Thalius coordinated a deal between the two courts. Both sides believe it to be a good match." She paused for a moment, "Not everyone, of course, but most."

"Who knew about this deal?"

"Very few. Thalius, the head of the Court of Reflection, Fayma, Rai, and the king. Brida, as much as I'd love to answer your questions, this isn't the most important thing right now. Alvar has been marked. His mark appeared during our meeting today; he will be king."

"Marked?" I asked her, "What does that mean?"

"It's literal. A mark appeared on his hand today during the meeting. We knew it was happening, it's supposed to be painful."

"What did he say about the marriage?" I asked, dreading how she might respond.

"He was opposed to it. As was Dainan, speaking of..." she paused, "*shit,* I'm running out of time. Brida, you need to wake up now." Her brow furrowed. "I'll be in touch if I can. Wake up, Brida. Now."

My eyes flew open, and I gasped for air. My breathing was labored. It felt as if my lungs had been filled with water. I'd been on the ground in the vision; however, it felt now as if I'd been submerged. I stayed bent over in the chair for several minutes as I gained my composure. Steadying myself, I rose from the chair and stared out the window. There were fewer stars in the sky than where I'd been. No crickets sang, no fireflies danced in the air around me.

I made my way over to Kadian, placed a kiss on his forehead, and whispered, "I love you, please wake up," and closed the door behind me as I left.

Alvar is to be king, I thought to myself. He seemed the logical choice. He was kind, considerate, and intelligent. I knew it was unlikely to have been Dainan, he was the youngest of the three, and according to Alvar, had shown zero desire to rule.

I didn't envy Alvar. The transition of a kingdom now rested on his shoulders. Continuing a longstanding peace that the king had battled for, killed for. The eyes of the world would be on him. And me, as I would be doing his work in the shadows.

I would help him in whatever way I could. He'd tried to stop the marriage between Rai and Lil. For that alone he had my gratitude, but beyond that, I believed Alvar and I were becoming friends.

Reflecting in the torch light, a shiny black envelope lay on the floor outside of my bedroom. The seal on it was blood red, the seal of the Court of Shadows.

After opening the door to my room and lighting the candles on my desk, I ripped open the envelope.

Dear Inductee,
It is with great pleasure that His Majesty King Elidas announces the engagement of his second son,
Prince Rai Luchien to Lilianna Towler of Lesalia, niece of Thalius Towler.
His Majesty also wishes to announce the engagement of his third son, Prince Dainan Luchien, to Iona Vorren of Azmeer, daughter of Deter Vorren.
In honor to celebrate their engagements, a ball will be thrown in their honor on the twelfth day of next month.

I held the letter over the open flame and watched it burn.

CHAPTER
THIRTY-EIGHT

My marriage was not the only thing decided today.

His words replayed themselves in my mind.

My marriage was not the only thing decided today.

Lil was to marry Rai, Alvar was to be king, and Dainan...

You mean absolutely nothing to him; he is trying to make a point. This is a fucking game to him.

"Bri?"

You mean absolutely nothing to him; he is trying to make a point. This is a fucking game to him.

"Bri?" I heard faintly.

"I'm not sure she hears you?"

I knew that voice.

My marriage was not the only thing decided today.

"Brida!" I snapped out of it as my body was jostled. Oz and Tamra looked at me, their eyes wide and full of shock.

They're in my room? How are they in here?

"You're going to need a new handle," Oz said as he determined what I was trying to figure out. I leaned back to look around them and saw my door handle in pieces on the floor.

"You weren't answering... We had a feeling something might be wrong," Tamra said, pushing my hair from my face.

"What time is it?" I finally managed to ask.

"You missed breakfast, if that's what you're wondering," she replied as she gestured to the plate of pastries she'd placed on my bedside table.

I noticed Oz pacing around the room, looking for something.

My marriage was not the only thing decided today.

"If you are looking for a black envelope with a red seal, you won't find it here," I said, his eyes shot to me.

"*Shit,*" Tamra said, "you saw it then?"

I nodded without uttering a word.

"Did you know?" Oz cocked an eyebrow at me. "About Lil, that is," he added.

"I didn't, not really," I pulled the covers from my legs and rose out of bed. "Thank you both for coming to check on me and..." I looked back at the pieces on my floor, "breaking my handle to make sure I was okay," I smiled at the two of them. "I'm fine. I need to get ready now if I'm going to be on time for the House of Shadows." I made my way to my bathing chamber.

"Do you want me to wait to go with you?" Tamra rose from the bed.

"That's sweet of you, thank both of you, but I'm fine." I paused to see the non-believing looks rest upon their faces, "Truly. I'm okay."

They stood for a moment longer before they each nodded. "If you need anything," Oz said.

"Anything," Tamra reiterated, "don't hesitate to ask."

"Thanks," I said, closing the door to the bathing chamber behind me.

I was a mess. Despite washing my hair only yesterday, it looked as if it hadn't been cleaned in weeks. My eyes were puffy from crying, and my face was swollen. *A good look*, I thought to myself.

I sighed, and made my way out through the broken door. I

needed to stop by Illerium's office before making my way to the House of Shadows. I had no idea how to get a new handle.

I knocked on Illerium's door, "Come in," he bellowed.

"Magister Illerium," I stepped inside. He wasn't alone.

"Yes, Brida?"

"I wasn't sure who to ask this question to..." I began to say as Marsh looked me up and down.

"Yes?" He asked.

You mean absolutely nothing to him; he is trying to make a point. This is a fucking game to him.

"Ms. Larrow, I don't have all day. Spit it out."

"Sorry, Magister," I tried to stay focused, "There's been an issue with my door handle and it broke. I'm requiring a replacement."

He sighed, "I'll put in a request, is that all?"

I nodded, "Very well," he said, brushing me off with his hand. "Marsh, you can go too. Report back when you know more."

I didn't have to look behind me to know Marsh was now inches from me, I could feel his presence.

"Brida?" He closed the door behind us.

"*Hm*?" I turned to face him.

"Are you alright?" He asked, taking a step towards me.

I lifted my gaze to meet him, his brows furrowed. I must've looked as terrible as I assumed. "I'm fine," I said, forcing a smile.

He stood in silence for a moment as he placed his hands into his pockets, "How's Kadian?"

"The same... I need to get going Marsh." I turned to leave.

"Brida, if you need anything, please come find me," he took another step towards me, his arm having reached out until he thought the better of it.

"Thanks," I smiled and left.

☽✳☾

Good afternoon, Brida, the door purred.

“Good afternoon to you too, whoever you are,” I could have sworn I heard it laugh.

There was no one waiting inside when I arrived. The walls shone, and the shadows hissed in whatever language they were using to speak to each other. I felt a shadow begin to swirl up my leg. It wasn’t the first time they’d tried to do this. In the past when they had reached my knee, they stopped. One shadow was more adventurous today as it swirled from my leg up my torso until it reached my side. It paused there for a moment before retreating back down towards my arm. It circled my wrist for a few moments before beginning to play with my fingers.

“Hello,” I said as I lifted my hand to my face.

I heard a slight hiss and felt a tingling sensation. “Nice to meet you, too,” I whispered. A moment later, it traveled back down to the floor where it sat as if waiting for me. “Do you know where Prince Alvar is?” It began to slither across the floor towards the stairs.

I’m beginning to go insane, I thought, watching the shadows. I gave in to that insanity and decided to follow. The shadows proceeded up the stairs, the opposite direction of Alvar’s rooms and the library.

We hadn’t gone this way when I’d been given my tour, sticking to the main floor and the two floors below. I knew there were countless levels in here, you’d need more than a few hours to see all of it.

As I neared the level where the shadows stopped, the heat emanating from the walls intensified. I heard shouting. Fifteen feet ahead of me, an entryway to a partially open door caught my eye. The shadows crawled towards the doorway and hissed, as if telling me to march that direction.

The voices grew louder, “How could you let this happen. You, of all fucking people, how the fuck could you let this happen,” the voice screamed.

“You know that I have very little say in the matter. I did what I could in the moment and will continue to look into it. In the meantime, I am sorry.”

"Sorry? You are fucking sorry. You are not the one who is going to be stuck with *that.*"

I was mere feet from the door now. I could see Alvar sitting in a chair while Dainan paced back and forth. Running his fingers through his hair.

"You can stop this, Alvar; you can put an end to it. You have the mark."

"The mark just appeared yesterday, and as you yourself know, it's not complete yet. I cannot force its completion, and I don't have the final say until that time."

Silence lingered for a few moments. "What am I supposed to do?" Dainan asked his brother, pleading in his voice.

"You will have to grin and bear it. Your life will not appear too different on the surface."

I heard a scoff. "That's easy for you to say, you have Asana."

So they are involved.

"You will get through this, Dainan. But as I said, until the mark is complete, my hands are tied."

I heard Alvar rise from his chair and begin to step towards the door. I backed away, not wanting them to know I'd been listening.

"Brida," Alvar said in a jovial tone.

Too late. I smiled at him as he pulled the door open wider, revealing Dainan inside. His expression was bleak, and his complexion ashen. Before another second passed, Dainan shadow-stepped and was gone.

Alvar raised his eyebrows after looking back to where his brother had been standing before returning his gaze to me. "How did you know I was up here?" He asked with a small smile on his lips.

"The..." I began to say, "the shadows told me." I didn't wish to lie to him. Besides, it could very well be known that the shadows do in fact communicate.

"*Did they*?" He chuckled. "Well," he continued as he stepped out of the room, gesturing us towards the stairs.

"I'm most apologetic for my absence yesterday. A few unforeseeable events needed tending to."

"It seems you are to gain two new family members. Congratulations."

"*Hmm*," was all he responded. It was uncharacteristic for him not to offer more.

"Did you hear much or all of the conversation upstairs?" He asked as we continued to descend.

I kept walking, but I didn't answer him for a moment, "All," I admitted.

He laughed, "I had a feeling. Dainan can be quite boisterous when he's upset. I'm surprised the entire House of Shadows wasn't outside waiting to see who would come out the victor."

"You appeared rather calm and collected."

"Yes, well," his tone was somber, "I deal with things in my own way."

"In the spirit of friendship and all," I turned to face him, "if you ever wanted to talk to someone."

His smile returned. "Thank you, Brida. In the meantime however, I do believe I asked you to retrieve some books for me yesterday, and it seems now that we also have some planning to do."

"Planning?"

"Yes," he groaned, "my father has bestowed upon me the task of organizing this *ball* for my brothers."

"Why would he assign that task to you?"

"He claims a king should know what sort of preparation goes into these things. In some way, I suppose he's right."

"Does that mean you're to be king then?"

He raised an eyebrow at me, "Come now, Brida. I think we both know that you already knew the answer to that question," he smirked. We continued down the stairs, "But yes, it seems the crown will fall to me."

"Is this because of the mark that you were discussing with Prince Dainan?"

"*Prince Dainan,* such formalities," he laughed. "Yes, the mark appeared yesterday, but it remains quite faint. It will darken once I am king."

"And in order for that, your father..."

"Has to die, yes." We reached the floor of the library when he stopped to look at me. "I know you didn't expect to be on a party planning committee of sorts when you accepted your placement here, Brida." He laughed, "I myself would not have predicted this either. But, I think we can make it something rather spectacular, that is," he offered me his hand where a faint mark now rested, "if we plan it together."

"I'll do my best to assist you, however I can," I offered him my hand. He clasped it and intertwined our arms.

"Excellent!" He walked us towards the library, "there is a planning room we can use to get ourselves sorted. Now, Brida," he began as he guided us forward, "I am a strong believer that even though there is to be dancing, there should be excellent food as well. Let us begin with canapés."

☽✳☾

Following a lengthy discussion on whether shrimp or lobster vol-au-vents would be better, it was decided that both would be best.

Scattered on the table in front of us were pages of notes, ideas—mostly food, and potential guests. "All of the inductees will be allowed to attend," he said firmly. "This begs the question as to where the ball will be held."

"Would it not be held...in the ballroom at the center court?" I asked him while laughing.

"Yes, Brida," he couldn't hide his sarcasm, "it most certainly would; however, I think it's time we spice things up a bit, don't you?"

"Spice things up how?" I asked , readjusting myself in my chair.

"I think we should hold it here," he said with a grin on his face.

"Here?" I asked, "In the library? I'm not sure how the books would feel about that, they are known for preferring quiet."

"Funny," he smirked, "there is a ballroom here. Come, I will show it to you."

"What, now?" I asked, looking down at the mess we'd made.

"Yes, this," he waved his hand at the papers, "can wait, it will be here when we come back."

"Will that be before tomorrow?" I asked, trying to organize everything.

"Do you always worry this much?" he gestured to the door.

"I've been known to worry every so often."

"Well, we'll have to break you of that habit, won't we! Come now, let's go."

I rose, looking back to the table once more, and left the room.

The ballroom was up on the sixth floor of the House of Shadows, and I found myself trying to memorize the way there.

"Are you always that anxious?" Alvar asked as we approached the third level.

I nodded, "A lot of the time yes. I wasn't always, but..." I felt myself stop.

"You lost someone?" He asked.

"My mother."

"Ah," he said, "on that note, I can sympathize. I too have lost my mother," he said, sadness coating his words.

"How old were you when you lost her?" I asked

"Compared to your human years I would have been quite old, but in Fae years I was still young." He smiled. "I was sixty. It was not long after that my father married Rai's mother." He continued.

"So each of you has a different mother?" I asked him. "All of them coming from the Court of Shadows?"

"Yes," he said as his eyes found mine, "a king is expected to marry within. Of course, my father was not yet a monarch when he and my mother were wed, but it is a tradition upheld by the majority of court members."

"How old were you when your father was crowned king?" He laughed, "If you must know, I was one hundred and thirty-seven when my father came to the throne."

I walked in silence attempting to do the mental math. "I am four hundred and seven, Brida," his laugh deepened. "Still young, but older than most people you know," he winked at me.

Gods. That tightening feeling began to creep back into my chest. He was older than most of the buildings in Escalia. "What happened to your mother?" He asked a moment later.

"She just...died." I said, trying to regain a hold of myself.

"They never offered any explanation?"

I shook my head, "I went to school and kissed her goodbye. I came home, and she was gone."

"How old were you?"

"Seven." We stared at each other for a moment before looking once more to where we were going.

"That must have been very hard. I'm sorry."

"It was. But as I'm sure you know, life goes on."

He agreed.

"What about your mother?" I pressed.

"She was a casualty of one of my father's wars." Bitterness laced his words. "My parents," he continued, "were not a love match. Like Rai, and Dainan." He said as if exasperated, "it was an arranged marriage. One that neither of them wanted. Rai's mother was then given to my father, but it was not long afterward he met Dainan's mother." He sighed, "arranged marriages didn't suit my father. I'm hoping my brothers will fare better."

"Is there much of an age gap between Rai and Dainan?" I wondered.

"They are separated by five months and two days," he smiled. "Their mothers' pregnancies were an awkward period here in Azmeer."

"I can imagine," I muttered under my breath.

"In the spirit of friendship," I said and he laughed, "I take it that Asana is someone that you have chosen to be with."

"You really did hear everything," he cocked an eyebrow at me, "Asana and I have been together for some time. I care for her deeply, and if she'll have me, I want her by my side."

Two black onyx doors embellished with blood rubies were what separated us from this supposed ballroom.

"This ballroom," Alvar said, "is an exact replica of the one at the Court of Shadows." He reached for the handle and opened the doors.

We took a few steps inside, "I can't see anything, Alvar." I chuckled.

"Ah, yes, of course," he waved his hand. A wall of cascading torches welcomed us.

Unlike the other walls in the House of Shadows, these walls did not possess the veins of fire. These walls were shrouded in darkness.

"What is this place?" I said as I walked into the center of the room, unsure where to look first.

"Beautiful, isn't it?"

The ceiling was a vast expanse of darkness, populated with shimmering constellations that mirrored those in the night sky. Each star pulsing with a luminous energy, each star offering an ethereal glow.

The circular dance floor in the center of the room was flanked by obsidian columns that reflected the flames twirling on the walls as if inviting you to dance.

"Why does no one ever use this room?" I whispered. I tilted my head back, watching a shooting star go by.

Alvar chuckled, "I know. It's a shame. I don't believe we've held more than five events here during my lifetime."

He made his way to stand beside me. "Have you thought about which court you would like to be in, Brida?" He inclined his head towards me.

"Of course," I began to say, "and I'm honestly not sure." "Do you feel comfortable *here*?" He asked as he followed my gaze.

“It would be difficult not to feel comfortable here, with such a wonderful host.” I inclined my head towards him and was met with a mocking stare.

“Yes,” I found myself saying, “I’m not going to lie and say that it’s what I expected. I didn’t think that I would be as comfortable here as I am, but,” I continued, “I find solace in the darkness, in the shadows.”

“It is when one learns to embrace the darkness and shadows that one is then able to see light.” He smiled, “it’s always a balance.”

We stood in silence for a few moments longer. “I think,” I began to say, “this ballroom will do quite nicely.”

“I’m glad you think so, Brida.” He smiled at me, “however, we still have quite a bit of planning to do.”

“Do you always worry this much?” I asked.

The soon to be king did not answer me as we both became lost in silence and the beauty of the stars that danced above us.

CHAPTER THIRTY-NINE

Hey Dad,

I got your last letter, I'm thrilled to hear that you have been feeling okay. Has Flora got you moving? I looked at a book last week that noted the importance of continued movement. I've attached a copy that I transcribed.

I have begun my placement in the House of Shadows. I'm not sure if I told you that we had been offered a choice, well, at least I had, and I feel as of this moment that it was the right one.

In addition to being allowed to look through the books in the house's library, I have also been working side by side with the man that is going to be king. That is not something I would ever have thought to put down on paper, and even more to my astonishment, I find myself considering him a friend.

I'm not sure how much longer we will have in our placements. They told us that it would be a few months, but with a possible upcoming coronation, it may be shorter. I'm hoping that I will have more answers soon.

In the meantime, be sure to keep up with your teas, and be well. Give my best to Flora.

I love you,

Bri

☽✳☾

Over the past couple of weeks, I'd gone from fetching books and taking notes to assisting Alvar with planning the ball. Days flew by. I tried to avoid being consumed by my thoughts. Thoughts of Lil, and by extension Kadian, thoughts of which court I may belong to, and whether I would be disappointed if it wasn't the Court of Shadows—considerations of how it would work to be part of the Court of Shadows with Dainan, and Iona.

I hadn't seen or spoken to Marsh, as he'd traveled back to Hadash. I found I missed speaking with him, but not as much as I once had. I keenly felt Kadian and Lil's absence. Kadian, my oldest friend. I wasn't myself without him. I knew there was a possibility when we came to Azmeer that we would be separated, especially if we found ourselves in different courts. I hadn't anticipated him being taken from me so soon.

Tamra and Oz had become my regular companions, joining me for dinner every night and sitting on my balcony with me. When I had free time, I popped into the library to see Addie, but she was busy gathering scrolls on lineages, necessary documentation for the royal weddings.

Despite appearing healthy, Kadian hadn't woken up. Magister Thorne advised me, for my own well-being, to take a few days off from visiting him.

I reluctantly consented and harbored guilt for finding pleasure in spending my days with Alvar.

"You realize you're coming up on six months here," he said, handing me a bite of sandwich. Despite Tura's protestations about us bringing food into the library, she relented when Alvar brought some for her as well. *"Almost anyone can be persuaded by bacon,"* Alvar had said.

"Hard to believe it's been that long," I took a bite.

"How are you feeling?" This line of questioning didn't catch me off guard. Over the past few weeks, we had gotten to know each other quite well. I learned his favorite color was, to no one's surprise, red. His birthday fell on the eighth day of the eleventh month; he had a peculiar fondness for anything with pickles, and despite being terrible, he loved to dance. He was easy to talk to, and our conversations made the long hours pass in the blink of an eye. He was kind, even in infuriating situations.

"I'm not sure how I feel about it," I let out a sigh.

"Why do you think that is?"

I paused for a few moments, "I feel for the past several years of my life that I've been wandering through an existence," my hands began to fidget, "and I haven't known what my place is in the world."

"What do you mean?" He leaned in closer to me, inclining his head.

"The last several months have felt like an emotional balancing act. My mind races and teeters between the familiar shores of my life before and the possible waters of the future."

"Or flames," cocking an eyebrow at me, a small smile formed on his lips.

"Since arriving here," I ignored him, "everything I thought I knew has been put to the test in some way. The ground has felt unsteady beneath my feet, and my normal guide posts haven't been there to help me navigate the way, and as you know," I found his gaze, "I'm terrible with directions."

He smiled.

"Even in the midst of this chaos, there is this glimmer of a possibility, a spark. Do you know what it is?"

He shook his head.

"It's hope," I sighed, "this little speck of resilience that refuses to be extinguished, that forces me from my bed each morning, pushes me into those unchartered waters. I've come to love that spark," I looked back to my hands, they'd stopped fidgeting. "Well, I love and fear it."

"Why would you fear it?"

"Because nothing is permanent," I said, "as you said, six months have already gone by and soon my time here will be complete. I have no idea if I'll be asked to join a court, and if I am, which it would be. But for now, there remains a hope that this time will just continue to go on."

"You will be alright, Brida," he put his hand on my arm, squeezing lightly. "That is," he continued, "if planning this party doesn't kill us both."

"Now now," I chimed in, "it's a *ball,* a party makes it sound frivolous,"

He laughed.

"Do you think we'll be able to finalize everything in the next ten days?" He returned to his lists.

"Do you always worry this much?" I cocked an eyebrow. "If you need a break, I'm happy to look over the guest list one more time. After I leave here, I'll put in a word with the Court of Whispers to get the message to everyone."

"You don't mind?" He looked exhausted.

"It's no problem. I'm happy to do it." I leaned across the table, taking the papers from him before sitting back down. There were many names on these lists. It had taken us a week just to come up with who we should invite so as to not incite discord amongst the courts.

"I haven't seen Asana in days, I can maybe convince her to skip out for a while. Wish me luck," he said as he reached for the handle of the door, "Brida, it will be how it is supposed to be." He winked at me, and then he left.

☽✳☾

I spent the next several hours analyzing names, double-checking, and comparing lists to ensure that no one important was forgotten. I packed the papers and folders and placed them into the leather satchel the library loaned its guests for transporting their work.

Shadows greeted me as I closed the door to the room. They'd become friendlier in the past few weeks, to the point I'd often forget that they were slithering along me as I walked. After careful study, I determined that they were, in fact, hissing, almost as if they were cats who had been frightened or touched in a spot they didn't approve of.

The library was deserted, not even Tura remained at the front desk. I decided to leave some of the folders in Alvar's room. He had altered the wards a few days ago, allowing me to enter them *in the spirit of friendship,* he'd told me.

I knew he seldom used these quarters, opting to stay in the royal quarters or Asana's rooms. His rooms were immaculate. I'd been fooled into thinking this is how Alvar was when in reality, it was just due to his lack of presence.

Everything in the room was the same as this morning, except for a small red velvet box that sat on the desk.

One peek won't hurt. I opened it and saw the most beautiful ruby ring. The gem itself was imbued with magic as every few moments, shadows danced within.

I breathed and tensed.

"Why are you here, Dainan?" I closed the ring box and placed it back on the desk.

"I'm flattered you knew it was me," he leaned against the doorframe. Of course, I knew it was him. His scent was impossible to ignore. "I see you don't need my assistance with getting into this room anymore," he held me with his gaze.

"Yes, I made sure I wouldn't need you again," I said, my voice curt.

I shuddered as his eyes trailed up my body, inspecting every inch of me while stopping to linger on my curves.

Time to go. "You're blocking the door, and I need to go to dinner," I said, trying to stay firm.

"To dinner?" He looked surprised.

"Yes, I don't believe I misspoke," I stayed where I was. I didn't want to risk getting too close.

"Dinner ended hours ago. You didn't miss much," he continued, "it was the chef's take on liver this evening."

Gods. I lost track of time.

"Fine, then I need to go to bed." With determination, I stepped towards him, but he shifted his body, blocking my path. I couldn't decide if it was a clever move or simply irritating.

"Are you going to let me pass?" I finally asked as he refused to move.

"I'm not stopping you."

I sighed, "Why are you here, Dainan?"

"Isn't it obvious?" He arched an eyebrow as I stood silently, "I sleep next door," he tilted his head down the hall.

"Tired of the royal quarters?"

"I haven't been sleeping there as of late." His voice was tight, clipped.

"Well, no doubt your betrothed can find you here more easily. It's nice, you two have so much time together." I didn't know why I was saying this. The connection between my mind and my voice severed yet again.

"Do you think I wanted this engagement? That I asked for it?" He practically spat as he took a step towards me.

"I have no idea what you did or did not ask for, Dainan. I'm tired, and I want to go to bed as I apparently missed a *very* delicious dinner."

"Getting feisty, *Ilia,*" he smirked.

"Don't call me that," the irritation evident in my voice.

"Why not? You seemed to like it the last time I said it to you."

"Was that when you practically mounted me in a doorway? The

same day the entirety of Azmeer and no doubt the continent was informed of your impending marriage."

You mean absolutely nothing to him; he is trying to make a point. This is a fucking game to him. I'm not here for this.

He stiffened, "I didn't ask for that," the flames that danced in his eyes were no doubt reflected in mine as my rage bubbled to the surface. All of the emotions that I'd been holding in for the last several months were rising, a wave ready to crash down upon me.

"Marsh was right, this *is* a game to you. You treat me as if I'm a prize to be won. What, you would have fucked me in the doorway, and then what, Dainan?" I took a step towards him, refusing to back down. "Why do you keep seeking me out? Why is it you can't seem to leave me alone?"

"What did Marsh say to you?" He snarled.

"What does it even matter to you?"

Instantly, he was in front of me.

"What did he say to you, *Brida?*" His eyes locked on mine, fire and the shadow mingling once more.

"Like I said," without moving an inch, "what does it matter to you?" My eyes remained on his.

"He is lying to you," he hissed. "I've told you, this is no game. Instead, you choose to believe *him,*" he raised his voice, taking another step closer, "you have no idea what you're talking about, Brida. But yes, by all means, believe *Marsh.*"

He scoffed, "Do you believe him because he's not in the Court of Shadows? Is that why you deem him to be trustworthy? Because he does not have a shroud of darkness as his constant companion?"

"How could you think that when I chose to be here?" *If only he knew of everything I'd done to get here.*

Ignoring me, he continued, "To be clear, Brida," he wasn't calling me Ilia anymore, "I would not have *fucked* you in the doorway, as you so eloquently put it." He took a step closer, we were mere inches apart, I could feel the heat radiating off of him, warming my cooler skin.

Leaning in close, his breath tickled my neck as he whispered, "If this was simply a game, I could have taken you in that bar. Your scent..." His hand found its way into my hair, the other began to caress my face, "was dripping with arousal. You wanted me just as much as I wanted you." I looked up, the shadows were gone, replaced by the fire dancing in his eyes. "And if I had tried to take you the last time we spoke, you would have done whatever I asked you to do because you wanted me, *Brida.*"

He's right. I wanted him then, and I want him now. I refused to let go of his gaze, not sure if I wanted the moment to end or where we'd go from here.

His voice lowered, "I did not ask for this. I wish you understood that," he pushed the hair from my eyes. His touch was gentle. I saw the pain and anger etched on his face. He hadn't asked for this, and I was punishing him for it.

I stood in silence for a few moments longer, "I don't know what it is you want with me, Dainan," A sigh escaped me as tears welled in my eyes, months of anguish and despair desperately seeking an escape. He noticed as he gently cupped my face.

"The day the announcement went out, she warned me to stay away, that you were spoken for." My voice barely rose above a whisper.

His thumb continued to tenderly caress my cheek, "it wasn't known to me at the time."

From the first moment I had seen Dainan, standing atop the gate for the Court of Shadows, something about him had called to me. I had been lying to myself these past months that there wasn't some pull towards him. A tether I didn't understand. A tether I refused to release. Despite the warnings, regardless of why I was here, I could no longer deny it.

I opened my mouth to speak and was interrupted by a growling from my stomach. Dainan's expression eased, "seems like we need to feed you," he reached for my hand. I felt a jolt as our fingers intertwined.

"What are you doing?" I asked as he pulled me out of the room.

"Getting you food, I thought that was obvious."

I closed the door behind me and followed as Dainan led me down a hall I didn't recognize.

Shadows found me on our walk, playfully hissing as they mingled with Dainan's shadows, I was sure they knew each other. He looked down and smiled. "Seems like they have a lot of catching up to do." I wondered how many had seen him smile, seen the cold exterior draw back to show the man beneath.

"Where are you taking me?" I asked.

"You will just have to wait and see."

After turning down three more corridors, Dainan pushed open the double doors we stood in front of.

"Shall we see what we can put together?" He said, pulling me inside.

It was a fully functional kitchen, cleaner than any I'd ever seen. It was reminiscent of the kitchen at my university, save this one was styled in the Court of Shadows.

"*You* cook?" I raised an eyebrow, "*you?*"

"I've been known to make a dish or two," he let go of my hand, making his way over to an icebox. "So," he looked back at me, "what will it be?"

I was so taken aback that all I could mumble was "surprise me" and he certainly did. He was a natural cook and seemed so comfortable in the kitchen. The only times I'd been allowed to cook had been when Dad had been sick, or I'd managed to make it home before him to surprise him with a meal. I'd never watched anyone with skill cook.

"Who taught you how to cook?" It was mesmerizing to watch how he moved around. Touching the ingredients, sniffing spices, ensuring they were the ones he wanted to use. "The only time I have ever been in a kitchen like this was with Kadian. He had insisted we go to a party and he was so drunk that he stumbled into the kitchen thinking it was his room. He came to find me afterwards, dragging me down there to show me the cookies he'd found." I smiled at the memory.

"You are lucky to have someone like him in your life, Brida. Not everyone is as fortunate." He moved to find an apron, tying it across his waist. I nearly fainted at the sight.

To distract myself from gaping, I prodded further. "So who taught you to cook? Or should I be expecting an experimental meal?"

"My mother taught me, pardon my reach," he leaned around me to grab cloves of garlic that he begun mincing. I felt blood rush to my cheeks as his arm brushed mine.

"Not that I've had much exposure to royalty, well, save for you and your brothers," Dainan cocked an eyebrow at the word *brothers*, "but I wouldn't think many queens know how to cook."

Dainan let out a chuckle, "She wasn't always a queen, Ilia. That is not to say that my father did not always love her, but for many years, she..." he paused, "I don't mean to bore you with stories of her." He began sautéing the food.

"Please tell me," I leaned on the counter, "I want to know." He paused to stare at me mid-slice, "but please pay attention to what you are cutting," I said as I inclined my head to the cutting board, "despite my best efforts on a few occasions, I have not proven to be a successful nurse. I am happy to tell you what herbs may ease your ailments, but the administration of them leaves something to be desired. Unless it is in the form of tea."

A low laugh escaped him, wrapping around us like the warmth of the kitchen.

"What's so funny?" My heart fluttered at the sound of his amusement.

"I am imagining you as my nurse. It wasn't the outfit that I would have chosen for you, but I wouldn't object to it either."

My cheeks warmed at the thought. "Tell me about your mother."

"If I'm going to be distracted by telling you a story, then you will have to assist with cooking the meal." He moved behind me, close enough that I could feel the heat radiating from his body. It took every ounce of strength not to lean into him, to allow myself to be overcome by him, his touch, his scent. The memory of our dancing permeated my senses. *He can smell arousal on you. Get it together.*

"Does that sound like something you can help me with?" he whispered into my ear, and fire ran through my veins, igniting a yearning I had never felt before.

"I can't make any guarantees for the quality of the meal if you insist on my helping you." My voice barely managed to escape, a mixture of playful defiance and the desperate hope that he might keep this closeness. I felt a rumble in his chest as he pressed himself against me, guiding us toward his workspace. He knew what his presence was doing to me, but I didn't want him to stop.

"Be sure to do exactly as I say; that way, we can be sure that you won't hurt yourself. I don't want to add cleaning blood to the list of activities for the evening." His hand enveloped mine, guiding it toward the knife with a gentle firmness that sent shivers down my spine. He did the same for my other hand, leading me to grab an onion and place it on the cutting board.

"My mother," he began, his voice steady as he adjusted my position, "says that she always loved my father. From everything they both claim, it was love from the moment they met. My mother knew that one day she would be queen, but—" he paused, his breath a whisper against my cheek. "No, Ilia... Slice like this." He guided my hand in a smoother motion, and I couldn't help but grin at the compliment. "That's better."

"Go on, please." My words felt like an invitation, pulling him deeper into the story as he continued to instruct me.

"Do you know how my parents met?" His cheek brushed against mine, our bodies fitting together as if they were made for this moment. I could feel the warmth rising in my cheeks as we finished thinly slicing, the intimacy of the task binding us closer. "Place these in the pan now," he whispered, the command stirring something thrilling within me.

“There’s a rumor as to how they met,” I said, jumping back when a sudden sizzling from the pan startled me.

“We will have to get you cooking more often if you are going to startle at onions frying in a pan,” he said, folding his arms over his chest, amusement dancing in his eyes.

“I did warn you. Your meal will not turn out as you expect once you get me involved.” He watched me, his gaze a mix of teasing and appreciation, making me feel both vulnerable and exhilarated. He placed himself behind me again, drawing closer as he gathered the next set of ingredients.

“The rumor you’re referencing is the one where my parents met in a pleasure den in Riccia?”

I nodded, my pulse quickening as I leaned in closer, eager to hear more.

“I’m sure you will be disappointed to know that it is, in fact, incorrect. They met at a coffee house.” I turned to stare at him, surprised. “Ah, ah,” he corrected me, turning my chin back forward with a gentle hand, forcing me to focus. “No blood, remember.”

“So they met in a coffee house,” I reminded him, my heart racing at his touch.

He clicked his tongue, the sound both playful and exasperated. “So impatient.”

He has no idea.

“My parents met in a coffee house in Mazima.”

“In Mazima? But that’s in the North.”

“If you continue to interrupt, Ilia, we will never get to the end of this tale.” I sighed, feeling him laugh behind me, the sound like music to my ears. A song familiar to my soul. “My father was on a tour. He made a habit of going into local shops and establishments. You can say terrible things about my father, many of them being true, but he’s a man of the people. He attempts to know them, understand them. It’s why he changed the rules with the Courting, insisting humans be invited to partake; he wanted everyone united.” He paused, placing a cloth in my hand as we patted down fish together, our fingers brushing against each other, sending another thrill through me.

"What was supposed to be a quick stop on his way to—" He leaned in, his breath warm against my ear as if questioning my geography.

"Hesum, the last stop before the Tactras Mountains," I whispered.

"Very good," he praised, pressing his cheek to mine once more. This time, I couldn't help it; I arched into his touch. His words, his praise, it would be my undoing.

"My father made his way inside and ordered a coffee. The woman working that day happened to be my mother. What should have been ten minutes at most became the entirety of the day, and lasted long into the night. They spoke of their shared love of the land, of their hopes, their dreams, and that night before closing the shop, my mother granted my father a wish. He said he wished for something as sweet as she was. She presented him with a honey cake that she made from scratch while he told her tales of his travels."

I turned to stare at him, my gaze falling on his lips as I forced out the words, "And what happened after that?"

He shook his head, realizing he'd disappeared into the story. "These require salt and pepper." He stepped back from me, grabbing the spices before seasoning the fish, his movements fluid and confident, almost mesmerizing.

"My father said he fell in love with my mother the same moment he fell in love with her cooking. She knew he was married, but there had been consorts before. She assumed there would be ones after, but there haven't been. My father brought her along with him on his tour, and in each place, they met with the farmers, the merchants. They tasted the cheese from the goats of Asilda and boarded the boats of the fishermen in the Eridan Sea. In each place, my mother would use local ingredients and cook something new and special for my father."

The sizzling in the pan was the only thing to distract me from his story. The fish was nearly cooked, and Dainan moved to the stove, ensuring his dish come together, ensuring no ingredient was missed. "Despite living in Azmeer, there's a reason the king is never seen at mealtime, and it is because my mother cooks for him."

"Even still?" I couldn't help but smile at that, the thought of a queen in her kitchen bringing a sense of warmth. Dinner time had always been special between my parents; it seemed this was something we shared.

"Even still." His eyes held me captive, a weight of understanding passing between us before he gazed back at the pan, preparing to add the finishing touches. "Cooking is a passion of my mother's; it's something she insisted I learn—in case I was ever in a situation where the chef would decide to experiment with liver for the main course."

I laughed, a light sound that filled the kitchen. "The queen has incredible foresight."

Dainan gestured toward a stool in front of the island, "This was one of the first things I learned to make." The dish looked and smelled incredible.

I sat down, taking a bite, the flavors exploding in my mouth. "It's delicious." The meal surpassed my expectations, offering a level of satisfaction I hadn't realized I was craving. "Thank you for sharing that story with me. I knew when I saw your parents at the Festival for Giaxia that..."

"That?"

"That they truly love each other. The way they stared at each other... It's rare and beautiful to find someone who can look at you that way. Someone who sees your faults, your cracks, what makes you, what breaks you, and still loves you. Your father may appear weak and ailing to those around him but to her..." I paused, trying to articulate exactly what I felt, the emotion swirling within me. "Your mother watched him as if he was, is, her world. There was no one else for her at that moment. If the rumors exist regarding mates, I would think your parents to be the very definition. We should all be so lucky to find someone like that. Someone who would love us as deeply as she loves him, and he her."

I'd never spoken this way to anyone, not even Kadian. I lowered my gaze to my plate, embarrassment creeping in at my raw honesty. We ate mostly in silence, even though I could feel him watching me, the weight of his gaze igniting my cheeks. I wanted to say something, but following my grand proclamation, I didn't know how to broach any subject.

"Have you been reading anything interesting lately?" He finally asked.

Thank the Gods. Shaking my head, I replied, "Not recently. Alvar had me retrieving books for him, but that was before we began planning the..." I stopped myself before forcing myself to ask, "Do you want to talk about it?"

Dainan raised an eyebrow as he took a sip of the wine he'd poured for himself. "Do I want to discuss how I am being forced to marry when all I am interested in is the company in front of me?" He took another sip, his tone deceptively casual, but his grip on the glass and the tension in his voice were unmistakable. "Not particularly."

Grief and frustration were written across his face. His shadows began to spiral in different directions as if he'd lost control of them. It was as if they were reacting to his emotions, feeding off his turmoil, moving with an unsettling, erratic energy.

Maybe they have a mind of their own? I wondered, watching their dance, a mesmerizing yet disturbing sight, before pulling my focus back to the conversation at hand.

The shadows crept from Dainan, slithering across the island before rising up to meet me. They looked similar to the shadows that I'd come to claim as my own, save his carried his scent. I extended my fingers and they danced between my fingertips.

"I'm sorry," I found the words escaping me before I had a chance to think it through. I lowered my hand, and found Dainan's gaze burrowing into me.

"From everything Alvar has told me, I know there is a history of arranged marriages, and I know it isn't what he would have chosen for you... it isn't what I would hope for you." I knew I was treading on dangerous ground. I couldn't imagine being in his position—trapped by duty, by expectations that didn't belong to him.

The darkness in Dainan's eyes stared back at me, pulling me into their frightening depths.

"Thank you," he whispered, placing the glass down on the countertop with a delicate clink. The shadows receded back towards him, before disappearing entirely. "It's not what I would have chosen." His voice was low, tinged with a vulnerability that felt rare, almost forbidden. "She's not whom I would have chosen."

Silence stretched between us, an invisible thread being pulled taut, fragile and tense. The weight of his confession hung in the air, and I found myself at a loss for words. I wanted to speak, to tell him that he should make a choice for himself. But I knew what was at stake—what standing in his world meant, what sacrifices came with it.

I stared down at my hand, my knuckles turning white from gripping the edge of the countertop so tightly it hurt, grounding myself in the physical sensation to avoid being swept away by the emotional storm raging inside me. I forced myself to take a breath, slow and deliberate, closing my eyes for a moment to steady the wild pulse of my heart, the darkness behind my eyelids offering momentary solitude.

When I opened my eyes again, Dainan's gaze hadn't wavered. He was still watching me, and in that moment, I felt utterly exposed. Yet, I smiled—though I wasn't sure where it came from. Maybe it was a defense mechanism, or maybe it was the need to diffuse the moment.

"To return to our previous topic," I said, my voice softer now, but steady, "I do miss reading." It was a gentle shift, an attempt to pull us both back from the edge of something too raw, too close to unraveling.

Understanding the need to move the conversation elsewhere, Dainan leaned back in his seat, the tension between us easing. "Do you have a favorite novel?" His voice was lighter, but there was a flicker of curiosity in his eyes as he watched me.

I let out a breath I hadn't realized I was holding, relieved at the change in pace. "It's hard to pick just one," I admitted, finding comfort in the familiar subject.

"*The Trials of Thale,*" I smiled, "I reread it every year."

"She emerged from the storm with strength in her eyes and fire in her heart and soul,
Her scars whispered of the battles fought and the victories won.
Through the darkest of nights, she clung onto hope like a guiding star.
Like a diamond forged in the depths of the earth, she emerged radiant and unbreakable."

Dainan recited.

"You've read it." I said.

"I'm familiar with it," his eyes shone with triumph.

"I haven't encountered many people who are. It's a rare book to come by. We aren't even sure who authored it, it's so old. Probably one of the earliest Fae."

I leaned on the island, continuing to admire the version of Dainan I was seeing for the first time. "Do you believe it predates the Primals? I've always found that to be one of the more interesting theories." I asked as I pushed my plate away. I was stuffed and couldn't eat another bite. Unless he had a dessert hidden away, and then I would force myself.

"No," he shook his head, "I think it talks of a specific Primal, but," he looked at the clock, "that is a story for another time. You must be exhausted." He rose, grabbed my plate and brought it to the sink.

At the mere mention of it, fatigue overwhelmed me. "I should help you clean up," I stood and began walking towards him.

His hands found mine, "no," he stopped me, "you need rest, *Ilia,*" he caressed my face."I can take you back to your room," he said.

"Do you have to?" His pained expression told me everything. The night would end here.

His smile was meek, saddened. Perhaps if we had met in a different time, a different place, a different life.

"Take a breath," he whispered, wrapping his arms around me.

I opened my eyes to find us standing outside of my room, the hallway empty, Dainan still embracing me. We stood in silence. The shared rhythm of our breaths filling the space between us, neither of us making a move to break the stillness.

He lifted his hand, brushing the hair from my face.

"Thank you," I said to him in a tone that was so low I wasn't sure he could hear me.

"What for?" He sounded unsure as his eyes held me. It looked as if he was trying to etch every line of my face into his memory, as if he were gazing upon me for the last time.

"Tonight," I brought his hand and placed it over my heart, holding it to me for a moment. I moved to the tips of my toes and pressed a soft kiss to his cheek. "Goodnight, Dainan."

That night, I stood on the balcony longer than usual. Lost in my thoughts and the comfort of the evening breeze.

CHAPTER FORTY

The ball was three days away. Every time I thought about it, a knot twisted tighter in my stomach. It was supposed to be a celebration—of a future that wasn't mine. A future I could imagine with him. And yet, here I was, planning an engagement ball for Dainan and the woman who wasn't me. My hands had picked the food and the drinks, had chosen the entertainment, and it filled me with dread.

Alvar kept asking for my input, and somehow, I found the will to answer without choking on the bile rising in my throat. If I didn't focus too long on what the event symbolized, maybe I could almost convince myself that the night might be bearable. Maybe I could hide behind the busy work, the details, the small choices that kept me numb.

"The decorations need to be that of both the Court of Shadows and the Court of Reflection," Alvar told me.

"How does one mingle turquoise with black and red without it appearing hideous?" I raised an eyebrow at him.

"Hm," he murmured to himself, lost in thought.

"Why don't we have two separate tables in the back of the room," I said, pointing to the seating chart and map that we had made of the ballroom, “we don’t want any of the dishes with fish to be offered to the members of the Court of Reflection anyways,” I remarked, recalling how much Lil adores fish. “It may not have been wise for us to have so many pescatarian dishes.”

“Thalius and his ilk will just have to deal with it. Lil is marrying into the Court of Shadows, and we do eat fish,” Alvar said. At last, he pointed to where in the room we would place their table, a table that would have turquoise and white on it, and a table that we both agreed would be an eyesore compared to everything else we’d worked on.

“Now,” Alvar said between bites of sandwich as we sat down, “this will be the last time we meet before the ball as I will be held up in meetings, and I promised Asana a day of rest before this whole,” his arm swept around us, “event.”

I chuckled, “I hope you're somewhat looking forward to it. It's not like we haven't put any work into this,” I nodded toward the ever-growing stacks of papers, diagrams, and lists scattered across the table.

“I am and am not," he said. "I can’t forget that this event celebrates something I don’t want to see happen.”

You and me both.

“Do you not approve of the marriages because of your personal beliefs pertaining to arranged marriages, or because of who is entering your family?” I’d become much bolder in my questioning him, and to my surprise, Alvar had never refused to answer.

“I’m very fond of Lil, as you know. Not that I’ve seen her lately,” he wiped his mouth with a napkin, “we always had a wonderful time when she’d visit, mind you it wasn’t frequent, but we saw her enough that I felt I knew her. She’s young though,” his eyes veered over to the list of desserts.

“Iona is the same age. I am the same age.”

“*That one* has had her eye on Dainan from the first moment she set foot in Azmeer. She couldn’t have been older than ten,” he said as he put a star next to eclairs, a note for the chef to save him some.

"She's been visiting the palace for that long?" I asked, and he nodded.

"Deter, her father is a wealthy man, powerful even outside of his position in the Court of Shadows. He was by my father's side when he became king, and it was no surprise that he ended up here," his arm gesturing around us once more.

"He's cunning, clever, and knows how to achieve his desires, and in this instance," he sighed, tipping his head back, closing his eyes, "what he desired was his daughter's happiness, and what she desired was Dainan."

"What would—" I stopped myself.

He opened one eye, all the while keeping his head back. "Don't leave me guessing, Brida. We both know you can ask what you like," he smirked.

I sighed, "What would happen if someone were to be married only to discover their mate?" My throat felt hoarse.

He opened both eyes and sat up straighter, "*Mates*? What do you know about mates?"

He turned to face me.

"Not much," which was mostly true, "only that the bond is supposedly so strong that it can drive someone to madness."

After a few moments of silence, he folded his arms over his chest as he leaned back, "There have always been rumors. It's supposed to have originated with the Primals."

"Yes, Ollo and Giaxia"

"No," his tone was firm, "Vasenia and Ollo."

I sat there dumbfounded. "I was told Giaxia sacrificed her mating bond with Ollo in order to create the courts."

He waved his hand at me as if brushing me off. "Hogwash," he said, "believed by the Eternal Court. A way for them to make themselves feel superior. That they were the first Court and that *their* Primal made this monumental sacrifice when in reality she caused a millennia-long war."

"What..." I began to say, and he sighed.

"The rumor that Giaxia and Ollo were mates was spread by the Eternal Court, an effort to justify her actions. It was an attempt to rewrite history, to paint her deeds in a more favorable light," he remarked, running his hand through his loose hair.

"But you're saying that Vasenia and Ollo were mates?"

He nodded. "It was believed to have been a gift from the Primals of Life and Death, who themselves were mates."

We do not belong to the Primal of Death. "So there is a Primal of Death." His mouth curved into a slight smile.

"What do I always say to you?"

"Do you always worry this much?"

He chuckled, "No, Brida. The *other* thing."

"It's always about balance. Magic is always a delicate balance," I mused, and he nodded in agreement.

"Without life, there can be no death; without death, we do not value life. A balance," he said as he balanced a stylus on his finger. "It only works when they are in sync with one another."

"You said it was a gift."

"Vasenia was thought to be related to the Primals of Life and Death; their names have been lost to time," he said as he leaned forward, grabbing his jar of water from the table.

"And they thought the mating bond was *a gift*?"

"They were said to have found happiness in their pairing and wanted the same for her. What they did not foresee was the jealousy of other Primals."

"What do you..." A knock came from the door.

"Yes," Alvar shouted. Asana entered, Tamra not far behind her. "May I help you, Asana?"

Even though I was aware of their relationship and the eventual prospect of Asana becoming our queen, they preferred to keep their affection relatively private, especially during "work hours," as he put it.

"It's time for our meeting," Asana replied in a curt tone.

He turned his back to her, winking at me as he said, "Very well, please give me a few moments to conclude my affairs here. I will meet you outside."

Before she closed the door, I leaned back and waved at Tamra, who looked confused by the interaction she'd just overheard.

"It appears I'm being called out early," he cocked an eyebrow after he heard the door close. "I believe everything is settled. All should be well for the ball. I'm sorry to leave you with just a few days left."

"Everything will be fine," I gave his arm a squeeze, "you've planned well. Your organizational skills are something we can discuss another time," I chuffed.

"A fine party," he muttered.

"A *ball*," I corrected him.

"Very well, a fine ball indeed. Now," he picked up a few of the papers on the table, "if you would, please be sure..."

He continued to provide instructions for the next several minutes as if it were new information rather than a repetition of what we'd discussed over the past few weeks.

"I'll be sure to find you on the dance floor," he said. "Oh, and Brida," I looked at him as he turned back towards me, "it has been my honor and pleasure to plan this *ball* with you."

A moment later, there was a knock on the door. I smiled when I saw Tamra enter.

"What was *that* about?"

"Not sure." I would never say anything without Alvar's direct permission on the matter.

She nodded, "we have an hour or so before dinner."

Dinner. My mind immediately recalled the meal I'd shared with Dainan. I hadn't seen him since. It was for the best as there would be a ball in a few days to celebrate his impending marriage. A marriage that both he and Alvar had assured me he didn't want.

"Is there anything you'd like to do with our hour of freedom?" Tamra smiled as she peered over at the mess that remained in Alvar's wake.

"If it's okay with you," I began, "I'm going to go check in at the library and then go see Kadian. I'll meet you at dinner, though?"

"Okay," she led us to the door, "I'll see you at dinner."

We parted ways, and I stopped by the desk to speak with Tura, reminding her of Alvar's request to close the library during the ball. "I will not deny people access to books, Brida, I will not." Tura's age remained a mystery to me. Her timeless beauty suggested a long life, with long white hair and weathered lines tracing her experiences. Her face exuded both warmth and authority, most notably when enforcing the library's quiet zones, and a respect for the books.

"It's not me making this request of you, Tura. I would never think to tell you how to run your library, which you do exceptionally well."

She smiled at me, "Yes, yes, it's Alvar, I know. You tell him that I'll keep it closed to the general public, but I will be here, womaning my post."

"*Womaning*?" I stifled a laugh.

"Of course, *womaning*, have you seen what men do around here?" She laughed, making her way into the stacks behind her. It was an infectious laugh and not one she shared often. The sole occasion I could recall her laughing was when I overheard Tura informing Iona that the library didn't have any of the novels on her list and that she hadn't even heard of those titles. "*Dainan has sent you on a fool's errand, girl,*" she chuckled to herself. Iona's sigh was so audible it seemed to carry several floors up. Theirs was going to be a union of marital bliss.

As I ascended the stairs, my shadows greeted me, having taken to following me around the house. They playfully wound themselves around my neck, twisting in my hair, emitting soft hisses as if expressing their delight at seeing me. I'd grown to love them and looked forward to seeing them each day. They never followed me beyond the exit to the House of Shadows; they did not exceed its boundaries.

"I'll see you tomorrow," I whispered to them, bending down to stroke their ethereal forms with my hand. To any onlooker, it must have seemed like madness, but they responded to my touch with what almost sounded like purrs of contentment.

I opened the door to leave and froze when I saw two figures standing near the entrance.

"Brida," Rai said, his tone sneering as he stepped towards me, Lil on his arm.

Gods, Lil. She looked ashen. Her once beautiful skin had drained of all its color. "Lil," I found myself saying in a tone that conveyed how worried I was at seeing her like this. Rai took a step closer, cutting me off.

"I hear we have you to thank for the ball that's being held in our honor," he said, glancing back towards Lil as if to remind me who the "our" was that he spoke of. "Alvar has assured me it will be an event to remember."

"I've merely helped your brother with the responsibilities of its organization," I replied curtly. He smiled at my evident frustration.

"Indeed." He took a step towards Lil, brushing some of the hair from her cheek. *She flinched.* I wasn't sure that Rai even noticed. Gods, how often had he done that to her. Did Dainan or Alvar know?

Alvar said he hadn't seen Lil. Where had Rai been keeping her? What had he been doing to her...

"We're very much looking forward to it, are we not?" He said as he pressed his lips to her cheek. She stiffened.

Her body is fighting him.

"Your brother has done a wonderful job," I said, trying to draw his attention away from her, "you'll undoubtedly be pleased. We've even set aside a table for the Court of Reflection. Both of your families courts will be given their due respect."

He watched me for a moment, his eyes searching for something. His gaze lingered on a spot at my side. With a shake of his head, he regained his composure.

"I have no doubt that Dainan and Iona will appreciate your efforts as well," his grin grew sinister.

Did he somehow know that I'd had dinner with Dainan a few nights ago? We hadn't seen him, and to my knowledge, he had not even been in Azmeer for the last several weeks.

Ignoring me, he glanced at Lil, "Come. I wish to show you our rooms here," he said as he let go of her arm, making his way towards the door.

Lil stood motionless, her eyes glazed over. Her soft curves barely remained, her arms were frail, her cheeks sunken, and the gold in her hair had lost all of its luster and shine.

I wanted to reach out and shake her, to tell her that everything was going to be okay.

I'd taken the time to research on my own who had the authority to decree or annul royal marriages. The power rested with the king. Alvar would have no influence until his mark was complete and his father had passed.

"Lil," he called back to her, with frustration in his voice.

I took a step closer to her, and in an instant, it was as though a bolt of lightning had surged through Lil's body. She began to twitch, her arms and fingers jerking unnaturally, as if pulled by invisible strings.

"What's happening?" I whispered to her, my voice barely audible.

Rai appeared oblivious to Lil's distress, engrossed in conversation with the door. For once I blessed that loquacious nuisance for the distraction it was providing us.

"Tell me how to help you." I took another step closer to her. Lil stopped moving. She glanced down, her fingers twitching one by one. She shifted her stare from her feet, moving her hands and arms as if they had been frozen in place for hours. Then, with a slow, deliberate motion, she lifted her gaze, and her eyes found mine; the color had returned to her face.

Her eyes were now a vibrant aquamarine. The gold strands in her hair shone as if they had been plucked from the sun itself. The beautiful glow of her skin radiated once more with a slight bit of blush that landed on her cheeks.

Her eyes widened, a hand pressing against her chest. Stepping back, she drew in deep breaths, visibly shaken. Yet, after a moment, she straightened herself, regaining her composure as she stood firm once more.

“Rai,” her voice was sweeter than I’d ever heard it. Rai flung around to face us as if he hadn’t heard her speak in weeks. “Would you mind if I have a moment to thank Brida for the work she put in? Besides, I want to tell her of the dress that I’ll be wearing.”

Rai, absorbed in whatever the door to the House of Shadows was saying to him, dismissed her with a wave. Lil moved a few steps ahead, then grabbed my arm, pulling me closer.

“He's awake.”

CHAPTER FORTY-ONE

I'd never run faster in my life. I wove in and out of people as I made my way through the halls, occasionally bumping into the odd person. I didn't stop to apologize. Kadian was awake, and I needed to get to him.

"Brida," Magister Thorne greeted me as I ran towards him. "How di—" I cut him off.

"He's awake, Magister?" He stared at me before nodding. I didn't linger for another second. Stepping into the room, I saw the most beautiful green and amber eyes, wide awake, ready to greet me.

"Kad!" I shouted, lunging forward to embrace him. Tears ran down my cheeks, I'd missed him so much. I pulled back from him just a bit as I sat next to him, cupping his face with my hands.

"Gods," the tears continued to flow, "don't ever pull a stunt like this again," was all I could think to say.

He said nothing, offering only a blank stare.

"Kadian?" I said, feeling his forehead. He didn't have a fever; he felt normal. "What is it?" I asked him, worry growing in my voice.

"I'm sorry," his eyes found mine, "as much as I love to wake up to a," he looked me up and down, "beautiful, vivacious woman caressing my face, would you mind telling me who you are?"

I shot upwards. "You don't know who I am?" I asked him. It felt as if my body had turned as cold as ice.

"Am I supposed to?" He said as we continued to stare at each other. I had no idea what to do or say, I was paralyzed where I stood.

After a few moments, he said, "I'm just kidding, Bri," and gave me the biggest grin I'd ever seen. I could've punched him.

"You prick, you absolute prick," I said, hugging him once more. This time, he hugged me back, his hands wrapping around me, letting me know he missed me too.

"I've been so worried about you, Kad," I said in between sobs, "really, I don't think I've ever been so worried in my life. I didn't know what t..."

"It's okay, Bri," he whispered while brushing away as many of the tears as he could.

"Gods, it's not okay, Kadian. I brought us up there, if I hadn't insisted..."

"Stop," he sat up straighter in the bed, "you have never once forced me to do anything. In fact, I believe on most occasions that I've been the one dragging you into terrible ideas. For example, do you remember when I told you we were going to a bar, and instead, I brought you to a pleasure den in Asteros?" He smiled once more.

I couldn't stop laughing in and amidst my crying. "I do remember that."

"Do you recall the really handsome brown-haired guy that dragged you into the back room and..."

"That's enough, Kadian," I smirked at him.

He held up his hands, opting for a truce and it felt as if part of my soul returned to my body. A piece of me that was so integral that I don't know how I managed without it.

"How long have I been out?" He asked.

I told him of almost everything he'd missed.

"So you've been working with Alvar then?"

"I have. There's a ball happening in a few days time. Speaking of which, we need to..."

There was a knock at the door, and Magister Thorne entered the room at that very moment. "Ah, Kadian, glad to see you are still among us," he said a bit too cavalierly for my liking.

"Was it ever a possibility that I wasn't going to be among you?" He looked from the Magister to me, and I slowly nodded.

"We had no idea what happened and what the outcome would be..." I whispered.

Magister Thorne made his way over to the chair beside the bed. He was moving slower than he had been just a few weeks earlier. His hair looked grayer. *Gods, he looks just like Dad did before I left.*

"Ah, that is better," his voice cut through my thoughts, grounding me. "I'm wondering if you can tell me exactly what happened. It will be most valuable for our records should something like this occur again." He pulled out a stylus and paper from a deep pocket on his light brown robes.

"I would be happy to, Magister, but I have no recollection of what happened that evening beyond going out with Brida."

"Kadian," I whispered as I reached my hand out back towards his, "do you really not remember?" He shook his head.

"Not a thing." He said, leaning his head back on his pillow.

"A pity," Magister Thorne clicked his tongue after a few moments.

"Should you remember anything, please do let me know. We'll keep you here for the next few days for observation, and then you may go." It took him several minutes to rise from his chair and make his way towards the door. With that, he left us alone.

"You don't remember anything?"

"I told you, I don't remember," his expression was genuine.

"What's the last thing you do remember?"

"We were walking. We stopped in that hallway, the one with all the mirrors," he snapped his finger as if trying to recall our steps of that evening.

"The *Celestial Corridor*," I said.

"Yeah, that one." He moved on quickly. "We came to some hallway, and then everything goes blank."

"You don't recall the mist?" I rose to peer out the window. Below, in the courtyard, I could have sworn I glimpsed shadows shifting. I hadn't realized how tired I was or how late it had become.

"What mist?" He said as his eyes followed me throughout the room.

"There was blinding mist outside of the entrance to the House of Whispers. You took off into it, something was speaking to you," I said as I began to rub my temples.

"*Something was speaking to me*?"

I nodded. "You screamed and said 'they are waking up' before collapsing to the floor, and here we are," I gestured my hand all around us. "I thought you died, Kadian." I finally said, sitting next to him once more.

"I'm right here, Bri." The smile he offered me made my heart hurt.

He didn't remember what happened or what had been said to him, did he remember about Lil? Gods, what about Lil, and the ball, I had to tell him.

"*Uhm,* Kadian," I began to say, but there was a knock on the door once more.

"Yes."

"Visiting hours are over, my dear," the night nurse said.

"Thank you," I replied as I clasped his hand once more. "Rest," I kissed his forehead, "we'll talk more tomorrow." I cupped his face in my hands, all the while staring into his beautiful and familiar eyes, "I love you. Please don't ever leave me again."

"I'll do my best," he smiled at me.

"I'll see you in the morning."

Exiting the room, I was greeted to a familiar face.

"I heard he's awake," Marsh said as he smiled at me.

"Did Thorne tell you?" I asked.

"Thorne sent Xavius a message, and Xavius told me. I thought I would find you here," he said as he put his hands into the pockets of his black suit.

He looked good. His hair had grown out since arriving in Azmeer, in addition to the slight stubble that now lived on his chin. His familiar scent of honey, and something else I couldn't quite put my finger on hit me at that moment.

"Thanks for coming to check up on him," I said.

"I didn't come to check on him," he said, "I came to check on you."

He paused for a moment, "as much as I'm relieved to hear that Kadian is going to be okay, my main concern always has been and will always be you, Brida." He took a step closer.

I could tell he wanted to come closer, but I kept my distance.

"Do you think we could spend some time together?" His eyes were hopeful. "Maybe we could go for a run? I'll be here until after the ball. I'll be free for the next several days," Marsh said, his voice casual, but there was a thread of something taut. I nodded, barely hearing him. As much as I appreciated what Marsh had done for me, I had no desire to place myself in the middle of whatever simmering rivalry was unfolding between him and Dainan. Whatever games they were playing, I wasn't a pawn.

I'd been distracted enough from my purpose in Azmeer as it was. The selection would be upon us in a blink, and I could feel time slipping through my fingers like sand.

"I'll be spending my free time with Kadian," I said, the words coming out firmer than I intended. It wasn't a lie. I needed him. His presence was the only thing tethering me to a semblance of normalcy in this twisted place.

"Of course," Marsh said, nodding, but there was a flicker in his eyes, a shadow of something unresolved. Silence stretched between us, thick and heavy, before he finally broke it, his voice softer. "Do you think...that we might be able to talk over the next few days? I could look for you at the ball. I assume you'll be attending since you've been working with the House of Shadows?"

His question lingered in the air between us, like a thread he hoped I would pull. "Okay," I said, offering him a faint smile to ease the tension. "Look for me there, and we can talk."

His face softened, a glimpse of relief easing the lines of his jaw. "Maybe we can have a dance?" He took a small step closer, his eyebrow raising in that way that always seemed to ask for just a little more than I was willing to give.

"Don't push your luck," I replied, the teasing edge in my voice belying the thrum of discomfort in my chest. I stepped around him, my fingers already curling around the cool brass door handle.

"I look forward to it," he called after me, a wink in his voice as he vanished, almost as if he dissolved into the wind itself.

I exhaled, the weight of that conversation lingering on my shoulders like a shroud, and made my way to the inductees' quarters. Each step I took echoed against the limestone floor, a rhythm as familiar as my own heartbeat, grounding me in a world that often felt like it was slipping away.

Before returning to my room, I found myself standing in front of Tamra's door. The soft murmur of whispers and the occasional burst of laughter drifted from inside, warm and intimate. I hesitated for a moment, then knocked.

"Come back later!" Amera's giggle floated through the door, light and carefree. I smiled despite myself, feeling a small warmth spread through me. I was happy for them—glad that Tamra had someone in this whirlwind of uncertainty.

I moved on to Oz's door. No answer. But from within, I could hear the unmistakable sound of soft snoring, and I couldn't help the small chuckle that escaped me. Sleep had claimed him. I'd tell them about Kadian in the morning, when the world felt a little less heavy.

After soaking in a long, hot bath, jasmine and vanilla oils swirling around me like a delicate embrace, I stepped out onto my balcony. The cool night air kissed my damp skin, and I inhaled a deep breath, my chest filling with the scent of the garden mingled with the faint traces of magic that always seemed to hang in the air.

Above me, the sky was alive—brilliant and vast, a canvas painted with stars that glittered like diamonds, each one a tiny flicker of light in the infinite darkness. They danced, those stars weaving ancient stories in their timeless ballet. Altia and her serpent. Malize and his bow. The gods and their eternal watch over us. They seemed so distant, so serene, untouched by our mortal struggles below.

I felt a pang of something sharp, almost like envy. What would it be like to be free from the weight of mortal trials? To float among the stars, eternal and unburdened by duty, or fear, or longing?

I whispered into the night, almost without realizing it, "What would it be like to travel among the stars?"

The wind stirred, brushing against my face like a gentle caress. And then, as if the night itself answered, I heard a voice—soft, smooth, curling around me.

"I could show you the stars if you wish."

"Could you now?" I asked, keeping my eyes trained on the stars above, refusing to let him draw me back into his orbit so easily.

His answer came like a whisper on the breeze, teasing. "I can't wait to see you in a few days."

I said nothing. The wind wrapped around me, warm and familiar, but my mind was far away—floating among the stars, imagining what it would be like to slip away from all of this, to lose myself in the freedom of the endless sky.

I settled onto the balcony, pulling my knees to my chest, and lifted my gaze once more to the heavens, letting my mind drift. Maybe, just maybe, in another life, I could have danced with the stars.

☽✳☾

"Why didn't you wake me last night?" Oz asked, his tone somewhere between irritation and concern.

I shook my head, brushing it off. “I’m sorry. I was overwhelmed. Besides, visiting hours were over anyway.”

“Yeah, but I would’ve gone there first thing this morning,” he insisted, glancing toward Tamra, clearly hoping for some backup. But she shot him a sharp look, one that could have melted steel.

“We’re just glad he’s okay,” she said, her voice flat but tinged with frustration. Oz flinched under her gaze but held his ground.

“Just would’ve been nice to know, that’s all I’m saying,” he muttered, but before he could say more, Tamra jabbed him in the ribs with her elbow.

“Thank you,” I smiled at her, grateful for her silent support. “It wouldn’t have mattered anyway. Magister Thorne was examining him this morning. They wouldn’t let me in, even though Kadian said it was okay. I’ll be checking on him in a little bit.”

Oz chuckled, “I’m honestly shocked you didn’t bang the door down to get inside.”

I sighed, resting my elbows on the table and leaning my head against my hands. The weight of everything—the ball, Kadian, and especially Lil—felt heavier than usual today. “He doesn’t know about Lil,” I said quietly, the words coming out more like a confession than a statement. I took a deep breath, trying to steady myself. “I have to figure out how to tell him. So yes, I’m a bit of a coward for not breaking the door down this morning just to stare at him, knowing I have terrible news to share.”

Silence stretched between us, punctuated only by the clatter of dishes and the low hum of conversation from the other tables in the dining hall.

“I thought I'd go for a run, try to clear my head,” I added, gesturing to my outfit.

Tamra raised an eyebrow and smirked. “I did think you looked rather casual this morning.”

I glanced at Oz and Tamra. “Either of you care to join me?”

They both shook their heads in unison.

"I'm going to see Kadian," Oz said, pushing back from the bench and standing up.

"Don't say anything," Tamra said sharply, grabbing his arm before he could take another step.

"Of course not," he pulled his arm free, the hint of a smile playing on his lips. "I promise." Then he turned to me.

"Tell him I'll be there in a couple of hours," I said, taking a bite of toast.

After Oz left, Tamra launched into a recount of her night with Amera. "She asked me to go to the ball with her as her date." She said, her tone a mix of excitement and nervousness.

I smiled, taking a sip of my coffee. "Sounds like things are getting serious."

"Yeah, I guess I'll have to introduce her to Oz at some point soon," Tamra laughed, shaking her head. Never one to linger on the topic of herself for long, Tamra asked, "What are you going to wear to the ball?"

I shrugged. "I haven't thought about it. Probably one of the dresses they left in my closet. Same as I do with everything else." I'd been too preoccupied, constantly reminding myself of the reason this ball was occurring in the first place. My clothes wouldn't matter, none of it did.

Glancing across the room, I spotted Addie walking into the dining hall, her eyes searching until they landed on me. She waved, and I nodded toward her. "Addie's over there," I said, standing up. "I'm going to go say hi and then head to the gym. See you later?"

Tamra nodded, turning her attention back to her breakfast.

I wove my way through the crowded hall until I reached Addie, who greeted me with her usual bright smile. "I don't normally see you in here," I teased.

"I thought I'd catch you this morning. I heard the good news about Kadian," she said, pulling me into a quick hug. "How's he feeling?"

"Want to walk with me?" I asked, and she wrapped her arm around my shoulders as we left the dining hall.

I filled her in on everything, including Kadian's incomplete memory. Addie listened carefully, her brow furrowing with concern.

"If Magister Thorne doesn't advise against it, you should get Kadian to that ball," she said thoughtfully. "He hasn't been seen much since the accident, and the courts might find him more intriguing because of it."

"I'll make sure he gets there," I promised. Her words gave me something to focus on, a small goal amidst the chaos.

As we reached the entrance to the gym, Addie smiled and squeezed my shoulders. "This is where I leave you. Good luck with your run."

I rounded the corner to an almost empty track, relieved to see I could run in peace—until a flash of violet hair caught my eye.

Marsh.

He slowed as he spotted me, his smile wide as he approached. "Brida," he said, his voice light. "Twice in less than twenty-four hours? I consider myself lucky."

"I consider it somewhat stalkerish," I replied, though I couldn't help the faint smile that tugged at my lips.

He laughed, shaking his head. "Believe it or not, I was a runner long before you showed up."

I glanced at him, then back at the empty track. "I can run ahead of you if you want," he offered, mischief dancing in his eyes.

"It's fine, Marsh," I said, finishing my stretches. "Just...try to keep up."

We kept a steady pace as we ran together in silence, our feet falling into a rhythm that felt oddly familiar, even though it had been months since we'd done this. Each lap around the track passed without a word, the quiet between us both comfortable and tense.

"I know we haven't had a chance to talk since we went to Hadash. I'm sorry," Marsh said as we rounded one of the curves, his shaky voice breaking the silence that had hung between us for so long.

I glanced at him, my chest tightening, panting. I replied, "What's been happening there?"

"The earthquake caused significant damage to the cave systems," he began, his voice low. "Some of the caves collapsed entirely. Part of the Eternal Court was built over those caves, and it suffered the highest number of casualties."

I stumbled slightly at his words, regaining my footing. "Do they know what caused the quakes?"

He slowed to a stop, turning to face me. His violet eyes held an intensity that made my stomach knot. "They believe it originated from the Pool of Vitality," he said.

I stood frozen. The heat from the sun seemed to vanish, leaving me cold. "Are you telling me..." I took a step closer to him, lowering my voice to a whisper. "That we somehow caused that earthquake?" My pulse raced, and a sickening feeling spread through my chest. The deaths of all those people—could we have been responsible?

Before the trip, Marsh had reassured me that visiting the pool was a common practice among members of the Eternal Court. I hadn't thought anything of it. The idea that our visit could have triggered something so catastrophic felt unreal. But now, I wasn't so sure.

"I've been trying to investigate that," Marsh said, holding my gaze. "That's why I've been going back to Hadash so often."

I wiped sweat from my temple, the sun suddenly feeling unbearable again. "Have you found anything?" My heart pounded against my ribcage, the fear that we were to blame twisting inside me.

"The cave system with the Pool of Vitality is one of the few destroyed. Well," he corrected himself, "the entrance was. No one's been able to get inside since. It's as if the cave sealed itself from within."

I stared at him, the horror building in my expression. Was that even possible? I could feel the guilt creeping in, threatening to overwhelm me.

"Does anyone know we were there the night before?"

"No," he assured me, his voice steady. "I kept that to myself."

I prayed he was right—that this was all some terrible coincidence. The idea that we could have had a hand in so many innocent deaths was unbearable.

"Are you alright?" Marsh asked, his warm hand on my arm. I hadn't realized I'd bent over, my breathing shallow and labored.

Slowly, I stood up straight. "Yes," I said, though I wasn't convinced. His smile helped ground me. "What have you been doing while you're there?" I asked, hoping to focus on something else, anything else.

"At first, I helped with transportation. But when Qurasa suggested to Illerium that the quake might be linked to the Pool of Vitality, I asked to assist with the investigation," he said as we made our way toward the table with water. "For the first few weeks, we tried to find a way inside the cave. When that failed, we started looking through historical records to see if something like this had happened before."

He handed me a glass of water, which I downed in two gulps. "Have you discovered anything?" I asked, reaching for another glass.

"Nothing yet," he sighed. "We're still searching."

"I hope I haven't used up all my time with you," Marsh said as we neared the exit, "and that we can still speak at the ball."

"We'll talk in a couple of days," I replied, smiling faintly as we parted ways.

☽✳☾

I shut the door behind me, the heavy click echoing in the stillness of the room. The sight of Kadian standing, stretching by the window, thrilled me. The morning light cast a soft glow around him, catching in his hair, making my heart flutter in my chest. He was out of bed—finally.

"Hello, stranger," I said, trying to keep my voice light, but I couldn't shake the tightness in my throat. My heart raced, pounding so loudly I feared he'd hear it. "How'd you sleep?"

He smiled, the kind that was so effortlessly Kadian—bright, warm, like a dawn you wanted to step into. "I slept well. Better than I have in ages."

His arms stretched over his head, muscles rippling beneath his tunic. "This view," he laughed, nodding toward the window. "It's better than what I had in the inductees' quarters. It's a shame I've missed it for most of my time here."

I sat down on the edge of the bed, forcing myself to smile back. My stomach twisted, the words boiling beneath my skin, burning to be let out. "Kadian..."

He turned toward me, curiosity sparking in his golden eyes like sunlight on water. "Yes?"

I stared at him, and for a moment, I wanted to swallow the words back down. They felt too sharp, too heavy for the quiet, warm room. But I couldn't. Not anymore.

"We need to talk," I said, the words tumbling out, unstoppable. "I tried to tell you last night, but I couldn't...I don't even know how to begin, but I have to, Kadian. I love you, and you're my best friend. You need to know. And I would never, ever want to hurt you—"

"Brida," he said softly, sitting next to me, so close I could feel the warmth of him seeping through the space between us. "Slow down. Breathe."

I did, shakily, trying to pull in air that felt too thick to swallow. His voice was steady, calm. "You have my attention."

I twisted my hands in my lap, avoiding his gaze for a moment longer. "I told you yesterday about working with Alvar..."

He nodded, a small crease forming between his brows. "Yeah, you did."

I turned toward him, “We’ve been planning the ball for weeks, Kadian. It’s to announce an engagement.”

Something shifted in his face—his eyes widened and lips parted in surprise. He stood, moving away from me like he needed space to breathe. “You’re marrying Alvar?”

His voice was edged with disbelief, and I wanted to laugh, to break the tension. But I couldn't.

“No—” I started, but he cut me off.

“Gods, Brida, I thought you had a thing for Dainan. Or Marsh, even though I never quite saw that one. But you—Alvar?” He smirked. “You’ve only ever had a thing for dark-haired men, and Alvar, well...” He trailed off, amusement flickering in his voice.

“Kadian.” I tried to keep my voice steady, but it wavered.

His grin grew as he paced in front of me. “So, you're to be a royal now? Will I have to bow and call you ‘Your Majesty’? This is all happening rather fast, isn’t it?”

“Kadian!” I stood, reaching out for him, desperate to pull him back to where we were, to ground us in the conversation I needed to have. “It’s not to announce *my* engagement.”

He stopped, the air stilling around us. His confusion was palpable as he stared at me, the humor draining from his face. "Oh... Well, that’s a relief. So, who’s getting married then?”

I sighed, the weight of the truth pressing down on me like a thousand stones. “It’s to celebrate two engagements.” I hesitated, the words sticking in my throat. “*The first*...is for Prince Dainan and Iona.”

Kadian’s eyes darkened, his lips curling in distaste. "That obnoxious redhead?"

Gods, I loved him for that. "Yes," I said, managing a weak smile. “She’s had her eye on him for ages. And what Iona wants—”

“—Iona gets.” he finished for me, his tone dripping with disdain. His gaze softened, a question still lingering in his eyes. “And?”

My breath caught, a knot tightening in my chest as I met his gaze. His eyes, usually so warm, felt like molten gold, burning with the intensity of his question. They danced with light, but I could feel the storm gathering behind them.

Here it goes.

"The second is for Prince Rai." I paused again, my hands trembling as I clasped them together. "Prince Rai is going to marry Lil."

For a moment, the world stood still. His expression was unreadable, a blank mask. No rage. No outburst. Just silence. It stretched on, wrapping around us, suffocating. Then, his lips parted, and he said, "I think Lil will be suited to royal life. She loves Azmeer."

My heart stuttered. "What?"

He smiled, walking toward the window where the light played across his features. "Lil loves it here. We've known that since the day we met her. She wore jewels to our induction meeting, for Gods' sake." He shrugged as if it were the most obvious thing in the world.

What is happening? I blinked. My mind scrambled to make sense of this.

"You're...happy for her?" I asked, my voice barely a whisper.

He turned to me, confusion flickering across his face. "Of course I'm happy for her. As long as she's happy, I'm happy for her."

I collapsed into the chair beside the bed, my mind reeling. This was not how it was supposed to go. This wasn't the reaction I had braced myself for.

"So... What's the big deal? This ball is for Lil, and—" His eyes widened, his hand coming to rest on my knee as he knelt before me. "Oh...Brida, are you upset about Dainan's wedding?"

I stared at him, utterly baffled. "Kadian... What was the last thing you told me about Lil?"

He paused, thinking, then shrugged. "I don't remember. Was it important?"

He doesn't remember. How can he not remember?

I forced a smile, my chest tightening as I fought to keep my composure. "The ball's in two days. Magister Thorne says you'll be able to attend."

I stared at him, a hollow ache gnawing at my insides. He didn't know. He didn't remember.

Kadian's laughter tugged at my heart, the familiar sound wrapping around me like a comforting blanket, pulling me away from the storm that brewed inside. "Great!" he said with a grin, taking a bite of the sandwich left untouched on the tray.

"Looks like I'll need to shave before the big event." His eyes lingered on me for a moment, his tone suddenly softer. "You okay, Bri?"

I swallowed the lump forming in my throat, willing the tension to unravel itself from my chest. "Sorry," I murmured, forcing a lightness I didn't feel into my voice. "I went for a run this morning. Guess the heat got to me."

The heat wasn't what was suffocating me, though. It was the words. The truth I'd been choking down.

Kadian didn't seem to notice. He'd already pulled out the shaving kit from the bedside table, smiling at me as if everything was as it should be. "It's warm here," he said, opening the razor with practiced ease. "As much as I love the cold, I can't hate this weather. There's something comforting about it, you know?"

Comforting. I wished I could find comfort in anything right now.

"I'll let you be, I wouldn't want you to make a mistake and cut your pretty face," I stood and stretched my legs.

His smirk widened as he pointed the razor at me. "Hey, it's a *handsome* face, Bri. Maybe even *beautiful.* Use the proper terms."

I chuckled, but it was hollow. Stepping closer to him, I inhaled deeply, catching nothing but the earthy scent that had always been him. It was strange—too strange. The salt that had clung to him for weeks had vanished, like a memory I couldn't quite grasp.

"I'll come back after dinner," I said, needing to escape the warmth of his room, the warmth of his presence. "Maybe Oz and Tamra can join us."

"Oz is only allowed back here if he brings the money he owes me," Kadian quipped, turning back to the mirror, the familiar humor in his eyes. "I kicked his ass at cards this morning."

My heart squeezed tighter, the light banter doing nothing to lessen the weight pressing down on me. "I'll see you later," I whispered, knowing he wouldn't hear the tremor in my voice. He was already focused on shaving, wiping away the last trace of the weeks he'd spent bedridden.

I stepped out into the hallway, barely registering where I was going. My mind was a whirlwind, thoughts colliding and crashing like waves against rocks.

Buzzing with a frantic energy, my fingers trembled as they reached for the door handle to my floor. Entering on the other side, I was stopped in my tracks—a large black box lay propped up against my door. It was sleek, with a blood-red ribbon tied around it, the seal of the Court of Shadows pressed into the attached card.

I swallowed hard, shifting the box into my arms as I pushed the door open with my hip.

With a deep breath, I placed it on the bed, my hands shaking as I broke the seal. The words written in bold, elegant script:

For a Lady of Shadows.

☽✳☾

Around lunch time on the day of the ball, Kadian was discharged from the infirmary and escorted back to his rooms by Oz, Tamra, and myself.

"I cleaned while you were gone," I said as we walked through the doorway, "please, try to keep it this way for at least an hour."

"Not a chance," he winked at me.

"So, what time does this party start tonight?" Oz collapsed on the bed.

"Whatever you do, if you see Prince Alvar around, be sure not to refer to it as a party in front of him. It starts at sundown. We have a few hours to get ready."

The conversation drifted into plans and hopes for the night, the anticipation weaving through our words. As time ticked on, we drifted apart to prepare ourselves for the evening.

My hair, having grown over the past six months, cascaded down in gentle waves. The red in my hair was more visible than it had once been, edging my hair closer to auburn than black. I ran my fingers through it, feeling the soft texture that seemed to shimmer with its own vitality.

The black gown now hung in my closet, a silent reminder of the night looming ahead. I hadn't wanted it to wrinkle—not that I felt much like wearing it. The moment I'd seen the gift, the blood-red ribbon, I knew Alvar had a hand in this.

I had planned to wear crimson—something striking but also safe. But when I mentioned it to Alvar, he was appalled. "You're to be part of the Court of Shadows," he had said, his brow furrowing in that disapproving way. "You should look the part."

And so, here it was: the most beautiful black gown I'd ever seen. The fabric was like liquid night, sleek and heavy, with intricate stitching that shimmered under the light. He'd gone to great lengths to ensure the measurements were exact—when I slipped it on, it fit as if it had been sewn onto me, hugging my curves and flowing effortlessly down to the floor.

I ran my fingers along the bodice, feeling the smoothness of the fabric, the weight of the gown pulling me toward the floor like an anchor. The black onyx earrings that had come with the dress—delicate spears—dangled from my ears, cold against my skin. I caught a glimpse of myself in the mirror, and for a moment, I almost didn't recognize the woman staring back.

She looked...elegant. Regal, even. But there was something hollow in her eyes, a flicker of dread that no amount of makeup or jewelry could hide.

My heart pounded as I fastened the last clasp, my hands trembling slightly. I paused, forcing myself to take slow, measured breaths. *You can do this,* I whispered, more to the reflection than to myself. *You have to do this.*

But the words felt empty, bouncing off the walls of my mind, offering no comfort. My chest tightened, and I could feel the sting of tears welling up behind my eyes. For a brief moment, I considered letting them fall. Maybe they would ease the weight pressing against my ribs, the guilt gnawing at the edges of my thoughts.

But I blinked the tears away. *No. Not tonight.* I couldn't afford to let the cracks show. Not when everyone would be watching.

I wiped at the corners of my eyes, careful not to smudge the makeup I'd spent far too long perfecting. The dress, the earrings—I had to look perfect, as if I belonged.

My feet ached already in the heels I'd chosen—delicate black stilettos that completed the ensemble but felt like a form of quiet torture. Flats wouldn't have sufficed. Not with a gown like this.

When I finally stepped out into the hallway, my legs felt shaky beneath me, as though they could give out at any moment. I walked slowly, the soft rustle of the gown trailing behind me as I made my way toward the entrance of the House of Shadows.

The doors were already open, an unusual gesture on Alvar's part. He'd insisted that they remain open throughout the night so that no one would be left waiting outside, risking the door's whimsical decision to bar latecomers.

I swallowed hard, my throat tight as I climbed the stairs. Each step made me more aware of the ache in my feet and the knot in my stomach. I could hear the faint sounds of music drifting through the air as I approached the ballroom—the musicians practicing their pieces, the notes echoing softly down the hallway. The scent of roasted meats and hors d'oeuvres followed soon after, wafting toward me as if to beckon me inside.

I paused just outside the ballroom, my heart racing in my chest. *I am more than my fear,* I told myself. *I am the story I choose to write.* And with that, I lifted my chin, squared my shoulders, and stepped forward into the gilded light of the ballroom.

Entering the ballroom was like stepping into a dream. The grandeur of it all seemed to swell around me, even more breathtaking than the first time I had seen it. The sight of Alvar, poised and impeccably dressed in a fitted black jacket and a deep red shirt, caught me by surprise. His attire revealed a glimpse of his chest and muscles, a detail I often overlooked but now found startling.

"Brida," he took a few steps toward me, "you look stunning. I'm so pleased you didn't opt for red, it would have been a ghastly decision with your hair."

I couldn't help the smile that bloomed on my face. "I suppose I have you to thank for this," I said, gesturing to the dress that seemed to shimmer with the essence of the night sky, its constellations woven into the fabric. The thin straps and low cut, coupled with the daring slits up to mid-thigh, made it perfect for dancing.

"As much as I would love to take credit for this look," his eyes traced me, "I cannot. I have been far too busy. Besides, Asana may be forgiving in most things, however dressing my protégé would be where she draws the line." He laughed.

Who sent this to me then?

"Come with me." Alvar ushered us to the table for the Court of Reflection. "Do you think it's the right shade of blue?" His arms were crossed as he stood back, judging the table as if it were being tried for murder.

"I'm not sure it really matters," I told him. It *was* the wrong color. It wasn't the color we'd selected, but it would have to do.

"That doesn't answer the question, Brida," he took a step towards it and began to rub his fingers over it in inspection.

"I'm not sure feeling the fabric is going to change its color, Alvar." He shot me a look. He was not in a playful mood.

I could hear him groan as he stood back once more, "it will have to do."

By the time we checked the other tables, the musicians, and their instruments—Alvar was an expert in tuning, in addition to stopping by and reminding the chef that he was to save Alvar each type of eclair, guests had started to arrive.

"Okay," Alvar took a deep breath. His hair was pulled back into a low bun this evening. It highlighted his features, and tonight, anxiety was the strongest feature of them all.

"Do you always worry this much?" I asked him as he grabbed a glass of champagne from a tray, downing it in one swig.

He paused for a moment and smiled. "Everything looks beautiful, Brida. You did a wonderful job. Even though the table is the wrong color."

I placed my hands on his arms, "*we* did a wonderful job."

I looked to the entryway, and in the midst of the crowd, I saw Asana enter; the look on Alvar's face was one of pure admiration and love. "Go, before everyone sees you and realizes just how in love you actually are," I said as I laughed, "you look like a love-sick puppy."

His grin turned wicked, "Save a dance for me?" He made his way towards her, grabbing another glass of champagne as he went.

I smiled.

If he continues to drink champagne like that, it'll be the most entertaining dance of my life.

Guests trickled in, their murmurs and gasps weaving through the air like a soft symphony of awe. They marveled at the House of Shadows, their eyes reflecting the grandeur that had become standard to me. The walls pulsed with live veins, veins that flickered with an ethereal glow, light dancing in every corner. Shadows slithered around the guests, curling around my ankles and climbing my legs like affectionate serpents. I felt their touch on my arms, a reminder of the House's living magic.

I waited for Oz, Tamra, and Kadian to join me, the crowd's conversations forming a constant, undulating background hum. Fragments of conversation reached me:

"I didn't know Prince Dainan was even entertaining marriage."

"He was not. The rumor is..."

"Thalius was the conspirator behind this arrangement. You know how he can be when he gets an idea in his head."

"Have you tried the roasts?"

"Have you seen the king?"

The heat of the room and the endless chatter became overwhelming, a press of warmth and noise. I sought refuge on one of the balconies, stepping outside into the cooler embrace of the evening air. I leaned against the railing, taking a deep breath as the warm breeze swept over me. The view was breathtaking—lanterns outside the city walls glowed like distant fireflies, their soft light twinkling in the darkness.

"Escaping to get some quiet?" a familiar voice interrupted my solitude.

I turned to find Marsh standing beside me, his presence as comforting as it was unexpected. His black suit made him look effortlessly handsome.

He joined me at the railing, his gaze lost in the expanse of the city below.

We stood together in silence, the hum of the party a distant murmur through the glass doors. His presence was calming, a soothing counterpoint to the evening's chaos.

"This doesn't have to be awkward, you know," he nudged me, his tone light but sincere. "Not unless you want it to be."

"I'm sorry," I said, my voice catching as I faced him. The weight of my earlier actions felt heavier now. "I've been pushing you away, not only because I was mad at you but also because I've been mad at myself." My eyes met his, searching for understanding. "I meant it when I kissed you, Marsh. I had no idea what I was doing when I danced with Dainan. It complicated things for me, and I'm sorry."

He paused, his fingers tracing idle patterns on the railing. "Do you..."

"Go ahead, ask your question," I urged, leaning back against the balcony and closing my eyes, trying to steady the tumult within me.

"It's none of my business," he said quietly.

"Can I ask you a question?"

"Of course," he replied, his expression relaxed but guarded.

"Why do you and Dainan hate each other?" The question slipped out before I could second-guess it, and I watched as his face tightened, his gaze growing distant.

He hesitated, then gestured toward a nearby bench. "It's a bit of a long story. I've known Dainan for a long time. My father helped his father in the Battle of Talvig."

The name of the battle brought a twinge of recognition. The battle that had cemented Elidas's claim to the throne.

"Our fathers worked closely together, and even though Dainan was still young, he was already a fierce warrior. He spent most of his early years away from home, training in Hadash or the Tactras Mountains." He continued, his voice steady but shadowed with memory. "When he arrived at the Court of Whispers, we became good friends—the three of us."

"The three of you?" I asked, curiosity piqued.

"Yes, the three of us." He exhaled, his smile faint and sad. "My best friend was a girl named Cyria. You remind me of her, actually," he said, his eyes softening. "She and Dainan became close. It wasn't encouraged, her family wasn't affiliated with the Court of Shadows. When it came to the Battle of Talvig, Cyria and I were sent to the Western Front while Dainan stayed on the Southern Flank despite us having trained together."

I nodded, urging him to continue.

"Our side suffered many casualties. During the chaos, Cyria and I got separated. I didn't find out what happened to her until later that day when I went searching for her." His face contorted with grief. "By the time I got there, Dainan had already found her. She died in the fighting, and Dainan blamed me for not protecting her."

"I'm sorry," I said softly, my hand rested on his arm. "I can only imagine how terrible that must have been. For both of you."

"Thank you," he said. "But that was a long time ago. Dainan

hasn't let it go. Since then, he's gone out of his way to pursue any woman I show interest in."

"Has that been many?" I asked with a smirk, trying to lighten the mood.

"No," he chuckled, the sound bittersweet. "Well, I wasn't expecting to have this conversation tonight." He offered me his hand, a gesture of camaraderie and perhaps something more.

"Do you think we could share a dance this evening?" Marsh's voice was hopeful as he took a step closer.

"If we do," I began, "I would like it to be as friends."

"Brida Larrow, I accept," he said with a bow, his smile warm and genuine.

"I need to go find Kadian. Come find me later, and we can have that dance," I said, smiling as we parted ways.

I soon found my friends by the food table. Oz and Kadian blended in in their black suits, each exuding a distinct charm. Tamra, dressed in a deep red suit that highlighted her warm complexion, looked stunning.

"Gods," Tamra exclaimed, her eyes wide as she took in my appearance.

"You look fucking incredible," Oz added, his voice filled with admiration. I felt a flush of warmth spread across my cheeks.

Kadian pulled me into an embrace, pressing a soft kiss to my cheek. "You look amazing. Anyone who says otherwise is out of their Gods damned mind."

The intensity of their stares made me squirm. "It's not like I don't put effort into my appearance most days," I said, trying to brush off their praise, though their laughter filled me with a sense of pride.

"Yeah, but," Tamra said, her gaze sweeping over me appreciatively, "this is different."

Maybe she was right. I did feel different. But as the night went on, I couldn't shake the feeling that something was lurking beneath the surface, ready to unravel the evening.

CHAPTER FORTY-TWO

The evening air was alive with a gentle hum of music and conversation, a symphony of voices blending into a pleasant backdrop. Amid the chatter, one question seemed to be on everyone's lips: where are they?

Despite the success of the evening, I couldn't help but be reminded as to the reason that we were all here. After showing Oz and Kadian a brief tour of the ballroom and surrounding areas, I decided to seek solace in the library. I left them on a balcony and made my way downstairs, gathering a plate of food before descending to the calm sanctuary.

Tura, ever the diligent librarian, was stationed at her post. "Library's closed," she yelled. Her presence was a comfort amidst the evening's chaos.

"Just checking to make sure that is truly the case," I said.

"What are you doing here?" she asked with a mixture of surprise and curiosity as she lifted her gaze to greet me.

"I thought you might be hungry," I said, offering her the plate of food. "I know Alvar is the one who usually brings you food, and he's your favorite..."

She waved me off with a dismissive gesture. "I like you just as much now," she grabbed the plate and began eating.

"Tura, do you mind if I ask how long you've worked here?"

"I'm the second librarian to have worked in the House of Shadows," she said proudly while taking a bite of lemon tart. "And I will remain at my post until the end."

"Until the end?" I echoed, puzzled by the cryptic note in her words.

She nodded, a strange, somber light in her eyes. "Thank you for the food, dear," she said, placing her hand on mine in a rare gesture of warmth.

Just then, I heard the distant shuffling of footsteps. "Have you been letting people into the library?" I teased. "When Alvar explicitly told me to tell you not to."

A tight tug found Tura's lips. "Other than you, only one has found their way here tonight. He's wandering around the third floor," she said, raising her voice, an unfamiliar edge to it. "Making more noise than he should as he shouldn't be here in the first place."

Cocking an eyebrow, I began to ask who she was speaking to but stopped short when I felt a familiar tickle on my leg. My shadows, drawn to me, began their usual playful dance, curling up my legs and climbing my arms.

"Hello to you too," I said as they wove their way to my neck.

Tura's face paled, and she began to retreat.

"Tura? Are you alright?"

"Yes, dear, I'm fine," she said hurriedly, stepping back into the stacks behind her desk. "Thank you again for the plate. I'll see you tomorrow."

I watched her go, puzzled. My shadows, however, were growing increasingly restless, hissing and moving with greater urgency. One of them leaped from my shoulder and onto the floor, guiding me towards the stairs.

"That isn't the exit, and I need to get back upstairs," I said, but they hissed louder as if insisting. "Fine," I muttered, following the path they were setting for me.

The shadowy guides continued to lead me, directing me to a part of the library I had never seen before. The room was warm and inviting, resembling a cozy cabin with a fireplace and leather furniture. A large window framed the evening sky, the view as beautiful as ever.

So they do have windows here.

In front of the window stood a figure in a black suit, back turned to me. His posture was rigid, and I could see the strength and tension in his stance even from behind.

"What are you doing here, Brida?" he asked without turning.

"How..." I began, surprised by his presence.

"Jasmine and vanilla," he said, his voice steady but tinged with an edge of sadness.

I moved to stand beside him, the moonlight casting a soft glow over his features, highlighting the depth of his distress. The night sky stretched out before us, a stark contrast to the turmoil within the library.

"What are you doing here, Brida?" he asked again, his voice carrying a note of both weariness and curiosity.

"Back to calling me Brida, I see," I said.

He turned towards me with a smoldering intensity that set fire to his eyes. I took a deep breath, trying to steady the whirlwind of emotions swirling inside me.

"I suppose it's rather inappropriate for me to have an affectionate nickname for you when I am to be chained to another." His voice was formal—something I had never heard from him before. "I ask you again, what are you doing here?"

"The shadows led me here," I replied, my voice tinged with frustration and fatigue. I raised my arm to show him the shadow that had slithered up me once more. "They insisted," I said.

Dainan took a step closer, his hand reaching out with a tentative grace. He held my hand, the warmth of his touch sending shivers up my arm. The shadow inspected him before slipping from my wrist to curl around his arm.

"It likes you," I said with a nervous laugh, but the silence that followed felt heavy. "I tried to leave, but it demanded that I find you first," I gestured to the shadow.

He nodded, his gaze drifting back to the window. I could sense his struggle to maintain control, a battle I knew all too well.

"I never asked you," I said, trying to bridge the silence, "what is your favorite book?" I caught the slight curve of his lips, a fleeting smirk that seemed to soften his stern demeanor.

"I have many," he admitted, "but if I were forced to choose," he met my gaze, "I think I would choose *Vietta*."

I cleared my throat:

"Amidst the boundless span, love's flame shall stay,
Neither time nor space can quench its fervent ray.
Though skies may weep and oceans wildly roar,
Their souls, united, bask in love's sweet lore."

He looked at me, astonished. "What can I say," I said, holding his gaze, "I love the classics." I smiled as his eyes remained wide, a silent acknowledgment of our shared passion.

"I wouldn't have pegged you for a lover of plays," I continued, moving to one of the leather wingback chairs. I propped my feet up on the ottoman, trying to ease the tension that crackled between us.

"And what do you think would be my preferred genre?" he asked, following me and sitting beside the chair, appearing unbothered by the proximity.

"Something dark." I chuckled, "Maybe a murder mystery." His smirk widened.

"I'm a bit deeper than that," he said, his tone laced with a hint of vulnerability he seldom shared. "Not that many around here would know it."

I felt a pang of sympathy. "I'm sorry," I whispered, my eyes locking with his. "It must be very difficult to feel that you are not seen for who you are."

His expression softened, a rare glimpse of his inner self. "How do you see me?" His fingers began to trace along my shin, and I was taken aback by the ease with which my body responded to his touch.

For a fleeting moment, I wondered if this intimacy had ever felt this natural with Cyria. Were they mates?

"I think that is a dangerous question, given what is going on upstairs," I said, emerging from my thoughts as his hand continued its slow, deliberate journey up my leg.

"Fuck," he murmured, pulling his hand away and pacing the room, his agitation palpable. "I can't do this, Brida." His frustration was evident as he ran a hand through his hair.

"No one is—"

"I can't do this when you are here, and you fucking smell the way you do," he said, his expression torn with pain.

"I'm sorry," I said softly, rising and heading for the door. But before I could leave, shadows surrounded me, closing in like a protective shroud.

Dainan was inches from me, his presence commanding, his hand braced against the shelf now behind me. "Gods," he said, his eyes burning with an unspoken need. "It's nothing you've done, Ilia." He gently brushed my hair from my face, his touch tender.

"Dainan..." I murmured, my voice trembling with the uncertainty of why I had been drawn to him tonight. But a deep part of me knew I was where I needed to be.

He brushed his thumb against my lower lip, and I moved instinctively towards him. His scent, now intoxicatingly close, enveloped me.

"I need you, Ilia," he whispered, his breath hot against the nape of my neck, eliciting a moan I couldn't contain.

Guilt surged through me, mingling with the fire that his touch ignited. What about Marsh? What about Iona, his marriage, the ball happening upstairs in honor of that marriage? As his lips pressed against my neck, my worries melted away, replaced by a primal need.

He lightly grazed his teeth along my skin, sending tremors through my body. His low, sultry laugh reverberated through me, heightening the intensity of my desire. I pressed myself closer to him with every kiss and touch, feeling the length of him against me. I brushed my fingers over him, and he growled in response.

"Fuck," he whispered, "if you touch me, Ilia, I can't promise I'll maintain control. I'm on the edge as it is."

"I want you unhinged," I breathed, my desire burning bright in my eyes.

His hand began to make lazy circles up my leg, his kisses trailing over my neck, each touch pushing me closer to the edge. "Dainan," I whimpered as his hand inched closer to the top of my thigh, the heat between us growing unbearable.

His eyes met mine, a question hanging in the air as he moved my undergarments aside, creating a blissful friction. I dug my fingers into his arms with every movement, low moans escaping me.

"Tell me to stop, and I will," he whispered, pressing a kiss to my neck. I knew he meant it. He would stop if I asked, but I needed him. Needed this.

"Don't stop," I managed to gasp, my voice raw.

With a low growl of approval, Dainan slid a finger inside me, his movements slow and deliberate. I moved my hips in rhythm with his fingers, craving more. I ran my hand through his fiery waves, pulling him closer.

"Do you think you can handle more of me?" he asked, his lips brushing the nape of my neck.

My pleas grew louder, a cry of desperation.

"Use your words, Ilia," he urged, his thumb rubbing my clit while his fingers continued their rhythmic exploration.

"More," I begged, and with that, he added a second finger, moving deeper, harder. The intensity was overwhelming, each stroke drawing out sounds and noises I had never made before, and never would again. Not unless I was with him. Nothing compared, no one would compare to this. I was lost in the sensation, the pleasure building within me until I felt I was on the brink of an explosion.

"Look at you," he growled, "fucking beautiful." His mouth found mine. Our tongues clashed in a desperate dance as I drowned in his scent, in the completeness of him.

He pulled back, his eyes searching mine. "Is this how you like it, Ilia?" he asked, pressing himself into me, his fingers continuing their relentless rhythm. The pleasure was almost too much to bear.

"That's it, Ilia," he said, his voice thick with approval. "You're getting close."

The tension inside me coiled tighter with each stroke of his hand. "Come for me, love."

My scream was swallowed by his mouth as he pulled me over the edge. My breathing ragged as my body trembled. Dainan's expression was feral as he watched me, his eyes a dark, smoldering blaze. I opened my mouth to speak, but he interrupted me.

"I need a minute," he said, his voice strained. I didn't move, though I longed to reciprocate, to touch him, to take him further. He remained still, his eyes filled with need but not pressing me for more.

After a moment, he whispered, "You're so beautiful." His thumb brushed along the nape of my neck, trailing lower toward my collarbone, his touch feather-light but searing.

"Dainan," I murmured, my voice trembling with a mix of desire and hesitation. As much as I wanted to lose myself in the moment, the worries I'd been trying to suppress came rushing back. "We should..." I began, struggling to give shape to the storm of conflicted feelings rising within me.

"We should..." he echoed softly, his lips brushing mine one last time before he pulled away. The kiss lingered like the faintest ember, setting fire to something deep inside me.

"There's a bathing chamber just around the corner," he said after a beat, his voice tinged with a note of restraint—or regret. "We can clean you up there."

"That was..." I began, attempting to steady my breathing and grasp at words that refused to come.

He smiled—a slow, effortless curve of his lips that made my knees falter. "I'm just sorry it took this long," he said, his fingers finding mine as he led the way.

"We need to get you back upstairs," he said as we emerged from the room.

"What about you?" I asked, my voice laced with reluctance, not wanting to let him go.

He took a step closer, his fingers grazing my cheek as he brushed a strand of hair away. The touch sent a shiver within me that screamed for more of him.

"Thank you," he murmured, his tone softer, more vulnerable than it had been before.

"For what?" I asked, trying to sound light-hearted, but the intensity in his gaze held me captive.

"For trusting me with you," he said, placing a kiss on my neck. The warmth of his lips against my skin made me melt, my body reacting to him with a fervent need that seemed to override all reason.

"Dainan..." I whispered, my voice faltering.

He continued to gently trace his thumb across my cheek, his touch tender and lingering, as if he, too, was reluctant to let this precious time slip away. "I can bring you back upstairs," he offered, his gaze dropping to my shoes with a hint of frustration. "It might be less painful than having you climb up in those," he added, a trace of annoyance evident in his voice.

"It's okay," I said, caressing his face one last time. He leaned into my touch, a silent acknowledgment of the connection we shared. We stood there, a silent struggle between departure and staying, our mutual hesitation to be the first to leave palpable.

I cupped his face in my hands, my eyes searching his. "I see you, Dainan. As you are," I said softly. Shadows of anguish flickered across his face, turning his fiery gaze into an abyss of darkness as if he was bracing himself against a storm within.

"I knew," he whispered into my ear, his breath warm against my skin, "that dress would make you look like a true Lady of Shadows. You look beautiful, Ilia." And with those words, he was gone.

Of course Dainan had sent the dress to me. The night had turned into something I hadn't expected.

"Where have you been?" Kadian asked when I returned to the ballroom.

I offered a carefully edited version of events, concealing the intimate details of what had transpired between Dainan and me. The secret was mine alone to keep, and a foolish one at that, given the circumstances.

Kadian saw the anxiety on my face beginning to build and insisted we dance. "I've got you, Bri." He whispered into my ear as he twirled me away from my thoughts and fears.

CHAPTER
FORTY-THREE

The ballroom had thrummed with life—an orchestra of laughter, clinking glasses, and the soaring notes of Strayers' Seventh Symphony. The strings had swelled, their melodies wrapping around the guests like silk, drawing them into the rhythm of the night. My pulse had matched the tempo, a silent drum under my skin, as I watched the dancers whirl like fireflies. Light, graceful, elegant.

And then—nothing.

The music had ebbed like a wave retreating from the shore, leaving only the ghost of its sound behind. A shiver ran through the crowd, heads turning as one toward the doorway.

There they stood.

The king and his queen entered with deliberate slowness as if each step they took pushed aside the air itself. The sea of guests parted like a veil, revealing the royal family as they crossed the floor with a grace that commanded reverence. And behind them, the Princes of Azmeer followed, shadows in their wake.

Alvar walked ahead, alone, his expression carved from stone. Rai trailed him, a softer contrast with Lil on his arm, her dress a waterfall of silver under the chandeliers. But it was Dainan who stole the breath from my lungs. Night cloaked in human form, fury etched across his features, his steps more predatory than royal. His eyes were dark, turbulent—wholly focused elsewhere. My heart faltered, ice spreading in my veins as I followed his gaze to Iona, whose victorious smirk made bile rise to my throat.

They reached the center of the room, and the king spoke, his voice cracked and worn, echoing the weight of years.

"Good evening." His eyes, pale and tired, swept over the room, collecting every soul within it.

"On behalf of my sons and my soon-to-be daughters-in-law," he bowed his heads towards Lil and Iona, the words crawling through my skin, "I thank you for making the journey to Azmeer for our little...get-together."

A wave of relief sloshed through me. *Thank the Gods he didn't call it a party.*

"Azmeer is lovely this time of year, is it not?" He smiled at his wife, his fingers grazing hers—a touch so gentle it hurt to witness. It was the smile of a man making peace with his goodbyes. "We are in a time of great change." he said, pausing as if weighing each word, "In addition to the marriages of my sons, I wish to make an announcement."

My heart clenched. *Not now, not here.*

"It was made known in these past weeks that I will be succeeded by my son, Alvar."

Alvar's skin blanched, the shock rippling through him as though someone had yanked the ground from beneath his feet. I knew from our late-night talks that, despite their tempestuous relationship, Alvar was already mourning his father. The man who was more king to him than kin. The man whose crown he would one day inherit.

"I have no doubt," the king said, his voice steady and deliberate, "that he will guide you into a peaceful transition." His gaze lingered on Alvar, a silent summons for him to step forward.

Applause erupted like a tidal wave, crashing against the walls and swallowing the room whole as Alvar moved into the spotlight. His composure teetered, a thread pulled taut, but he held firm.

He cleared his throat, his hands clasped tightly in front of him. "I...hadn't planned on giving a speech this evening, as tonight is not about me."

Ha, I thought. It never was with Alvar. Lil had warned me about the princes, but she couldn't have been more wrong about him. He was kind, funny, and unfailingly selfless. A rare blend of humility and strength.

He will make a phenomenal king.

The faces in the crowd were painted with respect and awe, their gazes fixed on him like he'd already earned their trust.

"But I am honored," he continued, his voice carrying the weight of the kingdom on his shoulders. "Though this will be a time of great sadness, I hope to usher in a period of peace and stability." His eyes darted to his father, and the briefest flicker of vulnerability passed between them. "As for tonight," he gestured to the band, "I ask that they play Vilmer's Tenth Symphony for the king and queen's first dance."

The conductor lifted his baton, and the soft, rumbling chords of the symphony began to fill the room. I watched the king turn to the queen, staring at her as if she were the only thing tethering him to this life. They moved into the waltz, their bodies becoming one, swaying to the rhythm in a final, bittersweet dance. Rai and Lil followed next, their movements precise, rehearsed, almost too perfect. Then Dainan and Iona joined the floor, their dance stilted, an uneasy clash of grace and tension.

And then, suddenly, Alvar was in front of me. His smirk was disarming, the gleam in his eye far too mischievous for the occasion.

"That was a fine speech." I said.

"You owe me a dance," he replied with a smirk.

I blinked, thrown by the abruptness. "Now? You cannot be serious."

"Oh, but I am." His hand was already outstretched. "You helped plan this *ball*, Brida. It's only right."

I glanced at the floor, the couples moving in seamless synchrony. Heat rushed to my cheeks. "I..."

"I won't take no for an answer."

With a sigh, I took his hand. "I hate you for this."

His laugh was rich, rolling over me like thunder. As he led me onto the floor, I caught sight of Oz and Kadian in the distance, their smug expressions making me wish the floor would swallow me whole. My skin prickled under their amused stares.

And then there was Dainan. His gaze, fierce and unyielding, sliced through the crowd like a blade, locking onto mine with an intensity that made my stomach twist. Next to him, Iona's eyes burned with pure, undiluted hatred.

"Turn and face me," Alvar said, snapping me out of my spiraling thoughts. He positioned me, one hand on my waist, the other clasping mine. His touch was firm but gentle. "Ready?"

Before I could answer, he guided me into the dance, spinning us into the flow of the music.

Everyone's watching. My breath hitched, my heart thudding painfully against my ribs.

"Look at me," Alvar whispered, his voice pulling my attention back to him. His eyes were warm, grounding me in the storm of my nerves. "Keep your eyes on me, and you'll forget they're even there."

I tried. Gods, I tried. But the weight of the stares, the burn of Dainan's eyes, the icy venom from Iona—it all pressed down on me, suffocating me.

"I can't believe you're making me do this," I muttered as we spun once more, the room blurring around us.

Alvar grinned, leaning in to whisper, "I've just done you the biggest favor of your life."

I raised an eyebrow.

He twirled me gracefully, his next words slipping into my ear like a secret. "Every court will want you now."

"Huh." The word slipped out before I could stop it, a fleeting glimpse into my emotions. I hated this—hated the attention, hated the charade. But beneath that frustration, I couldn't deny the cleverness of it all. I didn't want to give him the satisfaction, but it escaped anyway. "Well, as much as it pains me to say it...thank you."

His laugh rumbled, low and amused. "You're very welcome." There was an ease to him, a confidence in the way he guided me, even as the weight of everyone's stares pressed down on us.

"You're good at this," I muttered as we continued our journey across the floor.

"I did tell you that I loved to dance, Brida. I may be many things, but a liar has never been one of them."

"Will Asana be offended that you asked me for the first dance?" I blurted out, desperate for anything to distract from the tightening knot in my chest.

Alvar's eyes glittered with mischief. "I informed her yesterday. I know better than to play with fire." His tone was light, teasing, but there was a sharpness in his gaze, a flicker of something I couldn't quite place. "Everything turned out wonderfully, Brida. You did a spectacular job. Even if the color of the tablecloth is incorrect."

"I ordered the correct color," I muttered, my voice tight as he dipped me low, "It's not my fault they sent the wrong one. And *we* did a wonderful job."

His chuckle sent a wave of warmth through me, but it did little to ease the nervous flutter in my arms and legs. I glanced around the room, my gaze catching on the sea of faces, all watching us. My heart stuttered. *Too many eyes. Too much focus.*

"Please...distract me." The words tumbled out, a whispered plea as I gripped his hand a little tighter.

"I'm not sure what more I can do than continue to whirl you around this ballroom, Brida." His voice vibrated through me, steady, grounding. But my mind was elsewhere, drifting.

"Pick a subject, something, please." I begged.

I searched for an anchor, something, anything to pull me back to solid ground. Lil's face flashed as Rai spun her, her lips pressed into a thin line, eyes narrowed with disapproval. My heart sank. She was furious.

Kadian, oblivious as ever, stood in the crowd, grinning like a fool. How could he not see what this was doing to her?

"You promised we'd finish our conversation about the Primals," I said, clinging to the one thread of familiarity I could find. "Mates. Vasenia and Ollo."

Alvar's expression softened, his smirk fading into something more thoughtful. "The Court of Shadows believe that neither wanted the bond because Ollo had been in a relationship with Giaxia."

I nodded, my mind latching onto his words, letting them drown out the noise around us. Anything to escape the prying eyes.

"Giaxia hoped the bond would have snapped into place for her and Ollo, but it never did. When she got word that it did for Ollo and Vasenia, she went mad."

We spun, the movement dizzying, but his voice remained steady, drawing me back from the brink. "The story the Eternal Court tells, about Giaxia being assaulted by another Primal and thus sparking a war, is not one we adhere to. It is our belief that Giaxia kidnapped Vasenia, as retribution against Ollo spiting her, and that's what led Ollo to war."

I blinked, the weight of the story sinking into me. "She kidnapped Vasenia?"

"Indeed. The Primals chose sides. Some believed Giaxia and Ollo were true mates, that Vasenia had bewitched him. Others knew the truth."

The world around us faded as his words wrapped around me, pulling me deeper into the tale. "What about Giaxia establishing the courts?" I asked, my voice just above a whisper as he twirled me again.

A dark glint crossed his face, his lips curving into a grim smile. "Another myth. The Pool of Vitality...it demands blood for any request. Life for life." His gaze locked with mine, his words heavy with meaning. "We believe Giaxia offered Vasenia's blood to the pool. She offered the bond between Ollo and Vasenia, not her own. Giaxia didn't have one."

A chill crept over me despite the heat of the room. "Wouldn't the Pool of Vitality know it wasn't Vasenia offering her own blood?"

His expression was all the answer I needed. "The pool isn't sentient in that way. It understands the nature of its magic, not the identity of the one making the offering. It took Vasenia's blood, broke the bond...and that magic is what formed the Courts."

I swallowed hard, the weight of the revelation pressing down on my chest. "What happened to Vasenia?"

My eyes flicked toward Dainan, dancing across the room with Iona. Something in his posture, the tension in his shoulders...he looked enraged.

"Many believe Ollo never recovered from the bond's breaking. When word reached Giaxia that Ollo had died, it was said she killed Vasenia in revenge. But no one knows for sure. Some think Vasenia's spirit waits to be reborn in a descendant. Others believe she's still alive, hidden somewhere."

Alvar's grip tightened, pulling me close. His breath brushed against my neck, sending a shiver down my spine. Was he...sniffing me? My heart pounded in my chest as I pulled back, creating distance between us just as the final notes of the song were played. The applause erupted around us, but I barely heard it.

"Brida," Alvar started, his brow furrowing. His voice was hesitant, questioning. "Why do you smell like—"

The crowd's cheers drowned him out, and he froze, his words lost to the noise.

I didn't wait to hear what he had to say. "Thank you for the dance and the story, Alvar." My voice was clipped, rushed, as I released his hand and hurried off the dance floor.

My feet moved of their own accord, weaving through the crowd as the stares followed me. Alvar's plan had worked. Too well.

I didn't stop until I found Kadian and Oz by the food table, their smirks greeting me like old friends.

"Don't say a word," I warned, my voice tight, teeth clenched.

Kadian grinned, tossing a canapé into his mouth. "Way to lay low, Bri."

I shot him a glare. "Where's Tamra? I need support, not your nonsense."

He feigned hurt, pressing a hand to his chest. "I've been asleep for a month, and you already prefer Tamra over me? I'm wounded."

I rolled my eyes but couldn't help the small smile that tugged at my lips. "Don't make me regret missing you." I reached for a glass of champagne and downed it in two gulps.

His arm slid around my shoulders, pulling me close as he whispered, "You looked like the Goddess of Night out there." Warmth flooded my cheeks at his words.

"Please." I nudged him with my hip, but his laughter was contagious.

"I mean it. But you know what I noticed more? Iona trying to get Dainan's attention while all he did was watch you."

Oz nodded, a knowing look on his face.

I forced a laugh, brushing off the comment as Kadian extended his hand. "Come on. Dance with me."

With a sigh, I placed my hand in Kadian's, letting him lead me back onto the floor.

"You're going to have to let me lead this time, Brida. I can't lose face in front of everyone here," he teased.

We'd taken a dance elective back at school—Kadian had insisted we do something "less academic and actually fucking fun" for a change. Though we both had a knack for it, I always enjoyed switching roles, leading him around the dance floor with playful defiance.

Kadian spun me around for what felt like seven songs, and with each twirl, the fog in my mind began to clear. His easy laughter broke through the tension that had been coiling in my chest, grounding me in the moment. Sensing the turmoil beneath my smile, he said, "I'm here if you want to talk about it."

"You're showing off now, Kadian." We finished our last dance with a dramatic dip, one that had taken us hours of practicing to finesse.

His booming laugh filled the room, and as he pulled me up, he kissed me on the cheek.

"I'm flushed from all this attention," I said, adding a bit of humor to my voice.

"Go cool off, then. I'll catch you in a bit," he replied, already making his way toward Oz, who was surrounded by a group of Fae women. I chuckled, turning my steps toward the balcony, eager for a moment of quiet air.

The night air embraced me as I stepped outside, away from the heat of the dance floor. A familiar breeze seemed to swirl around me, like an old friend waiting for me to confide in it. The calm was broken by Marsh's voice.

"I was wondering if I'd find you here again," he said, his presence warm and grounding as he joined me on the balcony.

"It's stifling in there," I muttered, continuing to gaze out at the city down below.

"That's what happens when you're packed in with a bunch of Court of Shadows members." He leaned against the railing beside me, exhaling heavily.

I turned to face him, intrigued. "What do you mean?"

He ran a hand through his hair, a smirk playing on his lips. "Members of the Court of Shadows run hotter than the rest of us. Being around them...it raises your temperature. Great tactic to get people to cave to their wishes—overheat them until they give in."

"Anything else they do that makes you feel warm?" I teased.

His eyes darkened for a moment, his response far more serious than I expected. "Yes," he said quietly, "but that's a conversation for another time. I was promised a dance."

I sighed, playfully exasperated. "Always keeping secrets, Marsh."

He grinned. "That's what keeps me interesting." He extended his hand, leading me back inside.

As we moved back to the dance floor, Marsh launched into a story about how his father had once made him stay up late for a ball at the Court of Whispers. His storytelling was easy, natural, and I found myself sinking into the rhythm of it until Tamra appeared beside us.

"I'm supposed to tell you that if you want one of the eclairs Alvar insisted on saving, you better find him now. Otherwise, he's going to eat them all and, I quote, 'won't feel guilty at all.'"

I laughed. "Did Asana make you bring me that message?"

"Yes," Tamra said, rolling her eyes. "And I was in the middle of dancing with Amera, who has since disappeared into this mess of people."

"Go find her," I urged. "We're good here."

She smiled, disappearing back into the crowd as Marsh turned to me, his violet eyes sparkling with mischief. "Ready?" he asked.

We slipped into the next song effortlessly, our natural rhythm returning as if it had never left. His stories of childhood and court life wove around us as we danced, the songs melting away. I didn't keep count of how many times we'd spun around the floor, but each new song felt like an extension of the last.

"And that's when I decided I could never eat peas again," Marsh finished, making me laugh just as a strange, unplaceable feeling surged within me, subtle at first but growing stronger.

As we turned into the next movement, I caught sight of Dainan and Iona rejoining the dance floor. I forced myself to stay focused, following Marsh's lead, but my eyes kept wandering back to Dainan. He moved with a grace that was almost unnerving—fluid, controlled, beautiful. I found myself thinking of when we'd danced before, of how it had felt to be pressed close to him.

Focus. I reminded myself, but Marsh's words were drifting away as my shadows stirred.

They slid up my back like serpents, resting on my neck, whispering. “Lady,” they hissed, their sound like a low breeze. I tried to ignore them, focusing instead on Marsh's story about the Redarian Sea, but the whispers persisted.

“Lady,” they called again, louder this time.

I glanced back, wondering if my shadows were speaking to me, truly speaking. Until now, their sounds had never been anything more than a hiss. But this sounded like words, actual words. “Turn around,” they demanded.

On instinct, I spun with the next step of the dance, and my gaze locked with Dainan’s across the room. A tremor shot through me, sudden and terrifying. My body began to tremble uncontrollably.

“Brida?” Marsh’s voice cut through the noise, concern in his eyes as he slowed his movements.

A fire, hot and relentless, tore through me. I could feel it burning beneath my skin, spreading from my fingertips to my chest like molten lava. My breath hitched, and I clutched at my chest, gasping for air as the pain deepened.

“Brida!” Marsh’s voice seemed distant, muffled by the thundering pulse in my ears. I couldn’t respond.

A sharp, tearing sensation ripped through me, and I felt something deep inside snap. It was as if my very essence had been split apart. The air around me grew thick, the taste of smoke, citrus, and salt filling my mouth as I gasped desperately for breath.

I heard Marsh call my name again, but before I could reach for him, a scream split the air. It seemed far away, yet everything felt far away now. My body trembled, too weak to hold itself up. Without an anchor, I collapsed.

CHAPTER FORTY-FOUR

The mist was suffocating.

I opened my eyes, but all I could see was white, thick and endless. It felt like I was floating—or maybe I was standing? My legs trembled as if unsure whether they would hold me or give in to the weight of my confusion. I tried to blink away the fog clouding my vision, but it was everywhere, like a prison with no walls, trapping me in its boundless nothingness.

Then, that voice. *Its* voice.

We meet again.

It slithered into my mind, cold and familiar. I recoiled at the sound, instinctively wrapping my arms around myself for protection, but there was no escape from it.

"Where am I?" My voice rasped, hoarse as if I'd been screaming. My throat burned—*had I been yelling into this void, and no one had heard?* Panic gripped me, my heart racing in my chest. The silence was unbearable, suffocating, until its laugh echoed all around me.

"Tactras," the voice whispered, curling around the edges of my thoughts like smoke.

Tactras? Home of the Court of Whispers, a place shrouded in secrets and danger. Fear gnawed at me. I swallowed hard, trying to stay composed, but my voice trembled as I spoke. “Did you...cause what happened to me?” I could feel my heart pounding in my temples, the question barely escaping my lips.

The laugh returned, chilling and mocking. “In a way.”

My skin prickled with dread. I clenched my fists, trying to muster any sense of control. “What does that mean? Don’t play games with me,” I snapped, but my words felt weak, hollow.

“Why am I here?” I asked, rubbing my temples as a dull ache settled in. I wanted answers, but the fog in my mind was thickening, making it harder to think. Panic started clawing at the edges of my sanity. *Gods, what is happening to me?*

“I brought you to my home.”

My home. The words made my heart skip. This mist—was it from *Tactras*? Had it followed me, creeping into Azmeer? The thought of it haunting me, watching me this entire time, made my blood run cold.

“Okay...” My voice cracked as I tried to steady myself. “And why would you bring me here?” My chest tightened as if every breath was becoming harder to draw. The air felt too thin, too heavy. The longer I stood here, the more I felt like I was falling apart.

“There are things you must know.” Its voice was smooth, yet it chilled me to the bone. “If you recall, you made a deal with me. There will be a time when I call in that bargain. Today is not yet that day. ”

My breath hitched. *The deal.* My stomach twisted at the memory, the one I had pushed to the back of my mind, hoping it would fade away. But deep down, I’d known it wouldn’t. I couldn’t escape it. Not now. Not ever. “I remember,” I whispered, my voice barely audible.

The mist swirled around me, tightening its grip. “There are things you must learn.”

Before I could ask what it meant, the mist parted.

I dropped to my knees.

Standing before me was a man towering over me at least seven feet tall. His hair was blonde, shimmering with streaks of violet and white, as if the storms themselves had braided lightning into his locks. His presence was suffocating, charged with power and danger. The mist wrapped around his broad, muscled frame like a lover's embrace, tender yet deadly.

My breath caught in my throat as I gazed up at him. His eyes were violent. *A storm.* Clouds of purple and gray churned within them, flecked with shards of black and white, lightning flashing in the depths of his gaze. With every step he took toward me, thunder rumbled through the endless sky above us.

I couldn't move. I couldn't breathe.

"Who...who are you?" My voice trembled.

He laughed—a sound so powerful it shook the air, vibrating in my bones. "Is it not clear, Brida?" He lifted his arm, pointing towards the skies.

My gaze followed his gesture. Above us, a polar stratospheric cloud appeared, colors swirling like glass, rippling in the sky. The winds howled, growing stronger, more vicious. My body swayed, struggling to stay upright as the tempest roared around us. Thunder boomed, and I flinched, nearly collapsing under the weight of the fear surging through me.

Ollo. This was Ollo. *The Primal of Storms.*

My thoughts scrambled, desperate to make sense of the situation. I was kneeling before a being that could tear me apart with a mere thought.

I did the only thing I could think of. I lowered myself to the ground, my forehead pressed against the cold, hard earth. *If only Addie could see me now.*

"You can look at me." His voice was gentle as if amused by my submission.

I trembled as I lifted my head, but I didn't dare meet his gaze. I kept my eyes on the ground, every nerve in my body screaming in terror.

He walked to a nearby rock and sat, lightning flickering beneath his skin. His presence radiated power, more ancient and terrifying than anything I'd ever imagined. He was a living storm, and I was nothing more than a speck of dust caught in his fury.

"How..." My voice wavered as I struggled to find the words. "How is this real?"

"This is my home, Brida. Where else would I be?" His voice rumbled, a storm in itself.

I couldn't speak. Couldn't think. All I knew was that I was at his mercy.

And there was no escaping it.

"You can look at me."

I hesitated, lifting my head with the utmost caution, my heart hammering in my chest. Every crack of lightning in the distance jolted me, and I could barely stay upright. The Primal of Storms loomed over me, a breathtaking and terrifying presence. Lightning coursed through his veins, illuminating his skin in stark contrasts. He was more ethereal than I could have ever imagined.

"Am I allowed to speak?" I asked, trying to keep my voice steady as I looked at the mountain range that stretched endlessly before us. The sight was mesmerizing and overwhelming, the snow-capped peaks shimmering under the bright sun. Yet, it only added to my sense of displacement and fear.

"Of course, you may speak. I wouldn't have asked you to sit if I planned to prohibit it." His eyebrow arched, a mix of amusement and authority in his gaze.

"Okay." I paused. "Is this really happening or am I dreaming?"

He laughed, the sound booming across the skies and rattling through me. "What do you think is happening, Brida?"

"I'm not sure," I admitted, my voice quivering. "I'd like to think it's real and that I'm somehow still alive."

"You're still alive, Brida. There's plenty of work to be done yet."

"Work?" I echoed, my mind racing to process his words.

"Yes," he said, gesturing to the rock next to him.

"What sort of work?" I asked, confusion and fear mingling in my voice. This couldn't be real. *I had been at the ball. There had been pain... and then this.* I couldn't reconcile it all.

"That is the question, isn't it?" he replied, a smirk playing on his lips.

"Do all Gods speak in riddles?" I muttered, frustration bubbling beneath my fear. "Do you know what happened to me before," I waved my arm around us, "we got here?"

He nodded. "Yes."

"Do you plan on telling me?"

"If you ask the right questions," he said with a smile that seemed oddly familiar yet filled with enigmatic intent.

I felt trapped, the oppressive mist swirling around me, closing in. *Is this a dream? A game?* My mind struggled to grasp the reality of the situation. I had no connection to the Court of Whispers or to Ollo. Why was he speaking to me? "If this is really happening..."

"It is," he interrupted, his voice firm and unwavering.

"Why, of all people, have you chosen to speak with me?"

"Because everything is as it is meant to be."

I ran my hand through my hair, and realized that I was no longer in my dress. "What happened to my clothes?" I found myself asking and was greeted to his laughter.

"A fine question indeed. We couldn't very well have you looking like the night itself in the land of the Dawn, now could we?" He winked.

Stay focused. "You said there is work to be done."

"Yes," he confirmed, his smile widening.

"Am I purposed to complete this work, or task alone? Is this our bargain?"

"I did tell you that was for another day. But to answer your question, there are others."

"Others. Others to work with? Do I know them?"

"It would be far less interesting if you didn't," he said, his gaze shifting to the horizon. The sun was dipping lower, casting long shadows and turning the sky into a canvas of deepening colors. "We don't have much time left, Brida. Even though I am here, I am not truly here. Not yet."

Everything around me began to dissolve into white once more, the darkness encroaching rapidly.

"Listen to me, Brida," he said, his hands still on my shoulders, grounding me despite the vanishing world. "War is coming. You must be prepared. Like I told your friend, they are waking up."

"Who are they?" I asked, panic rising as the mist closed in.

"The rest," he said, beginning to fade from sight.

"What am I supposed to do?" I cried out, my voice swallowed by the encroaching mist.

"Make sure you have the Wind by your side," his voice grew distant, barely perceptible. "Close your eyes, Brida," he instructed as his presence started to disappear completely.

The mist enveloped me, and his final words echoed in my mind as the world around me dissolved into white.

☽✳☾

"Brida!" A voice exclaimed. "Brida, come on, Brida, look at me." I began to feel hands on my face, touching me as if they were examining me. I was so tired. My eyes fluttered back shut. "Stay with us, Brida." It was a familiar voice, a feminine voice.

Addie, I thought, that sounded like Addie. Where was I? My vision cleared, and I saw a familiar window to the left. I forced myself to blink. With each lift of my eyelids, the room came more into focus.

Addie and Magister Thorne were in the room with me. Addie was seated on the bed beside me, hands on my face. The Magister, who looked like he was seconds from death, sat in the chair that I had so many times before.

"She needs water."

Magister Thorne poured the water with shaky hands into the glass jar, handing it to Addie.

"Here," she propped me up with her left hand that she placed behind my back, pulling me towards her. "You need to drink this, Brida," she placed the cup at my lips. I did as she said. After finishing the glass, Addie placed it down on the table next to me.

"How are you feeling, sweetheart?" She leaned me back down towards the pillows.

How am I feeling? I have no idea what's going on.

"Confused." I sat up a bit straighter in the bed. Magister Thorne looked like he'd fallen asleep. "What happened?"

"What's the last thing you remember, honey?" Addie clasped my hand in hers.

"I was in pain," I said. "A lot of pain, and then I heard a scream. Now I'm here."

Addie nodded. "You seemed to have had an attack of some sort, the pain from it caused you to pass out. Do you remember what you felt?" Her eyes held mine.

I looked around the room. It hadn't been long since Kadian lay in this bed, with me pacing beside it, day after day, fervently wishing for him to wake. Reading through books, scouring for information as I sat in the chair that Magister Thorne slept in now. I couldn't help but wonder if Addie had done the same.

"How long have I been here, Addie?" My voice was low.

"Four days."

Sitting up straighter, my eyes focused on the doorway, and I found that there was no longer a door there, but a wall of shadows. "What is that?" I moved her so I could get out of the bed.

"Bri, be careful,"

The shadows hissed with a strange, almost tender sound as I approached. I extended my arm toward them. One shadow jumped from the others and began to swirl around my wrist, leaving a slight hole in the mass that I could see through. Dainan paced outside. I turned back to Addie, her expression grave, hinting at the seriousness of the situation.

"How long has he been there?" She remained silent. "How long, Addie?" My tone grew firmer.

She sighed, "He has refused to leave."

The shadow slithered down my body, rejoining the ones that blocked the door. Humming as it did so.

"He hasn't allowed anyone else inside and has insisted on keeping the shadows in place as a form of protection."

"Protection?" I echoed her words, "Protection from what?"

She opened her mouth but was interrupted by the snore that escaped Magister Thorne. She gestured her arm to the bed, demanding that I sit down.

"Addie, what's going on?" I asked as she pulled the covers over my legs once I crawled back into bed.

"The king is dead," she pushed my hair behind my ear.

"Oh," I whispered. *Poor Dainan, and Alvar. Gods, his wife.*"It was expected, was it not?" I leaned back.

Gods, I'm tired.

"The king's manner of death is what was not expected." She said, "The king and queen... She is still being monitored, but it doesn't look good."

The scream, I'd heard a woman's cry before collapsing.

"How?"

"Poison," Addie said as she clasped my hand.

"They're sure?"

Gods, how was Alvar? Dainan? Has Alvar's mark solidified in the last four days?

"Yes," she nodded, "they're sure."

"How were they poisoned?" I finally asked, noticing she was avoiding my gaze. "Addie, what are you not saying?"

She rose, looking at me, "The king and queen were each given an eclair for dessert to celebrate a successful evening. Prince Alvar had requested some be set aside for him. However, it was only at the last minute that the king had decided to attend the ball..."

"Gods, someone tried to poison Alvar?"

She began to pace, "Yes. It's believed the poison was not intended for Elidas but for Alvar."

Someone tried to poison Alvar? That didn't make sense. Alvar was beloved, I saw it the night of the ball.

"Who..."

"We still don't know. Whoever it was managed to somehow sneak into the kitchens and inject the eclairs with poison when no one was looking." She made her way to stare out the window.

"Addie," I whispered, "who brought me here?" She said nothing. "Addie," I said more sternly.

"Prince Dainan ran to you and shadow-stepped you here."

"I need to speak with him."

She turned to face me, "I'm not sure that's the best idea right now, Brida."

"What's that supposed to mean?" Frustration growing in my voice.

"Something's been happening to Dainan for the last several days," she said, her concern evident in the dance of emotions in her eyes. "His behavior has gone beyond normal levels of protectiveness in regards to you. He practically tried to kill Kadian when he came to see you. He needs rest. He's undoubtedly under stress from the news of his father, his concern for his mother, and *you*."

She sat beside me on the bed, "His caring of you is no longer secret, Brida, and his fiancé and her father are not pleased by this development."

I rubbed my face in my hands.

Alvar is king. Will the marriages even take place?

"I need to see him now, Addie."

Before I could hear Addie protest, I stood in front of the shadows, "move," I commanded. They slithered to the sides, allowing me through the doorway before closing on Addie as she tried to follow.

The scent of Dainan hit me as I stepped through. Within moments, he was in front of me, his presence overwhelming. The dark circles under his eyes spoke of sleepless nights.

"Dainan..." My voice was a breath of relief as he pulled me into his arms. His embrace was both desperate and comforting, one arm cradling my lower back while the other cupped my head, holding me close. I savored the warmth of his touch, the strength of his arms. For a moment, the world outside ceased to exist.

He pulled back slightly, his eyes a tempest of flame and shadow, each vying for dominance. "You're alright?"

"I think so," I replied, my hand resting on his cheek.

"Don't ever do that to me again." His voice was laden with the weight of his worry, his fear.

"I heard about your father," I murmured, my fingers threading through his hair. "I'm so sorry."

He remained silent, his gaze unwavering, reflecting his exhaustion. He had been a vigilant guardian, a sentinel who had not left his post.

"Dainan," I began, "something happened the night of the ball..."

"Bri!" Kadian's voice shattered the moment as he, Oz, and Tamra burst into the room. His face was a mask of worry, and his eyes darted between us, "Are you alright?"

Blocking me with his body, Dainan snarled at Kadian.

"Whoa," Kadian lifted his arms and took a step back, Oz and Tamra mere feet behind him. "Easy there, big fella. We've been through this."

Darkness began to emerge from Dainan, slowly extending its tendrils toward Kadian.

"Dainan," I said calmly as I placed my hand on his chest, "it's just Kadian. I'll be fine," he didn't move an inch. I moved myself in front of him, clasping his face in my hands. "Dainan," I said more firmly as I saw the flames surge in his eyes. "Look at me," I repeated until he pulled his attention from them and moved to me. "I'm okay, look at me, I'm fine and here. I'm in front of you right now," his breathing was ragged, a hunter ready to kill its prey.

"Bri..." Kadian said.

I turned around to see the three of them standing in complete shock.

"Kadian, stay there until I tell you it's fine." I sensed that even though Dainan's immediate impulse to attack was diminishing, it wasn't gone completely.

"Dainan," I ran my fingers along his jawline, pulling his face towards mine. "Please go rest, I will see you in a bit. I'm going to speak with them."

His eyes finally released them and found mine. He didn't move for several moments. "*Dainan,*" I whispered, almost a plea, until he nodded, the shadows receding.

He turned to me and pressed a light kiss to my forehead, "I'll come see you in a bit." He shadow-stepped out of the room, his departure freeing Addie as the barrier dissolved.

"What in the Gods' names is going on out here," Addie said as she came rushing out of the room.

I walked towards Kadian and embraced him. "I thought I was the only one allowed to pull stunts like this," he whispered. I couldn't help but laugh.

He raised an eyebrow as I pulled back. "What?" I asked him.

"We brought you something," Oz interrupted as he pulled a jar out from his pocket.

"I swiped it from the dining hall," he said, handing it to me. "It's wolfberry," he smiled.

"Did you bring me just a jar of jam?" I could feel the smile on my face.

"Ah, and..." He reached into his other pocket, "a spoon!"

"Thank you," I laughed as I looked at each of them. "Now, who is going to fill me in on what I've missed for the last four days?"

"No one, because you need to be back in bed," Addie said as she arrived beside me.

"I'll stay with her," Kadian answered as he looked at Tamra and Oz, who nodded. Addie didn't look convinced, "you know I'll make her stay in bed, Addie."

"I know no such thing, Kadian Taldot." Addie let out an exasperated sigh. "The last time I watched you two, you informed me you were headed home from the night and I found you at three in the morning, huddled under a blanket in Brida's room while she read to you. She was so tired the next morning that her face fell into her bowl of oats."

"Well, I promise this time to be good." He smiled. "I'll come to you guys later." He whispered to Oz and Tamra who nodded their goodbyes.

Making our way back into the room, Addie woke Magister Thorne and helped him walk from the room.

"He's looking fucking terrible," Kad said as he sat down next to me in the chair.

"I thought so, too. It's strange," I said as I leaned my head back against the pillows, "I feel like I just saw him and he looked nothing like that."

Kadian rose from the chair, and made his way to sit down on the bed next to me. "What happened, Bri?"

"I don't know what happened exactly," I said to him as I closed my eyes.

"Try to tell me what you remember," I heard him say.

"I saw Dainan..." I yawned, "and it felt like my body was being ripped apart." I was beginning to fade. In a whisper I said, "before *something* snapped."

I felt the darkness creeping closer, coming to lure me into a dream state. I welcomed it. I was just on the verge of sleep when Kadian said, "Did you say that something snapped?"

"*Mm?*" I replied as I fell into a deeper state of relaxation.

"*Snap...Snap... Snapped,*" I heard Kadian whisper. "Gods." His tone changed, and my eyes shot open.

"Lil," he ran out of the room.

CHAPTER
FORTY-FIVE

"Kadian!" I screamed as he bolted from the chair. I was in no condition to chase after him. *Do I even have shoes in this room?* I didn't have time to look and forced myself to follow him. Kadian wove in and out of the crowds, hitting the odd person, not stopping to apologize. I knew where he was going; I did my best to keep up.

I felt a slight shake begin in my legs as we rounded the fifth or sixth corner. My body was crippled with fatigue and was fighting to stay awake with every step I took. I lost sight of him on the final turn, but I heard him moments later.

"LIL," he screamed outside of the entrance to the Court of Reflection. The hallway was empty, save for us.

The trembling in my legs crept upward, reaching my knees. Standing became challenging. I leaned on the edge of the Mirrors of Reflection for support.

"LIL," I heard him yell once more. "Someone better open this fucking door," he slammed his hand against it.

"Kadian!" I tried getting his attention, but nothing broke his focus. My body gave out next to the pathway to the door. I rested on my knees while the small ledge that contained the Mirrors helped support my upper body. "Kadian, I'm begging you," my voice was barely a whisper.

He doesn't realize I'm here. I looked into the water and saw a ripple begin to form, similar to the last time. My eyelids were growing heavy, I needed rest, I needed... *Dainan... Stop him. Please, please stop him.*

The ripple in the water began to grow, and its color changed. What once had been a beautiful pale blue was now crimson that was mixed with something else. I was struggling to stay awake. After a few moments, Kadian's voice began to fade as the darkness claimed me.

☽✳☾

"You have been causing quite a commotion," Alvar said as he sat in a chair at the foot of the bed.

Why is there a chair at the foot of the bed? What room am I in? I closed my eyes and listened. I heard the soothing sounds of water. "Did you move me back to my room?" I asked him as a small smile plastered itself on my face.

"I wanted you to be somewhere comfortable. A general room in the infirmary does not fall under that category." He smiled as he rose to come stand by me. "Initially, I thought of bringing you to the royal quarters so that I could watch over you, but alas, things have been a bit chaotic."

"Are you here to tell me that I've been let go from my position?" I placed myself in the middle of the bed.

He laughed as he gestured for me to move over and sat down next to me. "On the contrary. I have classified the past few days as medical leave." His hands sat atop each other.

I found myself staring. "Your mark hasn't darkened." He nodded, "it will once I've been crowned," his voice became solemn.

"I'm sorry about your father."

Gods, what about my father? Had anyone informed him as to what had happened to me over the last week? Was he okay?

"Alvar," I said as he looked out the window, "how long was I asleep this time?"

An amiable silence fell over us until Alvar murmured, "I insisted those desserts be set aside," his voice no higher than a whisper.

"This wasn't your fault, Alvar," I reached for his hand, "you weren't to have known."

"A king would have been on alert," he said, lost in his thoughts.

"You were not yet a king, Alvar," I said as I squeezed his hand, "But you will be a wonderful king when the crown sits atop your head."

He shook his head as if he returned to the conversation we were having rather than the one he was having with himself. "I need to speak with you about something that some would consider...*delicate*," he said, his tone firmer than I was accustomed to hearing from him.

"Brida," he began, "something happened the night of the ball. I only noticed it in the final moments of our dance."

He remembers.

"Now," he continued, "I don't need to know the specifics, but I believe you and I need to be clear on a few things." I nodded, "should you choose to come back to work, *which I hope you do*," he smiled, " we need to be on the same page."

I nodded.

"Dainan is in a rather precarious position now that he is betrothed to Iona. And as much as we both know that he does not wish for that marriage to take place, as of now, there is nothing to be done to stop it."

"I don't know what he's told you..."

He raised his hand at me to stop.

"Several people saw Dainan leave Iona in the middle of the room, rushing to your side as you fell."

I laid my head back on the pillows.

"I've attempted to lessen the damage by insisting Dainan acted chivalrously as he knew how close you and I became after working together these past months." He said, "And while that has helped stave off some of the whispers, rumors have begun to circulate."

"Alvar..." I began to say, and he raised his hand once more.

"I've spoken with Dainan and told him that he's to maintain his distance from you, at least until things are sorted."

"*Sorted?*" I repeated back as I arched my eyebrow at him.

"Yes," he smiled, "I've been attempting to break this pact between Deter and my father. However, the only person who can break a marriage decreed by a king is another king."

"I believe I've heard this part before," I said and he smiled.

"You have." He rose from the bed and strode over to my window. "You have one of the lovelier views," he said as he turned back to face me. "Brida, what is the last thing you remember before you collapsed?"

I sat in silence for a few moments. *Shit, Kadian.* "Is he okay?" I pulled the comforter from my legs and attempted to leave the bed.

"Ah ah," he clicked his tongue in response as he shook his head. "You stay put," he said as he sat back down in an attempt to block me from moving.

"Your *friend,*" his brow furrowed.

"Kadian," I interjected.

"Yes, Kadian. He, too, has been causing a bit of a ruckus," he sighed, "when you collapsed, Kadian was in the midst of slamming the entry to the House of Reflection. As they are a levelheaded people, you might imagine that they did not respond well to this type of behavior."

Gods, what has he done?

"Thalius was rather put out when he opened the door and found someone he did not know demanding to see his niece. His niece, who is presently engaged to a crowned prince."

I shuddered. "Is he okay?"

"He is. However," he rubbed his temples, "since this debacle, I've been in meetings with Thalius practically around the clock as he is insisting that the wedding be expedited in order to prevent any more...*incidents*."

Kadian had done so much more damage than he realized.

"Are the weddings going to be sooner than expected?" I finally asked.

"It's yet to be determined, but it's possible. Thalius can be quite persuasive within the Courts, and Deter has, of course, learned of this and has been attempting similar tactics."

I sat in silence. *If Kadian remembered, which he no doubt did, would he begin to diminish as he had before?*

A sudden pain rippled through my chest. It lessened after a moment, but I was left with the sensation of a gentle pull that tugged at the very core of my being. It was new but familiar. As if it had been there all my life, waiting to assert itself. I placed my hand on my chest and forced myself to close my eyes.

Breathe. You're okay. Alvar is here. Listen to the water outside. Dainan is fine. Kadian is fine.

Alvar just stared at me, admiring what I was doing. "Are you alright?" His voice was calm and smooth.

I nodded.

"Be honest." He said, "In the spirit of friendship."

"Alvar," I asked him after several moments of silence, "where's Kadian?"

"He's in his room down the hall," he said as he remained looking outside. "He's been given a sedative these past several days to assist in keeping his outbursts to a minimum."

"*Several days*?" I whispered.

He turned to me and held me with his gaze, "You have been asleep for seven days, Brida."

Seven days.

"Is..." I started to ask him as my vision began to blur.

"Go ahead and ask your question," His smile was genuine.

"Is Dainan okay?" I felt a tear escape and run down my cheek.

"*Fascinating,*" Alvar said as he approached the bed, wiping the tear from my cheek. "No, I would not say that he is okay. But," he continued, "my hope is that he soon will be."

"Anything else of major import I missed this past week?" A small laugh escaped me.

"Nothing worth mentioning," he looked at the clock in my room. "I must be going. I have meetings, sadly. Don't push yourself too hard these next few days, Brida. Only return to the House of Shadows when you have recovered. I will do my best to come check on you, but if it's not frequent, I do hope that you'll forgive me."

"Alvar?" I asked him as he made his way to the door, "Everything will be as it is supposed to."

☽✳☾

I continued to rest over the course of the next few days. My days were filled with naps and visits from Tamra, Oz, and a subdued Kadian.

I didn't yet have the energy to leave my room. I found food waiting for me each morning, and some nights, I could have sworn that I heard the hissing of shadows close by.

Addie came to see me each day and offered information regarding what was happening outside of my bedroom walls. I'd missed Hild's festival while I'd been sleeping. According to Addie it had been successful, without any major issues.

"What happens at her festival anyway?"

"The ritual, traditionally performed in the Hydratas Sea at the actual Court of Reflection, is that you strip naked and submerge yourself in the water." She took a sip from her cup, "The idea is that She cleanses you of the previous year and absolves you of any wrong-doings. It's a way to start the year fresh."

"And what do you do when you are not near the Hydratas Sea?" She raised an eyebrow at me.

"*Oh Gods,*" I said after she refused to answer. "They go to the pool naked?"

She laughed as she nodded. "I have news," Addie said as she put her cup down on the bedside table. "Alvar is to be made king in ten days."

I found myself holding my breath.

Ten days.

"Aren't the weddings in four weeks?" I asked.

News had begun to circulate that neither Thalius nor Deter wanted to be viewed as lesser than the other. Therefore, a compromise had been struck that both weddings would occur in the same room, at the same moment, in four weeks' time.

She nodded.

Maybe he would be able to put a stop to this after all.

"I wrote your father," Addie brought me out of my thoughts with that remark. "I didn't tell him everything," she said as a look of worry took over my face. "He knows that you're okay and that you have been busy. I told him that you would write when you could."

"Thank you."

We reminisced for the remainder of her visit. Stories of when she and Mom had run away and found themselves in a cove that had been surrounded by sirens when they were little. And when dad had nearly burnt the house down when he tried to make a leek and onion tart.

Every night, I sat on my balcony and gazed up at the stars, drawn to them in a way I couldn't explain. The quiet, the peace of the sky. Occasionally, I would hear words on the wind, but it had been less frequent these days.

Marsh had gone back to Hadash. He'd left me a letter saying that I would see him at the coronation, and that he hoped we'd be able to speak more when he'd returned.

Addie brought me books while I remained in bed. The one that I had been most eager to continue reading was a book of poetry, a compendium of many of the myths and stories that had been detailed in *Teraler's Anthology*, a personal favorite of mine.

I'd left off reading about Egaber and his relentless search for the fountain of youth—a blessing and a curse, as he'd unknowingly traded something precious for his eternal beauty.

That tale was followed by the story of Pelia, who braved the depths of the sea to explore the elusive underwater kingdoms. Each story captivated me, drawing me deeper into a world of wonder and danger, each more enchanting than the last.

I turned the page, breathless after a harrowing battle between giants and men, only to pause as the next title caught my eye: *Shadows of Thale: The Veiled Truth.*

My heart skipped. I'd never seen Thale mentioned outside of *The Trials of Thale*. I turned the page and saw that the entirety of the story was eight lines.

In the realm of Elyria, where legends take flight,
Lived Thale, enduring trials with unwavering might.
Through battles untold and hardships profound,
Her spirit soared, unyielding, unbound.
In whispers they spoke of a woman revered
Her trials and struggles had always been mirrored
For beneath the stories remained a heroine's fame,
Thale, or Ilia, for both were her name.

CHAPTER FORTY-SIX

Thale, or Ilia, for both were her name.

Thale and Ilia were the same person? What was it that Dainan had said to me?

I'd asked him if the book had predated the Primals, and he'd said, "No...I think it talks of a specific Primal."

Did he think Ilia or Thale was a Primal? If so, which one was she?

Why had he given me *Ilia* as a nickname? Was it that I reminded him of her? Thale had been described as having hair similar to mine; beyond that, I wasn't sure what the comparisons could've been.

I'd asked Addie when I arrived in Azmeer if there were other books on Thale in the library and she had thought not. This had been a fluke chance.

Is it possible the house libraries possess volumes that contain valuable information in regard to Thale or Ilia? My mind couldn't view them as one, not yet, anyway.

☽*☾

Good morning, Brida. The door whispered to me as I approached.

"Good morning, *whoever you are,*" I whispered back.

There was no chuckle or response beyond the door opening and welcoming me back inside. The shadows that roamed within the House of Shadows gathered at the door to greet me, each hissing in turn as if saying they missed me. I kneeled towards them and extended my arm as a few of them began to dance along my fingertips before journeying up to my shoulder and neck. "There's someone we need to see," I whispered as I made my way to the stairs.

Tura stood behind the desk as she always did. Her face lit up when she saw me. "Hello dear," beautiful lines crinkled by her eyes when she smiled. It illuminated her face in the most endearing way. Despite all of the ageless beauty that roamed the halls of Azmeer, I was transfixed by Tura.

"Hello, Tura," I said as I reached the desk. "I've missed you," I offered her a smile.

"It has been a lonelier place without you here the past few weeks, love," she smiled back at me. "I must admit, though, that I wasn't quite expecting to see you just yet." She leaned in a bit closer, "Alvar has been keeping me apprised of your health, and he made it seem as if you were still quite tired."

I placed the book on the table, "I was wondering if you could perhaps do some research for me. I checked in the main library but..."

"Oh, their selection is trash," she reached for the book, looking at its spine. "You want to read poetry?" She raised an eyebrow at me, "This is a bit of a surprise."

I laughed. "Do you not think of me as a romantic, Tura?"

Her face didn't change.

"It's not really poetry," I gestured to the book and she handed it back to me. I opened it to the page and pointed, "This story mentions Thale, from *The Trials of Thale*, are you familiar with it?"

"Of course, I'm familiar with Thale."

"My apologies, I just wanted to be sure."

She smirked.

"This book mentions someone named *Ilia* and how she and Thale are, in fact, the same." I handed the book back to her. "I was wondering if it would be possible for you to see if you could find anything on this. Prior to this book, the only mention of Thale I'd ever seen was the Trials, and I'd never heard of *Ilia* before last night."

"The name sounds familiar," Tura clicked her tongue while thinking. "I'll look into it and see what I can find."

"Thank you."

My shadows waited for me at the base of the stairs and slithered alongside me. They'd become my constant companions while in the House of Shadows. I found myself staring at them as I walked, listening to the conversations they appeared to be having amongst themselves. The tones of the hisses changed as we reached the halfway point on the stairs. What had been faint hisses grew louder.

"What's wrong?" I said, kneeling to the floor. The shadows began to swarm around me, as if forming a barrier. "What are you doing?" I muttered as they continued to increase in their volume.

"*What the fuck is this*," I looked up and saw Iona standing above me. I rose to my feet, and the shadows followed suit. I'd never seen them do this before. The shadows formed a living shield in front of me, one that was in constant motion and talking in a language that they understood.

After taking a step back, she snarled, "*Where is he?*"

Something looked *different* about Iona, I wasn't sure what it was. I cocked my head to the side and stared at her, all the while saying nothing.

"*Where is he*?" She repeated herself, her tone growing firmer, vitriol dripping from each syllable.

"Based on the level of possessiveness in your voice, I can only assume you're speaking of Dainan," I took a step forward, my shadows moving with me.

She stepped back, not taking her eyes off them.

"I'm sorry to disappoint you, *Iona*," her name tasted like poison in my mouth, "but I have no idea where he is as I haven't seen him."

She held firm and didn't move.

"If you want to find him, it seems that all you need to do is ask your father. He makes sure you get exactly what you want. Even if it's someone that doesn't want *you*." I snarled at her. "If you go near him..."

"You'll do what?" I laughed, "Last I heard, you weren't to be his wife for another few weeks." I'd said the wrong thing as her grin grew sinister.

"You appear to be misinformed, Brida." She leaned in as close as the shadows would allow, "Like I said, stay the fuck away from him." Turning on her heel, she walked away.

The shadows recoiled and crawled up my body as if attempting to nuzzle themselves against my neck.

"Thank you," I whispered to them as I made my way to the door.

☽✳☾

The tapping of my shoes against the limestone floor, once a comforting rhythm, now served as a painful reminder of everything that had unraveled since my arrival in Azmeer. Every step echoed not only through the empty halls but through the cavernous void within me. I'd come here for my father, hoping to find some way to help him. But somewhere along the way, I had begun to hope, to believe that this place—Azmeer, these people—could be something I wanted for myself.

Yet that hope seemed like a distant memory now.

I had thought I'd found friends. Oz, with his mischievous charm; Tamra, whose calm strength had been a quiet source of stability; Lil, who had become so dear to me that the thought of her absence was a constant ache. And Emia... I'd written letter after letter to Emia, hoping for some word, some sign of life in response to her last cryptic message. But there had been nothing—just silence. Her ominous message, "Dawn," lingered in my mind like a weight I couldn't shake. What had she meant by that? Was she warning me, trying to protect me, or had she gotten too close to something dangerous? I didn't know. And not knowing gnawed at me, adding to the pile of things I had yet to face, things I couldn't yet untangle.

Opening the door to my room, I was surprised to see a familiar face.

"Good morning, Brida." Alvar rose from the chair at my desk.

"Your majesty," I responded, my voice holding a teasing lilt I couldn't quite suppress as I closed the door behind me.

Alvar's lips curled into a small, amused smile. "My my, so formal this morning. You know you may always call me, 'Your Royal Majesty.'" He stood, his posture relaxed, but there was a heaviness in his eyes that set my nerves on edge.

Without warning, he moved toward me, arms outstretched, and before I could register what was happening, I was enveloped in his embrace. It was warm, steady—but it startled me. Alvar had never hugged me before. We were close, yes, but there had always been an unspoken boundary between us—until now.

I pulled back enough to look at his face. His eyes, though similar in shape to Dainan's, were different—calmer, softer. Where Dainan's gaze burned with an intensity that could set the world alight, Alvar's always seemed as if they were holding the world together, piece by careful piece. He was never ruled by his emotions the way his brothers were. It made me wonder about his mother and how much of her lived in him.

"What's wrong?" I asked, a growing knot of anxiety forming in my chest as I made my way to sit down.

"I'm happy to see you out of bed," he said, but there was something guarded in his tone. He wasn't meeting my eyes.

I raised an eyebrow at him, pressing further. "You might as well spit it out, Alvar. Is one of us dying?" My attempt at humor felt thin, forced.

He gestured toward the space beside me. "May I?"

"Of course." I nodded, even though the unease inside me tightened.

Alvar crossed his legs as he sat beside me, hands resting one on top of the other, his usual composed stance, the perfect presentation of a king.

“There are a few things I wanted to share with you before the Court of Whispers releases the information later today.” His voice was calm, but the way he said it set my heart racing.

“I wanted us to have a chat, as the next several days will be busy.” He smiled, but it didn’t reach his eyes. There was a flicker of pain there, just beneath the surface.

“I hope this isn’t your way of asking me to help you plan a *party,*” I joked weakly.

A low rumble of laughter escaped his chest. “If only it were.”

But the levity was short-lived, his expression somber now. “Firstly, I wanted you to know that placements are officially over as of this afternoon. Each of the inductees will be informed by the person they have been working with—at least, they will be in the House of Shadows. I’m not entirely sure how the other Houses handle it.”

Placements are over... The thought sent a cold rush through me. *But Kadian—he’s barely had any time within the Eternal House. How could it be over already?* Panic sparked in my chest, but I swallowed it down, focusing on Alvar’s words.

“To be offered a final position in a court, it is, of course, not solely the decision of one, but several. Each house will congregate this evening, and discuss who will be offered a position and where. Once there has been a final tally, the decisions will be given to the Master of Trials.”

I nodded, my throat dry. “When will we be informed of the final decisions?”

“In two days' time. It will be handled in the same manner as the Eternia. Names will be read. You will make your way up to the front and be told which court, or courts, desire you.” He smiled, but it felt distant like there was something unsaid lingering between us.

"And then?" I asked, trying to ignore the growing fear that I wasn't ready for whatever came next.

"And then you will declare before everyone your choice."

I could feel the sweat gathering at my back, a cold, uncomfortable sensation that only heightened my anxiety. I stood abruptly, unable to sit still anymore. "I'm guessing there's a banquet of sorts to celebrate?"

Alvar rose with me, his movements smooth, composed. "Typically, yes. However, there has been a slight change in the plans this year."

"A slight change?" I echoed, the words hanging in the air like a warning.

He hesitated, just for a moment, and then his gaze softened. "I assume by now you've heard that I haven't been successful in what I sought to accomplish since our last conversation."

So this was what Iona had meant.

"Unfortunately," Alvar continued, "a soon-to-be king has very little power until he is actually king. It seems I'm being overruled by the Courts regarding whether these marriages should be allowed to take place." He sighed heavily, the weight of it all clear in his expression. "It has also come to my attention that you had a rather unfortunate encounter this morning."

My stomach twisted. "Iona, you mean?"

"Word came to me that you had returned to the House of Shadows, which I was most pleased to hear," he said, a small smile gracing his lips. "However, I was told that Iona cornered you on a stairwell."

No one else had been there. Who would've seen...

Unless...

"Did the shadows speak to you?" I asked, my voice quiet but edged with suspicion.

"A very interesting theory, Brida." A low laugh escaped him, easing some of the tension between us. "But no, they did not speak to me."

Then how did he know?

I exhaled, though the unease still clung to me. “What was the slight change you were referring to?”

“Ah, yes.” Alvar clasped his hands behind his back, his regal composure slipping into place again. “Typically, new court members are ushered to their respective courts as part of the evening’s celebrations. Some are then given posts within the courts themselves, while the majority return to Azmeer to begin work the following morning.”

“Okay...” I said, my voice trailing off, my mind still racing to keep up with everything he was telling me.

“The weddings are to take place in three days’ time.”

The words hit me like a blow to the chest. The spark of hope that had flickered in me earlier was now smothered, replaced by a suffocating sense of dread.

“In order to ensure that everyone is here for the royal marriages, the dinner will be postponed to the night of the wedding. Drinks are served in the ballroom, however the wedding feast is traditionally reserved for members of the royal family,” Alvar explained, though his tone was gentle.

“I see.” My voice sounded distant, not quite my own. “Thank you for letting me know.”

“Brida,” Alvar said softly, taking my hand in his. “I want you to know that you were an unexpected gift.”

His words stunned me. I blinked up at him, my vision blurring as my emotions warred within me.

“In all my years,” he continued, “to which you have reminded me, there have been many.”

I forced out a laugh.

“You are the sole person to have requested me during placements. It has been my privilege to get to know you.” He lifted my hand to his lips and pressed a soft, reverent kiss to it. “I have valued our time together, and look forward to many more years of friendship.”

He squeezed my other hand before letting go and retreating to the door.

"Alvar," I called, my voice barely above a whisper.

He turned back, his expression open, waiting.

"I read that in previous years, family members were invited to the Courting ceremony. Is that true?"

A grin spread across his face, warm and understanding. "Why yes, Brida. It is."

I felt my throat tighten as the weight of my father's illness pressed down on me.

"I'll see you at the ceremony, Brida."

CHAPTER FORTY-SEVEN

No one spoke, but the energy was undeniable, pulsing through the crowd, a shared fear of the unknown. Every single one of us was wondering the same thing: Will my name be called? What would happen if it wasn't? What would my life look like after today?

For most—the children of court members and esteemed officials—this day would end in reassurance. A quiet affirmation that they were, as always, exactly where they were supposed to be. For them, this was merely a formality, a ritual carved into stone before they were even born.

For those of us who didn't grow up in the protected embrace of the courts, for those of us who clawed our way up from the dust of lesser families, this day was everything. Everything. It wasn't just a ceremony. It was the culmination of every drop of sweat, every moment of sacrifice, every ounce of determination we'd poured into getting here.

My stomach churned with a nauseating mix of anxiety and desperation. I clenched my fists at my sides, trying to steady myself, but my hands were slick with sweat. I rubbed my palms against my dress, but it didn't help.

Magister Illerium, cloaked in his dark robes, moved to the head of the group. His steps were slow, deliberate, each one echoing with the weight of authority. The only thing separating us from whatever awaited us inside the chamber was the gargantuan wood doors behind him—doors that, in this moment, felt more like the gates to my destiny.

His cold, sharp eyes scanned the group, and when he spoke, his voice was like the crack of a whip. "Attention."

The room fell silent. Not a whisper, not even a breath, dared to break the quiet. My heart, which had been hammering wildly in my chest, seemed to stall for a beat.

"We are moments away from the Selection," he said, his tone measured, void of emotion. "Following your entry into the chamber behind me, you will be seated in the center of the room until your name is called."

His words hung heavy in the air, settling on us like a weight. My skin prickled under their oppressive weight. For most of us, seeing that room again would mean a life of servitude, of climbing, of endless challenges.

"He never got better at this, did he?" Kadian whispered.

Despite the anxiety clawing at me, I felt the corner of my mouth twitch in response.

Illerium continued, undeterred. "The Master of Trials will call your name if you have been offered a place." His eyes flickered over us, assessing, calculating. "Each court has its own ceremonial rite, which you will perform during the Selection. I will not detail it here, but you will be expected to complete it to secure your induction to the court."

Ceremony? Induction? My stomach lurched again, harder this time. Illerium's gaze was sharp, warning against any questions. He offered no further explanation, only stepping aside and nodding to the guards flanking the doors.

With a groan, the doors began to part, the creak of their slow, deliberate opening cutting through the thick silence like a blade. My heart lodged itself in my throat as the room beyond the doors came into view. It wasn't like anything I had seen before. Nothing in Azmeer compared to this.

Each corner hummed with the essence of a different Court, as though the very walls bore the soul of the Houses they represented. To the northeast, a towering mass of volcanic rock burned with a molten heat, glowing a deep, fiery red that danced with life. The sheer force of its heat was palpable, even from here, as if the rock itself was alive, pulsing with untamed power. Across from it, quartzite walls glowed with a soft, earthy light, tree roots curling and weaving through the stone, their presence a strange and eerie reminder that life—and magic—were woven into the very bones of this place.

I forced my eyes to move further to the other corners of the room. In the southwestern corner, a waterfall cascaded, its waters pouring into a dark, bottomless pit that swallowed the water whole. Its sound was a soft, melodic murmur that filled the air.

But it was the corner belonging to the Court of Whispers that sent a shiver down my spine. It shimmered with an iridescent sheen, the light bending and warping as if the space itself was in constant motion. And beneath that shimmering surface, a melody, haunted and beautiful, just barely audible. It beckoned, pulling at something deep inside me, a call I didn't fully understand but couldn't ignore.

Beside me, Kadian was pale, his warm skin now drained of color. The anxiety that clung to me was mirrored in him, only he didn't hide it as well. His fingers twisted and his eyes darted from one corner of the room to the next, as though he were trying to memorize every detail.

He's as worried as I am.

It wasn't just Kadian. All of us were on edge, but his situation felt particularly fragile. The others, those born into their placements, had been groomed for this, prepared for it. We were outsiders, clawing for a chance to belong.

"We'll be fine," I tried to reassure Kadian as much as myself. But the words felt hollow.

We took our seats in the center of the room, each of us casting nervous glances around. I tried to focus on the beauty of the space, on the intricate carvings that adorned the walls, the way the light filtered in from unseen windows, casting a soft, ethereal glow. But my mind kept drifting, my gaze returning to the dais at the front of the room. The long table that stood before it gleamed under the soft light, polished and immaculate. And for a brief, fleeting moment, I swore I saw something familiar—

But my thoughts were interrupted as the officials began to file in. They moved with an air of authority, their steps deliberate and slow, as though they were savoring the weight of this moment. The Master of Trials entered, his face a mask of impassivity.

And then, the princes.

Rai entered first, with Lil on his arm. My chest tightened at the sight of her, though I had been bracing for it. Lil looked as composed as ever, her expression unreadable, her steps in perfect sync with Rai's. I had no idea what her placement had been like—if she had even had one.

Then Dainan.

It was the first time we'd seen each other in weeks, the connection between us sparking to life in a way that made my pulse quicken. His expression was unreadable, but the intensity in his eyes burned, sending a tremor coursing through me.

But something was wrong. My stomach dropped as I searched the crowd. Where was Alvar?

I scanned the back of the room, my eyes darting from one face to the next, but there was no sign of him. People were filing in now—family members, friends—but Alvar wasn't among them.

"Good afternoon." The Master of Trials began. My back straightened involuntarily, my body responding to the authority in his voice.

"Today marks the end of the Courting. Those who have proven

themselves worthy shall reap their rewards—not only a position but the attributes that accompany it."

Magic. My heart skipped a beat at the thought. We had heard whispers, rumors about the kind of magic that would be bestowed upon those chosen by the courts, and when. But no one knew for sure. Not even Alvar had shared that information with me.

"Should your name be read, proceed to the table, where you will be provided further instruction." The Master of Trials' voice echoed in the chamber, but his words barely registered. I found myself half-listening, my mind too occupied with scanning the room. *Where is Alvar? Where is Addie?* The absence of both of them gnawed at me, creating an uneasy pit in my stomach. As much as I'd hoped my father would somehow manage to be here, I knew the journey was too arduous for him.

The Master's voice cut through again, louder this time as if he sensed the growing tension in the room. "Let us begin."

Sweat trickled down my back, pooling between my shoulder blades, my hands fidgeting restlessly in my lap. My fingers had taken on a life of their own, tangling and untangling as I wrestled with the anxiety that was threatening to swallow me whole. Just as I was about to lose myself in the spiral of my thoughts, I felt a familiar warmth—a steadying presence. Kadian's large hands clasped mine.

"We've got this, Bri," he whispered, his voice soft yet sure, just loud enough for me to hear.

I wanted to believe him, to cling to his certainty. But the dream—our dream—of everything we had worked for felt so precariously close, yet still out of reach. We were seconds away from knowing if we had made it, but the uncertainty was suffocating. More than anything, I found myself consumed with worry for Kadian. What would happen to him if his name wasn't called? Would he go back to Escalia? How would they treat him there, knowing that he had failed? How long would he last without Lil, without the promise of what the Courts offered?

What if he was assigned to a different court altogether? I shuddered at the thought. The lines between the courts were distinct, rigid, and though it had remained ambiguous to us inductees, the separation was undeniable.

They will never break that bond. We will not break. I clenched my teeth and squeezed his hand tighter, a silent vow forming in my mind. We were bound. No court, no ceremony, no decree could change that.

I must have been nodding without realizing it, as Kadian's gaze softened, his eyes flickering with that quiet, familiar acknowledgment. He leaned in closer, our foreheads pressing together in a moment of solidarity. "I know," he said quietly, his breath warm against my skin.

I inhaled, trying to steady my nerves just as the first name was called. "Osforth Kadem."

All heads turned toward Oz, who let out an audible sigh of relief. Oz looked to Kadian, and gave him a slap on the back. "You'll be next, brother." With a grin that barely masked his nerves, he stood and made his way to the front of the room.

"He's never going to let you live it down that he was called first," Kadian whispered to Tamra, who responded with such an exaggerated eye roll that I found myself stifling a laugh.

The Master of Trials' voice cut through again, formal and cold. "Osforth Kadem, you have been offered a position in the Eternal Court. Should you accept this offer, proceed to..."

We all leaned forward, trying to see past Oz as he stood before the table, blocking our view. But then it happened—a palpable, almost electric force seemed to radiate through the floor beneath us. I could feel it in my bones, a hum of power that made the hairs on the back of my neck stand on end. Oz turned back to us, his once light-colored eyes now a deep, molten gold.

"Please join your Court," the Master of Trials instructed.

One down. My heart pounded harder in my chest as I gripped Kadian's hand tighter, my knuckles turning white. Name after name was called, and I held my breath with each one. The Court of Whispers had gained two new members, the Eternal Court three, the Court of Reflection one, and the Court of Shadows—none.

As I continued scanning the room, my gaze landed on Kadian's family. They stood near the back, pale and stiff with concern. With each name called, they seemed to grow more pallid, their worry etched into the lines of their faces.

Then, the next name.

"Tamra Kadem."

Tamra stood, glancing back at us with her usual confident smirk. "I'll see you guys on the other side," she said before making her way to the front.

"Tamra Kadem, you have been offered a position in the Eternal Court and the Court of Shadows. Make a decision."

The room hushed as Tamra hesitated, her eyes darting to Oz and then to her family. We all knew where her heart lay. Despite her love for her family and the weight of their expectations, she had found a certain peace in the Court of Shadows during her placement. And so, she made her choice.

With a decisive nod, Tamra reached for something none of us could see, but the rush of heat through the room told us that she had aligned herself with the Court of Shadows.

My gaze shifted to Oz. He stood frozen, his face expressionless but his eyes rife with disappointment. He had known this would be her choice, but that didn't make it any easier to watch. Their bond was strong, and now they were being separated—by choice, no less.

As Tamra became the first and only person to stand in the corner illuminated by the living flames, the Master of Trials continued.

"Lilianna Towler."

An audible groan rose from somewhere in the crowd, and I had to bite my lip to suppress a laugh. I turned to Kadian, whose face remained impassive, but his eyes never left Lil.

"Lilianna Towler, you have been offered a position in the Court of Reflection—"

Before the Master could even finish the sentence, Lil was already moving, her hand reaching out toward something on the table. A cool sensation washed over the room, and she made her way to her corner, positioning herself as far away from Rai as possible. She caught my eye as she moved, and I was rewarded with a wink—a small gesture, but one that reassured me. Despite everything, despite the trials and the separation, Lil was still in there. She was still fighting.

The names kept coming, each one sending another pulse of anxiety through me. Iona was next, joining Tamra in the Court of Shadows. Tamra didn't contain her distaste, it only made me love her more. Derek was the next to join their ranks, and I searched the room hoping I would see Emia, but to my disappointment, she was nowhere to be seen.

With each passing name, the group around me grew smaller and smaller. The thrumming of my heartbeat grew louder, drowning out the Master of Trials' voice.

"Bri," Kadian whispered.

Did he say something?

"Brida," he repeated, firmer this time, releasing my hands.

I glanced up at him, catching the unwavering smile etched across his face. "You'll be next, I know it."

Before I could respond, he pressed a kiss to the top of my head and strode to the front of the room.

"Kadian Taldot, you have been offered a position in the Court of Shadows."

Did he just say Court of Shadows?

I fought to remain seated, my mind whirling in disbelief. My eyes darted across the room, searching frantically. *Alvar. This had to be Alvar's doing.*

Without a moment's hesitation, Kadian reached for the object on the table, and the familiar rush of warmth surged through the room. Tamra greeted him with wild enthusiasm.

I sat frozen, my thoughts spiraling back to how I'd ended up here. I wouldn't be sitting in this room if it weren't for Marsh. I'd searched for him earlier, hoping to catch a glimpse, but he was nowhere to be found.

I shifted uneasily, glancing from one corner of the room to the next, watching as the numbers in each group grew. Tamra's hair had darkened, now almost pitch black. Kadian, though—his had taken on a reddish hue. Mom would have loved that. I could almost hear her voice, imagining what she would say, her eyes twinkling with pride as she saw me now. I wished she were here. All this time, despite my late-night trips to the library and every stolen moment spent poring over books, I'd found nothing about her in Azmeer. Another mystery—one of so many—waiting to be solved.

The Master of Trials was mid-sentence, his voice echoing through the tense silence of the room, when the faint creak of the wooden doors broke through the stillness like a crack in glass. All at once, the room seemed to shift. Every head turned in unison, curiosity morphing into silent anticipation.

There, framed in the doorway, stood Alvar. His figure was solid, familiar, but it wasn't him who captured my attention—it was who he led inside. My father.

My breath caught, and for a moment, I was certain my heart stopped altogether. His arm was looped through Alvar's for support, but it was him—it was my father, walking, standing. A wave of disbelief crashed over me, sweeping through the raw edges of my composure. The world around me blurred at the edges, the weight of the moment pressing against my chest.

I fought the instinct to run to him and throw my arms around his neck. But I forced myself to stay seated, my fingers gripping the edge of my chair to keep from moving. I was aware of every fiber of my being, each heartbeat echoing in my ears as I struggled to hold myself in place. My father—who I feared I might never see again—was here. And somehow, impossibly, he looked far better than when I'd last seen him, over six long, uncertain months ago. His presence was an anchor, tethering me to the present, filling me with a fragile, swelling hope.

Alvar moved with the quiet efficiency I had come to expect from him, gently guiding my father toward a chair in the back of the room. Alvar's head dipped in acknowledgment to the Master of Trials, but my gaze remained fixed on my father, unable to tear myself away from the sight of him.

"Brida Larrow."

I rose slowly, feeling the hot tear escape down my cheek. My eyes locked with Alvar's, and I mouthed a silent "thank you." Each step to the front felt heavy, weighted with more than just the decision that lay ahead.

"Brida Larrow, you have been offered a position in the Eternal Court, Court of Whispers and the Court of Shadows. Make your choice."

The Eternal Court? I didn't have time to question it now.

A flutter of appreciation rippled through my chest, soft but insistent, warming me in a way I hadn't expected. *The Court of Whispers.* Marsh had fought for me. Despite the distance that had grown between us, despite the unspoken words and unresolved feelings, he had intervened.

But as the warmth settled in, so did the weight of realization. Gratitude alone wasn't enough to change what I knew had to be done. My heart may have softened for a moment, but it wasn't a reprieve—it was a reminder. Marsh had helped me, yes, but that didn't change the course I had set for myself. I couldn't allow his influence to sway me from the path I knew I had to follow.

My eyes fell to the table, where four objects lay. A silver bowl with aquamarine water sat on the far left, shimmering with an otherworldly glow. The water pulsed gently, as if alive with an ancient power that demanded reverence. This was the object for the Court of Reflection. Even from a distance, I felt its pull, a subtle tugging in the recesses of my mind, beckoning me to gaze into its depths, to uncover truths I wasn't sure I was ready to face. I swallowed hard, resisting the urge to step closer.

Next to it, a rough-hewn rock jutted from the table, its surface etched with a single rune, bold and unmistakable. The rune glowed, its lines crisp and deliberate, as though freshly carved by an unseen hand. The stone hummed with latent energy. There was something primal about it, something that spoke of ancient rites and powers long buried beneath the surface of the world.

Beside the stone, parchment danced through the air, caught in a swirling current of wind that appeared from nowhere. The pages moved as though guided by invisible hands. Words scrawled in ink I couldn't read flickered across the sheet, vanishing before I could decipher them. Shifting to keep secret the raw power that the Court of Whispers could summon.

And then there was the dagger.

Its sleek, silver blade gleamed coldly under the dim light, sharp and lethal. I would have recognized it anywhere—Vasenia's dagger, the very one Alvar had shown me on my first day. The intricate hilt, embedded with deep red rubies, looked as deadly as the blade itself, its dark elegance undeniable. A weapon forged not just for war but for something far more personal.

My eyes fell on the bowl beside it, filled with thick, dark droplets of blood. The crimson liquid clung to the sides of the vessel, catching the light in a way that made my stomach twist. The metallic tang of blood magic filled the air, faint but unmistakable, its presence a clear signal that whatever ritual this belonged to was steeped in something ancient and forbidden.

I looked toward Dainan. He sat tense, gripping the arms of his chair so tightly his knuckles had turned white.

I reached for the dagger, its weight cool in my hand. I pressed the tip to my index finger, watching the blood bead up before it dripped into the bowl below. I waited, expecting the same warm pulse to fill the room.

Nothing happened.

I glanced around, searching for some sign, some instruction, but was met with blank, unreadable faces. The room was still. Lowering the dagger, I bowed my head and made my way to Kadian and

Tamra, their corner feeling so far away from the others. The lines between us—between all of us—were so clear now.

I slipped into the familiar warmth of the walls, feeling Kadian's arms wrap around me.

"Thank you," he whispered.

My gaze drifted to Alvar, who was deep in conversation with my father as I clung to Kadian, wondering if, in trying to save us, Alvar had condemned us both.

CHAPTER FORTY-EIGHT

As the ceremony drew to a close, the room seemed to settle into a tense, uneasy quiet. Forty inductees remained unselected, their dreams dangled before them to be snatched away at the last moment —like a cat playing with a helpless toy. The weight of disappointment hung heavy in the air, stifling and undeniable.

Kadian, ever the reassuring presence, gave my shoulder a comforting squeeze before stepping away to join his parents. My heart lifted watching him reunite with his family. His mother's arms wrapped tightly around him, her fingers threading through his newly auburn hair, a mark of his place in the Court of Shadows.

"Guess I need to go sort this," Tamra muttered beside me, her usual bold demeanor dimmed. She moved to greet her family, though Oz, still crestfallen from the events, remained lingering on the edges. His disappointment mirrored the lingering tension in the room.

I ran my hand through my hair, my gaze lowering to my fingers. I hadn't felt any change within myself, nor had I noticed any physical alteration. Perhaps it was because my hair and eyes were already aligned with the Court of Shadows' aesthetics. I pushed the thought aside, reminding myself I had someone important to see.

When I found Alvar and my father at the back of the room, they were laughing—full, deep laughter, as if the world beyond this moment didn't exist. Alvar was doubled over, his shoulders shaking, while my father slapped his knee in pure amusement. I couldn't help the smile that tugged at my lips, a deep warmth filling me. How could he look this well?

"Hey, Dad," I said softly as I approached.

My father's pale eyes welled with emotion the instant he saw me. He turned to Alvar, who gave him a silent nod of reassurance, before rising to his feet. I didn't hesitate; I rushed forward and threw myself into his arms. The feel of him, solid and warm, the familiar scent of home wrapping around me, was almost too much to bear. His embrace tightened, securing me in a way that made the months of worry and fear melt away in an instant.

"Hello, my beautiful girl," his rich voice whispered.

I pulled back just enough to cup his face in my hands, searching his features. The gauntness, the weariness that had plagued him was gone. He looked like the man I remembered, not the frail figure I had feared losing. I couldn't make sense of it. "How...?" I barely managed to get the word out, my voice thick with disbelief.

His hands covered mine, pulling them gently down from his face as he smiled at me, his eyes filled with nothing but love and admiration.

"Dad, the herbs I sent—they helped, but not this much. Tell me what happened," I pressed, desperate for an explanation.

Before he could answer, Alvar chimed in, his voice drawing my attention. "Apologies for being late to the ceremony. I hope you didn't think we'd abandoned you," he said, stepping forward with that familiar calmness though his smile was warm and genuine.

My father nodded toward him, his expression softening. "I owe this man my life, Brida. More than I can ever repay."

I blinked, looking between the two of them. It was clear there was more to the story, something unsaid lingering between them.

Alvar cleared his throat, motioning for me to step aside with him. "Brida, may we speak for a moment?" He helped my father settle back into his chair before guiding me a few steps away.

"What's going on, Alvar?" I whispered, my nerves on edge. The strange feeling that all of this could slip away, like a dream fading upon waking, terrified me.

Alvar gave me a reassuring smile, his eyes crinkling at the corners. "We couldn't very well have your father miss the ceremony, could we?" There was a warmth in his tone that made my heart ache, and I couldn't help but smile back, despite my growing questions.

"How did you bring him here?" I asked, swiping at the tears that had begun to gather again. "You can't shadow-step."

"Ah, no, I cannot." He leaned in, his voice dropping. "But I happen to know two people who can."

My heart stuttered in my chest, my breath catching. "Dainan and Asana?" I asked, the disbelief creeping into my voice.

He nodded. "They wanted to help."

I wanted to thank him, to express the overwhelming gratitude swelling within me, but the words tangled on my tongue. Alvar seemed to sense it, his expression softening as he spoke again. "There are a few things we need to discuss, Brida. First, families must leave this afternoon. The Wind Walkers will handle their transport back home, so use your time wisely."

I nodded, the weight of the day pressing in on me. I didn't want to waste a single moment with my father.

"And secondly," Alvar hesitated, his voice dropping to a quieter tone. "The weddings..."

"The weddings?" I echoed, my stomach twisting.

"They'll be held in the Center Court throne room. It's...for appearances. A show that everyone is equal," he continued, though I could hear the disdain in his voice. "I'd suggest spending the morning in the House of Shadows or the library. You'll find peace there."

"I'll do as you ask, Alvar," I said, though the words felt like a betrayal of myself. Inside, the fiery sensation grew as if my very soul was splintering under the weight of helplessness.

"He cares about you," Alvar whispered, his voice softening. "I've never seen him like this before."

"Not even with Cyria?" I found myself asking before I could stop.

Alvar blinked, taken aback. "No," he replied, his voice barely audible.

We stood in silence, and then, with a gentle squeeze of my arm, he pulled me back to the present. "Go enjoy the afternoon with your father, Brida. There will be work for you after tomorrow."

I met his gaze, a deep sincerity mirrored in his dark eyes. "Do you know what my official position will be? Will I stay in Azmeer or be sent to Mount Kaiver?" I asked though the thought of being separated from Kadian made my chest tighten.

"If I am to be king, I'll need someone by my side to keep things in order." He leaned in, lowering his voice. "You didn't think I'd let you work for anyone else, did you?"

Despite the tension in the room, I found myself embracing Alvar, the gratitude overwhelming me. "Thank you," I whispered.

"You have nothing to thank me for, Brida," he replied. "I will see you after the weddings. Be sure to be on time." With a wink, Alvar pulled away, making his way through the crowd to his brothers.

Turning, I made my way back to my father. "Let me show you Azmeer."

CHAPTER FORTY-NINE

"It's so good to see you," I guided my father into the courtyard outside my room.

I could see the wonder in his eyes—the same wonder I had felt months ago when I first arrived. Back then, the grandeur of this place had been overwhelming, like it could swallow me whole at any moment. It still felt too grand, too otherworldly, and yet, despite everything that had happened, it had become my home. That truth settled in me with a strange mix of pride and sorrow.

My father turned to face me, his smile soft but tired, and sat on the edge of the fountain. The gentle sound of the water filled the silence that followed. It was the same fountain where Marsh had waited for me right before we ventured to Hadash. The memory felt distant now, like it belonged to another life.

"This is where your rooms are?" He asked with disbelief as he looked around.

"Yes," I breathed, trying to take in the moment. The smells of the garden, the feel of the fountain beneath me, the sound of stones beneath my feet. "Though I'll be moved soon. To the House of Shadows." The weight of that realization sank in, heavier than I wanted to admit. It would mean leaving this space, the place where I'd found a sliver of comfort. I'd be far from Lil, from Oz. From everything familiar.

My father hands rested on his knees as he stared out at the garden, his gaze following the way the breeze stirred the leaves, his thoughts somewhere far beyond. There was a heaviness to him that hadn't been there before. It was in his eyes, the way his shoulders sagged ever so slightly like he was carrying something too heavy for too long.

"Dad..." I whispered, moving closer to him, my voice trembling as I spoke. "You need to tell me how you're here. How this is possible?"

I could see the struggle on his face, the way he tried to find the right words—words that wouldn't shatter the fragile peace between us. He nodded, his expression softening as he turned to look at me.

"Flora read me each of your letters. Every night." His voice was quiet but steady. "After we said goodbye when we walked to Lesalia...I started to decline. Slowly, at first. But then it became faster."

My heart clenched. I had known it. I had *felt* it, even from far away. "I knew you'd overexerted yourself that day. You didn't have to walk so far. I shouldn't have—"

"There was every reason for it, Brida," he interrupted, grabbing my hands. "If you couldn't have your mother to walk with you, then you would have me."

I swallowed against the knot in my throat. The emotions I had buried deep inside—fears, regrets, the overwhelming sense of loss—began to rise to the surface, and I couldn't stop them.

"I asked Flora to read your letters to me every night," he repeated, his voice a little softer now. "I thought...maybe if I could hear your words, it would help me hold on a little longer. But each day, it felt like everything started to fade. My memories, the colors...they started to lose their brightness. Your mother's red hair—it wasn't as bright in my mind. The black of your hair..." His fingers reached out, brushing a strand of my hair behind my ear, his touch so gentle it made me ache. "In my mind, it started to turn gray."

Tears spilled down my cheeks, unbidden. My hands trembled, my chest tightening with the weight of his words. I hadn't known. I hadn't known how bad it had been. "She never told me," I whispered, my voice breaking. "Flora never told me how bad it was. If I'd known... I would have—"

"Everything was as it should have been," he interrupted, his thumb brushing away the tears that streaked my face. "And look at you now, what you've accomplished."

His words should have made me feel proud, but instead, they made the ache in my chest worse. "Alvar..." I started, trying to change the subject, to shift the conversation away from the pain that was threatening to overwhelm me. "You and Alvar are on a first-name basis now?"

He smiled, the kind of smile that lit up his whole face, if only for a moment. "He insisted. Something about the 'spirit of friendship.' I couldn't say no to him."

I laughed despite the tears, the sound strange and soft in my throat. "He would do that."

"And Flora nearly fainted when she opened the door and found him standing there. Not just him, but a woman and a man who looked more shadow than Fae." My father chuckled at the memory, his eyes twinkling with amusement.

"And she's recovered, I hope?" I asked, my lips quirking into a small smile.

"She did, eventually," he replied, still smiling. "Once she let them in, Alvar took one look at me and insisted we go. There wasn't much I could do to argue."

I shook my head, amazed. "And when you got here...?"

"When we got here, I don't remember much. Only that when I woke up, I felt fine."

I stared at him, incredulous. "You felt *fine*?"

"Yes," he said as if it were the most natural thing in the world.

"Dad, you're going to need to give me more than that. What happened? What did they do?"

He ran a hand through his hair, pausing to think. "When I woke up, Alvar was there. He said whatever had been ailing me had been resolved, but when I pressed him for details, he said we were running late and that it was imperative we be on time."

I let out a soft laugh, shaking my head. "He does have a thing for punctuality."

My father chuckled. "That he does. But Brida..." His tone softened, and he reached for my hand. "He told me how much you've helped him. How proud he is of you. And Brida, I couldn't be prouder of you."

The words hit me like a wave, and I blinked back the fresh tears that threatened to spill over. For a moment, all the doubts, all the fears, melted away. I had done something. Something right. And for the first time in a long while, I let myself feel it.

"Now, as much as I would love to continue sitting here and talking with you, there's someone else I need to see while I'm here." Dad started to stand, but before he could move, I reached for his wrist, halting him.

"I know Addie will love to see you," I said softly, trying to keep my voice steady. "But before we go, there's something we need to discuss."

The weight of my words seemed to stop him in his tracks. My father lowered himself back down, his movements slow and measured. His eyes, warm and attentive, locked on mine, a silent invitation for me to continue. "What is it, Bri?"

My heart pounded in my chest. I bit my lip, trying to hold the silence as long as I could as if the words I had to say would shatter something fragile between us. But I couldn't put it off any longer.

"Dad," I started, my voice trembling, "why did you never mention that Mom had been to Azmeer before?"

For a moment, my father stayed perfectly still, his expression unchanged, as if I had asked him something as simple as the weather. The calmness in his face unsettled me like he had already anticipated my question.

"To my recollection," he began slowly, carefully, "your mother was never in Azmeer proper. We met while listening to a musician... but that's all I knew. That, and she had come to see her sister, but she was staying in the center square when we first spoke. Is that what you mean by being in Azmeer before, darling?"

His answer was so matter-of-fact, so...benign. But it didn't line up with what I knew, and my frustration bubbled to the surface, tightening my chest. I shifted in my seat, unable to stay still, my nerves making me fidgety. "Dad," I said, my voice growing more urgent, "I was *mistaken* for Mom while I was in Azmeer. To my knowledge, she had never even been here. So why would anyone think—"

Before I could finish, he rubbed a hand over his face and sighed, his weariness suddenly palpable. "It's possible that I knew something at one point, Brida," he admitted, his voice laced with exhaustion. "But despite what Alvar has done for me...the memories that started to fade, they haven't come back." He paused, his hand falling back to his lap, and gave me a small, reassuring smile. "Not yet, anyway. Maybe, with time, some of them will return."

He patted my hand, his touch full of love and understanding. "And should I remember, I promise we'll have that conversation."

I knew I couldn't push him any further, even though every part of me screamed for answers. His memories were like fragile threads, worn and fraying, and pressing him would only strain them further.

"Come," I said, trying to inject some humor into my voice, "prepare to be awed by the most drab version of Addie you've ever seen."

CHAPTER FIFTY

"You look great, Vale. I'd even argue better than the last time I saw you." When she finally released him, her gaze softened. "Gods, it feels like it's been forever."

"A few years," he laughed, "I can only imagine what Aela would say if she could see you now."

"She'd say I look like shit." Their laughter rang out.

"I'm sorry I couldn't make it this morning. I had some last-minute things to do for tomorrow." Addie said to me.

For the weddings.

Addie led us through the library, a space I'd come to know well. Still, she pointed out things I had missed, little details hidden in the towering shelves, and even revealed the entry to the archives, a doorway I'd somehow never noticed before.

For hours, we sat and talked, the three of us sharing stories of Mom. Addie brought up memories from her visits—stories I hadn't heard since I was a child—and we laughed over the time Mom got lost in the market for hours, refusing to ask for directions. As always, I felt that familiar ache whenever Mom came up, the void she left behind so vast, no amount of stories could ever fill it.

But all too soon, the bells rang. The day was drawing to a close, and I knew it was time for Dad to go.

"I'll do a better job of visiting," Addie whispered as she hugged him again.

"Aela would be proud of you, Addie." Dad's voice was steady, a warmth radiating from him as he gestured to the grand library. "This... Everything you've done here is impressive. The ladies of Azmeer," he said with a wry smile, looking between the two of us.

I reached out, offering my hand to Dad. He didn't need my help anymore, but I wanted to hold on to him, just for a few more minutes. Dad gently pulled me into a small alcove hidden away from the main hall as we made our way to say goodbye.

"Brida," his voice laced with concern, "before I go, tell me—what's really bothering you?"

I froze, suddenly finding it hard to look him in the eye. "What do you mean?" My fingers fidgeted with the edge of my sleeve, and I shifted uncomfortably.

His brow raised, his smile gentle. "I may have asked Alvar about the other young man who came to the house yesterday."

I blinked, caught off guard. "You mean Dainan?"

Dad nodded, his eyes twinkling.

"He's older than you think, you know." A startled laugh escaped me. "Well, he doesn't look it," Dad teased, that same mischievous grin I remembered from my childhood lighting up his face. "He seemed...interested. I haven't seen someone look at our home like that since I brought your mother over for the first time."

My chest tightened at his words, but I shrugged, trying to play it off. "Maybe he's just nosy."

Dad's expression softened further, and he reached out, resting his hand over mine. "Brida."

"There may have been a moment—fleeting, really," I began, the words spilling out before I could stop them, "when something might have happened between Dainan and me. But he's getting married tomorrow. That's what Addie's been working on." My voice cracked as the reality of it sunk in further.

Dad's hands gently squeezed mine. "You'd be surprised at how things can sometimes work out," he said with a knowing look. "Life has a way of surprising us."

I bit my lip, unsure of how to respond. It was all too much, and at the same time, not enough.

"Alvar showed me where to go," he said as he pulled away, straightening his coat. "This is where I leave you."

"Absolutely not." I shook my head. "I'm walking you."

"No." Dad smiled, a kind but determined glint in his eye. "The last time I left you, I needed someone to escort me. But now I'm capable. I'll be fine, Brida."

His words were gentle, but they tugged at something deep inside me. He had come so far—healing, regaining his strength. It should've been a comfort, but it only made this moment harder.

"Please, just let me—"

"I'll be okay." He reached out, resting his hand against my cheek, and I leaned into the familiar warmth of his touch. "I'm okay."

The reassurance in his voice settled over me as he pulled me in for a final embrace. I clung to him, holding on for a beat longer than I probably should have.

"You write to me soon, okay?" His voice was soft against my ear. "You'll do incredible things, Brida. Don't doubt yourself."

A soft laugh bubbled up despite the ache in my throat. "I promise I'll write."

As we pulled back from each other, I took in his face, trying to memorize every line, every detail. His face looked just like it had in the vision during the second trial—healed, whole, radiant in a way I hadn't seen in years.

"Good luck with wind walking," I joked, trying to keep my voice steady as I slipped my hands into my pockets.

Dad chuckled, leaning in to kiss my cheek one last time. "I have a feeling I'll be just fine, my beautiful girl." His eyes were bright as he stepped back. "I'll see you soon."

I nodded, biting my lip to hold back the tears as I watched him walk away. He carried himself tall and proud, with the same grace and strength I'd always admired.

He's okay, I reminded myself. *He's okay.*

☽✻☾

I need you.

You were given a gift. The gift.

Ilia.

Breathe.

Listen to the sounds of the water, Brida, just breathe.

You were given a gift. The gift.

How was this a gift? It was a curse.

Just breathe, Brida.

I opened my eyes the next morning, unsure of what I had been dreaming, but woke in a sweat, my heart pulsing as if trying to escape my body that held it prisoner.

Sighing, I rose from bed and got dressed before making my way down the empty halls to the House of Shadows.

I stood in front of the door. Nothing happened.

"*Hello?*" I said to the loquacious door. It didn't open. "Can you open, please?" I asked as I heard a faint hissing from behind it.

Silence.

"I'm not sure if you know this, but it took a great deal of energy to get here this morning, and I would appreciate it if you opened the bloody door."

"*You have no idea how bloody this door is, child,*" the voice answered. It was not its typical greeting. "*You should not be here.*"

I looked around me. The cavernous atrium remained empty, save for me and the voice that belonged to the door. "There's nowhere else I should be right now," I whispered.

"*You're wrong, girl.*"

Girl. Another had called me "girl" before.

"*Ollo?*" I whispered, and the door laughed.

"*Gods no, do you think I sound like him?*"

What is happening to me? I thought.

"Who are you?" Taking a step forward, I placed the palm of my hand on the cold obsidian door.

"*You will know soon enough.*"

Do they all speak in these riddles?

"*Not all of us.*"

I hadn't said that out loud. A laugh echoed through my mind.

How are you doing that? I thought.

"*It's one of my gifts,*" the voice purred, "*one of my many gifts.*"

I stood in silence, trying not to think.

"*Ollo gave you clear instructions.*"

"Clear?" I yelled, "Everything that man—I don't even know if I can call him a man—PRIMAL, said was cryptic."

"*Think about what he told you,*" it said as the door opened.

"Thank you," I muttered under my breath. My shadows began hissing in melody as I stepped through the threshold.

The House of Shadows buzzed with life. The air humming with conversations, laughter, and the shuffle of arriving guests preparing for the weddings. I weaved through the groups, keeping my head low, my gaze averted. Today, of all days, I didn't want to be recognized.

The library, however, was a welcome contrast—a sanctuary of silence amidst the commotion outside.

"Good morning, Tura," I whispered, careful not to disturb the peace.

"Brida," she greeted warmly, her eyes crinkling with kindness. "I was hoping I would see you today."

Tura had made this place feel safe. The library had become my refuge, and she, an unspoken confidant.

"I did some research after we last spoke." She bent down,

rummaging through a drawer, her movements quick yet deliberate. With a gentle thud, she placed a stack of five books in front of me.

"This is just preliminary, of course," she explained, her smile patient and understanding. "There may be more, but it will take some time to uncover everything."

I stared at the books, some so old they looked like they might crumble in my hands. "Thank you. This means more than you know."

Tura's hand found mine, squeezing it. "I know today is a hard day, love. I lit the fire upstairs and prepared a cup of tea for you, in case you decided to come."

"A fire, in a library? Tura, I never imagined you'd allow flames so close to your books."

Her laugh was soft and reassuring. "Those flames will not harm them, trust me."

I collected the books and placed them in one of the bags she kept at her station, the ancient texts settling into their new home with a quiet rustle. "Thank you, Tura," I repeated, my gratitude laced with my unease.

The familiar quiet enveloped me as I climbed the stairs to the third floor. I sank into the chair, and reached into the bag, pulling out the first book. Tura had marked several pages with tabs, her neat handwriting scrawled in the margins. I turned to the first marked page, the soft rustle of the paper soothing, and began to read.

Seventh Day of the Six Month

As I sit here penning these words, with the light offered to me by the flickering fireflies, my thoughts are consumed by her. Whispers are carried on the wind, and secrets dance in the shadows of Azmeer, and yet my mind returns to her. As I watched her from the shadows, a veil of secrecy shrouding my intentions, I felt drawn to her. She is a puzzle waiting to be solved, a riddle to be deciphered. A game to be won.

. . .

Nineteenth Day of the Eighth Month

There is a power that emanates from her, ancient and primal in nature, yet she continues on with an air of unknowing innocence. There is so little to go on, so few clues to unravel the mystery that surrounds her, and yet I cannot stop myself. I am a moth to a flame. Unable to break the bonds of the pull from her presence.

Second day of the Eleventh Month

There is a mystery that shrouds her, a veil of secrecy that hides the truth of her lineage. I have seen the power that lies within her, that will come from her. A raw energy that courses through her veins like the blood of the earth itself. She is no ordinary mortal, of that I am certain.

Did whoever wrote this think Thale, or Ilia, was mortal? I turned to the fourth tab.

First Day of the Twelfth Month

As I gaze upon her sleeping form, bathed in the soft glow of the moonlight, curled against my side, I am filled with a sense of awe and wonder. Although I may never know the truth, I will continue to love and cherish her for all of the days of my immortal life.

Fifteenth Day of the Twelfth Month

I dare not speak my suspicions aloud for fear of revealing too much to her too soon. I sit with her, my heart aflutter, a mix of longing and trepidation. She continues to be a mystery wrapped in an enigma, and I am determined to uncover the truth. No matter the cost.

. . .

Twenty-First Day of the First Month

I cannot help but wonder about her lineage, about the gods from whom she descends. She is strong, beautiful, and beyond compare, and yet she carries herself with a humility that belies her true nature. It is a paradox that both intrigues and frustrates me, for she seems to be unaware.

Third day of the Second Month

Could she be a descendant of Ilia? The elusive goddess of fire and shadow, or perhaps another of the ancient deities whose names have been lost to time?

Ninth day of the Third Month

My heart remains heavy with all I have uncovered. She, the woman who captured my soul with her radiant presence, has chosen to walk away from me. [Redacted] is a revelation that both terrifies and enchants me, for I have glimpsed the power that she holds, should she choose it. She walks a path that I can only imagine, her destiny entwined with forces beyond my comprehension. I would have tried, had she let me.

She is a goddess in every sense of the word, and though she may have left me, I will forever be grateful for the love she brought to my life. My love, my Aela.

I bolted upwards.

Who wrote this book? The cover was blank. I tore open the book to the first few pages: *This book is the personal property of Yezed Albahar.*

Oh Gods.

The book slipped from my hands, crashing to the floor with a muffled thud. My heart raced, each beat louder than the last.

Addie—Addie would've known about Yezed's beliefs. Why hadn't she told me? Gods, Addie.

Without another thought, I snatched the book off the floor, shoving it into the bag, swinging the strap over my shoulder. I bolted. I had to find her.

"Brida, dear, where are you g—" Tura's voice trailed off as I sped past her, too focused to respond. My mind spun, tangled in a web of questions and disbelief.

The door said nothing as I burst out into the open air, my shadows hissing at the sudden shift from the library's stillness to the chaos outside. I hadn't run like this in weeks, and I could feel the strain on my legs, the burn creeping up from my calves with each frantic step. But I couldn't stop. Not now.

The halls stretched endlessly before me, blessedly empty, allowing me to run without the inconvenience of dodging others. The bag thudded against my hip, the rhythm punctuating my scattered thoughts.

I rounded and skidded to a halt, my heart hammering against my ribs as I was swallowed by a crowd. They stood, waiting for something, a low hum of murmurs rippling through them like a distant storm. *Why is everyone just standing here?*

Before I could gather my bearings, a deep, resounding gong echoed through the hallway, startling me back into reality. The large double doors ahead swung open, and the crowd surged forward. I tried to push against the tide, my mind still screaming that I had to reach the library—but I was helpless, caught in the current of bodies.

I fought against it, but the sheer force of the crowd was relentless. I was pulled along, dragged through the threshold, and into a cavernous room lined with pews. The walls towered high above, imposing, and the chattering of voices ricocheted off the stone like a chorus of whispers, growing louder and louder.

I was somehow near the front now, swept to the very heart of whatever this was. Panic gripped me. *I need to get out.* The only exit was at the back of the room. My breaths quickened as I began navigating the pews, muttering a constant stream of "Excuse me, pardon me," my focus fixed on the aisle leading me to freedom.

Another gong rang out and a voice as deep and commanding as the first day I arrived in Azmeer filled the air. “Be seated.”

I froze. The voice rumbled through me like an order woven into my very bones. I willed my legs to keep moving, to ignore the command, but it was as though I had lost control. My body sat of its own accord, surrendering to the unseen force that compelled me.

Before I could comprehend what was happening, music began to play, delicate yet powerful. I glanced over my shoulder to the back doors, which had been closed moments earlier but now swung wide open once again.

There, standing in the doorway, were Lil, Rai, Dainan, and Iona.

And just like that, the pieces clicked together.

I had a front-row seat to the wedding.

CHAPTER FIFTY-ONE

I'd never been to a Fae or royal wedding before. Let alone one where multiple couples were getting married, where I craved one of the grooms, or where my best friend was in love with one of the brides. In terms of weddings that I'd attended—which, to be fair, had been few—this was by far the worst.

In my panic running from the library, I'd forgotten what was happening later this morning.

The music started—a dirge masquerading as a wedding march. The couples began their slow, excruciating procession down the aisle, thousands of eyes watching their every step. The air in the throne room felt thick, suffocating. It clung to my skin, the weight of my dread curling like smoke around me.

I scanned the aisle again. Alvar walked behind the couples with Thalius and Deter flanking him like loyal hounds. At the rear, Addie walked with a fellow scribe I didn't recognize. My heart seized. If I'd made it to the library, Addie wouldn't have been there anyway.

I scanned the crowd again, searching for familiar faces, for any sign of solace in this sea of judgmental eyes. The new court members were seated near the center. I spotted Kadian and Oz, but neither of them saw me. Tamra must have found a spot with Amera, and Marsh... Marsh wasn't here. He said he wouldn't be, not until the coronation.

My gaze flicked back to the aisle. Each bride looked perfect, pristine, and hollow. Their hair sculpted into elegant piles, their dresses works of art. My heart twisted at the sight of Lil. Her gown, shimmered like the sea itself, flowing with every step, crashing against the stone floor.

Iona, by contrast, was fire incarnate. Her dress flickering with reds, oranges, and blacks as if the flames danced and swirled at her feet, eager to consume.

The crowd whispered about their beauty, their status, and how they would no doubt produce "gorgeous heirs." I fought back the bile in my throat. *I shouldn't be here. I should've stayed in the library, surrounded by the comfort of dust and parchment, burying myself in anything but this.*

My eyes drifted down the aisle. Thirty feet. Dainan was thirty feet from me, and my world shrank to him. His scent hit me before I could brace for it: smoke, citrus, and salt. It was heady, intoxicating, and the effect was immediate. My body jolted to life as though every dead nerve in me lit up, burning like wildfire through my veins.

I tried not to stare, tried not to let my hunger show, but my gaze refused to pull away. His eyes met mine, and panic flickered in his eyes. He didn't want me here. I shouldn't be here.

"I'm sorry," I mouthed, though my apology felt like a brittle leaf in the storm of emotions between us. His expression hardened, his features tightening as if he'd just remembered who he was, who I was, and the unbreakable roles we had to play. I looked to Iona, desperate to see if she noticed, but she remained unaware, lost in the grandeur of her own wedding. Lil, on the other hand saw me. Her eyes flicked to mine for a second, too quick, and then back to the aisle, pretending she hadn't seen me. My stomach clenched.

The couples reached the front of the aisle, and an officiant appeared, accompanied by Asana. Everything was falling into place. The nightmare was starting.

The officiant began speaking, his voice echoing through the room, but the words muffled around me. I was drowning in the pressure. The air felt too thick; I couldn't breathe. He gestured to the couples, his hands outstretched like he was offering them up as sacrifices. And maybe he was. This wasn't a wedding—it was a spectacle. A political statement. A transaction.

"We begin with Prince Rai Luchien and Lilianna Towler," the officiant announced, and I could've sworn I heard Lil scoff. *Good girl. Keep fighting.*

The vows began, the ancient words binding them to one another with every recitation.

Out of the corner of my eye, I saw Addie rifling through her papers, her expression focused, intent. *What is she doing?* My attention flickered back to the front.

"Until the end," Rai repeated, and I could barely stand to hear it. My eyes drifted away again, settling on Addie once more. She smacked a paper as though she had just found some crucial piece of information. My heart pounded in my chest, a small, irrational hope.

The officiant finished. "May your union be blessed through the eternities."

Lil's married.

The reality crashed into me. Lil was married.

And now...now it was Dainan's turn.

I can't do this. I couldn't watch this. My stomach twisted, my vision blurred, *I need to leave.* The officiant turned toward Dainan and Iona, beginning to speak the same damning words. The sickness clawed at me.

But something wasn't right. Addie had moved, now standing beside Alvar. She pointed to something on her paper, her face sharp with urgency. Alvar's eyes widened, his face paling as he grabbed the paper from her. My pulse quickened.

Something's wrong.

I leaned forward instinctively, almost stumbling into the aisle as I strained to hear. Alvar approached the officiant, his hand on the Fae's shoulder. The room seemed to hold its breath as he spoke. "This has been a grave error."

The crowd murmured, a wave of unease rippling through them. Thalius shot to his feet, rage blazing in his eyes. He snatched the paper from Alvar and scanned it, his lips tightening. "It doesn't matter," he shouted, his voice echoing in the grand hall. "It's done. They are wed." He flung his arm toward Lil and Rai, both of whom stood frozen, confusion written across their faces.

Alvar didn't back down. "It can be undone," he said, his voice steady, his gaze locked on the paper. He held it out, gesturing toward Dainan. Dainan took it, scanning it before looking up, his eyes frantically searching the crowd.

Searching for me.

Our gazes locked. That flicker of hope ignited into a flame. This wasn't over. There was a way out of this.

The room seemed to collapse in on itself, every moment sharper, more frantic than the last. Thalius's face remained calm amidst the growing chaos, detached from Deter's shouts about propriety. I saw his lips move, a whisper aimed at Rai. Whatever passed between them was brief but shifted something in the air. Rai turned to face Thalius, nodding, a silent pact made in a room that was anything but silent.

I blinked, my mind scrambling to process the thousand threads of disaster weaving around me. I caught a glimpse of Addie, pale and trembling, still clutching those damned documents. The papers that were supposed to grant approval for the marriages, not condemn them. She stood there, frozen in her own confusion, as the storm grew around her.

But my attention didn't stay long. Deter's voice had risen into a full-throated scream, cutting through the room just as Iona's cries began to ripple through the crowd. Iona—Gods, her tears, her wailing—her grief was a physical force now, adding to the pandemonium. People were starting to turn their heads, shifting in their seats. But I couldn't let myself focus on her either. Lil. My eyes found her, inching away from Rai and Thalius, her steps too deliberate to be unnoticed. She was trying to reach Addie, positioning herself, separating from whatever calamity was about to unfold.

And then it happened.

Rai moved in a single, smooth motion, like a dancer taking center stage. He crossed the dais with purpose, and in an instant, his hand was on the ceremonial knife. My heart plummeted, my breath stalling in my chest. No, no, no. His movements were too swift, too controlled. Before anyone could stop him, before anyone could understand what was happening, Rai drove the blade into Alvar's chest.

The room collapsed into screams. Asana's voice ripped through the air, the sound of it more terrible than anything I'd ever heard. Alvar staggered, hands scrambling to cover the wound, but the blood was everywhere. It soaked his robes, pooling under him, red and slick. The sight was overwhelming, dizzying.

Then the storm hit. Gusts slammed into the crowd, sending chairs and people toppling. I was thrown to my knees, helpless against the sheer force of the wind. My hands clawed at the ground as I tried to stay upright, my body trembling with effort. The howling wind drowned out every other sound except the scattered cries of panic. The fury of it was unbearable, forcing me down further.

Alvar was dying—bleeding out faster than anyone could react. Asana hovered over him, hands glowing with frantic magic, but it was clear she couldn't save him. He was too far gone.

Wind Walkers appeared out of thin air, summoned by the violence as though they'd been waiting for this. And then Thalius moved again. My eyes snapped to him just in time to see him seize the knife from Rai's limp fingers. He didn't hesitate. With terrifying precision, he crossed the dais.

"ADDIE!" The scream tore out of me, but it was already too late.

The blade slid across her throat, blood gushing from the wound. The papers she held scattered like leaves in the breeze, and her hands flew to her neck as she stumbled.

Time fractured. I felt it crack and slow, freezing everything but the sight of her falling. My voice died in my throat, suffocated by the wind that now roared louder than my own thoughts.

Get to Addie.

My body screamed at me to move, but the wind held me down. I was paralyzed, trapped by the force of the storm and the horror playing out in front of me. Everything had gone silent—at least, it felt that way. I could still hear screams in the distance, but they seemed detached, far away from where I was. All that existed was Addie's body, twitching on the floor.

"Brida, do not move." The voice was unmistakable, cutting through the chaos like a knife. I turned—no, forced my head to turn—fighting against the wind. Marsh stood behind me, his face grim, the wind swirling but not touching him. He looked so out of place, calm amidst the chaos.

"Do not move," he repeated, his words cold and commanding.

"ARE YOU A PART OF THIS?" I shrieked, my voice hoarse, my throat raw. I wasn't even sure he could hear me over the deafening roar of the tempest. But his eyes answered me. There was something dark in them—something I didn't want to see. He was involved, somehow. I could feel it in the way he looked at me, in the way he stood so still while everything around us fell apart.

The wind around us shifted. He wrapped a barrier of air around me, pulling me to my feet. I was face-to-face with him now, but my eyes darted over his shoulder to Dainan. Dainan's face twisted with rage when he saw Marsh. His entire body tensed, fury radiating from him as he fought against the windstorm to get to us.

Dainan stepped closer, shoulders squared and eyes dark, anger radiating off him in waves, as if his very body was braced to unleash something raw and untamed. "She's mine." The words tore from Dainan, a feral, guttural snarl that sent a shockwave through the air.

His voice was a razor-edged whisper of rage, vibrating with a primal intensity that seized every nerve in me.

Marsh tightened his grip on me, pulling me closer. “We’ll see,” he said, his voice smooth, unbothered by Dainan’s threat.

My heart was pounding so hard I thought it might burst out of my chest. My eyes darted back and forth—Lil, Addie, Thalius, Rai. Oh Gods, Rai. Rai and Thalius were making their way toward Dainan, and Dainan wasn’t paying attention. He didn’t see them coming.

I tried to scream again, to warn him, but the wind swallowed my voice. Everything was Chaos. Everything was unraveling.

I opened my mouth to scream but it was swallowed by the wind.

CHAPTER FIFTY-TWO

I lay on the cold, damp ground, its chill seeping through me. *Where am I?* I blinked, my vision blurry, and the room around me indistinct.

"Ah," a voice drawled, "you're beginning to wake."

I stared up at the ceiling, the unfamiliarity gnawing at me. I wasn't in a cell, at least not one I recognized. Slowly, I turned my head to the left, my gaze landing on a wall made of iridescent light.

I rubbed my head, trying to make sense of the throbbing. I didn't think I had been hit, but my body felt like it had been tossed and turned. My mind scrambled to remember—*I had wind walked.*

I sat up too fast, my pulse racing, and saw him sitting in the corner of the room, legs crossed, wearing a black suit, his posture far too relaxed. "Glad to see you've rejoined the land of the living, Brida," Marsh said casually, inspecting his nails as if speaking to me were beneath him.

"Where am I?" My throat was dry, my voice hoarse. *Had I been screaming?*

He glanced up, his tone incredulous, as if I should already know the answer. "I should think it would be obvious."

I took a few unsteady steps toward him, but a gust of wind knocked me back. A shimmering light blocked my path.

The Court of Whispers.

Marsh's smile widened. "I'm sorry it had to be this way, Brida," he said, standing and slipping his hands into his pockets as though this was routine.

My heart raced, memories crashing over me like waves—*the throne room, Lil, Dainan, Addie.*

"You killed Addie," I whispered, but my voice gained strength, twisting with rage. "You killed Addie!" I felt a tear slip down my cheek, but it did nothing to cool the fire burning inside me.

Marsh sighed. "Addie was an unfortunate bystander in a series of events that would have played out with or without her interference." He took a step closer, his tone calm, almost soothing. "I am sorry. I grew to like Addie."

The words stung like acid, and I felt something snap inside me. Rage surged, wild and uncontrollable. I slammed my fist into the light barrier in front of me, feeling the heat from the impact burn my skin. The barrier flickered, a hole burning where my fist struck it, but it sealed up in seconds.

"Interesting," Marsh said, watching the burn mark fade with curious fascination. He stepped closer, ignoring the anger rolling off me. "You'll be happy to know that your prince managed to escape. He even took Lil with him," he said with a dark chuckle.

My heart twisted, the images of the throne room flashing before me.

I couldn't comprehend the shift in him. The Marsh I knew, the one who had helped me, eased my burdens, was gone. This man standing before me was someone else entirely.

"Why?" The word barely escaped my lips, but it was all I could manage.

His eyes narrowed, and his voice dripped with a darkness that chilled my blood. "I knew from the moment I saw you." He took another step forward. "You look just like her."

Confusion and dread warred within me. "Who?" My voice trembled.

"Your mother," he sneered. The venom in his words made my stomach lurch.

I stumbled back, reeling. "You knew my mother?"

He laughed, the sound cold and mocking. "Oh, yes."

My mother? The thought sent my mind spiraling, but I tried to hold on, tried to steady myself. "Why am I here, Marsh?" I demanded, my voice trembling with anger.

A low chuckle rumbled from Marsh as he took in the sight of me. "Something has been long lost to this world. And we need it back, Brida." His eyes gleamed with twisted satisfaction. "You have already unleashed a chain of events that can no longer be stopped."

He took a step towards me. "Everything in this world has its balance, Brida. And you offered us exactly what we needed."

Offered? My blood ran cold as the memory of the ritual with Giaxia surged to the surface. *The pool. My blood.*

I took a step back, my heart pounding in my chest. "What did you need my blood for?" I growled through gritted teeth, barely able to contain the fury rising within me.

He clicked his tongue, amusement dancing in his eyes. He turned, taking slow, deliberate steps toward the door. "In time, you will come to trust me. And perhaps then, I'll tell you what you wish to know."

As he turned to leave, he gave one final, mocking nod towards the bed in the corner. "In the meantime, get some rest. It's a new Dawn, Brida. It's a new Dawn."

The door clicked shut behind him, and the sound of his footsteps faded, leaving me alone in the cold, silent room.

A wave of anguish crashed over me, and I fell to my knees, a broken sob tearing from my throat. The sound of my wailing filled the room, raw and guttural, echoing off the iridescent walls. Every breath felt like it was being ripped from my chest.

I pounded the floor, my hands bloody and bruised, my cries of frustration and helplessness growing louder, more frantic. I hit the ground again and again, as if I could shatter this prison, as if somehow, I could escape.

But nothing changed.

And so, I screamed until exhaustion overtook me and sleep pulled me into its dark embrace.

☽✳☾

The cold gnawed at me, creeping into my bones as I lay shivering beneath the thin blanket. It was the middle of the night, and the icy air felt like a cruel stranger, unwelcome after the balmy summer evenings of Azmeer. I missed the gentle breeze that swept through my balcony, brushing against my skin like a whispered promise of safety. Now, it seemed so far away, like another life altogether.

I wondered if the stars wept for the palace tonight. For Prince Alvar—the king he should have been but never would be. Would they mourn his loss, too, or had they become indifferent to the tragedies that unfolded beneath their eternal gaze?

A knot tightened in my chest as I thought of him, my friend. He had tried to guide me, protect me, even save me from myself. And now, he was gone. The mark of the king would have to choose a new victim. My thoughts spun between Dainan and Rai. *Would it be Dainan? Could he even rule after fleeing his own kingdom?*

I couldn't stop wondering where he had gone. Somewhere far, I hoped, somewhere safe. At least he had managed to take Lil with him, sparing her from the murderous rage of her husband. But the look on Rai's face after he realized what he had done—it still haunted me. His eyes had shifted from shock to a hollow emptiness, and I couldn't forget the sinister whisper from Thalius right before it all fell apart.

My breath hitched, and I struggled to steady it. *Stay calm, Brida.* I needed to stay sharp. There was no room for fear now, no room for mistakes.

"Make sure you have the Wind by your side," Ollo's voice echoed in my memory. How naive I had been. The wind had been plotting against us all along, using me without my knowledge.

I clenched my fists, a wave of nausea rising within me. *How could I have been such a fool?* The weight of my actions sat heavy on my chest, making me sick to my stomach. I squeezed my eyes shut, hoping sleep would rescue me from this nightmare. Yearning for the darkness to take me, in the hopes I could mingle with shadows.

Just as I felt myself drifting, something brushed against my cheek—a soft, tender touch. I froze, my heart pounding in my ears. It felt so familiar, so intimate.

"I am with you, Ilia."

My eyes snapped open, and I bolted upright, the voice lingering like an echo in the cold air. *Ilia.* The name Dainan had whispered so many times. My mind raced, piecing together what I had missed. Ollo's words resurfaced: *Make sure the wind is by your side.* The wind —*it had never meant Marsh.*

Dainan.

Dainan is a wind whisperer. But how? He wielded shadows, not wind. No one alive had ever held the power of two courts. Yet, as the truth sparked within me, it carried something unexpected: hope. A hope that had been buried deep beneath my fears, finally kindling to life.

A pull surged within me—so strong it nearly knocked the breath from my lungs. My veins felt as though they were set ablaze, warmth spreading through me for the first time in what seemed like an eternity.

I am more than my fear. I am the story I choose to write.

The thought pulsed through me, and with it came a flood of strength. The fire in my blood, the force in my chest—I would harness it. The fear was gone. No longer a leash tethering me to its mercy. I would bow to no one.

Marsh thought he had me cornered, thought I was defeated, fragile. I'd let him believe that, let him think he'd won. I would play the part, be what he needed me to be—just long enough to unearth his plans, his secrets.

And when the time came, I would fight. With everything I had left.

And I would win.

READY FOR MORE?

SNEAK PEAK

The story continues in
Tides of Memory
Book two in the Shattered Sky Saga.

For sneak peeks at upcoming books, bonus chapters, and exclusive content, subscribe to Laura Blake's newsletter at
www.laurablakeauthor.com

CHAPTER 1
TIDES OF MEMORY
-KADIAN-

"What do you think is happening up there?" I whispered to Oz, squinting at the front of the room where a piece of paper seemed to be passed from hand to hand. At least, I thought it was a piece of paper from what I could make out.

Lil looked fucking beautiful. My eyes kept drifting toward her, unable to focus on anything else.

"Maybe someone forgot to order a shrimp cocktail for the reception," Oz said, leaning back in his chair, craning his neck for a better view. "I'd be pissed too if people forgot one of the best food items."

"That's not a menu." I scowled at him as he shrugged. Oz could always make light of anything, but something about this didn't feel right.

I scanned the room, trying to spot Bri. Normally, she was easy to find, but the crowd was thick today, making it nearly impossible to see her.

"It can be undone; it says so right here."

Had I heard that right? Did they mean the wedding?

"Hey, do you—"

"Shh." I swatted at Oz, needing to hear more of what was being said up there. If this wasn't happening, maybe...

A strange pull tugged at my chest, not quite there but not absent either. They'd been giving me tea for weeks now—something to "relax" me, they'd said—but I wasn't sure that was all it was doing.

Lil had moved away from her uncle and Rai, heading toward a scribe.

Addie? Is that Addie up there?

It was impossible to see anything clearly from where I sat.

Then the screaming started.

"Holy shit," Oz muttered beside me.

"What the fuck is happening?" My eyes darted between the dais and the crowd, searching for Lil. Chaos erupted, figures moving in all directions, and Asana's piercing scream echoed through the room.

Like a violent windstorm, a sudden force pressed us into our seats. No one could move. Figures in purple cloaks emerged from the shadows, and my heart sank.

Wind Walkers? What in the gods' name is going on?

Someone stood in the aisle now.

Brida.

Why is Brida here, and why the fuck was she involved?

"Is that Brida?" Oz shouted over the roaring wind. I could barely hear him.

How is she even standing right now?

Where is Lil?

I forced myself to stand, battling the invisible tempest holding me down.

Lil was next to Addie, and her uncle was making a move to grab her. *Get to Lil*—that was all I could think. I had to reach her.

"Holy fuck," Oz whispered as I saw Thalius slice Addie's throat.

Gods. Brida.

My eyes found her again, but before I could react, a Walker appeared behind her.

Marsh. I'm going to fucking kill him. If he hurts her, I'll kill him.

I glanced back at the dais and saw what had caused the initial screams. Alvar lay dead, Asana cradling his body. *What is happening...*

Where did Brida go? She'd been there, but now she was gone. And Dainan was standing in front of them.

In a blink, Dainan shadow-stepped to Lil, and they vanished.

Lil...

The wind died down, and Oz tugged at my sleeve. "Sit down," he whispered. I collapsed onto the bench, my mind spinning. *Where are they?*

"What in the gods' name just happened?" Oz asked, his face pale.

"Alvar's dead," I muttered. "And Addie."

"Brida's aunt?" Oz raised an eyebrow.

I nodded. I had no idea why she was involved or if Brida even knew.

"All hail your new king!" A voice boomed from the dais, and Rai's arm was thrust into the air, supported by Thalius.

The crowd buzzed with murmurs, but I could only think of the mark. Alvar had been marked. Didn't a king need the mark? *Maybe it didn't matter if the throne was taken by conquest, but the story of King Elidas and the mark had always been clear. There had to be one.*

A gentle wind brushed against my cheek, whispering into my ear, "Do not fear what you've seen today. Everything is as it was meant to be."

I glanced around, seeing others nodding, eyes glazing over as they accepted the words.

"They can't believe this," I said to Oz, whose eyes had the same dazed look.

What is happening?

Asana rose to her feet, her voice dripping with rage. "You have no idea what you've done!"

Walkers moved toward her, but before they could reach her, she collapsed. A shadow engulfed her and Alvar, and they vanished.

The palace was no longer safe for Asana. Everyone had suspected something deeper going on between Alvar and the Speaker of the Court of Shadows. This confirmed it.

The wind's voice returned. "Refreshments will be served in the dining hall. Please enjoy tonight's festivities."

As if nothing had happened, the crowd stood and began to file out.

"Good thing this is over; I'm starving," Oz said casually.

"Oz..." I began, but the flow of people was already sweeping us along.

"What just happened?" I asked, unsure what answer I'd get.

"Rai was named king, man. Were you not watching?" Oz gestured toward the dais, now blocked off by Walkers.

"Yeah, but what about everything before that?"

"What are you talking about?" He clapped a hand on my shoulder. "Let's get some food into you, Kad. It's coronation day."

Coronation day. What the actual fuck.

"I wonder if the food will be as good as the ball. Brida did amazing work with that one. They should've asked her to plan this, too."

Brida. Lil. Where are they?

"Whoa, look at me, Kad," Oz said, his voice cutting through my fog.

"What?" I snapped, blood humming through my veins, the pulse of it drowning out all other sounds.

"Your eyes are really intense right now. Let's go get food. Maybe Tamra and Amera are there." He added with a laugh, steering me toward the door.

As we walked, the halls buzzed with chatter, everyone seemingly forgetting the two murders we'd just witnessed.

"I think Rai will make a fine king," someone said.

"He was always the right choice," another murmured.

Except the mark didn't appear on him.

The dining hall was decorated in an awful mix of blues, reds, blacks, and whites—*symbolic of the Courts of Reflection and Shadows and the unification of two courts, not of a coronation day.*

I rubbed my chest. The sensation that had been tugging at me earlier was back, stronger now.

Guests mingled, piling their plates with food as if nothing had happened. *How can everyone just stand around like this? How does no one see through this facade?*

Oz returned with a plate for me, snapping me out of my thoughts. "Got you a plate."

"Thanks," I muttered, barely noticing the rain outside. It had only rained a few times since we'd arrived in Azmeer, the last time being the day we'd looked into the Mirrors of Reflection. When I'd seen Lil...

"You think we should bring a plate to Brida?" Oz asked between bites.

Gods, he really didn't remember.

"She'll be fine," I said, forcing a smile. *Will she? Will Lil? I have no idea where either of them are.*

I wanted to leave, to figure out some kind of plan, but Walkers guarded the door, watching our every move.

Rai and Thalius eventually made their rounds, shaking hands with officials. Rai didn't even wear the crown. How were people falling for this?

After hours of parading through the crowd, the Walkers finally eased up, allowing people to leave.

"You look like shit," Oz said as we reached our floor.

"I'm just tired." The tea—over a day without it now—had left my head pounding.

"Well, get some sleep. Maybe tomorrow I'll finally beat you at the rock wall," Oz laughed, slapping my shoulder.

"Night, Oz." I fumbled with my door handle, pushing into the darkness of my room.

I lit a candle, and my heart stopped.

A wall of living shadows stood before me, hissing as they swirled downward, revealing the shape of a woman.

"We need to talk."

~

Want to know what happens next? Preorder Tides of Memory, book 2 of The Shattered Sky Saga now.

Acknowledgments

The idea for this world first hit me during a guided meditation on the app *Insight Timer*. I'd gone in for a quick five-minute break and found this beautiful, tribal music. Eyes closed, I was instantly carried away by the drums' beat, my pulse thrumming right along with it.

What I pictured was a young girl dancing around a fire, while a bird's cry echoed, calling to her and her people. After five minutes, I sat there thinking, "What if a whole group of people were ruled by fire? Connected to it, wielding it?" And just like that, my brain decided it had something to obsess over.

When I got home, I grabbed some colored pencils (I was committed) and mapped out a whole world on paper. At first, my main character was going to be a girl named Eosse, a woman (whose people would eventually go on to become The Court of Whispers) living under a dictator. That eventually transformed into the Court of Shadows. I even wrote a few different beginnings, most of them starting with big battle scenes, only to find myself asking, "Wait, why? Why do these people hate each other? What's their goal?" And, of course, "Where's the story?"

So, like most of my ideas, this one got pushed to the back of my ADD-riddled brain and sat there ruminating for years. Every few months, I'd leaf through notebooks or mention to my husband, Josh, that I'd come up with "the thing that'll finally tie it all together!" I still didn't have a clue.

In 2022, when my daughter was born, I realized I needed something that felt separate from motherhood. I found it through my booktube channel, building a community with amazing fellow nerds who loved fantasy as much as I did. Inspired, I co-organized a writers' group to meet weekly and review each other's work, which, of course, meant I had to bring something to share. I had to write.

When I finally sat down at my computer, words started pouring out. Was it the book I'd wanted to write? Absolutely not. I somehow ended up writing a satirical sci-fantasy, which—fun fact—still isn't finished. I worked on it through 2022 and 2023 until life threw a few curveballs. At the start of 2024, I needed time to rest and recharge. That's when I turned to romantasy—a genre I'd always avoided because "romance in fantasy wasn't my thing." Turns out, it's my favorite.

In March 2024, as I made my way through the gauntlet, and wandered through Pyrthian in my imagination, I felt something click —a way to connect the magic of this world with the one I'd first dreamed up. I told Josh I'd finish the draft by June. I was done by March 27th. It felt like the words had been waiting, bubbling up, desperate to spill out. Characters and place names changed, but the world's essence was exactly what I'd imagined.

Since that first draft, the book has, naturally, been put through the editing wringer, and I'm thrilled to finally be able to share it with you.

To my best friends: Jasmine and Vanessa —thanks for pushing me into romantasy, even though I was stubborn. To Najil, I look forward to you reading this in 2037.

Esmay Rosalyne, my forever cheerleader and the only person who's seen every draft, giving honest feedback every time. Thank you for being a beacon of light in this world. Caleb Clarke, for reading this book more times than he thought he ever would, for being a fantastic member of our writers' group, and for being great company on Wednesday nights. Nikki Callan, thanks for helping me zoom out and see the big picture! My mom, Dianna, for instilling in me a love of reading; and my dad, David, who always told me I could do whatever I put my mind to and cheered on every idea I threw his way.

To my beta readers: thank you from the bottom of my heart. What a privilege it was to share this with you, and thank you for helping me make it better.

To Kendra Silver, whose insights shaped this world, and Valeria Eden, whose feedback brought richness to the story—thank you. Tabitha Chandler, thank you for your incredible edits and keeping me in line!

To my sweet girl, F., thank you for teaching me about love, life, and patience on the days I spent more time on my computer than with you. Maybe one day, I'll let you read this.

To my husband, the guy who told me to keep going, who held me up every time I fell. You're the butter to my bread and the breath to my life. I love you.

To Ty and Tibby. We miss you more than words could ever express.

And finally, to you, dear reader. Thank you for joining me on this journey. There are no words to express my gratitude for spending time with Brida or wandering through Azmeer. Putting a first book out feels like walking on a tightrope over a canyon. But if, like Brida, you ever feel scared, I hope you face it head-on. And remember, it's okay to feel the fear—and then do the damn thing anyway.

ABOUT THE AUTHOR

Laura's journey has taken her down many unexpected paths, but her love for stories and fantasy has remained constant. After detours as a classical historian, history and religion teacher, and small business owner, she is thrilled to have fulfilled her lifelong dream of becoming a storyteller.

Originally from Montreal, Laura now resides in rural Maryland with her husband, daughter, and five energetic rescue cats. When she's not writing, you can find her experimenting with new recipes or passionately discussing books with anyone who will listen.

If you enjoyed The Forgotten Dawn, I would love it if you let your friends know so they can experience Azmeer as well. If you leave a review for The Forgotten Dawn on the site from which you purchased the book, Goodreads, or your own blog, it would mean more to me than you possibly know.

Want more goodies? Be sure to sign up to my newsletter here.

www.ingramcontent.com/pod-product-compliance
Lightning Source LLC
Chambersburg PA
CBHW030550310726
48979CB00011B/2103/J

* 9 7 8 1 9 6 7 3 8 9 0 0 1 *